THE CRANE MAIDEN

THE EMBER LILY ARC
BOOK ONE

M. H. WOODSCOURT

True North Press

Edited by Sarah B.

Map by CartographyBird Maps

Cover design by MiblArt

Published by True North Press

www.mhwoodscourt.com

Paperback ISBN: 978-1-959619-19-2

Hardback ISBN: 978-1-959619-20-8

To all those who stand tall in their beliefs,
no matter what storms may come. No matter what mockery.
No matter what fear.

Also to Joan of Arc,
the timeless heroine who inspired this story.

CONTENTS

PRONUNCIATION GUIDE

PEOPLE

Afallon – ah-full-ON
Alain Clayre – uh-lain clair
Aluem – AH-loo-em
Aveyal – Ah-VAY-ell
Bastin – bass-tin
Baya – bay-uh
Bregger – breg-er
Cetta d'Arc – kett-uh dark
Charton – CHAR-ton
Dulen Thame – DOOL-in thaym
Duron – der-RON
Edrin d'Arc – ed-rin dark
Evella – ee-VELL-uh
Firro – feer-oh
Frey – fray
Gilim – gill-im
Heshi d'Arc – HESH-ee dark
Huvarn – hugh-varn
Ilua Nuvan – eye-loo-uh NOO-vawn
Issa d'Arc – ee-suh dark
Jekan d'Arc – je-KAHN dark
Jenai d'Arc – jen-NAI (soft "j" sound)
Kilay – kee-LAY
Kirio – kee-ree-oh
Ladia – LAW-dee-uh
Limmar – lim-MAR
Lio – lee-oh
Lucen d'Arc – loo-SHEN dark
Mardry – MAR-dree
Mercer – mer-ser
Mirrasae – MEER-uh-say
Ney'Nenamyn – nay-NEN-uh-min
Onrin Tarie – on-rin tar-EE
Orry – OR-ee

Phren LeGre – fren la-GREE
Priarre – pry-AIR
Robarr – row-BAWR
Rowan d'Arc – RO-win dark
Runi – ROO-nee
Runin – ROO-nin
Sharisse – shar-EES
Silian – sil-ee-un
Thiavos – thee-uh-VOS
Tristel – triss-till
Tryla – TRY-luh
Tullo – TOO-low
Varide – vuh-reed
Varyon – var-ee-ON
Yenntevar – YEN-tuh-var

PLACES

Amri – AW-mree
Annonenfa – ah-non-NEN-fah
Boyan – boo-yan
Candalar – KAN-duh-LAR
Darr – dawr
Cethera – keth-uh-ruh
Domrem – DOM-rem
Fraelin – FRAY-linn
Hesh-Kassal – hesh-kass-ALL
Leyn – layn
Londolin – LAWN-do-linn
Lorion – lor-ee-ON
Lorrae – lor-RAY
Lué – loo-AY
Lué-de-Trul – loo-AY deh trool
Pira – PAI-ree
Rishom – ree-SHOM
Shinon – shee-NON
Simaerin – sim-MAY-ree
Thargundy – thar-gun-dee
Ilid – ill-idd
Valcinay – VAL-sin-nay

TERMS

Dreyvio – dray-vee-oh
Epian – ehp-ee-ehn
Fraeli – FRAY-lee
Lilerayai – lil-eh-RAY-eye
Simaeri – sim-MAY-ree
Trul – trool
Vien lo Fraelin – vee-EN lo FRAY-lin

Hear ye, hear ye. No magic shall be used within the mighty realm of Simaerin, by order of the Crow King.
ILID
SWAN CASTLE
MISORIL PROVINCE
MOUNT VINWEN
VINWEN PROVINCE
SIMAERIN
DOASMEN HEIGHTS
DELESAR RIVER
GLASHON PROVINCE
LONDOLIN
KEEP TALBETHÉ
CROWE
VAYMEER SEA
RIS

FRAELIN
HARGUNDY
PIRA
LORION
THRAY
ALCINAT
DOMREM
SHINOX
MS
ISLES OF AMRI
THE MANY LANDS OF
CHEND
MAPPED IN THE PRESENT AGE

FOREWORD

The idea for this story came to me in January 2024, straight out of "Nowhere". Which is always where the best stories come from, if you ask me. That realm likes to hoard treasure.

I've always had a fondness for the real-life heroine Joan of Arc. When I was young, my sister and I watched some mini-series or other about her life and I was enraptured. I'd also grown up on the classic 50s movie starring Ingrid Bergman. I can't remember a time when I wasn't aware of the Maid of Lorraine to some degree.

Did I have any notion I'd pull strongly from her life story to write a parallel but fictitious version of events? Certainly not! That is until "Nowhere" dropped the idea into my lap and said "Ta-da!"

You see, I'd been re-watching the Ingrid Bergman *Joan of Arc* movie for my birthday. And, as always, I was analyzing story beats, because that's what professional writers do for fun. Then suddenly: WHAM! I realized the story was following those beats *perfectly*, even beyond being a historical drama. To be fair, Hollywood took liberties with that film, as they always do, in order to make it compelling for its era and audience. But even so, stripping away the fluff, the bones beneath were simply *perfect* for a novel.

I spent the last half of the film taking notes and daydreaming about a parallel world set in a realm with dragons and unicorns. Naturally.

Thus, the story of Jenai d'Arc took root in my head. Few stories have ever come to me so easily. I dived into research, trying to understand Joan of Arc more intimately, in order to make my version as compelling, rich, and authentic as possible. My main source of inspiration comes from the biography *Joan of Arc: By Herself and Her Witnesses* written and compiled by French historian Regine Pernoud and translated by Edward Hyams. Largely it's comprised of historical accounts (with commentary), just as the title implies. From Joan herself I learned of her history, her bravery, her pain, and her faith. From her witnesses, I learned of her authenticity, her sacrifices, her strategies, her implausible knowledge, and her ultimate martyrdom.

That said, this is most definitely <u>not</u> a *historical fantasy* novel. I haven't crafted a magical background for France, nor is Jenai straight up copied from Joan. This is *high fantasy,* strongly inspired by real life. (I did something similar with the Wintervale duology which is set in the same fictional world set centuries following this story.)

If anyone picks up *The Crane Maiden* expecting historical fantasy and all that entails, they will be disappointed. This isn't set in our world. It's not an alternate Earth. I took liberties, I added elemental magic, and I built the world of Chend from scratch years ago. But I also borrowed heavily from Joan's life. Certain figures and their interactions are *very* much like history depicts them. But names are changed, locations are changed, and other facets are changed.

Those not familiar with the history of Joan of Arc may ask several questions as they read this novel: Did Joan of Arc really have a sister? Actually, history doesn't know for certain. (I used that gray area to build on Jenai's motivations in this book.) What did Joan reveal to the Dauphin to convince him of her divine mission? No one will ever know. What was Joan's relationship to the duke in real life? Friendship is all we know. Is the Fairy/Blessing Tree real? Yes! Did Joan wear a red dress and become well-known for it? She certainly did. Did she hear divine voices? She definitely believed so, as do I. Was there really a prophecy surrounding her during the 100 Year War? Evidence does speak of a prophecy given years before which Joan seems to have answered the call to fulfill.

Ironically, when I sent this manuscript to my early readers —from alpha to beta feedback and even my editor—the reactions proved fascinating: The least believable aspects of Jenai's story found herein, the parts that early readers questioned, are those parts that came directly from history itself. I've had to justify, embellish, and expound where history merely remarked. Truth really is stranger than fiction.

As I've written and edited this book, I've often wondered whether *The Crane Maiden* would find an audience. Some readers may be upset by my treatment of Saint Joan. Others may scoff at my borrowing from a greater story for something so superficial as fiction. Others still may see potential for a story that I didn't tap. Some may find the themes contradictory. But I felt moved to write this *as it is*. That shelf in "Nowhere" dropped this story into my lap for a reason (one I personally feel is divinely appointed). One thing is certain: I have no regrets.

Will some readers take issue with Jenai's unflagging faith? Will they scoff at her hordes of faithful followers? Will they sneer at her abilities in war? Will they take offense at the corruption of the church as depicted in these pages? Certainly, on all counts. But I caution those readers in advance: The least believable moments may just be the most accurate. That's what makes Joan's life so miraculous and timeless, and why I *had* to write a story based on that remarkable life.

Another question that has and will continue to come up is the following: Is *The Crane Maiden* a Christian Fantasy novel? My firm answer is no. Though it's inspired by a Christian-centric historical account, I didn't set out to tell a tale by a Christian for Christians. I meant to tell a timeless tale that could inspire a wide audience whatever their individual beliefs. Joan's example is one that has moved souls around the world, be it for her faith and martyrdom or her bold stand as a woman in man's domain. She speaks to every heart in different ways.

I definitely didn't want to limit the reach of this book by catering to one crowd of readers—even those of like-mind. I wished to pay tribute to a brave and inspiring woman. The church depicted herein has Christian influences, yes, but it's not a depiction of Christianity itself. Joan is a woman of faith surrounded by many who worship as she does and many who don't. I tried to be fair and balanced by depicting multiple worldviews around her. *The Crane Maiden* is a story of faith, certainly, but what form and value that faith has I leave to the reader to decipher.

At its heart, this is a novel about a brave soul who stands against the odds to make a difference. It's an underdog story. It's an account of courage and sacrifice. It's a tale of good versus evil. And that, I think, is why it's worth the telling.

—M. H. W.

THE CRANE MAIDEN

One woman shall sunder this land by her falsehoods.
Another shall save it by her faith.

— PROPHECY OF THE EMBER LILY

PROLOGUE

The old church bells rang out, shattering the peace of dawn in the village of Domrem. Their peals carried across the rural fields, over the wooded hills, reaching for the crisp sky of early autumn.

Jenai jumped up from the hearth stones she'd been scrubbing and raced to the cottage window. Her little sister, Cetta, was kneeling below the window in the vegetable patch, harvesting turnips. Straightening from the muddy garden plot, the ten-year-old girl glanced at Jenai who was a full three years older than her. The bells tolled on.

"It's not Reverence Day," Cetta said, sounding unsure. "Is it?"

Jenai shook her head. "It's not anything today." She pulled the gray kerchief from her head, smoothed back strands of her long, plaited black hair, then started to untie her apron. "Head for the church, Cetta, and see why the bells are ringing. I'll see if Mama knows—"

The little girl was already off, jumping over the tidy rows of vegetables. Her long dark braids beneath her blue kerchief drummed against her back. She scattered chickens, hopped

"

the stone fence, then raced up the hard-packed highway toward the church on the hill overlooking the town.

"Do not let Cetta go." The voice that spoke was soft, almost a whisper.

Jenai froze, then looked around for her brothers. Where had that voice come from? Did she imagine it? She shook it off as nerves and strode through the tidy cottage, past the oaken table, past the hearth, and past the three little bedrooms, stepping out back. Mama was milking the cow in the barn while the sun lazily hefted itself over the eastern tree-laden hills. Strands of light filtered through the tall elms bridging the yard and field where Papa and his sons threshed the golden barley.

"Mama!" Jenai rounded the well and parted a gaggle of honking geese. "Mama! The church bells are ringing!"

The thin woman looked up from her work, hands still working the cow's teats, a bucket of frothy milk already half-full. "And what's so strange about that? Why aren't you scrubbing, child?"

Jenai reached the open stall where the cow patiently chewed cud. "Is today a holy day?" Jenai wasn't well educated, but she thought she knew every Reverence Day of the year and all the Saints' Days besides.

"Of course it's not." Mama stooped over her stool to focus again on her milking. "The priest must be testing the bell ropes. They fray, you know."

"But they haven't stopped, Mama. Listen."

Mama's hands fell still, and she canted her head, frowning. "Send Cetta to see what's happened."

"I did."

Motion drew Jenai's attention toward the field where Papa was crossing the ditch between the yard and his two virgates of barley. Jenai's three brothers and the farmers under Papa's watch were following close at hand, wielding sickles and flails. They'd left the threshing sledges in the field.

"Issa! That's the battle bell! Where's Cetta?" Papa called.

Jenai froze, fear crawling up her skin. The battle bell? Did that mean the Thargundians had crossed the boundary into the Province of Lorrae for another raid? But why? Thanks to Count Duron, there'd been a tentative truce for the past three summers between the Fraeli and the traitorous Thargundians who were allied with the filthy Crowsmen of far-off Simaerin.

"*Go after Cetta.*" The strange voice came again, stronger. Cetta had gone to the church. Was she in danger? The needles up and down Jenai's flesh grew sharper and colder. She whirled around and started toward the front yard.

"Stay, Jenai!" Papa shouted. "Help your mama get the animals into the stalls."

She turned toward him, torn between the insistent voice and obeying her father. Meeting his stern, fierce stare, she flinched beneath the weight of his authority. Jekan d'Arc wasn't a man to defy. She nodded and moved toward the goats busily trimming weeds, even as a protest bubbled up her throat. "Papa—"

Ignoring her, Jekan turned away and barked orders at her brothers and the other assembled men to round up their horses and prepare to answer the bell's call.

Jenai tripped to Mama's side while rubbing her hands against her skirts. "Cetta went to the church, Mama."

The woman grimaced. "She's smart enough to keep out of the way. We need to let the men have the road."

The voice returned, more insistent. It chimed like crystal in Jenai's head. "*Go after Cetta.*"

She hesitated. What was this strange voice?

Is it from Sweet Afallon, or merely my imagination?

"*You will be too late,*" the voice said gently.

Jenai twisted toward the church on the hill. The bells still pealed, loud and long.

"Jenai, grab that hen!"

She scooped the chicken up and rushed it into the coop, all the while trying to ignore the knotting of her stomach. But the voice's gentle insistence dug in like a hot brand, and she imagined Cetta cut down on the road by the bloodthirsty Thargundians.

She dumped the chicken among the others, then raced toward the road.

"Jenai, come back!"

"I'm getting Cetta!" she called without looking back. Her long legs carried her fast, and she soon sprang over the stone fence and onto the road. The bells pealed on, though smoke plumed from the church's roof. Jenai's heart stuck in her throat. She ran faster than she ever had in her thirteen years. Where was Cetta? Where had the girl gone?

She should be back by now!

Horse hooves thundered from up the road, near the church. Jenai didn't slow, even as she squinted to make out the heraldry the three riders wore. Red. Red tabards and shields. Red, red, red. Thargundians. The enemy. The silhouette of a white stag against the red filled her vision.

Choking back a sob, Jenai pushed herself harder. There, in the field near the Thargundians, Cetta ran from the horsemen. Her blue kerchief stood out against the gold of the nodding barley.

Jenai tried to scream. Tried to reach out and stop what happened next—but she was too far away. Cetta stumbled. The closest horseman in the red heraldry leaned over his horse, the silver of his blade flashing in the sunrise. Blood spurted the air. A muted shriek cut short.

The air froze in Jenai's lungs.

"Jenai, drop where you are." The voice was gentle but firm.

With a sob, Jenai dropped. Her knee struck a stone. She barely felt the pain. Her vision swam with tears. Behind her, on the road, the din of horses throbbed against the hard-packed earth. Voices rose in shouts. Papa and the other farmers had assembled and were coming fast. They whipped past Jenai on horseback, one or two men catching her eye with looks of regret. They'd seen Cetta's death, too.

The Thargundians wheeled their horses around and retreated. Papa gave chase. The other farmers followed.

When the horsemen were nothing more than clouds of dust headed northwest toward the province boundary, Jenai staggered to her feet. Her chest was tight, and her hands shook. That was all she felt as she approached Cetta's prostrate form. The ground around the girl was dark where blood had soaked in, and drooping barley spikelets glistened red. Jenai knelt beside Cetta, set one hand on the lifeless body, and wept.

She'd seen too much death from plague and starvation to convince herself that her little sister might stir. She'd seen the cruelty of the Thargundians before now. They'd raided her village before, and they'd do so again.

We can't let them keep doing whatever they please!

"Afallon above," Jenai whispered, "please liberate Fraelin and its people from our conquerors. Drive out the Crowsmen and their sympathizers."

"*Heed the Voice,*" came the soft answer. "*Heed the Voice and you will be Fraelin's salvation, Jenai. Do not disregard the warnings again. Be obedient and wait with patience for the guidance to grant Fraelin liberty. Say nothing of my Voice or your mission unbidden, not even to your kin. Do you understand?*"

Jenai curled over Cetta's body. "I do. And I will obey until my dying breath. This I swear upon Afallon's life. I'll do whatever you require of me. Anything."

# Part 1

1

THE BLESSING TREE

Four Years Later

The fairy song drifted toward the branches of the Blessing Tree, brightening the leaves. Hands clasped with the other young women of Domrem, Jenai danced around the tree in the chain circle, singing the springtime chants that heralded the planting season. The boughs overhead bobbed in a pleasant evening breeze, and the frogs in the nearby brook harmonized with the girls' chanting.

Fireflies weaved near Jenai's ankles, and she smiled. After a harsh winter, the province of Lorrae needed a good planting year. The tradition of dancing around the Blessing Tree was an old one. Hardly anyone in the province held to the tradition, declaring it sacrilege to call upon the mythical power of the Weave instead of Afallon. But Jenai, and most of Domrem, felt that Afallon and the Weave were connected. Indeed, the old priest of Domrem subscribed to many of the old customs. He'd shown Jenai that prayers often used magic to meet their ends. The priest could conjure water, and he'd used it following the raid four years ago to put out the flames that had nearly destroyed the church.

"If Afallon is the Creator of all good things," the old priest once told her, "then that must include the wholesome magic of the Weave."

"But what about dark sorcery?" Jenai had dared to ask.

"That comes from Afallon's enemy, Thiavos, the Fallen One. You can recognize his magic easily, Daughter, for from it comes nothing whole or fair. Thiavos offers the promise of ease and comfort to ensnare us but never love or honor. His ways lead softly, ever softly, to a bitter end."

The old priest's words resonated within Jenai. She sought his counsel often, sometimes leaving the field at midday to attend High Reverence. His words were how she knew that the Blessing Tree was from Afallon, not Thiavos.

Sweet Afallon, give us a bounteous crop this season, she prayed silently, even as she chanted aloud.

The tree brightened more, pulling Jenai's eyes from the fireflies twirling in the grass. Her heart swelled. The leaves glowed gold now, and the bark was a luminous bronze. The other girls faltered, their chants fading—but this was a sight they saw every year. A miracle, yes, but not one that should prevent them from finishing what they started.

Jenai lifted her chin and sang louder:

> 'Blessed by root, bough, and bond,
> Be ever true—stand proud and strong.
> Bless the fields and rivers bold,
> And turn our harvest into gold.'

Glancing at Jenai, the others regathered themselves and began to dance properly in the unbroken circle. Beside her, Jenai's friend Sharisse smiled and leaned close between chants, her brown eyes twinkling while her soft brown curls bobbed around her shoulders.

"Phren has been looking for you."

Jenai glanced at Sharisse, then began the next stanza:

> 'By this tree and by the sword,
> Let us never be forsworn.
> Grant us hope and courage true,
> Bring us strength and honor, too.'

The dance grew more complicated, providing a break from the chant. The Blessing Tree was glowing even more, and the harmony around them surged like the fairies of the woods had come to join in the magic—though none appeared.

"What could Phren want with me?" Jenai asked, frowning.

"Only one thing I can think of." Sharisse gave her a significant look, then turned back to carry on another portion of the chant.

Jenai sang out as her stomach twisted. She'd known Phren for years. He was bold and outspoken, always getting into scrapes with the other young men of Domrem, usually with him in the lead. He'd teased her endlessly for being so devout to the Old Faith. But Phren was eighteen now, and he'd grown a little sense, at least. He'd also stopped mocking her after Cetta's death.

A hollow in Jenai's heart gaped wide, and memories of her little sister's death flooded the space, but she plunged into the dance, pushing back her regret and grief. They served no purpose now. Cetta was gone, and the Voice had promised Jenai the chance to end the conflict against the Thargundians and Crowsmen if she was patient. She'd been patient for four years and would continue on so.

The Blessing Tree chimed. The golden light trembled on every branch and leaf. The girls of Domrem finished the chant's last refrain, then ceased their dance. They remained clutching hands, still and reverent. Jenai smiled.

Blessed be Afallon and the Weave.

Together, the village girls intoned a final prayer, one the priest had instilled in them since they toddled:

'Blessed be our Sweet Afallon who aids the
    weary,
comforts the forlorn, and guides the lost. Finia.'

Sharisse released the hand of the girl beside her and tugged Jenai away from the brilliantly glowing tree. "Come. The boys always watch on the far side of the brook."

Jenai jerked back, trying to free herself, a note of panic in her head. "They do?"

Her friend glanced behind her, laughing. "You didn't know? Dear, innocent Jenai. They *always* watch us dancing at the Blessing Tree. It's as much a tradition as it is to have the village maidens dance in the first place."

Jenai's panic gave way to indignation. "That goes against the ceremony, Sharisse. No one is meant to watch. Certainly not boys like Phren."

Her friend's smile turned sly. "Boys like Phren become handsome and eligible men. I think he fancies you."

Jenai frowned and managed to pull free. "I can't attach myself to anyone."

Sharisse grimaced. "This piety of yours has really gone too far, you know. You can't live in your father's house forever. An old maid is a burden even he can't afford." The young woman sighed. "Why do you refuse to dream about marriage and family like the rest of us?"

"I can't explain," Jenai said gently, "nor would you understand if I tried."

"You think I'm a fool, don't you?" Sharisse halted. "Well,

I'm not. *I* can see the worth of Phren LeGre—even if you can't. Who's the real fool, Jenai?" She darted off, her skirts streaming out behind her, long curls bouncing down her back.

Jenai watched her childhood friend's retreat, torn between hurt and exasperation. Sharisse had always had a flare for melodrama and a healthy interest in the opposite sex. Meanwhile, Jenai had no interest in settling down and rearing children. She had a different mission, one ordained by Afallon. Nothing short of that cause would she accept.

Sighing, Jenai smoothed her red dress—her finest, meant for special occasions and Holy Days—and walked along the path leading from the Blessing Tree toward Domrem. Fireflies flickered in the meadow grass bordering the trail. Behind her, the other village girls remained at the tree for an evening picnic and games. Before Cetta's death, Jenai and her sister had joined in the festivities, but it didn't feel the same anymore. Since hearing the Voice, nothing had been the same.

Footsteps scuffed along the path behind her. Jenai glanced back, expecting to see one of the more reserved village girls retreating from the picnic—but it wasn't a girl at all. Phren LeGre strolled along the path toward Jenai, hands behind his back, a broad smile on his face. Jenai supposed he was handsome in a rugged, scruffy sort of way. His brunet hair was tousled, and his clothes were wrinkled and untucked. She turned back to the trail, not slowing her gait.

The footsteps increased their speed, then Phren reached her side. "Good evening, fair Jenai."

"Good evening, Phren." She kept her tones level, ignoring the writhing twist in her stomach.

"I enjoyed your singing tonight."

"You shouldn't have been watching."

Phren chuckled. "Even the priest knows we watch. By Afallon's bones, I'm certain when he was a lad—"

Jenai whirled on him. "Do *not* swear, Phren LeGre. Would

you use the name of Sweet Afallon so disrespectfully before the priest?"

He blinked. "I— My word, Jenai. You're more a saint than any priest. How did you ever bring yourself to dwell among mortals as you do? Even the legendary Crane King Varyon would have trembled at your holiness."

Cheeks warming, she turned and started along the path again. After a moment, he caught up.

"I spoke with your parents about an important matter this afternoon," Phren said.

"Indeed?" She didn't glance at him.

"It was about you."

Her step caught, but she pressed on. "In what way?"

"By Afallon—slow down, Jenai."

She halted and turned a narrow look on him. "What did you say?"

"I... n-nothing. I didn't say anything." He grimaced, then shrugged. "All right, I swore. I'm human, Jenai, but after we marry, you can spend a lifetime helping me become something better."

Prickles crawled up her spine. "After we what?"

"Your parents agree it's a good match," he went on. "You're beautiful and hardworking. Being the youngest of your family, you won't inherit any of your father's land or coin beyond your dowry, so it makes sense to marry into the other influential family of Domrem. We'll be united. Our lands already connect. This merger will—"

"I won't," Jenai said quietly.

He frowned. "You won't what?"

"I won't marry you."

He stared, then a grin started across his face. "I understand a maiden's desire to play at disinterest in these matter—"

"I won't trifle with your heart," Jenai said firmly. "I don't intend to marry—not you or anyone else. I'm sorry." She turned and kept walking.

His hand caught her arm, and he jerked her around to face him. "Your parents already agreed—"

"But I didn't." She met his dark blue eyes. "Good evening, Phren." Pulling free, she hurried up the path.

"This isn't over!" he called after her. "Your parents already gave their consent!"

As she walked, she kept her eyes fixed on the church with its blackened roof tiles and ancient belltower. She didn't look back until she reached Domrem proper and crested the hill to enter the church. It was quiet inside the musty old building. The pews, worn down from ages of use, stood in two columns leading to the pulpit and altar at the head of the vaulted chamber. Beyond that, the bell ropes hung, forlorn and unguarded. An urge to pull those ropes and make the bells peal swelled inside Jenai's chest. Anything to banish the hollow feeling inside her.

Instead, she sank to her knees before the church's altar and traced the symbol of Afallon: The Straight Path ran from right to left, across her chest, then she tapped her heart with two fingers. She then fell into deep prayer.

"Please, Sweet Afallon, when will my patience bear fruit? When will I be called to set Fraelin free from our conquerors? I'm ready to depart this village this moment if it would serve you best." She halted, refusing to beg further and try her Lord's tolerance. Willing her mind to calm, she centered herself on the miracle of the Blessing Tree and crafted a prayer of gratitude. Midway through the prayer, a breeze stirred her long, loose black hair. Jenai looked up, but there was no open window or door to let the draft in. It came again, brushing against her.

The Voice also came, close and gentle. *"Prepare yourself to depart Domrem at month's end. You will go to Lord Robarr at Valcinay, and he will set you on your way. Await the sign of the sapphire horn and go thence."*

Tears spilled down Jenai's cheeks. "Thank you. Oh, thank you. I'll be ready."

2

WAITING FOR THE CALL

"Jenai!" Papa's roar shamed the morning wind.

Looking up from feeding the chickens, Jenai smoothed the white kerchief on her head and stepped around the pecking birds to answer her father's call. "Coming, Papa!" Veering around chickens and goats, she brushed her gray work dress clean of oats and corn.

Papa stood with his eldest son, Rowan, like they'd been discussing the planting, but his dark gaze was fastened on Jenai. Curtsying, Jenai waited for the man to speak.

"Your brother just came from House LeGre. Explain yourself, daughter." His voice was quiet thunder now.

Jenai didn't flinch, but she kept her head bowed in proper deference. "Last night, Phren LeGre proposed marriage. I refused him."

The silence that followed her statement was deafening. Bracing herself, she glanced up. Papa's face was a brewing storm gathering strength. He marched closer, grabbed her arms in his strong fingers, and leaned down to meet her gaze.

"Must you plague me sleeping and waking, child? Your

duty is to marry, and soon! If not Phren LeGre, then someone else."

"I would rather not, Papa."

"Rather not?" He scoffed. "You'll be wed by summer's end, do I make myself plain?"

Fear wrenched Jenai's gut. Drawing a breath, steeling herself for the full fury of the storm, she quietly said, "In all things possible, I would obey you—but in this I cannot and will not comply. I'll not marry."

At that moment, Mama stepped around the house, arms full of the morning's wash. She halted and stared between her husband and daughter. "What is this, Jekan d'Arc? Would you bruise your own daughter?"

He jerked back, releasing Jenai with a bewildered look, as though he'd just come to himself. Dragging a hand down his dirt-smudged cheek, he drank in air, then jabbed a finger at Jenai. "She refuses to do her duty and marry. I told you, Issa. I told you she would come to ruin. Did I not foresee it?"

Chills caught Jenai's skin. "What do you mean, Papa?"

He whirled on her. "Never you mind. Just stay away from the Crane Prince's army. And hear this: you'll wed before autumn if I must haul you to the church like swine to market. That's my final word on the matter!" He caught up the buckets of seed at his feet and marched off. Rowan glanced at his sister, a frown on his lips, then he followed his sire toward the fields.

Jenai stood stunned. Always, she'd been an obedient daughter, even when it had cost Cetta her life. But in this, she couldn't possibly submit to her father's will. She swayed on her feet, her heart torn in two.

Mama drew near, still clutching the wet laundry. "His anger will blow over, Jenai. He's agitated by a dream he had, that's all."

"What dream?" asked Jenai meekly.

Mama hesitated. "Nothing, Jen—"

"Did it have to do with me? Is that what he meant about me plaguing his sleep, and why he told me to stay away from the Crane Prince's army?"

Mama's cheeks went red. She tried to turn away, but Jenai caught her elbow.

"Please, Mama. Tell me."

Mama's shoulders slumped. "He dreamt that you'd marched to war against the accursed Duke of Thargundy. I told him that simply wasn't possible, but he wouldn't be comforted."

Jenai's stomach wrenched again, this time with guilt. She released Mama's arm, unwilling to offer any reassurances that it was merely a dream. Fortunately, Mama didn't seem to need any. The woman shifted her load of dripping clothes and moved toward the line to hang them.

Jenai rubbed her hands on her gray skirts, then headed for the horse pasture. Halfway there she changed direction, aiming instead for the church on the hill. She needed to seek guidance, to understand how she should proceed. How could she follow Afallon's will without dishonoring her father?

Must I choose between my faith and my family?

She sent a silent prayer heavenward, asking that she might avoid such a choice. As she neared the church, a meadowlark sang out. The little yellow bird stood on a post near the stone fence of the neighboring field. The sweet, trilling notes soothed Jenai, and she smiled faintly, then continued on.

A huddled form sat on a large stone near the church's entrance. A worn scarf covered the figure's head, but the stranger looked up, revealing a gaunt face. The woman stretched out a hand. "Alms, kind lass?"

Jenai dug into the pouch at her belt and handed over a silver sol she'd earned doing a neighbor's darning. "May Afallon keep you."

"And you." The gaunt woman pressed the coin to her lips before hunching over again. She rocked back and forth like a broken reed in the wind.

Jenai stood still, watching the woman for a long moment. She knew that gauntness and look of loss. Memories of Cetta cluttered Jenai's thoughts, but she shoved them down and moved into the dim church, making her way to the altar. In the air, she traced Afallon's sign. Kneeling before the altar, she began to pray.

The faint shuffling sounds of the priest's approach didn't bring her head up until she'd poured forth her gratitude and her inquiry: Must she disobey her father? At last, she looked up from her pleas.

"Always so faithful," the priest said. "I've heard what the others your age say of you, sweet Jenai. That you're too pious and too pure. Do their words sting, my Daughter?"

She smiled, shaking her head. "If only it were true—but I sinned only this morning, Holy Father. I spoke against my papa's wishes, and I must disobey him if he tries to force me into something I can't accept."

"Do you mean matrimony?" asked the priest.

"Yes, Father. I mean not to wed."

"A life of purity is an honorable one, but also lonely," he said. "Do you have no prospects?"

"None I would choose unless Afallon willed it."

He rubbed his chin. "I will speak with your papa and tell him to give you time. Perhaps in a few years you'll change your mind."

Jenai hesitated. "Perhaps, but I don't believe so."

The priest moved to the nearest pew and sat on the polished wood. "You're a remarkable woman, young Jenai. I've met no one like you. Surely, Afallon has called you to something great—something I don't comprehend myself."

"Nor do I yet," Jenai confessed. "But I'll do what He directs."

"Of that I don't doubt."

Footsteps outside the church brought Jenai around. When no one entered, she looked at the priest again. "Who is the beggar at the door?"

"Ah, her. She was a high lady in the city of Moxwen, but the Thargundians learned that her husband was loyal to Fraelin, and the family was attacked in their home at night. She lost her three children. Her husband was executed the next morning—but by Afallon's will, the poor woman survived. Her mind is shattered, just as her heart is. She collects coin not for herself but to feed the children she no longer has."

Jenai set her jaw, fury coiling in her chest. It was a familiar anger. This wasn't the first account of brutality coming from the conquered lands of Thargundy in the north of Fraelin. The civil war had gone on for the last fifteen years, since the death of the previous Crane King. His son and heir—Crane Prince Chartan—had the rightful claim to the throne, but his cousin, Kon—son of the Duke of Thargundy—had declared Prince Chartan illegitimate. Considering the Crane Queen's insatiable appetites, it was all too possible. The claim had split the kingdom, and many called Prince Chartan cursed.

In Fraelin's disarray, the Crow King of Simaerin across the channel had offered his services to the traitorous duke's son in exchange for one thing: All of Fraelin must bow to the Crow King. If Lord Kon Dragonclaw paid tribute to the Crow King, he could rule Fraelin beneath the sovereignty of Simaerin across the channel. Once his father died, Kon implemented his plan of attack.

Fraelin's loyalties had split between the two principalities: Thargundy in the north, and Lorion in the south. Lord Kon then marched on the great cities in central Fraelin, swallowing Reems—where all Crane Kings were crowned—then Pira, then finally the city of Lorion, named for the southern principality. Without shedding any blood, Kon took Lorion for his own, and the Crane Prince fled southward, hiding in Shinon, the last bastion against the Thargundian traitors.

Most Fraeli believed it was only a matter of time before their lands were absorbed into Simaerin forever. Few still fought. The Crane Prince had withdrawn his forces from the borders of Thargundian rule, leaving most of his people to whatever fate decreed.

But Jenai, and those in the farming villages near the conflict, defied the Thargundian advance. They still prayed fervently—most to Afallon, some to the Weave—for deliverance from bloodshed. Had Lord Kon not involved the tyrannical Crow King of Simaerin, perhaps a truce could've been reached, but now war was the only choice if Fraelin didn't want to be wiped off the map.

The priest rested a hand on Jenai's shoulder, stirring her from her reverie. "All will be as Afallon wills, Daughter."

"I know, Father. But most times, He uses us to accomplish His ends—and if we don't answer His call, He won't force us." She turned to the door just as it opened, revealing her second oldest brother, Lucen. He poked his head around the half-ajar door and smiled at her.

"I thought you'd be in here," he said, then inclined his head to the priest. "Holy Father."

"My Son," the priest said. "Blessings to you and your house."

"Thank you, Father. Come, Jenai. Papa's upset enough already. If he learns you shirked your chores—"

"I haven't shirked them. They'll be done as always. First, I had to pray and confess." She turned to the priest, curtsied, then strode down the aisle to her brother's side. "Shall we?"

Side by side, she and Lucen walked outside and across the church grounds, toward their home, circling wide to avoid the spot where Cetta had died four years ago. Neither spoke until they reached the road.

"Did you really refuse Phren's proposal?" Lucen asked.

"I did."

"Good. He's a pompous bull."

Jenai cast him a reproachful look. "It isn't kind to speak that way of Afallon's creatures."

"Afallon created the Crow King, didn't he?" Lucen shrugged.

Put that way, Jenai had no rebuttal, so she kept her peace.

"Do you still plan never to wed?" asked Lucen, his gaze boring into her.

"I won't have the time."

"Time? You're a farmer's daughter. Every farmer's daughter—or son, come to that—has time. That's no reason." He shrugged. "I intend to marry after harvest."

She glanced at him. "Have you asked someone?"

"Not yet." His cheeks turned pink. "But I think Sharisse would make a fine catch."

"She's not a fish, Lucen," Jenai said gently.

"You know what I mean."

"You should ask soon, otherwise she'll say yes to someone else."

Lucen sighed. "I know. But..."

She smiled at her shy brother. Outside the family circle, he barely spoke a word if he could help it.

They reached the stone fence guarding their fields, and Lucen sprang over it, then helped Jenai to cross in her skirts. Together they traversed the field toward the yard.

"Promise me something," Lucen said after a moment. "Promise you won't go off by yourself."

"But I do so frequently," she said.

"You know I don't mean that. Promise you won't run off to the war camps."

"There are hardly any of those left."

"Mama told me about Papa's dream when she asked me to fetch you back. Promise you won't run off to help the Crane Prince."

Jenai halted, eyeing Lucen's back before he stopped and turned to face her.

"What is it?" he asked.

"I can't promise that, Lucen. I will do what must be done."

THE MAGISTRATE'S SUMMONS

The knock on the door at supper brought every head up mid-prayer. Two weeks had passed since Jenai last heard the Voice, and she still waited for the sign of the sapphire horn. Could this be it?

Papa stood up from the table where the meal of mutton and turnips coiled with steam. He glanced at Mama, then moved to the door, cracked it open, and spoke quietly with someone on the other side. Jenai folded her napkin into her lap, smoothing its creases over and over. Her stomach danced. Inexplicably, she knew the conversation had to do with her.

"*What?*" Papa's voice cracked like thunder.

Jenai flinched, as did Lucen. Her two other brothers, Rowan and Edrin, didn't so much as blink. Rowan's wife, Hethi, dropped her fork with a clatter, face paling. Mama rose and moved to the door, but Papa slammed it shut before she arrived.

"What is it?" Mama asked.

Papa marched to the table, his gaze pinned on Jenai. "Daughter."

Jenai stood up, resting her napkin on the table. "Yes, Papa?"

"This." He held out a parchment. "This!"

Jenai frowned. Even if she could read—which she couldn't—it would be impossible to know what the parchment said with the way Papa squeezed it.

"What's happened?" Mama asked again.

"A summons, that's what." Papa slammed the parchment down on the oak table, his gaze never leaving Jenai's. "Phren LeGre has laid charges against you, child. He claims you broke your troth to him."

Jenai glanced between the crinkled parchment and her father's red face. "But I didn't," she said calmly.

Papa spluttered. "Didn't you?"

"No. I never did."

"Jenai doesn't lie, Papa," Edrin said. "But that dolt Phren lies all the time—which you well know."

"It hardly matters," Papa said, the red draining from his face. "Your sister has been summoned to the magistrate's court."

Her eyes snapped onto the parchment, her nerves settling. The magistrate was in Valcinay. That was where Lord Robarr, governor of Lorrae Province, lived.

But I've seen no sign of the sapphire horn yet.

Even so, she knew in her heart that this was the means provided to meet with Lord Robarr.

Thank you, Sweet Afallon.

She smoothed her skirts straight and asked in a calm voice, "When must I be ready to depart?"

He picked the parchment back up to read it again. "End of the week. Fortunately, we've time enough to finish planting before I must stop my work." Papa's wrathful gaze softened. "You can still reconcile with Phren, Jenai. Marry the lad and set his path right with Afallon. You're the one to do it."

"I'm sorry, Papa," Jenai said. "I won't marry him or any other."

"Stubborn fool!" He crushed the parchment between his vise-like fingers until it almost appeared to writhe. "Your duty is to home and family."

"I've forsaken neither," Jenai answered.

"You abandon your chores to wander off to that church of yours."

Every eye flicked between father and daughter. None dared to speak out. They barely dared to breathe.

"Have I ever failed to complete my chores by day's end?" asked Jenai gently.

He stared, then his shoulders slumped. "No, daughter. You work harder than your three brothers altogether."

A smile slipped onto Jenai's lips, and she stepped to her father's side. Tucking her arm around his, she stood on tiptoe to kiss the tall man's cheek. "That's an exaggeration, but I will always do my part while I remain in your house."

Papa sighed. "I want more for you than that, Jenai. You're a beautiful woman with more faith than I. You'll make a good wife and mother. Won't you stop and consider the honor in that?"

"I've always seen the honor in it," Jenai said. "I respect Mama for all she's done, and Hethi is a good wife to Rowan. I have great admiration for the women in Domrem who diligently fulfill their duties, as I do the men who fulfill theirs. That's not an issue."

"Then why?" he asked. "Why will you delay your duty?"

"I cannot tell you." She pulled free of him. "Forgive me, Papa. But I can't."

He scowled and held up the parchment. "What of this summons?"

"I will answer it," she said. "I've broken no troth. The magistrate will learn that, and the matter will be dismissed."

"You sound so certain."

"I am." She stood waiting for Papa to decide whether to let the family eat or not. He continued to study her as though she were one of the woodland fae folk—the Ilidreth—who'd gone into hiding long ago when the first Crow King hunted them down. Smile deepening, Jenai tipped her head toward the table, and Papa blinked, likely recalling the food and those gathered around it.

"Enough of this for now," he said. "Let's not let your Mama's good food be wasted."

They walked to the table and sat down. Papa started the prayer over, and soon everyone was digging into the cold meal, pretending it was still piping hot and delicious. Conversation was light and trivial. Listening to the tones rather than the words, Jenai's thoughts traveled beyond the confines of her cottage, out into the gathering darkness of evening. Soon the fireflies would be bobbing among the spring blossoms, and the Blessing Tree—though no longer glowing—would shake its boughs and settle its roots for the night.

After the meal, Jenai helped Mama and Hethi wash and dry the dishes while her brothers wiped the table of crumbs, then swept. Papa smoked his pipe at the fire, overseeing his family while they tidied. Edrin brought in more wood since the nights were still chilly though it was nearly summer.

When the work was finished and most had settled around the hearth for Hethi's stories, Jenai wrapped a shawl around her shoulders and slipped out the front door. The fireflies had come early—and likely they regretted it with the nip in the air—but they still danced defiantly near the growing hollyhocks and ember lilies.

Jenai left the yard and started up the road for the church, but something compelled her to continue past it. She walked through Domrem. Lights shone in the front windows of the thatched cottages while the bakery, chandlery, butchery, and other such shops were all dark. She strode on, passing the perfume of the early lilacs, making her way toward the path that led into the woods and eventually to the Blessing Tree.

No one was out this late. She had the world to herself, and she reveled in it. Days were so busy, spent around chattering farmhands, clucking chickens, the clamor of tools, the laughter of children. She enjoyed it, but the silence of the evening was a welcome change. Rarely could she be alone, even in the church.

Ahead, the Blessing Tree loomed. It was a dark shape against the blue-black sky where the first stars were faint pinpricks. The burble of the brook greeted Jenai like an old friend. She smiled, grateful. Since Sharisse had learned that Jenai had "foolishly" rejected Phren's offer of marriage, the girl had been avoiding Jenai, as though the decision had personally offended her. Jenai didn't understand that—but then, she hardly understood people. Since Cetta's death, she'd felt apart from them, like an observer watching from beyond the bounds of everyday life.

A twig snapped in the trees. Jenai whirled toward the noise, half afraid, half curious. It wouldn't be a villager. No one entered the woods at night. They knew better. Too many fallen logs or hidden burrows could cause a person to trip and break a bone. Jenai had spent her childhood wandering the pathless woods with Lucen when there wasn't work to be done, but even she wouldn't brave that place in the dark.

Yet someone approached her now. A light came toward her—brighter than any lantern she'd ever seen. Jenai stood still upon the path, straining for another sound, but the brook drowned out the noise of the approaching...something.

Moving to the path's edge, Jenai squinted to make out the shape at the center of the light. Her breath caught. That was no lantern, nor was it a person.

"Blessed Afallon be praised," she whispered.

A unicorn stepped from the trees, its white coat shining like moonlight, its mane a silvery hue. Its horn shone like sapphires twining around gold. The fragrance of herbs and wet stone accompanied the ethereal creature. Jenai fell to her knees, hands clasped before her. She'd heard of unicorns all her life, but never had she dared to dream she would ever see one.

'Greetings, Jenai d'Arc, chosen of the Weave.' The unicorn's voice entered Jenai's head directly, sounding like sprinkling rain and water lapping against a sandy shore. It wasn't *the* Voice that had spoken with her several times before, but it was gentle and welcome all the same. *'I am Mirrasae. I have come to aid you.'*

Jenai's lungs unlocked, allowing her to breathe. She reached out, aching to touch the unicorn's glowing coat—but she stopped herself. Unicorns were everything pure and holy. Even the church, prone to shunning the magical such as Ilidreth or dragons, revered these divine creations of Afallon.

'You may stroke my coat if you wish,' the unicorn said. *'We shall be companions in the coming days, so long as you remain pure in heart and grounded in mind.'*

"You will come with me to see the Crane Prince?"

'Just so. But you must seek a method to gain an audience with him. I can carry you upon my back, but I cannot interfere in human politics.' Amusement flooded the link between their minds. *'Not in obvious ways, at least.'*

Jenai inched closer and set her hand upon Mirrasae. The coat was trim and short but softer than a rabbit's fur. It was also cool to the touch, like soothing salve on a burn. Jenai beamed as she traced her fingers across the delicate unicorn's flank. She brushed the gleaming mane. It was silken like water running over a stone.

"I'm honored and humbled to think of riding upon your back," Jenai whispered. "Afallon is good to me."

'*Your Afallon does favor the just and the merciful,*' answered Mirrasae. '*As does the Weave.*' The unicorn's eyes—the color of seafoam—met Jenai's hazel gaze. '*We will not leave until you are destined for your time in court, but I shall linger nearby. Waiting until week's end to begin our crusade is no hardship for me. Your mortal time is short.*'

"Will you require food? Shall I—"

'*That isn't necessary, sweet Jenai. We unicorns always find sustenance, though we rarely need it. Now, return to your home and sleep peacefully, child. Once we set out to free Fraelin from the evil gripping its shores, you will find little rest. Collect what you can of it now, and relish your family's nearness. Soon, you will ache for it, and it will be far from you.*'

"I understand." Jenai's chest panged with fear, but she pushed it aside. Her capabilities were limited, her education sparse, but Afallon would make up for her defects—of that she had no doubt.

With regret, she left Mirrasae's side. Twice she glanced back to look at the unicorn. Mirrasae glowed bright enough that she might've swallowed the moon. Smiling at that thought, Jenai turned and hurried back through Domrem to her warm bed. Troubles would come, but for now, she clutched peace and relief close, soaking them in.

That night she dreamed of walking across water while crystal stones hummed beneath her dry feet. The unicorn walked with her, singing a song of starlight.

4

THE PRISONER

The dripping of water was a noise Alain had grown so used to, he rarely noticed it in the dank, dismal cell. But today he lay on his stone bed and watched the water drip in the corner while the half-rotted straw scratched at his threadbare garb. It must be raining outside. He welcomed the idea of a storm. It suited his mood.

The sniffing and scuffling of rats in the walls were less welcome. One rodent poked its nose out of the tiny hole near the water. Alain shot upright. "Out. Out!" His voice startled the filthy rodent back into its hole.

Alain had waged a private war against the rats for half a decade. His only relief came in the brief excursions to the world above when he was allowed to bathe once a month— the single perk he had due to his noble title. He couldn't be allowed to rot—not while he might be a useful bargaining chip.

He grimaced. *My life in exchange for Fraelin's imprisonment.*

Apart from those few excursions, he was trapped in this dismal little cell, fighting the rats for every moldy scrap of bread, lump of cheese, and metallic swallow of water. He'd even had to chase the rodents out of his chamber pot—the nasty little snipes.

Settling back against his sparse pile of straw, Alain tried to find a more comfortable position. He always tried. It was something to work for. A cause he still had—though one as futile as Fraelin's efforts to win against the Duke of Thargundy and the Crow King of Simaerin.

Alain lifted his eyes to the stone ceiling and glowered at the world above. Simaerin. He'd been imprisoned in this foreign land, surrounded by enemies, for five excruciating years. It was everything he could do to keep his mind sharp. He drilled himself in war strategies and sword movements. He paced his tiny cell and used the stone bed to exercise, keeping his muscles honed. It was the hardest thing he'd ever done, especially on the piddling rations the guards supplied along with a healthy side of mockery.

The thud of boots approached the cell. Alain eyed the door, then rose onto one elbow. He had time to wait. The way noise carried in the corridor outside his cell gave him ample warning before the guards arrived. But why were they coming? He'd already had his daily meal, and his chamber pot wasn't due to be emptied for another two days. He'd also bathed last week.

Swinging his legs off his chiseled bed, Alain rested his hands on his thighs and waited to see if the boots would stop at another door before his cell. They often did, but today they kept coming, stomping past the closest cell with an occupant. Alain had tried to speak with his neighbor before, but the prisoner never replied. Only the opening and closing of the food slot and the weekly noise of a chamber pot being dumped assured Alain that anyone lived next door.

Grit crunched under the heavy boots. There were two sets —no, three. Keys brattled. The lock shrieked, then the hinges whined and the door was pushed inward.

"Prisoner Alain Clayre, stand up."

Too curious to muster defiance, Alain obeyed the command, checking his stance to make certain he stood like a proper nobleman should. Two figures stood in the doorway. He could make out the armored plate one man wore, glinting dully in a thread of orange light. They must've brought a torch with them, presumably in the hands of a third figure out of sight behind the other two.

"The Crow King has received ransom for you. You're to be freed and returned to your native land."

Blood drained from Alain's face. How much did that cost his cousin?

Too much. I'm going to strangle the fool!

Taking a step forward, Alain curled his hands into fists. "This isn't a mistake?"

"We don't make mistakes here," the man standing behind the armored guard said. He was dressed in the tabard of a knighted Crowsman, the black crow silhouette stark against the red. "They aren't allowed."

That Alain could well believe. "Am I to be released immediately?"

"Yes. This way."

Alain followed the guard from the cell. The man who'd spoken took the lead along the corridors, and his young page stayed close, wielding the torch. As they moved through the dungeon halls, Alain had a hard time comprehending his freedom. Five years. He'd spent five years in that cell, wrestling against animal instinct as the hunger and loneliness grew. He'd thought he'd done well to keep his sanity—but was he the same? Or had he broken despite himself?

Only time will answer that.

He strode up the stairs, as he had dozens of times, but now he wasn't going for the baths. This time he was heading for home. An impulse to run came over him, but he stamped down on the urge. At the top floor of the dungeon, where the black stone ended and the gray stone began, the officer in the red tabard turned west. Toward the baths. Alain frowned and halted.

"I thought I was going home."

The man glanced at him. "Don't you want to bathe first?"

Right. A bath was always a good idea. He pushed a crooked smile to his lips. "Surely."

"Then come this way, Alain Clayre."

Determined to contain his growing excitement, Alain steadily traversed the familiar corridor toward his final bath in enemy lands. All the while, he contemplated what the Crane Prince must've given up to secure Alain's freedom and marveled that it had worked.

5

GOING TO TRIAL

Under a cloudy sky at week's end, Jenai climbed into Papa's wagon and waited while he checked the harnesses. Lucen handed up her and Papa's belongings, neatly packed into two satchels. Rowan and Edrin loaded up the plow into the wagon bed. The plow had been wearing down, and Papa had decided to use the trip into Valcinay to hire a proper blacksmith to repair it.

"We'll be back as soon as we can," Papa said to Mama, then kissed her on the cheeks. It was the most affection he would show to anyone.

"Take care of our Jenai," Mama said, grasping his hand. "Promise me."

Jenai looked away, unwilling to witness that promise. Papa would do his best, but she would have to defy him all the same. She must seek out Lord Robarr, persuade him to give her a letter of introduction, and then make her way to the Crane Prince in distant Shinon in the south. No one save Afallon could protect her now.

Her three brothers stood beside the wagon, along with Mama and Hethi, all smiling encouragingly, though Mama had

45

a handkerchief on hand and her eyes were red-rimmed. No one spoke. Her brothers had used up their words last night—Rowan and Edrin attempting to persuade her one last time to accept Phren's hand, and Lucen telling her he'd pray for her. It was that prayer which she clung to most.

"Ready, daughter?" asked Papa, swinging into the wagon seat.

"Yes, Papa." She settled down in the wagon bed beside the strapped down plow and pulled her shawl tight. The wagon lurched forward and rattled along the rutted road until it reached the main highway. Looking back at the thatched cottage, she waved to her family and, with a burning throat, wondered if she would ever see them again.

THE CLAMOR OF VALCINAY WAS HOW JENAI IMAGINED THE roar of the ocean to be. She'd never seen that endless stretch of water in the southwest. Her one glimpse of great waters was the channel between Fraelin and Simaerin, but that had been years ago, when she and Cetta had traveled with Papa to buy special seed during a famine.

The streets of the city were bustling with people and clattering carts. Hawkers shouted their wares. Colorful awnings adorned stalls where an assortment of scents mingled, some welcoming, others repulsive. Jenai had been to this city twice before, and she'd never enjoyed the experience. She preferred open fields and tight-knit trees to looming buildings that leaned toward her and muddy streets that smelled strongly of manure.

Papa maneuvered the wagon through town as fast as he could, but the traffic made their passage difficult. At last, they reached his brother's house in the southside residential sector. Uncle Kerch greeted them from the stoop. His wife,

Aunt Ladia, ushered them inside. She wrapped Jenai in a hug, then dragged her toward the room where Jenai and Cetta had stayed with their female cousins as children. Those cousins were all grown and married now, so Jenai had the nursery to herself.

Ladia set Jenai's satchel on one of the narrow beds. "You look lovely, dearest. How are your nerves?"

"I'm well enough," Jenai answered. "I've done nothing wrong. The magistrate will see that."

Ladia swept Jenai into another hug, then excused herself to speak with the men. Sinking onto the nearest mattress, Jenai stared around the room. It contained the familiar humble furniture, worn rug, and gray curtains drawn aside to let in the dismal light. Clouds still covered the sun, threatening rain. That would make the streets even more muddy.

The court date was set for the following morning. Papa had declared he'd wanted to arrive in time to settle his business affairs beforehand. Doubtless he also wanted to give Jenai time to reconsider her stance. But she wouldn't. Flopping against the scratchy mattress, Jenai stared at the thatching above the rafters. Soon, she would meet Lord Robarr. Soon she would begin her mission.

Is Mirrasae in the city? Did she follow close?

Jenai had tried to keep an eye out for the unicorn, but she'd seen nothing of that glorious coat and horn. Rolling onto her side, Jenai closed her eyes, letting the stillness settle into her bones after the long wagon ride. The noises of the city grew softer. The patter of rain lulled her into deep darkness.

Her aunt woke her at dinner. Jenai ate mechanically, responding to inquiries only as necessary. When dinner was cleared, she helped wash and stack the dishes. Ladia kept sending her sympathetic glances. Jenai knew that the woman believed she was nervous about seeing the magistrate, and Jenai didn't correct her. Better not to admit the real issue: that she didn't know what to say to Lord Robarr to convince him to let her see the Crane Prince.

The Voice will guide me.

So she told herself as she slipped into her nightgown. So she told herself again when she brushed her hair, then slid into the cool coverlets. So she prayed before she drifted off to sleep again.

MORNING DELIVERED A RADIANT SUN. NOT A CLOUD stained the sky. Papa was reticent and surly at breakfast. He gave Jenai more than one sharp look, as though that would convince her to change her mind about Phren. She focused on her porridge and did her best to ignore him.

Halfway through her bowl, Papa slammed his hands on the table, then stood up. His chair screeched backward across the stone floor. "Time to go."

Jenai stood up, smoothed her red dress, and wrapped her gray shawl around her shoulders. "I'm ready, Papa."

He glowered at her, then marched toward the front door, muttering "fool child" under his breath.

Aunt Ladia embraced her, then Jenai followed Papa from the dingy house out into the bright street. The courthouse was across the southern residential area and three blocks north in the administrative sector of Valcinay. Father and daughter walked side by side, their steps brisk, crossing roads where the mud was less prominent. As long-limbed as she was, she had little trouble keeping up.

The northern half of Valcinay was fragrant with flowers, and the cobbled streets were clean. Gardens were tucked between several of the buildings. The scent of manure faded away, and Jenai drank in the clean air.

Their goal was the largest structure in the city's main square. There were other smaller buildings circling the cobblestone plaza, but according to Papa, they were guild houses. In the center of the plaza was a burbling fountain topped with the statue of a crane. Crane flags hung from every second story. Everything about Valcinay defied the encroaching Thargundians.

A quarter hour before Jenai was scheduled for court, they entered the grand stone building. Phren hadn't arrived yet. Jenai sat in one of the chairs resting in a row against a wall while Papa paced the flagstones. A skylight in the vaulted ceiling let in ample light, making the torches in their sconces redundant. The dark wood that framed the entrance hall was polished and gleaming. A blue ensign bearing a white crane hung from the middle beam. Jenai studied that banner with growing solemnity. She shouldn't be here in the courthouse—she should be wherever Lord Robarr was, pleading her case.

I don't even know where to go. Perhaps he's also here in the courthouse.

The double doors flung open, banging against the inner walls and startling Jenai to her feet. Heart hammering, she looked toward the entrance. In marched a bearded, heavyset man in a green velvet surcoat, a gold chain of office winking on his chest. He wore a hat, the kind that made him look official and important.

Lord Robarr. She knew it was him. *Afallon be praised.*

The man was surrounded by guild leaders, judging by their rich apparel and the lesser chains hanging from their necks. They resembled a flock of different kinds of birds—from tall, gangling herons to squat ducks, and everything in-between. Two women were among them, one as graceful as a swan, with light brunette hair and dark eyes. The other was a wood thrush, short and portly, with rare fiery red hair and a keen gaze.

As the cluster of town leaders started forward, Robarr argued with the redheaded woman. Papa lurched out of their way, earning a passing glance from the governor. Robarr's eyes flitted to Jenai, then drifted away. The contingent moved toward a set of double doors ahead, entered in a bluster, and shut the doors with a resounding boom.

Papa scoffed faintly. "Self-important, all of them. Yet without us and our taxes, where would they be?"

"Without their defenses, where would we be?" Jenai whispered back before she considered her words. Flinching, she wondered if that would earn her a flogging later, but Papa's gaze softened.

"True enough, lass," he said. "While it lasts." He eyed the Crane Banner rippling in the breeze and shook his head. "While it lasts."

6

OBEDIENT

The magistrate was a man in his autumn years, with a deeply wrinkled brow, a severe frown, and a white powdered wig. He wore the austere blue robes of his calling, and clutched his gavel like he might a cane.

"Order!" the man bellowed in a thunderous voice that belied his years. "The case of one Phren LeGre of Domrem versus Jenai d'Arc of Domrem is now in session. There will be order!"

He battled only silence. A handful of spectators sat on the polished benches to either side of the chamber. None were familiar to Jenai. According to Aunt Ladia, they were the chronic variety that showed up for every court session, drinking in the drama, then pretending it hadn't been worth the effort.

The juror stand was empty; none had been called for this trifling affair. The magistrate narrowed his eyes around the still room, perhaps seeking that one troublemaker who might interrupt his court and provide him a chance to use his beloved gavel.

No one gave him the pleasure.

With marked disappointment, the magistrate studied the parchments on his desk for a long time. No one stirred. No one coughed. The magistrate lifted his gavel and slammed it against the wood all the same.

"Order! Having reviewed the case, I now desire to hear from both parties. The petitioner, Phren LeGre, will step forward."

Phren sauntered to the stand in the center of the chamber, his chin high, his hair combed. He'd even taken the time to wash behind his ears and wear his Reverence Day apparel. "Your Honor, I come before you aggrieved that my future wife has abandoned her oaths. I demand she be ordered by this court to marry me as she promised."

The magistrate squinted down at Phren, his frown deepening until the grooves around his eyes were yawning furrows. "Demand, is it?"

"Yes, Your Honor."

"And when did the accused promise she would wed you?"

"O-on Blessing Day, after the eventide ceremony. We spoke and—and expressed our devotion to each other. We agreed then and there to be wed by summer's end."

"And when did she rescind her promise?"

"The following day, Your Honor."

The magistrate grunted. "Next day, eh?" He glanced toward Jenai, who waited calmly on the chamber floor where she'd been told to stand. Papa sat in the nearest pew behind her. The magistrate considered her for a long moment, then turned back to Phren. "You're both of age, are you?"

"Y-yes, Your Honor," Phren said. "I'm eighteen. Jenai is seventeen."

"And your parents—do they have views on this matter?"

"Jenai's parents gave their consent before I received her promise," Phren said. "My parents have always liked Jenai. We're an excellent match, Your Honor. I think poor Jenai is just too shy and needs an official court order to push her into what she truly wants in her heart of hearts."

Jenai fixed her gaze on her feet, resisting a growing urge to laugh at Phren's lies. He'd always been quick to conjure them, especially when he was little. The whole village knew he could create whoppers large enough to swallow Fraelin. Few still bought into them, all these years later. But it was possible that the magistrate would—and then she would be forced to wed Phren.

If it comes to that, I'll have to run away.

But surely Afallon would guide the magistrate away from that decision. She had a calling far away from this little province. The Crane Prince needed her.

I must simply put my trust in a higher power and let this go as it will.

"Do you have anything else to add to your statement, young man?" asked the magistrate.

"No, Your Honor. Only—that I love her."

The magistrate slammed his gavel down. "Irrelevant. Step back."

As Phren retreated from the stand, Jenai studied him. He didn't love her. That was a lie, too. He certainly wanted her, but that had begun as a whim and only turned more serious when she'd refused him. She knew him well enough to be certain of that.

"The accused will step forth," the magistrate called, shuffling his papers with one hand, the other still gripping his gavel.

Jenai glided to the stand, keeping her posture straight, not daring to lift her chin too high. If she did, the magistrate might think she was haughty and disrespectful. She clasped her hands before her, showing him due deference.

"State your name."

"I am Jenai d'Arc of Domrem."

"Do you know the petitioner?"

"Yes. He is Phren LeGre."

"Did you recently break your troth to this young man?"

"No, Your Honor." Her statement sent a murmur rippling through the small crowd.

The magistrate seized his chance, striking his gavel hard and fast three times. "Order! There will be order!"

The murmurs stopped. Shuffling settled into stillness. Several matrons leaned forward to catch the next exchange between the accused and the magistrate. After scanning the room for any further disturbances, the magistrate turned back to Jenai. "You mean to say you have *not* broken your troth?"

"There was no troth to break."

The magistrate lifted his gavel in anticipation, but no one had the courtesy to utter a single word. He grimaced and bore down on Jenai in retaliation. "It's a sin to lie in court, lass."

"It is a sin to lie at all."

Someone coughed. The magistrate didn't notice. He shifted in his chair, eyeing Jenai with newfound interest. "So it is. Your statement, then, is that you gave no troth to him. No promise. No intention."

"None, Your Honor. I refused him."

"Why?"

"I don't wish to marry him."

An onlooker snorted. The magistrate tapped his gavel, but not hard.

"What about your parents? Did they approve of the match?"

"They did, Your Honor."

"Then you have dishonored them in your refusal."

Jenai's shoulders drooped. "I'm afraid so, Your Honor, but they did not command me to wed Phren LeGre. I've not disobeyed them in that. Your Honor, I cannot and will not marry him."

"What if I ordered you to right now, this very moment?"

"Then as an obedient citizen of Fraelin, I will obey, Your Honor. But I beg you not to command me."

"Is he so repulsive to you?" The magistrate's voice gentled. "Has he tried to harm you, lass?"

"Beyond my reputation, no, Your Honor."

"Then why refuse him? Can he not provide a suitable home? The chance for your own space? A parcel of children?"

"Presumably, he can offer all of that," Jenai answered, "but still, I will not marry him."

"Is it a matter of love, child?"

"Yes, Your Honor. My love of Afallon over man."

Murmurs hummed like bees in a clover field. The magistrate rapped his gavel harder than ever. He looked at Jenai, narrowing his eyes until they were mere slits. He leaned over his platform, a scowl drawing lines around his mouth.

"Do you seek a life of seclusion? You wish to join a convent?"

"No, Your Honor. I seek to do Sweet Afallon's will."

He leaned back. The hardness fell away. "And what is His will?"

Jenai hesitated, feeling Papa's eyes on her back. But she wouldn't lie. "I can't tell you, Your Honor. That's between me, Afallon, and Lord Robarr."

The crowd's humming grew to stinging levels, but the magistrate only stared, his gavel forgotten. "You need to speak with Lord Robarr?"

"Yes, Your Honor. I must be granted an audience with him. It's urgent."

The magistrate set his gavel aside and motioned to the bailiff standing to one side of the bench. The two men put their heads together, whispering like snakes, then the bailiff trotted from the room.

Clearing his throat, the magistrate turned his attention back to Jenai. He searched her face, then pinned his sights on Phren. "The court has made its decision. In the matter of Phren LeGre against Jenai d'Arc of Domrem, the court rules in favor of the accused. No troth has been broken. The young woman is free of any matrimonial obligation. The court suggests Phren LeGre not make a habit of lying to Fraelin's officials in future, lest he risk the stocks. Dismissed!"

7

HER PETITION

The magistrate pounded the gavel with immense force, then stood up and moved to one side of the stand.

The spectators cheered, their applause ringing in the rafters of the large stone room. Relief soared in Jenai's chest, and she set her hand against her racing heart. She didn't dare glance back to see Phren's reaction, nor did she risk looking at Papa. She wasn't certain which man would be angrier at the verdict or her responses that had led to it. Motion by the stand caught her eye, and she found the magistrate waving her over to him.

Gladly, she crossed the chamber and curtsied to the magistrate. "Your Honor?"

"I've sent the bailiff to bring Lord Robarr here. If he's in council, it may be a while before he can slip away. Call it an old man's curiosity, lass, but I feel you deserve the chance to speak with him." He pointed to a door to one side of the chamber. "You may wait in my study until he arrives. Make yourself comfortable."

"Thank you, Your Honor!" To go from fear of a forced

marriage to earning a private audience with Lord Robarr? Jenai felt so light, she might fly.

Afallon be thanked.

She curtsied again and moved toward the door, wondering if Papa would join her or not. If he did, he would soon learn her destiny.

Reaching the door, she chanced a look behind her. Papa was speaking with the magistrate, his large hands gesturing wildly, while the older man frowned and shook his head. Jenai could imagine Papa's protest—demanding that she be made to see reason, that she be made to marry. But the magistrate folded his arms and looked down his nose.

Jenai slipped into the study and shut the door. The room had a window across from the entrance, framed by blue curtains. The paned glass looked out onto a private garden sandwiched between the courthouse and the next building. A gleaming wall of shelves to one side of the room brimmed with tomes and scrolls. A fire crackled in the stone hearth on the other side, and a banner with the emblem of the crane against a blue field took up the wall above the mantelpiece. A corner desk beside the books was stuffed with stacks of parchment and quills. In a glass case upon the desk lay a gavel broken in two pieces on a velvet cushion. A pair of chaise lounges were facing each other in the center of the chamber. A wide rug lay between them.

She sat down on one of the lounges, smoothed her red dress, then ran her hands through her long black hair while she waited, nerves dancing. Time stretched on. Papa never came in. He might argue with authority, but he'd never force entry. His loyalty to Fraelin ran too deep.

Distant doors opened and closed. Humming voices grew loud in the adjoining chamber, suggesting more spectators had arrived for the new show. Soon, the magistrate's booming voice and the accompanying drum of his gavel resounded from his perch. The din of the spectators tapered. Likely, the magistrate's new case was a much more important ordeal than Jenai's had been.

The minutes turned into an hour. The boos of an angry crowd ebbed and flowed like the tide, and the magistrate's gavel must have been half-worn out by the time he issued a thundering verdict of "Guilty!" to the crowd's uproarious approval. The sentence was death. The cheers roared even louder, with several sharp protests cutting through the celebrations.

Agitated by the bloodthirstiness, Jenai rose and hurried to the window. She threw the latch and pushed the window open. The fragrance of spring flowers and freshly scythed grass poured in. A bee zipped by, and a bird trilled in the oak tree at the edge of the garden.

The shouts in the adjacent room were replaced by the pounding of departing feet. Someone was sobbing and pleading with the magistrate. Another person shouted. Then doors slammed shut. Jenai had no idea what the affair had been about, or why death was the result. Perhaps a Thargundian sympathizer. That was the leading cause of execution these days.

Silence followed. The doors in the next room burst open. Two deep voices spoke, but they were too muffled to make out. Another moment, then footsteps approached the study. The door swung inward, revealing the magistrate. Just behind him stood Lord Robarr in his green velvet ensemble.

"Is this the lass?" the governor asked.

"Yes. Jenai d'Arc of Domrem."

She moved from the window and dropped to her knees. "Your Excellency."

Robarr strode into the study, eyeing her critically. "I have little time. What presses you to seek an audience with me, maiden of Domrem?"

She drew a steadying breath and bowed her head. "By your leave, my lord, I need a letter of introduction from you."

"To what possible end?"

"I seek an audience with the Crane Prince of Fraelin. I must lead his army to victory against Kon Dragonclaw of Thargundy."

8

SEEKING COURAGE

The stillness was deafening. Jenai stared at Lord Robarr's boots. Outside, the bird trilled again.

"Is this some jest?" Lord Robarr asked, sounding more bewildered than angry.

"No, my lord," Jenai said.

"She's an earnest lass," the magistrate said from the doorway. "Faithful and honest by my scrutiny. But perhaps she's simpleminded."

Robarr grunted. His boots twisted away, taking him toward the door.

"Please, my lord!" Jenai half-rose from the floor. "I'm not in jest, nor am I addled. I may be a simple lass from a small village, but I speak only what I know."

He turned toward her, his brows drawn together, a grave sort of derision set against his thin mouth. "Admit it. You wish to present yourself to the Crane Prince in order to see if the bachelor heir apparent will admire your beauty. Maybe even take you to wife. Isn't that so? I'm minded to flog you and throw you in the stocks for a day."

Jenai started forward. "Please, my lord, heed me. I must

be introduced to the Crane Prince in order to liberate Fraelin from our enemies. This is Afallon's own truth—I vow it."

Something in Robarr's face softened. "I see. Your earnestness has given you delusions. It's a fine thing you crave, Maid Jenai, but the war is all but over. The Crow King is content to let us rot in the south of Fraelin. Your Crane Prince will never be king, but he'll live a long and fruitless life, much as any of us."

The Voice came, gentle and whispering, bringing a warning.

Fear grew in Jenai's gut as she listened. "The war is about to worsen, my lord," she said. "A troop of Thargundians marches on Water-by-the-Rift not twenty leagues from here. The Crow King is *not* content to let us rot. He wishes to enslave us or destroy us. He'll never let us sit free."

Robarr's eyes hardened. "You go too far, lass. You can't possibly know what's going on twenty leagues off, nor can you predict the Crow's movements better than me or my soldiers. Off with you." He whirled toward the magistrate. "Is that her father out there?"

"Yes," the magistrate said, though his eyes rested on Jenai.

"Take her to him and tell them both to return to their living. I have more immediate concerns to handle here. I can't waste my time on delusions of grandeur. Out with you, maiden."

"Please, my lord. Look to Water-by-the-Rift. If—"

"I said out!"

She curtsied, then slipped around him and stepped into the courtroom. Papa was standing near the doors leading out into the audience hall. His dark eyes were blazing. Jenai held that gaze steadily. She'd failed today, but she would return as many times as it took to receive permission to see the Crane Prince.

THAT NIGHT, SHE STOLE AWAY FROM HER UNCLE'S HOME. Papa had switched between quiet wrath to rumbling shouts all through dinner. She'd embarrassed him. She'd ruined her chances of marriage, perhaps forever. How could she disgrace the family so? Jenai had sat in silence, eating her stew, doing her best to let the tides of his fury roll off her.

At last, exhausted, Papa had gone to bed after announcing that they would be leaving in the morning, even if the plow wasn't repaired. He'd probably change his mind when he woke up. Without the plow, he'd have to make a return trip, and that would cut into his work hours. Papa never let anything cut into those if he could help it.

In the darkness, the city of Valcinay was less intimidating. Most folk had retreated indoors, and the odors of churned manure and mud had settled down. The haunting fragrance of magnolias and lilacs floated in the air like familiar ghosts. Jenai found their company comforting.

She retraced her steps to the administrative sector and spotted the courthouse looming before the square's grand fountain. She strode past it and sought the garden hidden between its wall and the neighboring building. It was gated, but the gate wasn't locked. Gingerly, Jenai opened it and stepped into the green haven.

No birds sang in the darkness, but crickets had begun their nightly symphony. Half-grown ember lilies brought the promise of summer. Fireflies danced beneath the tree, reminiscent of the Blessing Tree in Domrem. With the recent memory came a stab of melancholy. Jenai found she was homesick, but not for her family. She hadn't been away from them long enough for that. She found she was homesick for before...everything.

Sinking to her knees in the garden's trimmed lawn, she bowed her head. "Sweet Afallon, I'm afraid. I know what You wish me to do, and I can do all things through You. But I'm still afraid. Forgive my weakness. Forgive my frailty. I miss Cetta. I miss my childhood. I miss its simplicity and peace. But I know that You faced hardships far greater than mine. And I know that when tyranny comes, someone must stand and fend it off. Why You've chosen me, I can't guess—but I will do my best. It's...all I have to give You."

'*It will be enough*,' came a voice like flowing water—not *the* Voice, but a welcome one, nonetheless.

Jenai twisted around, still on her knees, and found Mirrasae glowing beneath the pale moon. The unicorn's sapphire horn gleamed. Rising, Jenai approached the wondrous creature, trembling with relief and joy.

"Did the Voice send you to bring me strength, lovely Mirrasae?"

'*The Weave sent me, which may be the same source. I do not know.*' Mirrasae looked into Jenai's eyes. '*It is all right to be afraid if you do not let it cripple you. Fear lends clarity and keeps one alive. Without it, one may plunge into shadows and never see the danger.*'

Jenai rested her hand on Mirrasae's muzzle. The soft, cool sensation of the unicorn's coat quieted the ripples of unrest in her soul. "I'm not afraid now. You give me courage."

'*Seek courage in yourself, Jenai d'Arc. There is plenty of it to be mined.*'

She nodded, though she couldn't help doubting the unicorn's standpoint. Jenai was courageous about *some* things, but she still couldn't fathom why Afallon would choose her to liberate Fraelin. Still, she did have faith in her God, if not in herself.

"Lord Robarr refused my petition," she whispered.

'That is no surprise. Do not despair, Jenai. The Weave shall aid you.'

The Weave. The magic woven into the world. Jenai knew little about it beyond what the priest had told her—but the unicorn was proof that it was good.

"I won't despair now," Jenai said. "I'm no longer alone."

AT DAWN, SHE RETURNED TO THE COURTHOUSE AND requested an audience with Lord Robarr. Papa was still asleep when she slipped out. Jenai didn't doubt that when he woke to find her gone, a storm would brew over her uncle's home. But that couldn't matter.

She sat in the audience hall, darning socks she'd brought along to Valcinay to pass the time. All morning long, the names of other petitioners were called out, even those who'd arrived after her. At noon, she confronted the man stationed at the door to Lord Robarr's offices.

"Will I be called after lunch?" she asked.

"Name?" He unfurled his scroll.

"Jenai d'Arc of Domrem."

He scanned the parchment. "You're not on here, lass. Day's full. Come back tomorrow."

Jenai's stomach sank. "There must be some mistake. I came early this morning. I gave you my name."

He squinted at her, then blinked. "Ah. You. Lord Robarr said you concluded your business yesterday. Don't waste his lordship's time. Be off with you."

"I can't and won't. This matter is urgent. Please put my name on the petitioner's list again. I will wait all day."

"It's full," he said. "Come back tomorrow and try again if you must—but don't expect anything to come of it."

Anxiety tugged at her chest, but she hefted her chin and

held the man's dark eyes. "I will come back. I won't *stop* coming back until Lord Robarr grants me an audience. Remember my name: Jenai d'Arc." She turned and left the building.

She couldn't return to her uncle's house. Papa would be waiting, furious and ready to beat her. Instead, she wandered Valcinay. The city was bustling. The odors of manure and sweat were strong, mingling with baking bread and roasting meat. Jenai found herself following the scent of food. The few coins in her dress pocket acted as a tempting weight. She'd eaten nothing since last night, and the sun was in full splendor now, spreading spokes of light through dappled clouds.

Her steps brought her to a wide market bursting with stalls whose hawkers shouted out all manner of food, from fruit preserves, to baked goods, to mutton and beef. Jenai approached the first stall she could find where rolls were on display. A nearby stand of flowers wafted their perfume toward her. She bought two rolls for a better price than anything sold in Domrem's bakery. The bread was fluffy and soft, and she relished each bite, glad to quiet the grumbling of her stomach.

She passed by peasants in humble clothes, soldiers in gleaming armor, and nobles in their fine brocaded linens with glittering gems. The last of these perplexed Jenai. The province was impoverished. Everyone knew that. Even the Crane Prince had no money to fund his army. Yet these men and women strolled along, wearing what must be the last of their wealth, their noses in the air, as though somehow, they were still superior to the filth around them.

Afallon, forgive me the uncharitable thought. I shouldn't judge them.

"Hello there, lass." The man who spoke wore Lord Robarr's stallion crest upon his gleaming breastplate. He'd cut off her path while she was studying the nearby noblewoman drenched in blue silks and velvets.

"Hello, good sir." She curtsied, heart pounding. She'd never spoken with a soldier before. Had Papa sent him to find her? Had she addressed him properly?

"Are they any good?" The soldier nodded to her rolls. His eyes were a stormy gray, and his dark brown hair was held back in a tail. He couldn't be older than twenty-two or twenty-three years, and his face was handsome in a rugged way.

Hadn't he asked her something. She shook herself. "I'm sorry, um..."

"Your rolls?" he prompted. "Are they any good?"

"Oh. Yes. Very good."

"From which stall did you purchase them?"

She turned to retrace her steps, seeking the merchant. "That one. Near the flower girl."

"Much obliged." He moved off, another soldier—older by two decades—following him.

Jenai tracked their steps with her eyes until they reached the right stall, then she turned and continued circling the food market. A turkey leg tempted her, but she resisted. There was the chance her uncle would refuse to let her stay with him, and if she must remain in Valcinay for days or weeks, she needed to hold back the rest of her money to survive. Rolls would be her rations.

If I am to remain here, first I must convince Papa to let me.

But no matter how she nibbled her rolls and circled the square, no ideas came to her. She couldn't think of any way to convince Papa that her call was more important than returning home. Especially after his unsettling dreams about her in the war camps.

I'm forbidden to tell him of the Voice. Even if I could, he would never believe me.

She wasn't certain anyone would.

The sun was sinking behind the buildings before she turned her steps toward Papa and the storm waiting to receive her at her uncle's house. It was nearing dinnertime. Aunt Ladia would be worriedly ringing her hands. Papa would be pacing the flagstones. Uncle Kerch would be tending the fire, trying to assure everyone that Jenai was fine, even as he quietly fretted.

She reached the front door of the house. The wooden barrier sagged on its hinges, and the lintel whitewash was weathered. Jenai stared at the details of the slow wear-down for several moments, trying to build up her nerve. Few things frightened her so much as Papa's wrath, perhaps because he was usually a quiet man, good to his family—unless the tide inside him rose.

Afallon, keep me.

She stepped inside and shut the door. Standing near the table, Aunt Ladia whirled to face the newcomer, her expression just what Jenai had pictured. Uncle Kerch stood up from the fireplace where he'd been adding logs. But Papa was nowhere in sight.

"When you didn't come home after the courthouse closed, he went out looking for you," Ladia said. "Child, he's not pleased."

Jenai nodded. "I would be angry, too, in his place."

"Where have you been?" asked Uncle Kerch.

"I went to petition Lord Robarr, but he won't see me until tomorrow or later. After that, I wandered the markets."

"All day?" Ladia shook her head. "Jenai, you knew you were supposed to return to Domrem. The plow's repaired. You'll be leaving in the morning."

"No. Papa will, but not me. I must remain and speak with Lord Robarr."

"What could be so urgent, child?" asked Kerch. "You were

already acquitted of that idiot Phren's accusations." He hesitated. "Do you fear he'll harm you in retaliation?"

"No, there's no danger of that. Phren's too proud. He won't seek me out again."

"Then what can be so pressing that you'd disobey your father?" Ladia asked. "You've always been obedient, Jenai."

"I will always be so where I'm able," Jenai answered, "but in matters of Afallon's will, I must act regardless of anyone else's wishes."

Ladia approached, examining Jenai's eyes. "Speaking with Lord Robarr is *that* important?"

"It matters above all other things."

Ladia searched her face a moment more, then nodded. "Very well. Go to the nursery. Say nothing."

"Ladia," Uncle Kerch said sharply.

"Hush, husband. My niece has never lied to me." Ladia rested her hand on Jenai's arm. "Stay quiet. When your papa returns, remain hidden. We'll convince him to return to his fields and promise him that we'll continue searching for you."

"We can't lie to my brother," Uncle Kerch said.

"We will dance around any lies," Ladia told him. "Tend to your fire." The man grimaced but did as he was told. Ladia turned back to Jenai. "You're too good and too devout to be less than honest. I trust you above all others, niece. Go, now. Your papa will return at any moment."

Jenai embraced her aunt, murmured her thanks, and stole off to the bedroom. Sinking to her knees beside the bed, she prayed Papa wouldn't be too upset. She also asked for the strength to face him someday...if she lived long enough.

It was another hour before the front door opened. Lying on the straw mattress, Jenai held still, listening hard. Voices rose and fell, but Papa never shouted. The clatter of dishes followed. The scent of food wafted toward Jenai, but her stomach was in knots. The idea of eating anything was nauseating. She rolled over and fell asleep.

In her dreams, she wore bright armor and hefted a sword bearing ember lilies upon its hilt. A banner flew overhead, billowing in a strong wind. It bore three ember lilies upon a white field.

9

IMPASSE

Ladia woke Jenai near dawn. "Your papa's gone. He agreed to depart first thing this morning. He's furious with you, but he can't neglect his work any longer. We're to take you to him as soon as we can convince you to return."

Jenai hugged her aunt again. "Thank you. Afallon bless you."

"Enough of that. Be off to speak with Lord Robarr so that we can put this affair behind us."

Jenai climbed from the bed and slipped her red dress over her shift. "He may not listen to me, and I can't depart until he does."

"But, child—"

"Please don't ask me questions I'm not at liberty to answer." Jenai pulled on her slippers, then caught up a brush on the washstand to run it through her hair. "I know this is all very strange, but you must trust me to know my business."

"I do," Ladia said. "Just...be wise."

Jenai set the brush down and turned to face her aunt. "I have no wisdom in this matter. But through Afallon, I will be guided." She hugged Ladia again. "I must go now."

"Here." Ladia pressed a knapsack into her arms. "Something to tide you over today. Come back for dinner, whatever happens."

After thanking her, Jenai set off. The path to the courthouse felt familiar now, and the noises of the stirring city were less disconcerting after wandering so much yesterday. Jenai kept one eye out for her father in case he hadn't left Valcinay yet, but she never saw him. Approaching the courthouse, she slowed and looked around cautiously. He could be waiting there—but he wasn't. Papa was a single-minded man. His work came before anything else.

Satisfied, Jenai slipped inside the grand building and past the armored guards at the doors. She waited in the short queue for her turn to put her name on the petitioner list. When she reached the front of the line, the man glanced up, then froze.

"You came back?"

"I said I would."

Shrugging, he set his quill to parchment. "Name?"

"Jenai d'Arc of Domrem."

"Purpose?"

"An urgent military matter."

The man gave her a flat stare, then shrugged and wrote her answer.

Jenai moved to an empty seat to wait. She ate the apple and half the wedge of cheese Aunt Ladia had packed for her, saving the bread and other half of the wedge for lunch. The day progressed much like the previous had—with names called and petitioners coming and going. Just like yesterday, people who had entered the courthouse after Jenai were called before her. But she didn't leave. At lunch she stayed in her seat and ate her meal in silence. After lunch, when the city chimes sounded, the petitioners continued flowing in and out. Her name was never called.

When the five o'clock chimes pealed, the man with the list rolled up the parchment. "That's all for today. Come back tomorrow if it's so urgent." His eyes danced away from Jenai, but she approached him, nonetheless.

"I will return tomorrow," she said. "Remember my name: Jenai d'Arc."

He said nothing, and she departed.

At dinner, Uncle Kerch tried to convince Jenai to return home. "Lord Robarr is a busy man, and not someone to annoy. If he won't see you again, that isn't likely to change."

"Then I will have to see him outside the courthouse."

Jenai rose earlier the next morning and slipped on her red dress. Aunt Ladia had anticipated her and offered up another bundle of food. Jenai accepted it with quiet thanks. Trudging through the predawn mists, she hurried to the courthouse. The man with the list hadn't arrived yet. The doors were locked. Jenai waited.

At the seventh hour chime, two guards came to flank the doors. Next came the man with the list. He glanced at Jenai, then sighed, unlocked the doors, and stepped inside. Jenai remained on the stoop, waiting.

Lord Robarr arrived shortly with his retinue. He wore velvet again, this time burgundy. The same hat sat on his head while the same chain of office glittered in the pale morning light. He argued with a large, stiff man who could easily be mistaken for a boulder, from his thick chest to his meaty hands. Even the man's pate was bare and hard. They ascended the steps, Lord Robarr walking slightly ahead of the other fellow. He spared a glance toward the top stair, then froze. A glower darkened his face.

"You again. This is too much."

Jenai curtsied. "My lord, were it not of the utmost—"

"Annoyance," he cut across her. "That's what it is. Utmost

annoyance. Enough of this daydreaming, lass. Return to your fields, or I'll have you flogged."

A thread of fear coiled against her heart, but Jenai held his gaze all the same. "Flog me if you must, my lord. But then send me with your blessing to the Crane Prince."

"Nothing doing," he said. "Where's your father?"

"He returned home."

"Fool man," Robarr muttered. "Follow after him. Go home and find something constructive to fill your hours. War is man's province."

"Yes, my lord. And peace is Afallon's. I petition you on his behalf to let me go on an errand of peace."

Robarr snorted. "I thought you said you intended to defeat the Thargundians in battle."

"Yes, my lord, so that we can all stop fighting."

The boulder of a man took the last two steps and set his broad, heavy hand on Jenai's shoulder. "Out of his lordship's way. Move." His voice was surprisingly gentle.

Jenai obeyed him, her mind racing for another way to argue her point. "Please, my lord" was all that came out.

Robarr passed her, shaking his head, while his retinue of birds either ignored her or looked her up and down like she was a beggar seeking alms. The swan and the wood thrush didn't glance her way, but she felt their sharp judgment all the same. The door shut in their wake, leaving Jenai alone on the stairs.

With a sigh she stepped inside the courthouse. The retinue had already flown into their nests, leaving only Jenai and the man with the scroll. She strode up to him while he stared fixedly at his parchment, ignoring her.

"Jenai d'Arc to see Lord Robarr on Afallon's errand."

The man sighed, his shoulders drooping. "He won't see you."

"Please tell him all the same."

He nodded and scribbled on his parchment. "Sit, lass."

Jenai sat in the nearest chair to Lord Robarr's office, took a sock out of her knapsack, and began darning it. Other petitioners filed into the courthouse. The hall filled up. The old magistrate entered but never glanced her way. After that, a few prisoners in manacles came, then went, led between guards wearing the city heraldry. Now and then the raging thunder of the magistrate's gavel boomed through the hall amid gales of cheers or protests. The day progressed the same as the last two: other petitioners were called, but never Jenai. At noon, she remained in the hall, and Lord Robarr bustled out to eat, never sparing her a glance.

By evening, Jenai felt defeated, but she couldn't go home.

Afallon will provide a way.

On the walk back to her lodgings, she considered begging Uncle Kerch for directions southward. She could ride Mirrasae to the Crane Prince's abode in Shinon on her own—but that was foolishness. If Lord Robarr wouldn't listen to her, how could she ever seek an audience with the Crane Prince? Besides, the route to Shinon was treacherous. Thargundian sympathizers and ruffians alike haunted the byways of Southern Fraelin. They'd never let her through alive and unscathed.

There must be some way.

The Voice had told her to be patient.

I'm trying. But patience is harder than all other virtues.

Yet Jenai had no choice.

THE WEEK PROGRESSED IN THE SAME MANNER. DESPITE Robarr's threat of a flogging, he never followed through. But he did order the man with the scroll not to write Jenai's name down.

"It's too bad," the man said on the fifth day. "I know your name better than my own now."

"I'm sorry for troubling you," Jenai said.

"It's no trouble. I'm in awe of your audacity."

Jenai had never heard the word *audacity* before. Was it similar to being stubborn? "Thank you, I think," she said.

He grinned. "Trust me, it's an admirable quality."

She smiled. "Then I accept your compliment. What's your name?"

"Petray Havim," he said.

"I'm grateful to you for your patience, Petray Havim."

"As I said, it's no trouble. Perhaps one of these days, Lord Robarr will cave."

"Afallon willing."

Since her name was no longer on the list, Jenai didn't arrive at the beginning of each day and stay until dusk. She came and went at random, between times walking the streets, praying and meditating on another approach to convince him. To pass the time, she familiarized herself with the city. Several of the hawkers in the market squares now knew her by name. A few of the beggars she'd given coin to called out greetings when she passed.

Smiling, she hailed them all back, showing none of the turmoil in her heart. Time was getting away from her. One week became two. A letter arrived from home, written in Edrin's wobbly hand. He was the only one of Jenai's siblings who'd learned to read and write. It was addressed to Aunt Ladia in the event that the woman found Jenai. The hasty words, dictated by Mama, begged Jenai to return to Domrem. Uncle Kerch read them at dinner.

"Perhaps it's time to go home, child," Ladia said in the silence that evening.

"Not until Afallon wills it," Jenai replied.

The conversation ended right there.

In the middle of the third week, Jenai strode toward the courthouse. It was midmorning, with the promise of a beautiful day. She composed a message in her mind to have Petray write and deliver to Lord Robarr. She barely noticed the passersby or heard the carts rolling through the streets. Her head was bowed, watching the paving stones before her slippers. She carried her usual knapsack with bread and cheese and a water flask she always filled at the Crane fountain outside the courthouse.

A pair of polished boots stepped in front of her. "Hello again, lass."

She lifted her head in surprise. A soldier stood before her, a grim sort of smile on his face. Startling, she realized it was the same man from the food market her second day in Valcinay. He had the same stormy gray eyes and wore the gleaming armor with Lord Robarr's stallion crest stamped on the breastplate.

Jenai dipped into a curtsey. "Good sir."

"Those rolls were as delicious as they looked," he said quietly. "I appreciated your help that day."

"It was no trouble."

"I've seen you since," he said. "You visit the court district daily, don't you?"

She nodded, dread climbing her throat. Had Lord Robarr sent this man to stop her? Was she about to be escorted back to Domrem forcibly?

"People are talking about you," he said. "Rumor has it you've requested an army to escort you to the Crane Prince in Shinon for a private audience."

Warmth spread across Jenai's cheeks. How had the rumors gotten started? Only Robarr, the old magistrate, and her aunt and uncle knew anything regarding her mission. "I'd not be so bold as to request an army at my back."

He fell still. "Is the rest of it true then?"

"Yes," she said. "It's a matter of urgency."

"So the rumors indicated." He folded his arms over his breastplate, eyeing her like he hadn't seen anything quite like her before. "I understand Lord Robarr has refused your request—twice. Do you intend to continue seeking his aid anyway?"

"I do." She held the man's gaze. "I'll continue on until he relents. There is no other recourse."

"Couldn't you travel to Shinon without his permission?"

"The Crane Prince won't see me without a letter of introduction. I need Lord Robarr's stamp. Besides that, I don't know the route, and it's dangerous."

"The Crane Prince *does* take petitioners, you know."

"Not in time to act. Too many northern refugees would be ahead of me in the queue. I need to see him *immediately* once I arrive."

"You've thought this through, I see." He tipped his head to one side. "What compels you so urgently to see our prince?"

She hesitated, but something about this man's eyes made her trust him. If only she could explain...

"You may tell him of your calling," the Voice whispered.

Relief made Jenai's heart leap. Someone she could confide in. "I must convince him to let me lead his armies in a siege against Kon Dragonclaw at Lorion." She curtsied again. "If you'll excuse me, I must seek Lord Robarr again today."

She started around him, but the man caught her arm.

"You really mean that?"

"I'm not in the habit of lying."

"I'm Sir Mercer, Knight of Valcinay, serving under Lord Robarr. What's your name, lass?"

"Jenai d'Arc of Domrem." She looked into his eyes again.

"How did you know I was the woman spoken of in those rumors?"

He pointed at her dress. "Your apparel, Maid Jenai. Everyone along this stretch of Valcinay is speaking of the damsel in the red dress who won't accept Lord Robarr's no as his final word. As I said before, I've seen you. So has everyone else."

"I see." She glanced at her dress. It was the finest she owned—the only one she thought was fitting to see nobility in. She hadn't considered how it might make her stand out. She'd selected the red fabric and sewn it together intentionally—to remind herself of her purpose in fighting against the red of Thargundy. It was her statement against the traitors until she could don the royal blue of Fraelin and serve the Crane Prince.

"Please excuse me, Sir Knight," she said, dipping her head. "I mustn't delay, or I'll miss Lord Robarr. Midweek, he leaves early for meetings across Valcinay."

"Of course." He released her arm. "I'll walk with you if that's all right?"

"If you wish."

They strode together along the street. For the first time, Jenai was conscious of how she must stand out. Her nerves hummed, and she felt a hundred eyes boring into her, watching from the windows above and the alleys running opposite the main thoroughfare.

The knight, Mercer, was tall and muscular. Jenai was taller than most women by several inches, but she felt short beside him. The height difference was disconcerting, but her instincts didn't scream a warning in Mercer's presence. He felt genuine, and his conduct was gentle and welcoming.

"How long have you been in Valcinay?" he asked.

"Just over a fortnight. We met on my second full day."

"You're most persistent. May I ask you something, Maid Jenai?"

"If you wish."

"How do you feel you can lead an army in a siege? Do the maidens of Domrem learn combat and strategy?"

"We learn to work hard and trust in Afallon," she replied.

"Ah. You're devout, then?"

"Are you not?" she asked.

"I'm as devout as any soldier, I suppose."

"I've never met a soldier before," she said. "I have no method to gauge your faith by that measure."

He shrugged. "I've seen combat, Maid Jenai. I've seen death and worse. I've witnessed the ugliness of men on both sides of a conflict: looting, carnage, debauchery. I'm sure even you have heard of the exploits of the notorious General La Resh. I think such sights lead a man to wonder whether Afallon in His heaven really cares or even exists. I'm not saying I'm a non-believer, but I do have questions."

"We all have questions, Sir Mercer," Jenai said. "Afallon saw fit to take my younger sister four years ago. She died at the hands of the Thargundians. I wasn't certain I could live without her, but Afallon knew I could."

He said nothing. Their steps gently slapped the walkway.

"I'm sorry about your sister. There's no pain like that—losing close kin so young." He glanced at her. "You seem older than you look."

"War grows us up very quickly."

"You're from Domrem, you said? I think I've heard of it. Is it near the central boundary?"

"Yes. We've fought Thargundian invaders often since they broke the treaty."

He nodded. "My own village was wiped off the map two years ago. Luckily, we received word in time and most people got out. Only those who refused to leave their homes perished."

Nausea churned Jenai's stomach. "Why would anyone stay under such a threat?"

"Who can say?" They reached the courthouse and Sir Mercer halted. "I've been commanded to patrol this street today. Good fortunes to you, Maid Jenai."

"Thank you, Sir Mercer." She inclined her head, then strode up the steps and into the courthouse. The hall within was packed. The cry of children echoed off the wooden rafters, and several petitioners coughed at intervals. Every chair was occupied, and whole families huddled together on the floor. Many wore blood-stained bandages, and their clothes were dusty from travel.

Petray looked up from his scroll, blinked, then shook his head. He didn't make a note on his parchment before he shouted for the next petitioner to enter Lord Robarr's offices.

Jenai made her way through the hall, dancing around people, noting dirt-smudged cheeks stained with old tears. When she reached Petray, she waited for him to jot down another name.

"Lord Robarr already left for the day," the scribe said without looking up. "His assistants are the ones dealing with this mess."

"What's happened?" she asked, suspicions already rising. Thargundian attack. It was the most likely possibility.

"I don't ask questions," Petray answered. "I only take names."

"You haven't heard anything?" She glanced around the hall.

"Could you hear anything in this din? I'm sorry, Jenai, but today I couldn't possibly take a message for you, even if my lord was here. Please try tomorrow—or go home. That might be best."

She smiled at him. "You know I won't do that."

"No. You won't, stubborn girl." He sounded put out, but a faint smile twitched at his lips. "Either way, it's best you wait. Today, Lord Robarr's temper will be hot as a dragon's breath."

She thanked him, then weaved through the clusters of families. Several smelled of woodsmoke while others shook with fever and stank of blood. At the door, someone caught her skirt. A girl, perhaps ten years old, with mournful dark eyes so much like Cetta's. Jenai crouched beside her.

"Please," the girl croaked. "Water?"

Jenai had expected a plea for alms. Gently prying the girl's hand loose, she pushed the knapsack onto her lap. "Eat this. I'll fetch some water." She sprang up, gripping her empty water flask, and stepped out into the fresh air under a warm, bright sky. She'd forgotten to fill the flask, her routine thrown off by her conversation with Mercer.

Shutting the courthouse door, she scanned the vicinity. There, Sir Mercer was across the plaza, strolling toward the building opposite the courthouse. Jenai broke into a run, waving her hands to gain his attention. Near the fountain, she caught his gaze. He broke off his patrol and hurried over.

He searched her face. "Did Lord Robarr relent? Are you going?"

"No. I can't speak with him today. Thargundians attacked again, I'm certain of it. Refugees are crammed inside the hall." She glanced over her shoulder to the building she'd just left. "They're hungry and thirsty. Some are injured. Will you help me?"

He hesitated. "I can't leave the plaza while I'm on duty."

She pointed to the fountain, then thrust her empty water flask at him. "Use this. I'll bring more."

"Are you—"

She raced off, heedless of his question. She didn't have enough money to feed them all, but she could work off the debt if she needed.

Afallon guide my hands.

Jenai knew where these people had come from. Once Lord Robarr found out she'd told him the truth about the attack at Water-by-the-Rift, he would finally believe she was sent from Afallon.

STIRRING THE EMBERS

Not every merchant in the food district joined Jenai's efforts to feed the refugees—but more than half picked up their carts and left the market to parade to the court district. On arrival, they set up their carts outside the courthouse and formed a line, taking food inside. Sir Mercer had rounded up two pages and three knights to haul water from the fountain, each using his own water flask. Mercer carried Jenai's along with his own.

Once Jenai was satisfied that the food and water distribution was working well, she set about cleaning wounds and tending to fevers. It was midafternoon before they finished feeding the refugees. The empty carts rattled back toward their own district while a few volunteers remained with Jenai to finish ministering to the ailing. Sir Mercer patrolled outside the courthouse, but twice he sent a guard off to fetch more bandages.

When the evening bells chimed across the city, Jenai handed a slumbering infant back to his mother, then rose. She smoothed her red skirts and smiled at the refugees. "A kind woman has opened her inn to anyone in need of a good night's rest. Sir Mercer has agreed to lead everyone there. It will be a tight fit, but you'll stay warm. You can come back and wait to speak with Lord Robarr tomorrow."

"The Weave bless you," the young mother said, tears sparkling in her eyes.

"Thank you." Jenai stroked the baby's cheek, then slipped outside. She stumbled on the steps but caught herself. Every muscle in her body protested a long day spent crouching and then rising again, a hundred times or more—but she found herself smiling. Back in Domrem, she'd helped the midwife and the healer when she could, and she was grateful she'd taken the time to learn a little of each trade.

She strode toward her lodgings, keeping one eye open for any sign of Mirrasae, but the unicorn never appeared. When she reached her aunt and uncle's house, she found supper waiting. Aunt Ladia was beaming at her.

"Half of Valcinay knows what you did today. I've never heard of anything like it. The merchants hate each other, yet you got half of them to donate food to help people they've never met."

"Give credit to Afallon." Jenai sank into a chair, feeling wearier than ever before, even toiling in the fields or shearing sheep. She also felt...bright. Like her soul had expanded somehow.

She fell asleep halfway through the meal.

SHE WOKE IN THE NURSERY EARLY THE NEXT MORNING AND set out to visit the market square. Most merchants had refused her offer to work off the food they'd given away yesterday, but a few had taken the deal.

She expected to work hard for the rest of the week, but when she arrived at the square surrounding one of Valcinay's swards, she found only half the vendors set up for the day with no sign of any coming carts.

Moving to the stall where she bought her rolls, she caught the baker's eye. "Where is everyone?"

"Being conscripted, some of them," the woman answered, setting out trays of rolls and pasties. Three of her daughters were laying the baked goods out on more trays. "My husband's among them," the baker continued. "For once I'm glad I have only daughters."

Jenai's skin prickled. "When did the conscription notices go out?"

"Last night. Half the city is in an uproar. The other half is lying low. Lord Robarr is giving only a day's notice to enlist or be branded a traitor. My Orry went to the court district to sign up first thing, just as I told him to. Lord Robarr promised wages, but I don't know where he'll get them from. Not even the Crane Prince has a spare sol from what I've heard."

Jenai studied the golden crust of a pecan tart. "Did the notice say where the conscripted soldiers will march?"

"Water-by-the-Rift, I don't wonder," the woman said. "People are talking of payback—and I don't blame them. I have a cousin who lives that way. Even if he's escaped the carnage, I doubt his farm has. It'll be looted—and his children..." The woman dug out a handkerchief and nearly dropped the tray in the process. Her eldest daughter took the tray from her and set it on one of the shelves built into their stall. The baker blew her nose, then set her hands on her hips. "Don't go thinking none of our missing merchants is brave, lass. Most fled from the notices. No one cares to fight anymore. What's the point? We're starving already—just wait until the Thargundians burn our fields."

Jenai set a sol on the countertop and selected a pecan tart. The sweet aroma tickled her senses. "But that's why we must fight. There's a distinct line between starvation and death, and we shouldn't walk over that line like it's not there. If we give up, we certainly die—but if we fight, we have the chance to live. Afallon will save us."

The woman snorted. "Will He then? And why would He start now? Has He looked down from His cloud and finally remembered we belong to Him?" She slapped the counter hard.

Jenai set her free hand over the woman's. "Perhaps *we* are the ones who forgot to whom we belong." She spoke gently, earnestly, trembling under the rush of her faith and the fervor to answer Afallon's summons. She must reach the Crane Prince—and soon.

"I thought you'd be here." Mercer's voice came from directly behind Jenai. She whirled, dropping the tart, her nerves tingling. The tart struck the ground and oozed pecan filling. He winced. "Apologies, Maid Jenai. I'll pay for another of those." He untied a pouch at his belt, rummaged through it, then set another coin on the counter.

"Thank you." Jenai knew better than to reject his offer. It went against Fraelin custom to refuse a man's perceived debt. She took up another tart, then met Mercer's steady gaze. "Were you looking for me for a particular reason?"

"Yes. I've been asked to make certain you don't leave the city." He stooped to clean up the broken remnants of the first tart, using a rag the baker proffered to him.

She tensed. "Why? By whom?"

"Lord Robarr didn't give his reasons," Mercer said. "I merely have my orders."

"Are you going to escort me throughout the day?"

"Yes."

She bit into the flaky tart, relishing the burst of spices. After swallowing, she nodded to the market square. "I'd intended to work here today, but it seems I won't have the opportunity to pay my debt."

"I shouldn't think you owed a debt." Mercer straightened, holding the rag in both hands. The baker took it from him, tossing it in a rubbish bin beside her stall. He nodded to the woman, then turned back to Jenai. "How could you owe anyone after what you did yesterday for those refugees?"

The baker grunted her agreement. "So I told her, along with those who felt differently. Luckily, those who demanded recompense are the same cowards who fled their conscriptions."

Mercer sighed. "Fools. They'll be caught and quartered for deserting."

Jenai flinched, trying not to picture the gruesome imagery. She took another bite of her tart, then motioned to the stall shelves. "You should eat."

He took up a roll and set down another coin. "This will do."

They bade the baker goodbye, then strolled along the cobblestones edging the green. Neither spoke, lost in their own thoughts, eating their breakfast. Eventually, they reached the end of the square and Jenai took a seat on a bench. Mercer stood beside her, rigid.

"You can sit," she said, glancing at him.

"I'm on duty."

"Ah." She rubbed the residue of pecan filling from her fingertips, uncertain what else to say.

"I'd like to come with you."

She twisted toward him. "You mean beyond today?"

"Yes. I want to travel with you. I couldn't sleep last night."

"Did I cause that?"

"In a way," he said. "I couldn't put you from my thoughts. Your words yesterday...they *moved* me. Everything about you does that. And not just me. Others see it, too. They're calling you the Maiden of Lorrae. Some who know where you hail from call you the Maiden of Domrem."

"But why?" asked Jenai. "I've done nothing—"

"You call your work yesterday nothing?"

"I mean before that. Besides, anyone in my shoes would have—"

"No, Maid Jenai. Not *anyone*. Only you thought to feed those begging for aid. And your efforts have created ripples. Lord Robarr hasn't conscripted anyone after past attacks, even following skirmishes closer than Water-by-the-Rift. Not until now."

She looked down at her hands. "That feels more worthy of blame than praise."

"But don't you want us to fight?"

"Yes," she said. "When and where it matters. Taking the city of Lorion back from the Duke of Thargundy—that would make a difference. But sending farmers against their will to fight on the borders, against far greater forces—that makes little sense. They're not trained. They're frightened. And they have no symbol carved into their hearts to fight for."

"But you have such a symbol, don't you?"

She shook her head. "What I have is faith. What I can *give*—that will be their symbol."

"Do you mean yourself?"

"As Afallon wills."

They lapsed into silence, letting the growing hubbub of trade flow around them. The trees circling the square whispered in a mild breeze.

Mercer sighed. "Why I believe in you, I don't know. What it is about you—a simple maiden—that stirs the dying embers of patriotism, I can't say. But follow you I will, into the pits of Thiavos if need be."

She smiled up at him. "Thank you, Sir Mercer, from my heart."

They spent the day petitioning the various markets for more of the refugees' needs. One of the food merchants lent them a cart to gather supplies. Toward evening, Jenai and Mercer delivered what they'd collected—food, blankets, a few shawls and socks, hats, bandages, ointments, and other necessities—to the inn where the refugees were housed. Some camped on the meager lawn before the structure. All of them blessed Jenai and Mercer as they passed out the donations.

In the growing dusk, Jenai walked to her aunt and uncle's home. Mercer strode with her, whistling a soft tune. When they reached Jenai's lodgings, she expected most of the windows to be dark, but instead the house was lit up. Every lantern blazed while smoke plumed from the chimney. A carriage was parked outside the front door, with the driver snoozing in his seat, still clutching the reins.

Casting a glance at Mercer, Jenai raced up the steps and hurried inside, half-afraid something dreadful had happened to one of her relatives. Inside, she found the main room well lit—and there stood Lord Robarr.

HER FIRST EXAMINATION

The lord of Valcinay was draped in a fur cloak. A high collar hid his neck while his chain of office glittered in the hearth light. Two priests and a priestess stood with him, all robed in white with blue and gold accents. Jenai's aunt and uncle sat at their table, leaning on each other for support, their faces pinched and pale. She tried to offer them a reassuring smile, but her nerves were too taut.

"There you are, Maiden of Lorrae," the rotund man rumbled. "What kept you?"

Mercer stepped forward. "She was delivering supplies to the refugees from Water-by-the-Rift, my lord."

Robarr sniffed at that, eyeing Jenai for a long, weighty moment. "You're a kind woman by all appearances—but does devilry lurk beneath a varnish of goodness?" He gestured, and the clergy stepped forward. "You were correct about Water-by-the-Rift. There were only three ways that could be so. Since I've confirmed that no one in that valley knows you, it can only be one of *two* ways. Either you're sent by Afallon, or you're a witch serving Thiavos. Will you submit to an examination?"

Jenai bowed her head. "I'm your obedient servant, my lord."

The priests and priestess glided forward in their holy robes, and Jenai fell to her knees to kiss their sapphire rings. Each prayed over her in turns, setting their palms to her forehead. Then they questioned her.

"Who are your parents?"

"Jekan and Issa d'Arc of Domrem."

"Where were you born?"

"In the village of Domrem in the province of Lorrae."

"Have you been baptized into Afallon's one church?"

"Yes. As an infant."

On the questions ran, testing her knowledge of the faith and its many tenets. They asked after the priest in Domrem. She gave his name.

"Lastly," the priestess said, "are you pure, Daughter?"

"I have known no man," Jenai answered.

The priestess glanced at Lord Robarr. "Shall I examine her body?"

"No need." Robarr was frowning at her. "Are you all satisfied by her answers?"

The clergy nodded.

"We find her faithful and obedient," one priest said.

"Her eyes are filled with Afallon's love," the priestess added.

"What about her desire to seek out the Crane Prince?" the lord asked. "She claims Afallon is sending her there."

The priestess turned to Jenai, searching her face. "Rise, Daughter. Is this your desire?"

"It is Afallon's. He's sending me." Jenai stood, welcoming the tingling rush of blood in her legs.

"To what end?"

Jenai hesitated, uncertain how much to say. She'd *seen* things—things the Voice had shown her—but she didn't understand all of it. "To free Fraelin," she answered. "To remove the Crow King's taint from these beautiful shores."

The priestess's eyes widened, and her face paled. She turned toward Robarr. "My lord, this child speaks with authority greater than mine. Give her passage. Lend her horses and an escort."

Robarr stiffened. "You're certain?"

"She's no witch, but she has power from the Weave flowing through her. It must be granted by Afallon."

Robarr strode from across the room, eyes narrowed on Jenai. "You believe you've been called by Afallon to serve the Crane Prince in our war efforts?"

"Yes, Lord Robarr," she answered.

Sir Mercer stepped closer. "My lord, I respectfully request the opportunity to travel with the Maiden and serve her in her quest to free Fraelin."

Robarr turned to the knight, frowning. "Why?" His tone was sharp, as if he suspected Mercer's motives to be uncouth.

"I feel drawn to her cause like an Ilidreth to his first bow. If I might aid in defeating the bloody Simaeri and the treacherous Thargundians, I must try."

Robarr folded his arms and breathed out through his nose, contemplating Jenai and her companion. He glanced twice at the clergy, who in turn each considered Jenai.

At last, the lord of Valcinay nodded. "Very well. I will draft a letter of introduction to the Crane Prince in his court at Shinon. But, lass, don't expect much of a welcome. In the prince's estimation, I rank very low. Still..." He rubbed at his beard. "I wish you success as Afallon wills."

Hope swelled in Jenai's chest. She fell to her knees again and caught Robarr's hand to kiss his signet ring. "Thank you, my lord."

He gently tugged away. "I'll have the letter ready, along

with horses and men to ride with you, by noon tomorrow. Come to the court district then."

Jenai stood. "As you please, but I have my own mount. Give horses only to your men."

"Very well." Motioning to the clergy, he started for the front door. The priests and priestess trailed after him, whispering among themselves. At the door, the priestess glanced back, offering Jenai a kind smile before she slipped out.

"I, too, will take my leave," Mercer said. "I'll meet you in front of the courthouse tomorrow at noon. Goodnight, Maiden of Lorrae."

Jenai curtsied. "Good sleep to you, Sir Mercer."

He bowed his head to her aunt and uncle, then strode out of the house, his armor glinting in the firelight. When the door snicked shut behind him, Aunt Ladia flew to Jenai's side and clutched her arm.

"Child, how can you go to Shinon to see the prince? How can—"

"I must, so I shall," Jenai said.

"What will your parents say?" Ladia asked. "I received a letter from your mother saying that she'll reach Valcinay in two days to help search for you. Will you wait that long and at least say farewell?"

"No," Jenai said, fighting the tightness in her chest. "I leave tomorrow for Shinon."

Her uncle approached. "You would disobey your parents?"

"I must obey my God."

"What can we tell your mother when she arrives?" Ladia whispered.

Jenai pried Ladia's fingers from her arm and held the woman's hands with tenderness. "Tell her I'm on an errand for Afallon, for that is what it is."

"But what can *you* do for Fraelin?" Uncle Kerch demanded.

"Whatever I'm commanded to do." Jenai smiled at him. "If He can guide a seed to grow into a giant tree or teach a bumblebee to fly, can He not also grant me the courage and strength to accomplish whatever He desires? If I must take flight, He will give me wings." She turned to meet Ladia's gaze. "I'm not afraid."

Her aunt studied her, then sighed, offering a wobbly smile. "I can see that, Jenai. Truly, you've been called to this end. I won't stop you." Uncle Kerch started to splutter, but Ladia shook her head. "It's no use, husband. She'll not be moved—and we might be struck down by heaven for trying. Let her fulfill her purpose on the battlefield. Where men have failed to free Fraelin, let this woman walk."

FALSE PRINCE

Alain trudged down the gangway. Every muscle throbbed, along with his head. Crossing the channel between Simaerin and Fraelin was unpleasant in peacetime, let alone when foreign powers thought they ruled the known world.

Home. After five years in the dungeons of Crowwell, at last he was back in his homeland. The wind played with his pale hair, and Alain drank in the scents. After so long living with a hollow in his chest where his magic ought to be, the return of that magic felt almost...heavy. The Crow King despised magic—and he could somehow bar it from its natural wielders within his kingdom. No one in Simaerin could use magic of any kind.

Alain didn't glance toward the Crow banner fluttering on the ship's mainmast, even when the gulls of Fraelin screamed their manic welcome from the sky. He ignored the red-tabarded knights mingling with the citizens of Fraelin along the wharves of Thray. His sights were set on the fine coach perched at the end of the dock, its blue paint a little worn, but the presence of the crane symbol like a healing balm. He fingered the elongated lump in his cloak's inner pocket, glad of its weight.

Prince Chartan should've known better than to send a marked coach to collect him. It was too stark a reminder that the Simaeri invaders didn't own all of Fraelin yet—which could lead to skirmishes, or worse. Though the Thargundian traitors had allied with Simaerin, causing a kind of truce, it was as thin as a fraying rope and ready to snap at the first chance. Either side might give the tug that snapped that rope, unleashing all-out war.

Part of Alain longed for that, just to end matters. To let the war decide who owned Fraelin once and for all. But the part of him that still vividly remembered the terrible battle leading to his capture wanted to avoid that much bloodshed ever again. He rubbed at the scar on his temple.

Open war is inevitable, and you know you can't stand idly by to let others fight for you, Alain.

He reached the coach and smiled at the morose and ancient driver perched behind the four sturdy horses. "Here for me?"

"Duke Alain Clayre, is it?" asked the driver in a croak.

"The same," Alain said, with the first genuine smile he'd used in years.

"Then I'm here for you."

"I appreciate the gesture but—"

"Halt!" boomed a voice. Alain knew that kind of command like he knew his own heartbeat; shouts just like it had so often caused his heart to stop. The follow-up sound of marching boots and clanking armor approached. Alain wheeled toward the Crowsmen. Behind a dour-faced man with sandy-blond hair and a chiseled jaw followed a half-dozen soldiers in garish red bearing the silhouette of a crow.

"You're under arrest, Fraeli," the Crow captain declared.

Alain gathered himself up, every nerve catching fire. "What's the charge? I've only just landed."

"Consorting with the false prince." The captain's sneer seemed to bruise the man's face. He glanced toward the coach. "That's cause for execution around here."

"Is it?" Alain's voice was flat. Everything was clicking into place now. "I didn't know that." He glanced at the ancient driver, an unfamiliar face in a kingdom that Alain barely recognized, despite the traditional style of the buildings surrounding the port of entry. Despite the homey fragrance of honey that wafted in from the nearby clover fields. Despite the symbol of the crane on the coach. Fraelin was rotting at its core, allowing the Crowsmen to gain ground. The familiar sights were only a façade to disguise that fact.

That crane symbol was being used as a lure, to cage him again.

"I thought I knew the coachman," Alain said smoothly, "but he's a stranger to me. I meant no harm and certainly no offense."

The Crow captain frowned, squinting between the coach and Alain. "You intended to climb into this conveyance and meet with the wanted criminal claiming to be Prince Chartan. Do you deny it?"

"Yes. On my life, I had no intention of doing so." Alain would've lied, but there was no need. He'd had no intention of entering that coach. It was a death sentence. At least now he understood he'd been set up and his cousin hadn't been stupid enough to send the coach into enemy territory.

"On your life?" the captain scoffed.

"Truly. A man recently freed from the Crowwell dungeons knows better than to mark himself mere weeks later." Alain adjusted his face into his practiced smile, half-wondering if it had the same charismatic effect it'd once possessed. He'd been called handsome in his youth, but after years in an underground prison, he wasn't certain he'd aged well. He was twenty-five now. How much had he altered?

The captain listed his head to one side and chewed his cheek. At last, he shook himself. "I see what I see, Fraeli. You're still under arrest."

Alain sighed, his shoulders slumping. "Must we? I'd hoped to avoid an altercation so early upon arriving in my homeland."

"I'd recommend not resisting, lad." The captain's eyes were bright with the idea despite his claims. He drew his broadsword. Steel flashed under the sun.

Alain set his stance wide, fingering the lump in his hidden pocket. He'd traded most of his voyage food and a bar of soap that he'd swiped from Crow Castle's baths for a fine dagger. The pockmarked man who'd owned it had seemed eager to part with it.

The captain lunged, sword jabbing straight on. Alain flung out his cloak hem, disguising his leftward step. He drew the dagger and smashed it against the blade. Then he kicked out, tapping wind magic to strengthen his blow. His boot connected with the captain's temple, and the man flew sideways. The soldiers shouted, drawing their swords. Alain turned, inhaled wind, and blew out. As though he'd summoned a small tornado, they were flung backwards. One man overstepped the dock and splashed into the water, sinking like a stone in his armor.

Alain stooped to claim the captain's sword, then glanced at the coachman. "Nice trick, but I'm not *that* stupid." He winked at the old man, then strode along the cobbled road toward the center of Thray. He had a little coin that he'd won aboard the ship. He wasn't a gambler—he and luck had never gotten on well—but he'd been desperate enough to try.

Hopefully, the five sols would be enough to secure a horse. Either way, he had the feeling he wouldn't be eating until he reached Shinon.

THE ROAD TO SHINON

Jenai was ready to depart well before noon. With her few belongings gathered in her satchel, she sat down to wait for the appointed time. Uncle Kersh had already left to tend to his work in the stonemason guild house. Aunt Ladia said almost nothing as she made a hearty breakfast large enough to feed Jenai's absent family. Jenai ate what she could of it, then stood and gave Ladia a long hug.

"I don't know if I'll see you again alive." Jenai's voice was muffled by her aunt's shoulder. "Whatever happens, I love you, and I pray for Afallon's blessings on your house."

Ladia squeezed her niece tighter. "May Afallon and all His angels attend you, child."

They stepped apart. Jenai wiped at her eyes, then moved to the door, caught up her satchel, and stepped from the house. Before the stoop, Mirrasae stood in plain view, her sapphire and gold horn flashing under the midmorning sun. Jenai hurried down the steps.

"Should people see you so openly, Mirrasae?" she asked.

"Most do not see what I truly am. Only those of great purity or power recognize a unicorn. The rest see only a beautiful white horse."

Mirrasae tossed her mane. *"Come, Jenai d'Arc. It is time for our departure. Climb onto my back."*

Jenai gripped her skirts in one hand and used the lowest step to swing her leg over Mirrasae. The unicorn's silken hair was cool against her legs. She gathered up Mirrasae's mane, still clutching her satchel. "I'm ready."

The unicorn trotted up the street. Though her movements were fleet, Jenai felt secure atop the glorious creature. Mirrasae headed for the court district, turning heads, whether or not the people recognized what she really was. Jenai sat proudly, feeling the weight of the past weeks fade. She was finally on her way. Soon, she would meet the Crane Prince. Soon she would free Fraelin from the Crow King's growing shadow.

Upon entering the manicured square where the courthouse rose, Jenai started. Crowds had gathered. People turned to find her, and many pointed and shouted. A ripple went through the gathering as it parted to let her pass.

"It's the Maiden," someone breathed nearby. "She's as lovely as they say."

"Do you see that horse? Magnificent."

"That's no horse."

"What is it, then—a mule, you daft sod?"

"Look, son. Soon she'll be leading your papa into battle." A man hefted his toddler in his arms. "Try to touch her hem. She's got the luck of the Weave, she has."

Jenai's cheeks warmed, and she started to dip her head.

"Don't hide," said the Voice like a chime. *"You must stir them to victory. Do not be ashamed."*

Squaring her shoulders, Jenai fixed her sights on Lord Robarr standing with other officials at the top of the courthouse steps. The man was eyeing the crowd with a bemused frown, shaking his head while his cluster of colleagues whispered around him. One pointed toward Jenai.

Robarr angled toward her, his chain of office glittering against his large middle.

Near the steps, she spotted Mercer and three other men standing beside four saddled horses, with an extra horse carrying supplies. She'd been worried Lord Robarr would send them with a supply wagon, which would only slow them down on the road. Thankfully, the man had more sense than that.

"Welcome, Jenai d'Arc, Maiden of Lorrae." Robarr's voice rang out across the square, quieting the last whispers of conversation. "I have heard your request, and I gladly send you on your way—though the road is treacherous. These men are sworn to bring you safely to Shinon. Here is your letter of introduction." He motioned and the swanlike women in his retinue came forward, all smiles now, proffering a parchment scroll sealed with Robarr's stallion crest.

Jenai accepted the scroll, then dipped her head. "Thank you, Lord Robarr. May Afallon guard this great city from all threats."

Murmurs swelled behind her, carrying her words to the back of the throng. Someone shouted out a blessing for her safe journey. Jenai turned to find the voice and offer a smile, but it was impossible to locate them in the packed square. She turned back to Robarr, meeting his eyes.

"I still don't know whether you're called of Afallon or suffering delusions of grandeur," he said in a low voice. "Whatever the case, I do wish you success in your fight for our kingdom. Afallon and the Weave be with you."

"Thank you, Lord Robarr." She started toward Sir Mercer and the other men, but a familiar face on the stoop caught her eye. Shifting on Mirrasae's back, she met the magistrate's gaze. The old man, draped in his blue robes and white wig, grinned at her like a co-conspirator who'd fought on her behalf. She supposed he had. Beyond him, peeking outside the courthouse door, lurked Petray. She inclined her head to each man in turn, gratitude brimming in her chest. She turned back to Mercer. Mirrasae strode forward without the faintest nudge.

Jenai cast her eye over the men standing behind Mercer. The eldest, a grizzled man, wore knightly armor matching Mercer's. The other two, a middle-aged man and a young boy barely more than an adolescent, wore plain armor, signifying their ranks in the city guard. The youngest ogled Jenai like he'd never seen a girl before.

"We're ready to leave at once, Lady Jenai," Mercer said. "If we're not delayed en route, it will take a fortnight to reach the Crane Prince."

"Then let us depart."

A cheer rose up, as though the throng had been waiting for her to say exactly those words. Jenai's cheeks flushed again. She sat a little straighter but couldn't bring herself to look at the people at her back. A flicker of doubt crossed her mind. Could she do this? Could someone like her—with no battle experience, and no knowledge of anything beyond keeping house and tending fields—really hope to purge Fraelin of its enemies?

'*You are not alone,*' the unicorn said in her mind. '*Trust in the Weave.*'

Shoving aside her doubts, she clutched Mirrasae's mane harder. "I'm ready," she whispered.

Mirrasae pranced forward, her gait wide and graceful, barely jarring Jenai. The men followed. Their horses' hooves clattered on the cobblestones. The people of Valcinay continued their cheering even after Mirrasae turned the corner down another street—and Jenai soon saw why. More crowds had gathered. Hundreds of people. All of them cheering and shouting. Young girls threw flowers onto the street where no carriages or carts interrupted Jenai's march from the city.

"I don't understand how they can all know," Jenai said, loud enough for Mercer to hear above the din.

"There are no secrets in Valcinay," the knight replied. "The quieter you keep your business, the faster news of it will spread. I suspect it will be no different in Shinon. Word of your arrival will race ahead of you. Likely, the Crane Prince will have already decided if he'll grant you an audience. So it goes in politics."

Jenai shook her head. "I'm not interested in politics, Sir Mercer."

"That will hardly matter. You're in the political waters now, Maid Jenai, and if you don't find a means of navigating the current, you'll drown."

Fear crept through Jenai's heart and squeezed her lungs.

I'm not alone, she told herself. *Afallon will guide me.*

At last, the houses and shops gave way to open fields and a tree-lined road running on for miles to the south. The last of spring's blossoms scattered before them, floating on a breeze that raked its fingers through the apple orchards on the east side near a lazy river. Fingers of wind ran through Jenai's long black hair.

Mercer steered his horse to her side. "We'll reach the village of Candalar by dusk if we stop only thrice en route today. It will be the only inn along our journey. Few are willing to offer lodgings with the threat of Thargundians. It's possible this inn has also closed after the raid at Water-by-the-Rift."

"I can sleep on the ground well enough." Her mind flitted back to summer nights spent camping in the woods with her brothers. She'd never been bothered by the out-of-doors. Her job had been to cook and collect berries while the boys hunted game for the family's winter stores. It had been a welcome reprieve from field work.

"You're tougher than you look, Jenai d'Arc," said Mercer.

She frowned. He made a good point. Dressed as she was,

looking like a maiden, how could she convince anyone to follow her into battle? How could she garner the Crane Prince's confidence? She needed to alter the way others saw her.

"Does Candalar have a tailor and a barber?" She glanced at the knight.

"I'm certain it does."

"I will need each brought to me at the inn—if the inn accepts us."

"As you wish."

THEY REACHED CANDALAR AT SUNSET. STREAKS OF RED AND orange light gleamed off the closed shop windows. Ahead stood a brightly lit two-story building bearing a sign with a large hog in a nightcap. Words were carved beneath the sign. Jenai couldn't read them. They trotted to the building, where tavern music played cheerily and laughter wafted across the air.

"Welcome to the Sleepy Hog." Mercer swung from his saddle and reached for Mirrasae, but the unicorn danced backward. The knight smiled. "A bit jittery for such a well-behaved mount."

'Tell him not to touch me. I am not to be treated as a beast,' Mirrasae said, without malice.

Jenai faintly nodded. "She prefers only the touch of her rider."

"Ah. I've known mares like her before," Mercer said.

'Doubtful.' Mirrasae tossed her head, though she sounded amused rather than upset. Jenai smiled and allowed the knight to help her slide to the ground.

"We can get you a saddle and reins at first light," Mercer said.

"That isn't necessary. I'll ride bareback," Jenai told him. "I would rather you sent for the tailor and barber."

"It will be done." He hesitated. "What title should I give you, Maid Jenai? You're not a lady of court but saying your name without any honorifics feels wrong."

"I have no titles," she said, "and Jenai is my name. Please use it."

He grimaced. "Perhaps the Crane Prince will give you a title before we march on Lorion."

"Your faith in my ability to persuade him heartens me."

He searched her face. "Do you not think you can?"

"With Afallon's help, I will."

"Then my faith is warranted."

They walked into the Sleepy Hog side by side while the other three men saw to the horses. Mirrasae followed the beasts of burden into the stable without complaint, and Jenai briefly wondered what the fair creature would do among the common stock before she turned her thoughts to her own needs.

The innkeeper was a small man with a thatch of thick hair. He was quick to serve the knight and lady, not batting an eye when they requested three rooms in total. "You may have your pick, as you please," he said. "None are occupied." His gaze settled on Jenai. "You are she, aren't you? The maiden all are speaking of?"

"I hardly know," she answered.

"You seek an audience with the Crane Prince?"

"I do."

"Then you *are* she." He rubbed his hands together, beaming. "Everyone in Candalar is speaking of how you'll throw out the Thargundian swine and clean house."

She canted her head. "How could they make such claims? I'm not yet proven in combat."

The innkeeper's smile stretched wider, the light of

superstition in his eyes. "You moved Lord Robarr—no one does that. His retinue can hardly convince him to dig a new trench, even when he knows it's a good idea. But to obtain a letter of introduction to the Crane Prince? I heard two travelers speaking of your plight not three days ago. *Impossible*, they said. *She's daft*! And yet, here you stand in company with one of *his* men on the road to Shinon. It's a blessed miracle."

She smiled at the choice of words. "In that we're agreed, good sir. I have three more companions. Please see that they're made comfortable when they come in."

"It will be done."

The innkeeper showed them to their rooms. Jenai took the smaller room, and she shut herself inside for the night after the innkeeper promised to bring her a warm meal. She didn't want to enter the tavern's common room and find other travelers gossiping about her. She'd had no notion that her mission had been so widely broadcast. The idea that the Crane Prince might make up his mind against her before she ever reached him was disheartening.

Sinking to her knees, Jenai prayed to Afallon until dinner arrived. At the innkeeper's knock, she rose and answered the door. Mercer stood at his side, along with a beefy man wielding a pair of shears.

"This is Runin," Mercer said. "He's the barber."

"My lady." Runin bowed his head.

The slight innkeeper slipped inside the room and set the tray of lambchops and mashed turnips on the nightstand. He took his leave with a bow.

"What might these shears do for you, Maiden of Domrem?" the barber asked.

Jenai unbound her black hair and let it hang long, down to her thighs. "You may cut my tresses."

Both men stared.

She stood waiting, but neither moved. Running a hand through a lock of her hair, she smiled. "It needn't be cropped too short. Just enough that it wears well in a tail like young men of my age often wear. To the shoulders will suffice, I think."

Mercer stirred. "Ah, you mean to disguise yourself as a lad."

"I do," she said. "As I am, I stand out too much. We'll never reach Shinon unmolested, especially with rumors flying out before us. Besides, wearing a dress into battle, or letting my hair fly free, is impractical. Until the Crow King's influence is removed from Fraelin, and the Thargundians bow the knee to the rightful Crane King, I will wear the garb of a man when occasion requires it."

Mercer glanced between her and the barber, almost as though he expected a fight. But Runin shook himself, opened and shut the shears, then stepped forward. "If Afallon has called me to this end, I'll deem it an honor to cut your hair, fair lass. Please sit."

Jenai took the room's single chair and spread her hair behind the seatback. A twinge of regret caught in her lungs, but she breathed through the feeling. It was only hair. It would grow back. The cause was far greater than the cost.

The whispering hiss of the shears was followed by the faint rip and snip of blades running through hair. The barber's motions were quick, and every snip lessened the burden of Jenai's hair against her scalp. A few moments passed, then Runin stepped back.

"All done, Maiden of Domrem."

She reached back, fingering the short locks against her shoulder. They felt thicker, yet her head was strangely light. Her vision swam and another pang of regret washed over her, but she blinked back the tears, rose, and faced the two men with a smile. "Thank you, Runin. I won't forget your service to me."

The barber inclined his head, then stared at the floor where her locks of black curled around the chair legs. "With your permission," he whispered, "I will keep a lock of your hair to remember this night."

"If it pleases you." She stooped and gathered up a thick handful. "Here you are."

He accepted the gift along with payment, then bowed himself out as though she were a woman of noble birth. Kneeling to clean up the last of her lost hair, she tried to shake off the hollow feeling that threaded through her.

"Did it hurt?" asked Mercer in a quiet voice.

She glanced up, bemused. "A woman's hair is no different from a man's, Sir Knight. It will grow again."

"That's not what I meant." He knelt to help her, but when his fingers brushed the long, sheared hair, he flinched back like he'd been burned. "It's just...I recall that my mother said her hair was her one vanity. Her crowning glory. Are you sad?"

She tightened her clutch on the black locks. "A little. But as I said, it will grow. And it's nothing—*nothing*—to the sacrifices that lay ahead. Lives matter more than vanity. There's no comparison."

NEW SKIN

At dawn, Mercer knocked on Jenai's door. After throwing on her robe, she answered, peering out into the hall with bleary eyes. Alongside the knight stood a tall man with a balding pate. His eyes shone in the light from the candle Mercer held.

"I've brought the tailor as you requested," the knight said.

She stepped aside to admit them. The tailor sized her up, humming to himself. "By your leave, I'll take your measurements." Jenai nodded and held out her arms. He pulled out a coiled string from his pocket, unwound it, then set to work measuring her limbs. "The knight told me what you're after," he said. "Anything for the Maiden of Lorrae."

"Thank you," she murmured. "How quickly might you have something ready?"

"Give me 'til after breakfast, my lady. I've got work-clothes aplenty for my own lad. Just need to resize one or two of his old things. I'll bring 'em in for you, then bring 'em over."

"Thank you."

"An honor it is." Just like the barber, he bowed himself out and shut the door behind him.

Jenai turned to Mercer. "We must be ready to depart the moment I've changed into my new apparel." She brushed back her hair, startled to feel the shorter length. She shoved aside a fresh twinge of regret.

"I'll see to it," Mercer said, then left the room.

Jenai knelt beside her bed to pour out all her feelings of gratitude and joy for being on her way at last, as well as her trepidation for what might stand in her path.

"You will be guided true, Jenai of Domrem. Rise and do not surrender to your fear."

She obeyed the Voice and moved to the water pitcher to wash up. A short while later, Mercer returned, carrying a tray of food. She thanked him, then sat alone to eat. As she finished the last of her warm cakes drizzled in honey, another knock sounded. She abandoned her food and opened the door to receive the tailor.

"Not my finest work, but it will wear well, my lady." He proffered some folded clothing.

"It's fine enough for me," she said, taking it. "Thank you. One moment please." She strode to the bureau where her coin purse rested and dug out a sol.

"No, my lady. I couldn't. Y-you're a heroine, you are, what with you marching for Fraelin's sake—"

"You must feed your family meanwhile." She pressed the coin into his hand. "Even heroines should pay their way."

He bowed himself from the room, still stammering his thanks. Once he'd gone, Jenai stripped down and climbed into her new wardrobe. The leggings were a bit loose, but that made them more comfortable. The shirt was sized well, and the jerkin overtop helped to hide her slim shape without binding her chest. She finished it off by tying her hair back in the fashion of young men, then slipped on her boots.

Glancing in the mirror, she was startled by the transformation. Though she still looked lean, even petite, between the male trappings and her own height, she looked like a comely lad rather than the maid she'd always been. Passing a hand across her face, she smiled. She could do this. By Afallon's grace she could!

Her hand fell to her hip. She would need a sword soon. But that must come in its own time. Gathering her belongings, she stepped from her room to find Mercer waiting.

"Ready when you are," he said, his expression controlled. Whatever he thought of her new appearance, he kept it to himself.

"Then let's be off. We've a prince to meet, Sir Knight."

15

MARAUDERS

The lands beyond Candalar were once expansive woodlands used for lumber, but war had turned them into blasted fields and hills of charred tree husks. Jenai's heart throbbed. She rode along battered roads, passing entire villages reduced to bones and ashes. In some places, brave souls had returned to bury their dead, and the cemeteries in those towns were now larger than the village squares had been. In other places, the dead remained strewn among the rubble, worn down to white bone by weather or fire.

Mercer explained that, out in the wastes, the marauders were a greater risk than the soldiers of either army. "But don't think we're safe from those either," he added.

"Not safe from our own soldiers?" asked Jenai, surprised.

Mercer nodded, steering his stallion around a small boulder resting on the highway running between two shallow cliffs. "Prince Chartan can't feed his men. Most are desperate. Some are deserters still wearing their uniforms to intimidate common folk into submission. If we're waylaid, we may not fare well."

She searched the craggy surrounds. They'd left the

remains of a village at midmorning and now traveled along an area lined with cliffs: the perfect place for an ambush. She stretched her senses for hints of life, but she was no magic wielder. The unicorn trotted on, ears forward, tail streaming behind her.

Surely, Mirrasae would know if something were amiss.

They moved at a steady pace until early afternoon when the unicorn slowed. Her tail swished, and her ears cocked to the right. '*The marauders are ahead. There, in that cavity fifteen feet above ground.*'

Jenai spotted the dark, gaping hole. Her muscles tensed. "Sir Mercer, they're in there." She didn't risk pointing with her finger, but let her eyes guide the knight to find the same half-hidden hole.

His hand fell to his sword. "It's a strong possibility."

"It's a certainty," Jenai replied.

"*Jenai.*" The Voice flooded through her, filling her with light. "*Duck down.*"

She slammed forward against Mirrasae's silken neck. An arrow breathed past her spine and pierced the hard-packed road. Mercer let out a curse, wheeling his horse around to move in front of Jenai while the other three soldiers lifted crossbows toward the cavity. One loosed his bolt with a snap, and someone among the cliffs screamed.

More arrows rained down. Mirrasae danced out of reach while Mercer cut down several shafts with his broadsword. Jenai stayed low, letting the unicorn canter away from the attack. More crossbow bolts snapped free. Mercer was shouting orders. Someone above yelled counterattack formations.

Mirrasae reached a grotto half-shrouded by a twisted cedar tree. As the unicorn entered the little shelter, pebbles skittered under her hooves. Several yards within, the floor of the grotto gave way to a drop too dark to see the bottom.

Jenai sat upright, her scalp brushing the rock ceiling. The air was musty, almost metallic, and cold enough to lift the fine hairs on her arms.

"That was a near thing," Jenai whispered. "Will the men be all right?"

'They are here to defend you, Jenai,' said Mirrasae. *'Let them do their work—you will have yours to do soon enough.'*

Jenai's nerves were humming in her ears, almost drowning out the shouts and snaps of crossbow bolts. She drew deep breaths, trying to focus on any thread of comfort she could grasp in Mirrasae's gentle tones. She knew the unicorn was right. Mercer had come along to defend her, as had the other three. This was their responsibility. But she could pray for their safety. Bowing her head, she didn't cease to pray until silence filled the canyon outside.

Hooves clopped close. Jenai lifted her head, heart tripping against her ribcage. Beads of sweat trickled down her brow despite the cold.

"My lady?" Mercer called into the gloom. "You can come out now."

"Afallon be praised." Jenai patted Mirrasae. "Let's go." The unicorn walked toward the light where Mercer's dark outline on horseback stood in relief. "Sir Knight, are you wounded?" Jenai asked before she could make out his face.

"A bolt grazed my cheek, but it's nothing. The others are unharmed."

Moving into the light, Jenai blinked under the sun until her vision adjusted. "Afallon has been good to us today."

"The marauders are all dead. I had Bregger check. There are six corpses in total. I don't think we can bury them, though I suspect you'd prefer that. It's too rocky here."

"We can cover them with stones," Jenai said.

He hesitated, then nodded. "As you wish, but it will cost us time."

"Afallon will make up for that. We must honor the dead, no matter their faults in life. It's Afallon's way."

He nodded again and turned his horse to relay her wishes. The soldiers standing below the cavity argued with him for several minutes. One threw his hands into the air, but soon they all started back up the cliff to collect the bodies.

Jenai stroked Mirrasae's mane, searching the canyon, her nerves still taut. She couldn't bring herself to watch the soldiers using ropes to lower the bodies, one by one, down the cliff. Instead, she slid from Mirrasae's back and set about putting together a meal. It would help them to regain some lost time.

The men laid the corpses out on the roadside, close together, and began covering them up. Jenai carried the cheese, flat bread, and apples over to them, giving them a break midway through their labor. Mercer murmured his thanks while the other three crammed down the food in a few gulps then got back to work.

Jenai ate a few bites of cheese, then knelt beside the graveside to assist in burying the marauders. Three of the six were young men, barely grown, and one was older than her grandfather. They looked more hungry than sinister, and Jenai's heart squeezed until her head felt light. She deepened her breaths, fighting through the guilt, telling herself to give these poor souls some dignity in their death, since she could do nothing else.

Afallon, please take them into Thy protection.

Covering them up was slow, sweaty work, but between the five of them they finished well before evening, then moved on. No one spoke for a long time.

"We won't make it to the flatlands before nightfall," Mercer said. "We'll need to camp in the hills, which will be treacherous. Bigger groups of marauders will be abroad. I suggest no campfire."

"That seems wise," Jenai said. "We'll do as you suggest."

They carried on without any further conversation and didn't bed down until long past the twilight hour. Spreading out her bedroll beneath a sky glittering with crystal stars, Jenai murmured her nightly prayers, keeping the six dead men in her thoughts. Mercer unrolled his bed nearby but respectfully kept his back to her. Bregger, the middle-aged man with skin like toughened leather, sat in a cluster of rocks, keeping watch. The old knight was already lying down, his white hair fluttering in the night breeze while the young soldier, who sported unruly hair and pimples, kept stealing glances at Jenai. She couldn't read if he was angry or curious or something else.

Mercer shifted, turning toward Jenai. "Best steer clear of young Limmar. Even with short hair and boy's clothes, you're still a girl, and boys at that age are curious about girls."

Jenai's cheeks warmed. "Oh." Keeping all her clothing on, she slipped under her covers.

"May I ask you something, Maid Jenai?" Mercer kept his voice quiet.

"You may."

"How did you know about that ambush? Was it..."

"The will of Afallon," she replied steadily.

"I see."

"Good sleep to you, Sir Mercer."

"And to you, Jenai."

Though the day's work pressed heavily against her bones, Jenai found she couldn't sleep. After tossing for an hour, she threw aside her blankets and joined Mirrasae who was standing like a beacon under the dark sky. Resting a hand on the unicorn's muzzle, Jenai smiled sadly.

"I can't escape the memories of those men we buried."

'Death is a sorrowful thing to witness, no matter how often we see it.'

"Sometimes I've felt nothing at all, seeing it as often as I have," Jenai admitted. "Yet today, it cut me to my soul." A tear leaked from her eye, and she wiped it away. "I...had a sister."

'Yes, I know.' Mirrasae's voice in her mind was like the gentle patter of rain. *'I have watched you for years, Jenai. I came that day, called by the Weave, though I did not arrive in time to save Cetta. That is one of my deepest regrets in this age.'*

Jenai dipped her head, fighting back more tears. Her throat burned, and her chest tightened around her lungs. She didn't dare speak. Didn't dare look up, or she might burst into sobs. She stared at the ground, letting the weight of Cetta's death veil her: the guilt, the despair, the anger—all of it.

"That day," she said when the threat of tears had passed, "I swore to drive the Thargundians back and purge the vile Simaeri from our lands."

'Yes, and the Weave heard you,' said Mirrasae. *'I, too, seek vengeance.'*

Jenai jerked her head up, surprised. "You? But unicorns are purity itself."

Mirrasae stood still for a long moment. *'So they ought to be, but I am weakened by my grief. I lost my own sister to the Crow King. I have sought her for many years but may never find her. In my long search, I've grown wrathful toward the ruler of Simaerin. In that weakness, the Weave has sent me to you, that I may fight the tyrant king justly, rather than for my own vendetta.'*

Sympathy pulled at Jenai's heart. She rested her forehead against Mirrasae's muzzle, shut her eyes, and found herself humming a lullaby from her childhood. The unicorn seemed to hum with her, though it was more like the strings of a harp or the piping of a flute. How long they stood like that—Jenai drinking in the unicorn's windy fragrance, Mirrasae soaking in the music—Jenai couldn't say. When at last she pulled away, her heart felt lighter. She stared into the unicorn's ancient eyes, smiled with gratitude, then returned to her bedroll.

Nothing had changed in the world. War continued. People died. The Crow King still brooded in his dark tower across the channel while Thargundians plotted the fall of Fraelin's southern lands. The Crane Prince still had no throne.

Nothing had changed.

Yet Jenai felt stronger, and braver, and ready to tackle what must come next.

16

THE NEXT STEPS

They reached Shinon during a heavy rainstorm. The city spread below a swell of hills, and the rain painted the wild grass a darker hue of green. The stony road wending down the hill was a deep gray color. Jenai and her companions paused to survey the sight before them. Sir Mercer, Bregger, and the old knight had been this far south before, but they allowed Jenai and Limmar to gape for a few moments.

The buildings were two- and three-story structures with tiled roofs. A distant sward served as the town's main market. Under the gray deluge, the city looked sorrowful and beaten down. The Cathedral of Shinon rose to the west of the valley, a beacon on a hill, grand even at a distance. On the far side of Shinon, a chateau stood beside a sprawling vineyard to the east. Beyond the chateau grounds, a deep forest carpeted the distant hills.

Jenai tightened her hold on Mirrasae's mane, mustering the courage she'd found several long nights ago. It was one thing to prepare oneself to speak with the Crane Prince while traveling. It was altogether different when that impending meeting was an hour or so away.

"Ready, Jenai?" whispered Mercer.

She nodded, adjusting her sopping hood with one hand. "I am." She sounded more confident than she felt. Nudging Mirrasae, the company started down the last hill before the bottomlands where Shinon nestled.

Few travelers were on the road. Jenai glanced at a peddler and his cart as she passed him, then she turned her focus to what lay ahead. Prince Chartan, the rightful heir of Fraelin, hid in Chateau Darr. Even the Thargundians knew it. Fortunately, the enemy seemed content to let him rot there while they pillaged and burned the surrounding provinces. Their passivity would buy Jenai the time she needed to convince her prince to fight for Fraelin's liberty.

She straightened her shoulders, praying hard for guidance. She couldn't waste time in Shinon, as she had in Valcinay. She must muster an army to march against the Thargundians before more innocent lives were lost. Before all that remained of Fraelin was a single dreary province.

Entering Shinon proper, Jenai glanced at the sagging townhouses and the darkened shops. Everyone was hunkering down in the wet conditions, but it felt deeper than that. The air tasted of defeat. Even here, in the last bastion of hope for Fraelin's future, little of that frail dream remained.

That must change. She urged Mirrasae to trot a little faster. Her entourage kept pace.

Ahead, Chateau Darr loomed.

THE CHATEAU WAS AN ELEGANT, SPRAWLING STONE fortress, boasting a dozen chimneys and a handful of turrets. Windows, buttresses, and archways softened the severity of its five-story height. Jenai had never dreamed of seeing anything so grand up close.

Under the hammering rain, stablehands led Mirrasae and the horses to a nearby post, then the majordomo bowed the visitors into the chateau's shelter. Jenai dragged her dripping cloak from her shoulders and passed it off to a waiting servant while the majordomo spoke with Sir Mercer, then examined the letter Lord Robarr had sent introducing Jenai.

The head servant's lips pressed into a thin line. He glanced up. "Where is Maid Jenai?"

"I am she," Jenai said, brushing damp hair from her face.

The majordomo looked her up and down. Displeasure drew lines around his eyes. "Please wait here." He carried the letter off, leaving the visitors to drip in the grand vestibule.

Jenai admired the polished marble pillars, wooden reliefs, and bright tapestries depicting cranes, ocean scapes, fierce dragons, and Ilidreth forests. The colorful mosaic stone floor was covered with wide blue rugs, absorbing the water at Jenai's feet. The faint hint of burning incense carried in from the chamber where the majordomo had gone. The door was cracked open. Light spilled out from there, and voices—many of them—were raised as though in argument.

One voice lifted higher than the rest: "—have no time for Robarr's nonsense! Send the maiden away!"

Jenai's shoulder blades cinched. It would be no different from Valcinay after all. She squared her shoulders and started for the door, but a hand grabbed her arm.

"Not here," Mercer murmured. "We must do this through the proper channels."

She glanced at the knight, then back toward the door. It swung outward. The majordomo stepped out, his face a mask of indifference.

"The Crane Prince is otherwise occupied. He won't see you."

Jenai gently pulled herself free of Mercer's grasp. "I will return on the morrow, then."

The majordomo inclined his head. "It is likely he won't see you at all, but do as you will. There is the petitioner's hall. You can try that method to gain his attention." He shrugged.

"I intend to." She turned, grabbed her cloak from the waiting servant, and strode back out into the deluge. Wind yanked back her hood and whipped at her tied-back hair. Cold slithered down her back, but she ignored the discomfort. A fire had lit in her stomach. Deep down, she'd known seeing the Crane Prince wouldn't be simple, but she wouldn't let that stop her. If the Thargundians, Crowsmen, and the wolves of Unholy Thiavos all rose up at once, she would not be thwarted.

Untying Mirrasae from the post with slick fingers, Jenai cast aside the rope the stablehand had used to secure the unicorn. She swung up onto Mirrasae's bare back, then turned toward her men. "I thank each of you for escorting me to Shinon. Those of you who wish to return to Valcinay, go as you please. I'm safely arrived, and soon I'll meet with our prince. If you wish to remain here, I'm headed for the nearest inn and will wait as long as needs be to speak with our ruler."

As the unicorn trotted through the rain, Jenai didn't look back, but the sound of hooves followed.

The nearest inn was full. Jenai tried three more while her entourage stayed close. None left her, and under the stormy conditions she didn't blame them. Snatches of conversation led her to believe the old knight, at least, intended to return to Valcinay once the deluge stopped.

Rain whipped ruthlessly at their backs. The fourth inn— the Broken Nest—stood on the outskirts of Shinon. It was a ramshackle structure whose second story leaned into the street. A rough crowd took up every spare space in the smoke-filled tavern. Mercer moved ahead of Jenai and spoke with the proprietor. The man was weaselly, with gaps between his teeth and thin, oiled hair. They conversed in faint tones, then Mercer pressed several coins into the man's palm.

Returning, the knight nodded to a table on the far side of the tavern, occupied by only one person. "We can sit there. No one else will. There are two available rooms, and we can make do with the loft in the stable if we like. Stew is included with our fee, though I doubt we'll like it."

"A warm place is more than enough." Jenai caught Mercer's eye. "Thank you for staying, Sir Knight."

"I've already sworn myself to your cause. I won't leave your side." He moved between the tables, leading the way to the corner where the solitary figure resided. Fearless, Mercer strode up to the table. "Mind if we join you, stranger?"

The hooded figure turned, revealing dark eyes glittering in the light from a candle on his table. "Not at all." His voice was a soft baritone, with a kind of wandering quality, like he'd stepped out of a dream. He gestured to the empty chairs.

"Thank you." Mercer guided Jenai to the chair farthest from the stranger. There was a tension in his faint touch. She glanced at the knight. He was keeping one eye on the stranger. Jenai studied the shadows around the lone man's dark eyes, but she sensed only a lost soul. The stranger turned back to his mug of mulled cider, clutching the handle, though it looked like he'd drunk barely a swallow or two from the foamy liquid.

Her other guards sat around the table, and soon a barmaid arrived to take drink orders. Mercer ordered ale for everyone, along with the stew included in their room cost. The girl nodded, then, mistaking Jenai for a lad, winked at her. Jenai eyed her coldly, giving her no chance to mistake Jenai's disinterest. Flinching, the barmaid retreated, nearly tripping over herself.

"You should take the room with the single bed," Mercer whispered, "and the rest of us will split up between the stable and the second room. The innkeeper said the second room has two beds. Expect fleas."

Jenai nodded, saying nothing. She didn't dare give away her gender in a tavern full of unsavory folk. They looked hungry for more than liquor and stew.

Soon the barmaid returned, along with two others, carrying tankards and bowls between them. They set them down around the table, including a bowl for the stranger, while the barmaid shot a needled glance at Jenai before whipping away. Her friends also snubbed Jenai, instead winking at the youngest, Limmar, who blushed and watched the three young women sashay away.

Jenai studied her bowl of stew. It smelled of too many herbs and spices, like someone had been trying to disguise something rotten. She prodded the food with her spoon.

"It won't come alive," the stranger said. "I already tested it."

She smiled faintly at him, then returned to examining her meal. She wasn't convinced he was right.

Bregger sampled his stew, working his mouth for several seconds. "Better than me mum's, I'll give it that much."

Everyone chuckled at that.

"Don't trust Bregger's stomach," said Mercer. "It's tougher than most if he survived his childhood eating poison for meals."

"Truth!" Bregger lifted his tankard and drank deeply to that.

"What will you each do tomorrow?" asked the old knight. Jenai hadn't learned his name in their travels. He was the quietest of the group.

"S'what I wanna know, too," Limmar said, prodding his stew with faint disgust. "We leaving or staying tomorrow?"

"I'm staying," said Mercer. "The rest of you may do as you please."

Bregger lifted his tankard in salute to Jenai. "I'll stay. I wouldn't miss this slice of history if the Thargundians their own selves were beating down the Nest's front door. There's something mystic about you, lass."

Jenai blanched. "Quiet, Bregger." Her voice came out calm and low, though she didn't know how she managed that.

He blinked, then glanced around the tavern. "Aye, sorry—friend." He offered a crooked grin. "Relaxed my bones a bit too much if I'm spouting nonsense." He flicked a glance toward the hooded stranger, then away.

Jenai could feel the stranger's eyes on her. She dug into her stew, taking a bite that singed her tongue with its horrific combination of spices. Gagging, she chewed nonetheless, determined to eat and then retreat to her room. She shouldn't have come into the tavern at all.

"Easy there," the stranger said. "That's not palatable stuff for a growing lad." He stood, gesturing. The barmaid returned, all smiles. The stranger flipped her a coin. "Bring cheese and bread in plenty."

She playfully flipped back a strand of hair before she left. The stranger sat again, then pushed the bowls—all untouched but for Bregger's empty one—to one side of the scarred table. He smiled at Jenai. "Never order the stew. There's a reason it's complimentary."

"You ate it," Limmar piped up.

The stranger chuckled. "I've been away a long while. I'd forgotten, but I thought I'd pass along my ill-gotten remembrance before any of you took sick. They never empty the pot, you know. They just add new ingredients and keep it over the flames forever. Never-ending stew, it's called."

"The terrors of road-side convenience," murmured the nameless knight.

Bregger grunted his agreement.

The old knight shifted, catching Jenai's gaze. "I'll be

returning to Valcinay. My kin's all there, and if fighting commences, I want to help them. I've done my bit if you'll grant me leave."

"I already did," Jenai said. "And I thank you for your aid in reaching Shinon. Go with Afallon's blessing."

The old knight dipped his head, then rested a broad hand on Limmar's shoulder. "You'll come with me, lad. Your ma won't thank me if I leave you behind."

Limmar stammered a protest, glancing at Jenai for help, but she left the youth to his choice.

She turned to Mercer. "It may be some time before I accomplish what I must here. Will the coin hold out?"

"For a few weeks, it should. I'll find work if need be."

The barmaid returned with three loaves of bread and two wheels of cheese, along with butter and a carving knife. She dumped the spoils and skipped off to another table where someone was hollering for service.

The stranger's eyes fell on Jenai while Mercer and Bregger divvied up the food. She lifted her gaze to meet his, but he didn't look away. His smile was different now. Rather than friendly, it wore a kind of weariness, adding to the listlessness in his dark eyes.

"What business brings you to Shinon?" he asked.

Everyone at the table froze. Jenai, however, saw no point in lying. "The same thing as most, I should think. We seek an audience with the Crane Prince. What about you?"

"The same," he said. "I suppose the inns are full of all sorts of petitioners." He wrenched off a piece of bread with his teeth and chewed.

"May I ask an impertinent question?" asked Mercer, eyeing the stranger warily.

"Certainly. I'll even answer if I like it well enough. Make it a good one."

"Why is everyone in here avoiding you?" the knight asked.

"Ah." The stranger glanced over his shoulder. Several curious gazes around the room darted away. He turned back, his smile crooking. "I left a bit of an impression when I arrived. Speaking of which, I overheard you discussing your slight accommodations. I'd thought to stay here one more night, but I think I'll try to see the Crane Prince after our meal. Consider my room yours."

"We can't do that," Mercer protested. "Especially since it's doubtful you'll see the prince. We already came from Chateau Darr. The prince isn't seeing anyone."

"He already had company," Bregger added.

The stranger nodded. "I'll take my chances—but if I'm wrong, I might come back and sleep in the stables. Please accept my room." He set the bronze key on the table. "I won't take no for an answer."

Jenai reached out and dragged the key toward her. "We thank you, friend. What name might we remember you by?"

"Friend is good enough," the stranger said. "Indeed, it feels better than any name I've worn in five years." He stood up and moved around the table. In the candlelight, Jenai caught a flash of pale hair under his hood, contrasting with the darkness of his eyes. He offered her another smile—that wandering, wistful one—then swept across the tavern. Folk leaned away from him, then breathed out faint sighs as he passed. The proprietor looked relieved the moment the stranger stepped out into the pounding rain and rising mist.

The barmaid was back, collecting the bowls of uneaten stew.

"Who was that?" Mercer asked her.

"Duke Alain Clayre," she whispered. "Cousin to the Crane Prince. He was just released from the Crow King's custody in Simaerin. Fought his way here, they say. Thargundians chased him nearly to Shinon before he cut the last one down. He's a terror. Half-maddened. Did you see his scar?"

"No," Mercer said, then turned away from the barmaid to find Jenai's gaze. "I've heard of him. The Duke of Clayre was captured in the Battle of Rime five years ago. I thought he died. He and Prince Chartan were like brothers. He's one of the few high-ranking lords who hasn't tried to steal the Crane Prince's throne."

Something loosened in Jenai's chest. "And we met him tonight. That feels like a good omen."

"Maybe." Mercer's frown deepened. "But five years in prison can change a man."

"He seemed nice enough," Bregger said. "A bit odd, but not mad, methinks."

Jenai tore off a bite of bread, deliberating while she chewed. Would the Duke of Clayre assist them if they returned to see the Crane Prince tomorrow? Did he have enough sway for that? Would he even remember them after tonight?

Time alone would tell.

HOME AT LAST

Alain was sopping by the time he reached the front gates of Chateau Darr. He hadn't wanted to face this tonight, any more than he had the last several nights since arriving in Shinon. Somehow, reaching his destination had punctured any desire to return to Chartan's side. He loved his cousin—that wasn't the problem. Alain just didn't want to face what must've become of the rightful heir since Fraelin's fall into...

What do I even call this? It's not defeat. It's something worse.

Alain had spent the last few days in Shinon observing the despondency of its citizens. Once the southern city had been a thriving port, abutting booming wine vineyards, exporting goods to Simaerin, Hesh-Kassal, and even distant Amri and Rishom. Now it was a reeking cesspit full of fear and crime.

Five years had transformed Fraelin from fields of grain and thriving vineyards to a wasteland of despair and misery, perfectly matching Alain's soul. How had it changed Chartan? Alain hated to imagine the alteration in his cousin, but better that than to see it in person.

Yet here he stood, the bell rung, the gatekeeper trudging

from his warm lodgings in the guardhouse to answer Alain's summons. Peering out from his hood, the gatekeeper scowled.

"Go away, vagrant. Gates don't open until dawn."

"I realize that, but this is important." Alain wasn't certain he was telling the truth. Though Chartan had paid the Crow King's ransom for Alain's freedom, it didn't necessarily follow that the Crane Prince would appreciate his cousin barging in on a stormy night, looking like a half-drowned rat.

"Nothing is important enough to warrant waking the Crane Prince," the gatekeeper sneered.

Alain opened his mouth to protest, but the gatekeeper pivoted and marched off, splashing through puddles across the driveway. Muddy droplets splattered Alain's face. "Please come back! Or tell the prince Alain's come home!"

The gatekeeper didn't glance back.

Alain stood in the hammering rain, rivulets rushing down his cheeks. A burning sensation climbed his throat, like he might start crying. But he hadn't cried in years, not even when he'd received word that his mother had died while he was in a Simaeri dungeon. Not even when he'd been set free. He wasn't certain he was capable of tears anymore.

Sure enough, the burning in his throat died after a few swallows. Alain turned from the gate and made for the nearest alleyway to wait out the storm or for dawn's approach. Whichever came first.

MORNING LIGHT CARESSED HIS CHEEKS. ALAIN SAT upright, his back aching, his clothes damp and unpleasant against his prickling flesh. He glanced at his neighbor: a homeless man with several missing teeth who'd been kind enough to share his alleyway. The man was rummaging through a pile of refuse where half-rotten vegetables had been thrown out. Alain's stomach rumbled, but he wasn't desperate enough to eat the mushy-looking carrot the old man proffered.

Digging into his pocket, Alain pulled out the last coin he'd taken off the Crowsmen he'd slain en route to Shinon. He flipped the coin at the old man. "Use it wisely."

The homeless man clutched it to his heart, nodding his thanks. Alain suspected the man's tongue had been cut out, probably by Thargundians who'd found him insolent. Alain made a mental note to help the old man once he was back in a position to help anyone. Assuming Chartan had the means anymore.

How much money did you waste on freeing me instead of helping your people, you fool?

Alain left the alley and started up the hill for Chateau Darr. Sunlight rippled in the puddles, and water dripped from the eaves. The world was fresher after that downpour, and Shinon didn't feel quite so downcast. Though the night spent in the alley had left Alain drenched and weary, he was glad he'd been able to brighten the homeless man's day and give his room over to travelers who needed it more. He contemplated the strangers who'd supped with him. One of the youngest, a woman dressed like a lad, had intrigued him. He could only guess why she wore boy's clothes. Probably for protection on the road. Considering his own perilous journey to Shinon, he didn't blame anyone for taking precautions.

But it was more than her appearance that had left an impression. Something about her was...different. Radiant and otherworldly. Sitting in her presence, over a bowl of putrid stew, caged in a tavern reeking of smoke and spirits, Alain had felt as though he sat in a church—which he hadn't done in over a decade.

Reaching the gate barring entrance to Chateau Darr, Alain rang the cord that alerted the gatekeeper.

Behind him, in Shinon proper, bells began to ring. Alain whirled around, startled, before he remembered that in Fraelin the bells still rang on Worship Days. Like low clouds giving way to sunlight, the clarion peals did something for the depressed old city. That ancient song of faith seemed to transform the dreary streets, lifting an oppressive mist from the nooks and crannies. It was nothing literal, just a feeling, and Alain shrank from it.

"What'd you want?" the gatekeeper demanded.

Spinning, Alain met the old man's narrowed eyes beneath bushy eyebrows. "To see Prince Chartan."

"It's Worship Day," the gatekeeper said, then turned and started off through the puddles. Alain leaned back to avoid getting splashed again.

"Wait! At least tell him I'm here." He scowled. "That's an order, soldier!"

The man froze, then wheeled around slowly. "Did you just command me, peasant?"

"I'm not a peasant." Alain drew himself upright, remembering his years of training for his title's sake. "I am Duke Alain Clayre, returned recently from my captivity in Crowwell, and I demand to see my cousin the crown prince. Can I be any plainer, Gatekeeper?"

The man's frown deepened, then he moved back to the gate. Alain noted that the sentinel had a faint limp. Leaning close to the bars, the gatekeeper squinted out at Alain, his lips pressed tight. "You don't look like the duke."

"I've spent five years in prison, man." Alain shrugged. "That would make skeletons out of giants." He resisted shifting his feet under the guard's scrutiny. He kept his shoulders erect and his chin high—but not too high. The man stared on. Alain sighed. "Let me see the Crane Prince, and he can decide which of us is right. Hm?"

"That's one idea," the old man mused.

"A decent one, too. Do you have another?"

"Yes. You can get stuffed. I knew Duke Alain. Good man, great warrior. Never stank." The gatekeeper whirled away again and marched off, spraying muddy water at Alain, who didn't think to dodge in time.

The gatekeeper's name returned like a bolt of lightning, striking Alain with old memories of a man who liked to heckle young soldiers. "Like the unholy pits, I didn't ever stink! Have you ever seen a battlefield? Have you ever used a sword? Get back here, Huvarn, you goat-headed oaf!"

The gatekeeper halted, boots ankle-high in water, his back to Alain. His shoulders began to shake, then Huvarn threw his head back and barked out a laugh. He turned, still laughing, mirth brightening his worn face. "It really is you, my lord." The old man hurried back, agile despite his limp. He unlatched several locks, then threw the gates aside to admit Alain. "Welcome home, Your Grace. Glory to Afallon for his tender blessings."

Alain's smile twitched toward a grimace, but he batted that down. Let Huvarn credit whom he pleased. No one needed to share Alain's skepticism for the blessings from on high. They needn't experience what he had. He set his hand on Huvarn's shoulder. "You've gotten so old, I couldn't see your soul for all your wrinkles, you old fool."

Huvarn's laughter deepened until his entire frame shook. "You've gotten worse at your insults, Your Grace. They don't land as they once did."

"I'm out of practice. I'll work up a proper one for next time."

Huvarn's hand caught Alain's elbow. "Steady, Your Grace. Rest up first, then you'll have the wits. You've not got enough meat on those bones to land anything, be it fowl, insult, or lady."

Alain snorted. "Well, your wits haven't addled." He

clapped the man's shoulder again, then made his way up the private drive to the chateau's front doors. Ivy grew up around the old stone fortress, glistening with last night's deluge. The flowers along the drive had opened to devour the sunlight after a night of imbibing rain. A gardener rounded the side of the chateau, clippers in hand, but upon seeing Alain in his travel cloak he ducked back behind the house. Alain took the stairs two at a time, ignoring the strain on his legs. Despite trying to keep fit for five years, his lean diet had caused his muscles to wither. It would be some time before he was the warrior he'd once been, assuming Fraelin would be allowed to fight at all.

As he pounded on the door, Alain debated breaking inside. If he had to fight another servant for the right to see his cousin, he'd lose his temper. He was hungry, cold, and eager for familial affection. Prince Chartan was all he had left.

The door opened, and the majordomo peeked out, his wig askew. "What is this?"

"I'm home, Figg."

The majordomo's eyes widened, then his lips stretched in a strained smile. "Can you really be him?"

"Who else calls you Figg?"

"*Everyone*, thanks to you, Duke Rascal." Dropping all decorum, the lean servant flung his arms around Alain. Figg drew him into an embrace that a bear would envy, clapping Alain's back until it stung. At last, the majordomo drew back, moisture glistening in his brown eyes. "Prince Chartan said he'd paid the ransom, but I presumed you dead. I thought—" Figg shook his head. "What am I doing? Come inside, Your Grace. Hurry now. You look damp and hungry."

Alain allowed the majordomo to usher him inside the grand vestibule. Only when the warmth and woodsmoke from a blazing fireplace enveloped him did he realize how cold he'd been. Gooseflesh needled his arms, and his teeth began to chatter.

Figg looked him up and down, humming to himself, then he led Alain past the front audience rooms, into the backend residential area, and up a flight of wide stairs. Alain soon found himself in an ornate bedchamber untouched by Fraelin's years of poverty. The chateau stood like a memory of grander days. A lump of guilt swelled in Alain's stomach.

Rather than send for a housemaid, Figg drew Alain's bath. Despite being eager to see his cousin, Alain didn't argue. He needed to chase off last night's chill, and after years in a dungeon, he never wanted to feel dirty again.

Breakfast was sent up, and Alain ate it while he soaked the travel grime from his skin. When he finally dragged himself from the cooling water, he found fresh clothes laid out on the four-post bed. Slipping into the white blouse, blue vest and trousers, and supple gray boots, Alain felt more human than he had in ages. He ran his hand along the flimsy cloth of his baggy blouse sleeve and shook his head. He'd forgotten what luxury felt like.

Figg knocked, then entered the bedchamber at Alain's invitation. The majordomo held oils, a comb, shaving implements, and a ribbon. He first insisted on shaving Alain's pale whiskers, then convinced the duke to let him trim then tie Alain's hair into a tidy ribbon according to the present fashion. Alain accommodated him. Seated in a plush chair, he studied himself in the looking glass while the man worked. It wasn't surprising to see the gaunt face and haunted eyes. What did surprise him was that he didn't look past thirty, despite the abuse he'd endured. He'd fully expected to have aged into an old man.

"You'll soon have meat on your bones again," Figg said, tying off the ribbon. "Prince Chartan will see to that."

"I confess, Mardry's table is half the reason I came home. She's the finest cook in the world."

Figg smiled. "She is that. All finished."

Alain inspected himself in the mirror one more time, then stood up and rested a hand on Figg's shoulder. "Thank you for this. I..." Emotion swelled up his throat, and he fell still, letting it sweep over him. Figg caught his elbow again, waiting with the infinite patience the man always wielded. Figg had been with Prince Chartan for as long as Alain could remember. The majordomo was more like family than a head servant. Chartan and Alain had played with his children, treating them like cousins. In many ways, Figg was their surrogate father, as both had been robbed of theirs too young.

Alain pressed his emotions back down into their cage, then straightened his shoulders. "I'm ready to see Chartan. Does he know I'm here?"

"No," Figg said. "He's been in a meeting with the Arch Priest and the Duke of Thame all morning. His breakfast is cold."

Alain's elation withered. "What is that old goat doing here?" He'd detested Duke Dulen Thame for years, and he'd thought Chartan felt the same.

"I'm afraid Thame is all that's holding our last defenses against the Thargundians together. He's financing the soldiers."

Fire rolled through Alain's veins. "Of course he is. He's been hoarding wealth for years while the rest of us gave every last sol to the cause. *Now* he chooses to aid Fraelin? At what interest rate, I wonder?" Storming from the bedchamber, he marched down the stairs, aiming for the front offices. But the chateau was large enough that Alain could only guess where Chartan would hold his private meetings. He halted. "Figg, where do I go?"

The majordomo passed him by and steered Alain toward a

small study. The room was brightly lit by dawn. Blue velvet curtains hung to either side of the broad windows, and the wooden furniture gleamed with fresh polish. At the study's wide desk, the Arch Priest—a quill-thin, stooped, balding man in clergy robes—and Thame—a rotund man sparkling with gems sewn into every layer of his clothing—were both leaning close to a harassed-looking Crane Prince.

The image, so much like two vultures eyeing a fresh animal carcass, nearly sent Alain flying forth, blade drawn, but he'd left his stolen sword in his guestroom. Instead, Alain composed himself, drawing deep breaths. He tacked on a smile, spread his arms wide, and shouted, "Good morrow, cousin!"

The two vultures whirled to face Alain, eyes wide, mouths gaping. Their surprise mounted upon recognizing the Duke of Clayre. Alain danced between them, taking advantage of their stunned silence.

Prince Chartan jumped from his chair so fast that he knocked it onto its back with a resounding clatter. He seized Alain's hands in his, searching his face. The Crane Prince had aged, not unlike Alain. He already had five years on the duke, but now he looked forty rather than thirty years of age. His dark hair had thinned, and his features—never striking—were shadowed and dimmed by sleepless nights.

"By Afallon's bloody wounds, is it really you, Alain?" Chartan breathed.

"I dearly hope so," Alain laughed. "If not, I'm not sure *who* I am."

The prince released his hands and circled the desk to embrace Alain. "Brother of my heart, it does my soul such good to see you in the flesh! I sent that ransom months ago, then heard nothing at all. I'd have sent a coach to claim you if I'd been given notice."

Alain grinned. "The Crow King was good enough to send

one in your stead. I dare say he intended to imprison me all over again. Why wait until I reached Fraelin, I can't say. But he's a lunatic, isn't he?" He shrugged. "In any case, I'm here and all's well. Figg had the goodness to feed and clothe me, so I'm presentable. And with a little time, I'll have my strength back to beat the Simaeri from our shores and pound the Thargundians into proper submission."

The room grew heavy at his words.

"We were just discussing that," Thame said. "A letter arrived from the Duke of Thargundy—"

"Not now." Chartan glowered at the fat man. "My cousin has just returned from the abyss of Simaerin. Politics can rest for a time. I want to soak in this moment. Indeed, we should celebrate!" He started for the liquor cabinet beside the closest window.

Alain caught his arm. "Hold fast. What did the letter contain?"

"Demands to surrender, Your Grace," said the Arch Priest.

A chill nibbled at Alain's flesh, but he shrugged. "If they wish to surrender, all the better for us."

Thame rolled his eyes. "I see you still take everything as a jest, Your Grace. But this is deadly serious. Our armies are in rags. Half our forces have deserted. Our food supplies have been reduced to rotten cabbages. We're losing day by day."

"I survived five years in rags, eating rotten food, *Your Grace*." Alain drew himself up. "That doesn't equal loss. Suffering, certainly, but not loss. If we live on, we're victorious every day."

"A pretty sentiment," Thame sneered. "I would have thought the Crow's dungeons would shatter that rosy outlook, but it seems naïvety, for some, is a condition."

"Enough, Duke Dulen Thame." Chartan slammed the cabinet door shut, clutching a decanter of wine in one hand.

"My cousin has just returned to us, and I'll have no word laid against him. Do I speak plainly?"

The Duke of Thame hesitated, then dipped his head. "As my lord prince commands. But may I add a word of caution before I hold my peace?"

"You always do." Chartan sighed and moved to Alain's side.

"While none here would ever doubt the good intentions of the people's beloved Duke of Clayre, it's said that the dungeons in Crowwell break minds." Thame swiveled toward Alain, who stiffened under the crafty gleam in those dark eyes. "I'm not saying you don't *intend* to do right by Fraelin, but perhaps you ought to rest for a few months—"

"I've had enough of *resting*." Alain curled his hands into fists. "I've likewise had enough of coercion and politicking. You think my mind is broken, Your Grace? You think me incapable of sitting in on councils such as this? I've a right to be here, and I'm not leaving, whatever condition my mind is in. My cousin needs me, and so long as that remains the case—"

Chartan placed a hand on Alain's shoulder. "Easy, cousin. You're welcome here." He pressed a goblet of red wine into Alain's hand. "Drink, sit. I, too, have had enough of politicking for a while. Your Grace, Your Holiness, might you both leave us for an hour to reminisce about happier times?"

The portly duke opened his mouth, a protest gathering like a hurricane in his countenance, but the priest shot him a look. Thame snapped his mouth shut like a turtle, huffed through his nose, then bowed his head. "We'll return in an hour, Your Royal Highness." He whirled around and waddled from the room, taking the storm with him. The Arch Priest slithered out behind him.

Alain dropped into a chair only after the door shut. Letting out a low breath, he shook his head, then took a sip of the wine. Its dry, sour taste fit his mood too well. He set the goblet down with a grimace. "We used to supply the best wine in the world. We used to be a kingdom. Now what are we? By Afallon, what has Fraelin become?"

Chartan sat in the chair beside him. "Spare me your speeches, Alain. I hear enough from Dulen Thame every day."

"I'm not speech-making. I'm lamenting." But Alain didn't pick his words back up. He studied Chartan, letting the tension bleed from his shoulders, letting the warmth of the sunny study soak into his skin. "It's good to see you, cousin."

Chartan flashed him a grin that shaved off years from his face. "And you, Alain."

"But you shouldn't have ransomed me. I'm not worth giving up the last of your coin when others—"

"I *had* to," Chartan said miserably. "I needed someone I can trust. I needed a friend in my corner." He sighed. "Someone of rank, not Figg."

"Has it been that bad?" Alain could imagine the pulling and tugging all too well. "Do they all want to surrender to Thargundy?"

"No. No, no. That only came up because of Kon Dragonclaw's letter. Before that, it's been all about land-grabbing and changing up titles. Who supported me best at the battle of so-and-so or such-and-such, and should Garvay's barony be given over to the earldom of Lentari for his betrayal? It's as though everyone is content to play pretend—like we're not a kingdom at the brink of destruction. It's a political nightmare. Thame speaks loudest, and he has friends *and* wealth to back him."

"Why let him in?"

Chartan narrowed a look on Alain. "Did I not just say *wealth?*"

Alain scowled. "I can't help you there. My fortune died

with my father, and no title is worth sod without you on the throne of Fraelin. We must storm Lorion—take it back."

"We can't." Chartan shook his head. "We haven't the arms."

"Raise a new army."

"No one will come. I have no money to pay them, no throne to control them. I've lost my credibility. Only Thame has the means—"

"That's out of the question. He'd buy his way to the crown at Reems if money alone was enough. A man like that can't be trusted."

"Apart from you, who can I trust?"

A knock sounded at the door.

"Come!" Chartan called, glancing apologetically at Alain.

Figg stuck his head inside. "Forgive me, but the petitioners have gathered."

"Not today, Figg. I'm otherwise occupied, and it's Worship Day. Send them away."

Alain reached for his wine goblet, then remembered he hadn't cared for it. "Don't forsake your duties on my account, Chartan. Your people are waiting."

"My people are always waiting. And they all want the same thing: money. Which I don't have. How many petitioners must I hear and turn away before the rest understand that I can do nothing for them? I have no crown, no throne, no hoard of wealth tucked away like some dragon. The coffers are empty, and taxes have bled my subjects dry. I'm a pauper prince, and that's the straight truth." Chartan slumped back in his chair.

"You're also Fraelin's hope and purpose." Alain leaned forward, trying to catch his cousin's eye, but the man twisted away. "Chartan, if you could embolden the people, many would still fight for you."

"Yes, and die for me. Pointlessly." Chartan shrugged. "Forgive me if I'm more than weary of that predictable end."

"What's the alternative?" asked Alain.

"Not surrender." Chartan shifted to look at him. "I'm not so desperate as that yet. Believe me, Alain. I don't intend to give the Duke of Thargundy Fraelin now or later."

"Then you *must* fight."

"How?"

"Raise a new army and march on Lorion!"

"I suppose you want me to listen to that deranged Maiden of Lorrae or wherever she's from?"

"I don't know who you mean. I just want you to rally your troops and—"

"We're talking in circles." Chartan stood up and stomped behind his desk, keeping his back to Alain. "No, cousin. There's no army to raise. Only Afallon could intercede on our behalf, and He's forsaken my kingdom. Fight we will, but only in defense. It's all we can do."

"It's not enough, Your Highness."

"Then we die."

18

TRUE PRINCE

Jenai, Mercer, and Bregger stayed at the Broken Nest all week. The old knight and Limmar left after that first stormy night in Shinon, making it easier to feed those who remained. At the end of the week, Mercer was able to secure better accommodations at the Two Feathers inn near Chateau Darr. It wasn't a fancy establishment, but it was clean, and the patrons didn't look ready to skewer each other for a single coin. Jenai had her own room while Mercer and Bregger shared the room opposite hers.

Each morning, Jenai made her presence known at the chateau, just as she'd done in Valcinay. Mercer and Bregger took turns accompanying her while the other did odd jobs around Shinon to keep enough money for food and lodgings. Jenai remained in the waiting room—a vast chamber filled with chairs—where petitioners from across Fraelin gathered to meet their prince.

Each day, she sat near a window and watched the routine of the chateau's staff. Prince Chartan only saw between four and seven people daily. Just like in Valcinay, people who had come after Jenai were called upon while some who had been coming to the chateau longer than Jenai were still waiting. Many grew disheartened and left, but a few stubbornly arrived each morning just like she did.

Discouragement tried to set in, but Jenai barred it. Afallon wouldn't have sent her all this way only to fail. An opportunity would arise, perhaps as unexpected as her part to play with the refugees in Valcinay.

A fortnight after reaching Shinon, Jenai stood up from her seat at eventide, Mercer at her side. They moved with the stream of hapless petitioners toward the chateau's front door. As Jenai stepped through the chamber out into the vestibule, movement caught her eye. She turned and found Duke Alain Clayre slipping from the Crane Prince's audience chamber. He glanced toward her and froze.

He was dressed well, in fashionable blue and gray clothing, with his pale blond hair tied back in a tail. His brown eyes stood out against the fairness of his skin and his apparel. A faint smile caught his lips, and he started forward, then halted and glanced at the audience room behind him. He turned to her and mouthed 'Come back tomorrow.'

She nodded, hope fluttering through her chest like a dove's wings. The flow of petitioners pushed her toward the chateau's front doors, and she fell into their pace, losing sight of the young duke. Soon she was out-of-doors, standing next to her unicorn, lifting a prayer toward heaven.

Sir Mercer reached her, frowning. "You look happy. What happened?"

"Tomorrow," she said, half-afraid. Then she lifted her head, warmth flooding through her. "Afallon will work His will tomorrow."

Mercer's frown softened. "He's a slow worker. But I suppose He works through dawdling people."

"So He does." She stroked Mirrasae's silky mane. "Let's delay returning to the inn. I wish to visit the chapel first."

The knight helped her climb onto Mirrasae's back, then mounted his own horse. They left the chateau behind and trotted to the church just down the hill. It was old, large, and well kept. Already Jenai had spoken with the priest there—a man of middle years who treated her with kindness, even if he looked as though he questioned her sanity. She'd gone to him for confession thrice upon moving to the Two Feathers. After their first conversation, he'd ceased trying to convince her to return to her father's farm.

Mirrasae stopped at the end of the gravel path leading up to the church. Flowers bloomed on either side of the walkway, their fragrance welcoming and sweet. So far south, the ember lilies were already unfurled, presently snowy white. Toward autumn, the unique, long-lasting flower petals would be tipped with red.

Jenai swung down, murmured her thanks to the unicorn, then started up the pathway. Mercer remained outside, guarding her. Jenai allowed it, sensing that he needed to be useful even if there was no danger in Shinon.

Soon enough the dangers will come.

She slipped inside the hallowed building and drank in the faith humming in the very walls. Pillars lined the walkway between polished pews. Candles flickered in rows at the altar standing on the far end of the long stone chapel. The floor was a colorful mosaic much like Chateau Darr. The vaulted ceiling depicted angels surrounding Afallon in His glory. Jenai strode forward, her heart pounding. Why, she wondered.

Is it because tomorrow, at last, I will take another step toward defeating Fraelin's foes?

She found herself smiling grimly. Reaching the altar, she knelt and bowed her head. "Gracious Afallon, my Guide and Benefactor, let tomorrow be the hour when Fraelin takes back her banner. Direct me to defeat our cruel enemies and heal this broken land. Give me courage and strength. Give me purpose and foresight. Give me hope, and keep me gentle. Finia."

She took up a candle from the pile of unlit tapers and set the wick against one of the flickering flames. It sparked with light. She placed it among the rest, then knelt again to pray on. Hours passed. She didn't cease her prayers until past dark.

When she stepped outside, Mercer was still there, waiting on the path. The streets were lit for the night, though few people roamed so late.

"Ready?" the knight asked quietly.

"I am now." She climbed onto Mirrasae's back. "Let us return to the inn."

Mercer swung up into his saddle with a creak of leather. He waited for Jenai to lead the way, then followed close.

At the Two Feathers, Bregger didn't ask where they'd been. He studied Jenai's face, then grunted to himself. "Dinner's waiting."

"Let's eat together, then retire," Jenai said. "I must be fresh for tomorrow."

She ate only a little, then excused herself. In her room, she stripped out of her masculine clothing and slipped into a nightgown. Letting her hair out, she sat on the edge of her bed. A storm was rising outside. Wind howled through the windowpanes, and the silhouette of tree boughs danced against the opposing wall. Jenai watched the pitching shadows, torn between weariness and nervous excitement.

She lay down and stared at the shadows across the ceiling. "Let tomorrow go well, Sweet Afallon. I can't abide the waiting."

Turning over, Jenai tried to claim sleep, but it came with reluctance. By dawn, she'd only caught two hours of rest at intervals. At first light she rose and dressed quickly. Stepping out into the hall, she found Mercer waiting.

"Thought we'd be heading over early." He offered her a cinnamon bun. "Eat up, my lady."

She accepted the pastry with thanks, then strode at his side down the stairs and out into the chilly morning air. Mirrasae and the horse were waiting. They rode to the chateau at a quick pace. All the while, Jenai's insides writhed.

The majordomo ushered them into the waiting chamber like always. He didn't ask for her name—he knew it by now. She sat at her usual spot, heart hammering. Mercer stood beside her. A few familiar petitioners waved, and Jenai waved back.

Time crawled by. Other names were called, then none. Jenai fended off every doubt trying to creep into her heart. The duke had told her to come back. He'd remembered her. She'd felt Afallon's peace. Surely, this was the day.

Let it be today.

Seven petitioners had been called. What felt like hours had passed since. Prince Chartan never saw more than eight in a day. It was now or never.

Jenai shifted in her chair. Every nerve was taut.

Let it be now. Please let it be now.

The majordomo reappeared at the door. "Will Jenai d'Arc of Domrem please rise?"

Murmurs rose at that. Many of the petitioners knew her name and guessed her purpose. Rumors had chased her from Valcinay.

Jenai sat stunned. Had she heard right? Mercer nudged her, and she sprang to her feet. A friendly woman several seats down smiled at her. They'd been coming to the chateau for the same length of time. Likely, the woman saw this as a hopeful sign for her own petition.

Sending up a prayer to heaven, Jenai crossed the chamber, Mercer at her back. The majordomo glanced at the knight, then motioned them out into the vestibule. He turned back to the room at large. "There will be no more interviews today. Please depart." He slipped ahead of her and led the way toward the ornate door Jenai had been vying for since she'd reached Shinon. Beyond that scroll-worked barrier rose voices —a lot of them.

Jenai glanced at the head servant. "Are we meeting with a council?"

"The prince is entertaining dignitaries today in celebration of his cousin's long-anticipated return." The majordomo paused outside the door and studied Jenai's face. "The Duke of Clayre vouched for you. It's why you're being granted an audience so soon."

"May Afallon bless him for that," Jenai answered.

The majordomo frowned, then pushed aside the door, admitting her into a broad chamber filled with finely clad nobles. Their perfume and sweat wafted toward her, nearly strangling her. She took shallow breaths, set her shoulders, and stepped into the chamber. Mercer walked at her back. Every eye landed on her, taking her in, weighing her down under their judgment and curiosity.

At the head of the room, a short dais held a cushioned throne beneath an enormous Crane banner draped against the back wall. Upon that throne sat a man in his thirties wearing a circlet that was lopsided on his brow. A short cape was draped across one shoulder in a fashion Jenai hadn't seen before. He eyed her with a fierce frown, almost a scowl. The courtiers and nobles parted to let her pass along the center of the chamber. Several hid their faces behind fans. Whispers stalked her up the aisle they'd made.

Jenai approached the throne, trying to recall the petition she'd practiced since reaching Shinon—but something about the atmosphere, coupled with her own tight nerves, made it difficult to focus. Someone in the room giggled. Jenai halted halfway to the throne and glanced around. Mercer stayed close, saying nothing, though his gaze was heavy against her back.

Afallon, whatever is happening here, please guide me.

Starting forward again, she neared the dais. Looking up at the throne, she stared into the man's eyes. His scowl twitched toward a smirk, and Jenai frowned.

This isn't right.

"You're not him. Where is the Crane Prince?" She turned to face the room. Murmurs broke out across the chamber. Faces ducked further behind their fans and cloaks.

"Jenai, they are testing you," said the Voice. *"Seek the true prince in the crowd."*

She glanced around, taking in the dozens of posh dignitaries, seeking the man she would swear allegiance to. Among the courtiers, she glimpsed the Duke of Clayre. He watched her with curiosity, but no amusement.

She moved past the duke, searching each face. Each countenance. And then she halted. There, it must be *him*. He was similar in build and age to the imposter sitting on the throne, but this man was careworn, with straight shoulders, and a corona of light on his brow in place of a circlet. Jenai strode to him, parting people with a glance, then knelt before him.

"Yes, Jenai, this is your prince," said the Voice.

She caught his hand and kissed the signet ring. "My sweet prince, I've come to lead your army to victory against the Thargundians and to thrust out the Crowsmen from Fraelin. My life is yours to command under Afallon's will."

The murmurs climbed higher. Disbelief and scorn mingled with awe. She kept her head bowed, clutching Prince Chartan's hand, awaiting his word to rise.

"How did you know it was me?" he asked amid the din of voices, his expression mystified.

She lifted her chin enough to smile at him. "You're

marked by Afallon to rule Fraelin. You wear a crown that none can remove, save Afallon alone."

He hesitated, then stooped to take her elbow and lift her to her feet. "Silence!" he called into the growing noise. Everyone fell still to watch. Turning back to Jenai, he arched his brow. "You would lead my army to Lorion?"

"I've been sent by Afallon to that end, my prince."

"But you're a woman. You can't have any battle experience."

"If he sent a mongrel dog alone to fight, victory would be possible where faith walks." Jenai's smile deepened. "Send me to war, Crane Prince, and I will see you crowned king in Reems."

Voices filled the chamber. Eyes were glued on Jenai, some sneering, others curious, still others reverential. Finding the Duke of Clayre's face among the onlookers, Jenai was buoyed up by his quiet smile. She shifted her attention back to Prince Chartan, waiting. Mercer remained at her side, saying nothing.

The prince glanced toward someone in the sea of people. "Clear the room! Bring me the Arch Priest. Let's settle this matter forthwith."

19

BEFORE THE DAIS

The vaulted chamber felt more vast in the absence of the dignitaries. Jenai stood before the dais upon the mosaic stone floor, Mercer still beside her. Stained-glass windows spread prisms of light across the high, ornate ceiling. Portraits of past kings and queens adorned the walls at intervals, all looking proud and benevolent. All wore the same sapphire-bedecked golden crown of Fraelin.

The Crane Prince now sat upon his throne, his circlet returned and resting properly on his brow. He studied Jenai with a pensive frown, his finger and thumb rubbing the tip of his chin. "You must forgive my earlier subterfuge, Maid Jenai. Several of my advisors had heard rumors about you in Shinon and wanted to test the truth. People were calling you the Voice of Afallon. They seem to think you have supernatural powers. Do you?"

"I have no powers," she answered.

"Yet you knew who I was."

"That was revealed through Afallon's will."

The few men remaining in the chamber whispered at her back. One of them stepped forward. He was a rotund fellow, better dressed than anyone else, with a poofy hat on his head. Rings sparkled on his fingers. "Your Royal Highness, it's obvious the lass is touched in her mind. No doubt, it's caused by the fact that her village is so near the Thargundian borders. The horrors she must have seen." He shuddered dramatically. "Is there really any need to examine her? We should send her back to her home. Her parents must be sick with worry."

The Duke of Clayre stepped up on Jenai's other side, his eyes narrowed on the prince. "Lord Robarr of Valcinay sent her, Your Highness, and we all know how pragmatic *he* is. But these are all points that we've already discussed. Let the church examine her. Let us see what she's about without biases." He never looked toward Jenai, but she sensed his warmth like a hearth fire on a cold night. He was her one ally among the prince's retinue.

"I've already called for the Arch Priest," Prince Chartan said. "He will decide the girl's fate in this matter. There's no need to bicker, though it seems the two of you would seize the chance even over a hard biscuit."

"True, if it were the last one," the Duke of Clayre said, a grin flashing across his face. "Although I expect the Duke of Thame would need it far more than I."

The fat man snorted. "I'd thank you for the generous gift, but hard biscuits are *not* part of my lifestyle. I didn't earn my girth by consuming peasant food." He rubbed his protruding gut affectionately.

"If we don't end this war and earn the victory," Alain Clayre shot back, "then *everyone* will be eating peasant food—even rotting cabbages—including Your Grace."

"I'd prefer *not* to eat His Grace," someone behind them quipped.

That evoked laughter from the small crowd, but Jenai ignored them, studying the chuckling prince on his throne.

This was the man chosen to rule Fraelin. She was certain he had failings, as all humans did, but surely not so many as the disgruntled common folk expressed. In any event, she'd been called to clear his path to the cathedral in Reems, where tradition demanded any true king be crowned. She must see it done, or his reign would be plagued with doubts about his legitimacy caused by his mother's unseemly conduct.

As the general mirth faded, the prince turned his attention back to her. The pensive frown returned. "Have you ever wielded a sword, Maid Jenai?"

"No, sweet prince."

"Do you know battle strategies?"

"No."

"Have you ever witnessed more than a skirmish against the Thargundians?"

"Never."

He sat back. "I realize that your faith is great if you say a dog could lead the way to victory. But surely Afallon would call a student of war to the cause."

"Afallon calls those who listen. If your war generals don't heed the call, Afallon must send one who will."

"A well-considered argument," said a voice drifting toward the throne from behind Jenai. She turned and found a priest of older years, stooped and balding, clutching a staff for balance. He squinted at her, furrowing the lines of his face further. He made his way to her side, silver and blue robes gliding across the polished floor in his wake. "Are you a student of faith, child?"

"I pray we all are."

He grunted at that. "Then some are more apt than others." He shot a look past her shoulder, possibly in the direction of the Duke of Thame. "Who is the priest in Domrem, lass?"

"Father Priarre."

"Ah. I know the man. Gentle as a dove, except when provoked. And then he is fiercer than a dragoness guarding her hatchlings."

"You do know the man, Your Holiness." Jenai ducked her head reverently.

The Arch Priest's thick eyebrows dipped until they looked like brooding storm clouds. "You claim to have been sent by Afallon to lead Fraelin to victory against the Thargundians and the Crowsmen of Simaerin, yes?"

"Yes, Holiness."

"How do you know this to be true? In what way does Afallon manifest His will to you?"

Jenai hesitated. "I'm not at liberty to say."

The priest's brows lowered, thundering. "I am the Arch Priest of Fraelin. If you cannot tell me, then you are deceived, child."

"You're also a servant of the Crane Prince," Jenai said. "If he were to command you to share all that Afallon has revealed to you, would you obey him?"

"I could not," the Arch Priest replied. "My oath is foremost to the faith of heaven, and secondly to the rightful prince of Fraelin."

"So, too," she said, "I will keep my peace with One who stands higher than all of us, even His priests. If Afallon bids that I should reveal the way in which He communicates with me, only then will I tell you."

The storm broke across the Arch Priest's face. He sighed and turned to the throne. "Your Highness, I ask for more time to examine this creature. She is either a saint in mortal coils or a devil in stolen flesh. May I take her with me to the cathedral and exert the Council of Faith to assist me in this matter?"

Dismay caught Jenai's lungs, and she glanced at the Crane Prince.

"By all means, Your Holiness," Prince Chartan said. "But don't delay quite so long as your council is prone to do. If she is indeed sent by our God, I'd rather get on with winning my rightful crown and spanking the Thargundians hard."

The Arch Priest dipped his head, then took Jenai's arm. "My carriage awaits us."

Mercer inched closer. "My lady?"

"This is well," she said, though dread fluttered in her chest. "I have nothing to fear in an examination of my faith. Return to Bregger and await my word. Care well for Mirrasae in my absence."

He nodded and stepped back.

Guided by the Arch Priest's hand, Jenai was led from the chamber. She glanced back and found Mercer and the Duke of Clayre standing side by side, their expressions of concern identical. She turned her eyes forward and steeled herself for what was to come.

The Voice came to her. *"Be cautious, child, and say nothing of your mission to any lone priest. Speak only where witnesses stand."*

THE CARRIAGE RUMBLED ACROSS COBBLESTONES, SWAYING back and forth. Jenai felt the Arch Priest's eyes on her while she stared out the window between the parted curtains, watching the city of Shinon fly by. Evening encroached on the streets, conjuring long shadows. An early mist curled around the edges of the old buildings.

"Tell me about your journey here, my child," the priest said.

Jenai shook her head. "I will speak only before the entire Council of Faith. There I will have witnesses."

"You're not on trial, lass," the priest said more gently.

"Even so, I will do no dealings in the dark." She glanced at him to find him nodding slowly.

"A wise practice. How old are you?"

She turned away. "I will answer no questions tonight, Holy Father. Please."

The carriage rattled over several potholes, then climbed away from the city, up another hillside. Jenai pressed against the glass but could see nothing of the cathedral from her angle. After several minutes, the road curved, and the lit-up dark-stone building rose like a beacon beneath the red-streaked sky. The edifice was tiered, with a high tower and lower towers surrounding it, and grand flying buttresses arcing outward to either side. Stained-glass windows glinted under the influence of torches surrounding the structure in rows. The flames guttered in a wind stronger than any that swept through city streets. She'd longed to visit this cathedral, but not as a prisoner. Whether it was official or not, she felt like one now, chained to skepticism.

Afallon, guide my steps.

"*Do not fear,*" the Voice said. "*You did not come all this way to be prevented now. Only among witnesses, speak the truth, except where you are expressly forbidden.*"

She sent up silent thanks, then kept praying, for strength, for support, and especially for courage.

HER SECOND EXAMINATION

Dawn light blazed on the stone floor of the council room. Upon waking, Jenai had washed up, then climbed into her boy's clothes just in time to be escorted from her borrowed bedroom: a small, tidy chamber with a narrow bed, a washstand, and a chair and mirror. She was led down a long corridor, and into the wide chamber where she now stood. Two dozen priests sat in chairs in a semi-circle before her. It didn't feel like a tribunal, though she read incredulity and annoyance in most countenances. The thin Arch Priest sat at the center of the group, his face a mask of piety. She stood beside a chair, waiting for permission to sit.

"Daughter, this is the Council of Faith," the Arch Priest said.

"Yes, Your Holiness." She'd sorted that much out but didn't say so.

"What you say here will not be recorded, so feel—"

"Please, Holy One." She took a step forward. "I would prefer everything to be written down."

"This isn't a trial," he said with a thread of irritation.

"Nevertheless, I would prefer all questions and answers to be recorded officially."

The Arch Priest glanced at the man on his left, who nodded. "Very well. Be seated."

She sat.

"Let us begin with the basics. State your full name, birthplace, and where you were baptized for the record."

"I am called Jenai d'Arc of Domrem. There I was born and there I dwelt until I came away to fulfill Afallon's work. I was baptized in the church at Domrem by Father Priarre, the priest living there."

The scratch of a quill caught Jenai's notice. She eyed the priest seated at the edge of the semi-circle, parchment set on a small table at his side. Turning back to the Arch Priest, she waited for the next question.

"Tell us of your journey to Shinon."

She spoke briefly of Valcinay, then of the road, the marauders they'd fended off, and her companions. "Two remain here in Shinon, awaiting my fate as I do."

"Why do you dress like a man?" the High Priest asked.

The question unbalanced Jenai. She'd expected a different track. Shaking that off, she rested a hand on her sleeve. "It was to keep safe on the road to Shinon. It will also protect me in battle. Long hair and dresses are not practical for combat."

"You assume much," said a priest along the right side of the semi-circle. "Why would we send a maiden to fight a man's war?"

"Because man hasn't ended it on his own," she answered gently.

A few priests exchanged looks while others shifted in their chairs.

"You have a ready tongue," the man to the left of the Arch Priest said. "Tell us, Maid Jenai, how do you know you're on Blessed Afallon's errand?"

She hesitated, but the Voice had told her to speak openly. "A Voice comes to me with His will."

"Blasphemy!" shouted a man on the opposite end of the scribe.

"Do not pronounce judgment so hastily, Priest Varide," snapped the Arch Priest. "Let us hear the child out." He turned a stern look on her. "Your claim is a heavy one. To *feel* compelled to serve our Lord is one thing. To hear or see Him is quite another."

"I do not profess to see or hear Sweet Afallon. I am led by a Voice speaking on His behalf—that is what I claim."

"How does this Voice speak to you?" asked a younger priest.

"Words flow into my head and pierce my heart." She pressed a fist to her chest. "They feel warm and sweet."

"How long have you heard this voice?" asked another priest.

Jenai paused, grief rolling through her like a flood. "Since the day four years ago when Thargundians invaded Domrem and killed my little sister. That day I didn't heed the Voice, and Cetta was slain due to my disobedience."

"The voice warned you of her death?"

"Yes." Jenai lowered her head. "As the enemy was driven back, I knelt beside my sister's corpse and prayed for liberty from the Thargundian monsters. The Voice assured me it would be so, and that I would help bring victory to Fraelin." She looked into the faces before her. Some were sympathetic, others looked affronted.

"This *voice* guaranteed victory?" one priest scoffed.

"Can Afallon not wield a sword as well as wisdom?" Jenai asked. "'He does not abide the suffering of the faithful for long.'" The familiar words were from scripture, and saying them warmed Jenai, chasing off the nibbling shadows of fear.

There was a long silence. Then a chair squeaked under shifting weight. The man to the Arch Priest's left leaned forward, setting an elbow on his thigh to perch against it. "Tell me, Maid Jenai. You said you wore men's clothes to protect yourself from dangers en route to Shinon. Was it also to protect yourself from your companions?"

Jenai's mind flicked back to young Limmar. "It was not in my mind to do so, but it may have protected me from one, yes."

"*May* have?"

"Do I know the thoughts of a man?" Jenai countered.

"Are you a virgin, Jenai?" the priest asked.

"Yes," she said. "I've never known a man in that way."

"Are you betrothed?"

"I have given none my troth."

"Are you in love?"

"No, save with sweet Afallon. But that love isn't carnal in nature." She met the Arch Priest's eyes. "Is this relevant to my mission, Your Holiness?"

"Yes, Daughter," he said. "We must determine if you're pure. If you be so, then you speak the truth and have been sent by a higher power. If not, then you're deceived and must be cleansed by faith or by fire."

She nodded, relaxing. "Then ask your questions. I will answer."

Ask they did, forcing her to create a detailed sketch of her life through her responses. The man on the Arch Priest's left only asked a few questions, but he leaned in often to whisper into the head priest's ear. An hour passed, then another, and Jenai felt faint with hunger. Her throat was dry, but she didn't ask for water. She needed to show these men her strength and fortitude. If they perceived weakness, they might conclude that she was unworthy to ride into battle.

The questions persisted, though now they were variations on what had already been asked. The priests spoke in circles, but Jenai gave the same answers every time: yes, she was from Domrem. Yes, she heard a Voice. Yes, it came on behalf of Afallon. No, she was not betrothed. Yes, she was a virgin. Yes, she was faithful to the church. No, she did not converse with devils.

She felt vaguely dizzy in the growing heat. A distant bell pealed across the air through a window one priest had cracked open to let in a breeze. Jenai sat up straight, clearing the cobwebs from her tired mind. Was that the noon chime?

The priests stirred, shaking off their own weariness.

"I believe that's enough for today," the Arch Priest declared. "We will resume this examination tomorrow after morning mass."

Jenai's heart sank. How could they have more questions to present? She'd already detailed her life, reliving the painful moments of her sister's death, over and over, in words that sliced like a blade. Despite that, she hadn't cried. Tears were for private moments, away from judging eyes and scornful hearts.

"Maid Jenai d'Arc, you're free to return to your quarters," the Arch Priest said. "Food will be delivered to you shortly."

She rose. "Please, Your Holiness—am I to remain in my quarters like a prisoner? Or may I visit the chapel for prayer?"

The priests exchanged looks, then the Arch Priest nodded. "We will assign you an escort. You may visit the chapel and the grounds in company with him."

The man on his left leaned in to whisper. The Arch Priest frowned, then nodded. "True. That's true." He turned his gaze on Jenai again. "Upon consideration, we will assign you a priestess rather than a guard. That might be more appropriate, considering..." He looked her up and down, the faintest hint of disdain crossing his lips. "For now, the guard will guide you to your quarters. Please remain there until the priestess arrives."

Jenai inclined her head. "I thank you, Holy Father."

He waggled his fingers dismissively, and a firm hand fell on her shoulder. Jenai looked up into the face of her guard. The man was stern and stared straight ahead, rather than look at her. She turned with him, and they left the judgment chamber.

Back in her room, Jenai awaited lunch. It arrived within a quarter hour, then she was left alone. After eating, she wandered over to the window, leaned against the sill, and studied the swelling land cradling Shinon. From here, the despairing grayness of the city was lessened under the bright sun and circling green hills. The old buildings looked charming rather than depressed.

Her mind flicked to Mercer, Bregger, and Mirrasae, and she sent up a prayer of peace on their behalf. Then she lingered on her strange encounter with the Crane Prince and his entourage. Upon setting out for Shinon, she hadn't anticipated finding an ally in the prince's cousin, but Alain Clayre felt like a good man, and the chateau's majordomo had told her he'd helped her to gain that audience.

A knock sounded on the door. She turned, straightening from the window. "Come in, please."

A woman stepped into the room, clad in the blue robes of a priestess, her hair coiffed under her veil. She smiled demurely, holding a bundle of cloth in her arms. "You're Maid Jenai?"

"I am."

"I am Priestess Kilay. I will be your companion while you reside within these walls." She stepped over to the narrow bed and laid out the bundle. "I've been ordered to give these to you."

Jenai approached the bed, eyeing the bundle of cloth.

Dresses. All light gray with white trim, the sort of outfit used by novices intending to become priestesses. Jenai brushed her finger against the coarse cloth, smiling. "Thank you. I'll dress quickly."

The priestess slipped out to allow Jenai to change, then they walked together toward the chapel on the public side of the cathedral.

"This is one of the oldest holy edifices in Fraelin," the priestess told her in matter-of-fact tones. "Once the joyful news of Afallon reached these shores, and people converted to Him, they demanded a structure for the purpose of worship. In ancient times, Afallon walked in Londolin, the Silver City in Simaerin, but we in Fraelin desired to establish a sanctuary for newfound faith in lands touched by His divine hand even after His death. One of my ancestors was a carpenter. He carved the pews within the chapel."

"A beautiful legacy of faith." Jenai ached to enter the holy space as swiftly as she could. Never had she dreamed that she would enter the great Cathedral of Shinon. Even under guard, she was glad of the chance to view the stunning motifs crafted through love and worship.

The hallways leading to the chapel were wide, made of sparkling granite, with a vaulted ceiling. Long mullioned windows to one side revealed the buttresses jutting out like graceful spider's legs. Every stone, every arch, every length of wood was crafted with precision such as she'd never seen. As they neared the chapel, Jenai's knees weakened. A heavy warmth filled the air made by the layers of faith imbued into the framework of the grand cathedral. Ancient prayers still seemed to resound off the blocks of stone.

The priestess glanced at Jenai, then slowed her step. "Are you well, Daughter?"

"Yes, Holiness," Jenai whispered. "The hallowedness of

this place is astounding. I'm..." She searched for the right word. "I'm humbled to stand where saints once walked."

The woman gave her a long, searching look, then nodded. "Just a little farther, child."

They stepped from the corridor and into a wide, grand vestibule filled with stained-glass. Their steps echoed off the walls, then they slipped through a side door that accessed the chapel. Jenai stopped in her tracks, eyes wide. An impression, much like the Voice, filled her until she thought her lungs would burst. If the faith beyond this room had been overwhelming, then what could she call this feeling?

I dwell within an ocean of holiness.

The chapel was grander than she could dream. Standing near the nave, she had a clear view of the pews set to either side of a wide aisle. At the far side stood the altar where candles brightened a statue of Blessed Afallon. Beyond that statue, an ornate stained-glass window let in dazzling colorful light. The fragrance of beeswax was fused with the mineral scent of stone and the perfume of flower bouquets which had been placed at the foot of the altar. Mullioned windows rose to the high, rib vaulted ceiling.

Trembling, Jenai moved forward. Her heart swelled in her chest. No one else was within the chapel. Encouraged by that, she strode to the altar, sank to her knees, and bowed her head in prayer.

At once, the presence of the Voice filled her. "*Speak to the Crane Prince when he comes to visit you on the morrow. There is something you must tell him privately.*"

She nodded. *What shall I say?*

"*I will tell you at that time the words that you must convey. It will be enough to release you. From thence, you must travel to the Church of St. Cethera to retrieve the sword laid aside for your use. It shall be a symbol that will rally many to your banner.*"

"As you will," she whispered, then continued to pray until the priestess told her they must leave. As Jenai slipped from the chapel through the side door, she took in the grand architecture one last time, drinking in the ambient faith.

Back in her room, she collapsed on the bed, wearier than she'd ever felt after a long day in the fields back home.

FINDING A USE

"You can't leave her to the vultures!" Alain stood before the Crane Prince's desk in the sunny study both men preferred.

Prince Chartan offered him an amused look. "I'm the crown prince. I can do what I like."

"Very well, you pedantic ogre. You *shouldn't* leave her to the vultures."

The prince sighed and set aside his quill. "Sit, Alain."

The duke obeyed, dropping into the nearest chair. "I'm sitting, Your Royal Highness."

"Good. Better. Now, do you have something against the church that I should know about?"

Alain scowled. "Nothing in particular."

"Just a general dislike then?"

The duke shrugged. He plucked at the long hem of his blouse while coils of fury tightened in his chest. "So many priests are hypocrites and liars. If there's one thing that I learned in Crowwell, it's that priests can be bought with enough coin."

"Did you buy one?" asked Chartan with a twinkle in his eye.

"Did I have any coin? I might've tried if I did. It would've been nice to have an ally in that forsaken place. They call the shores of Simaerin holy, but I can tell you that doesn't apply anywhere near Crowwell."

"Did you ever see the ancient wonder of Londolin?"

"No. Not even a glimpse. Simaerin is bigger than it looks on a map."

The prince nodded while fingering the edge of the document he'd just signed. "If you're so disenchanted with the church, why such an interest in the Maiden of Domrem? She claims to be a messenger from Afallon."

"That's different. She's purity itself, or hadn't you noticed?"

"Pure. Yes, she did seem that. But innocent souls have been deceived by devils before." He searched Alain's face. "Are you sure you don't mean she's pretty?"

Alain considered that. "I suppose she is. Somehow, I hadn't noticed. I just feel...compelled to aid her. She's important, Chartan. She matters in this war. Can't you feel it?"

"No." The prince leaned back in his chair. "I can't say I do."

"Maybe you could if you stopped listening to Dulen Thame."

"I contemplate his council, just as I do yours. That's only fair."

"Yes, but you've not had the balance of both of us for five years."

"You're back now. And though some may think you unfit to attend me, cousin, I feel otherwise."

Gripping the arms of his chair, Alain bit back a waspish

comment about where those who mistrusted him could stick themselves. An outburst wouldn't help his case. "I didn't sell out to the Crow King."

"I know." Chartan restacked his papers out of habit. "I doubt many suspect you of that."

"No? They only doubt my mental faculties then, is that it?" Alain's voice was low, almost a whisper. He couldn't keep the bitterness from his tones.

"Some do," Chartan answered, "but I've always assumed you had the same doubts about them."

Alain's scowl cracked. "Your tongue is quicker than it was five years ago."

"Time transforms us all." The prince plucked up a parchment and scanned the page, then grimaced. "I do have a lot of work to accomplish this morning, Alain. Can we finish our discussion about the maiden later."

"They're calling her the Maiden of Lorrae, not just Domrem." Alain leaned forward. "News of her is flooding the streets of Shinon. Especially after last night and her ability to pick you out of the crowd. The gossip vine is thriving in your chateau, it seems."

"Well, at least they have something to gossip about beyond my empty coffers," Chartan muttered. "If they get too bored, they'll all leave, since I have little enough to pay them with. Despise the Duke of Thame all you like, but he's all that's keeping this edifice erect."

"I dislike his *charity*."

"It's not charity," Chartan said. "It's a loan."

"With what for interest?" Alain folded his arms. "Let me guess—his daughter for your bride."

"He's said nothing of the kind."

"Words are useless next to implications."

Chartan sighed and set down the parchment to sign it. "Both have their moments. But I'll not agree to wed anyone just to purge a monetary debt. To my mind, that isn't an equal trade, whatever tradition says."

"We must take Lorion." Alain set his fist on the desk. "Cousin, look at me."

Chartan hefted his eyes like they weighed forty tons.

"We must take Lorion, and Maid Jenai is the one to lead us."

"You can't seriously think—"

"Speak with her. Don't let the church alone decide her fate. People are flocking to Shinon. News of Jenai's actions—feeding refugees after warning of the attack at Water-by-the-Rift, then coming here, across dangerous fields unscathed, and then identifying you last night—it's an irresistible force. Don't you see that she's a rallying point?"

"And if she's a witch like Thame and his faction are declaring? If the church finds her unholy?"

"Then I'll eat my boot. Did you not look into her eyes and see purity? Whether sent by Afallon or her own delusions, she's no witch. She believes wholeheartedly that she can help Fraelin. Why not let her?"

"She could die on the field." Chartan shoved his quill into the ink pot. "She could be killed. What kind of woman fights?"

"Likely the same type as a man who fights. Not everyone is equipped for it, but some need to be. Just speak with her. Go to the cathedral, interview her for yourself, and show the church that you're interested."

"What if I'm not?"

"Aren't you?"

Chartan rubbed his temple. "Yes, I confess that I am. But I'm also cautious—a trait you seem to have abandoned."

"That's not true. I just don't waste my caution on things that don't deserve it. You do agree that, as things presently stand, Fraelin—as she's always been—is on the brink of collapse. Yes?"

"Yes," Chartan sighed.

"And something must be done to stir up the people to fight or we lose everything. Yes?"

"...Yes."

"Then why not this girl?"

"You propose I use her?"

"I propose you investigate her for yourself. Don't pretend you trust the church to be all holiness and light. There are good priests, yes, and there are sellouts. Liars. Politicians. Do you trust the Arch Priest implicitly?"

Chartan said nothing, his grimace returning.

"I thought not." Alain stood. "Think about it, Your Royal Highness. Consider whether you should trust the church's verdict, or whether you should give a little nudge to remind them that they're not the only power in Shinon. Examine the girl. See what she's really about. And then see if the church aligns with your feelings or balks against them. It will be telling, no?"

Chartan's sigh was heavier this time. "I will *consider* your words, Alain. Now, leave me. I have a mountain of paperwork, with petitioners beating down the door in the next room. I feel like a wounded rabbit with carrion birds winging overhead, awaiting my final breaths."

"Let me handle some of them." Alain glanced between the door and the Crane Prince. "If Figg can sort out those who don't need your direct involvement, maybe we can ease your burden. May I try? It's something to do."

Chartan pursed his lips, then nodded. "If it makes you happy, then very well. But don't tax yourself. You're still weak."

Alain snorted. "A weak man only gets stronger by moving.

High time I begin." He bowed, then slipped out of the room and started down the corridor. Figg was outside the petitioner's hall, conversing with a servant in the blue and gold of the Royal House. Upon seeing Alain, Figg motioned the servant away, then let his professional façade fall in favor of a genuine smile.

"How may I help you, Your Grace?"

"Do you keep a record of what the petitioners are seeking?"

"It's not comprehensive," Figg said, "but I do so when the petitioners are willing to open up. I try not to fill the hall with those we can't aid at all. Just yesterday a man came here seeking the prince's personal guard to avenge himself against a Simaeri man who eloped with the petitioner's daughter. They traveled to Thargundy. We can do nothing about that."

"Not yet, perhaps," Alain murmured. "I've offered to hear the petitions of those who don't need to see the Crane Prince directly. I think we can handle most of them and leave only the most pressing for him."

Figg's eyes lit up, but he rubbed his chin. "Are you up for such a task so soon?"

"Anything's better than sitting around waiting for the world to end." Alain shrugged. "I'll start with a handful, see how I feel, and plan from there. If you can organize them by need and prioritize by how long they've been waiting, we can begin as soon as I have a room in which to see them."

Figg glanced down the corridor. "What about a parlor setting?"

"That's fine."

Figg motioned for Alain to follow, and the two men strode down the corridor, away from the main vestibule. Figg opened a door into a cheerful chamber furnished with silver-threaded brocade settees and a small table for tea. The tall, muntined windows let in an abundance of sunlight and boasted a garden view. Silver drapes, accented with deep blue, framed the windows.

Alain stepped into the parlor, drinking in the sight with a smile. His boots sank into the fur rug. "Yes, this will do well."

"Very good. I'll assign guards for your safety and then send in your first petitioner." Figg bowed, then straightened. There was a proud glint in his eyes. He hurried off, leaving Alain alone in the parlor. Alain wandered over to the closest window, unlatched it, and swung it open, letting in a flood of floral fragrances and the rich green of summer. He dragged in a breath, centering his thoughts. The idea of listening to the problems of others wasn't appealing. He knew he'd hear unspeakable heartbreaks, and many he'd have to turn away, unable to assist them without proper funds—but he had to do *something*. To feel alive again. To have a sense of purpose.

If Afallon can make use of a snip of a girl, maybe he can make use of a broken man, too.

Alain turned from the garden view and picked an armchair for himself, leaving the straight-backed settee for guests. Soon two guards in glistening armor arrived, and Alain instructed them to station themselves to either side of the door on the interior. Shortly after that, Figg returned with an old woman in tow.

"Please be seated," Figg told her, then he moved to Alain's side and handed him a sheaf of papers. "Your petitioners for today."

Alain perused the first page. In Figg's neat penmanship, the old woman's name, age, home province, and reason for coming were succinctly listed. He nodded to Figg who bowed then retreated from the room, shutting the door softly.

"You are Widow Evella?" he asked, looking up.

The old woman, gowned in worn black clothing that had once been costly, nodded and pulled her shawl tight around her shoulders. "I am she."

"How long have you been waiting to speak with the Crane Prince?"

"Three weeks."

He fought down a grimace. "And what is your petition?"

"My grandson—Tristel—he was conscripted into the army three weeks ago. But he's the only kin I have in the world. If he marches to fight the Thargundians, I—" She cut off, digging a handkerchief from her pocket. "I...I'm so very sorry."

"Don't be." Alain shifted, uncertain how to comfort her. "You wish to ask the Crane Prince to free your grandson from conscription?"

Dabbing at her eyes, she nodded. "He's all I have left."

Alain glanced at Figg's notes about her petition: *Grandson is in the Crane Army. She is widowed and alone.* Alain's chest panged. He knew loneliness. He understood the fear—the paralyzing terror—but he was still young, spry, and recently freed from the dungeons where loneliness haunted the very stones. He still had kin, still had friends. This frail old woman had only her grandson.

"I can't guarantee that he'll be sent home," Alain said, "but I'll do what I can to protect him from battle. What's his name and age, and where was he conscripted?"

The old woman rattled off the information between sobs, then thanked him profusely for hearing her request as he led her to the door. "Afallon bless you," she said in parting.

"Better that He focuses on you, Evella." Alain slipped back into the parlor and took his seat, then glanced at the next sheaf of paper. A request for food to be sent to the town of Boyan following a bad mudslide.

He winced. *Where do I get food from?*

No wonder his cousin only saw so many in a day. The requests were endless, all were necessary, but what could they do to aid anyone? Everyone was starving. Everyone was desperate. All were suffering from the endless siege from the north.

Alain saw four petitioners, promising them he'd do what he could, committing to nothing, before he told Figg no more. When the majordomo sent away the guards, Alain slumped back in his armchair. He heard the pad of Figg's approaching feet, then cracked one eye open to find the man seating himself on the settee.

"If we don't take back the north, Figg, we'll lose this war within five years."

Figg nodded. "That seems a reasonable assessment, alas."

"*Alas* is right." Alain rested his forearm over his eyes. "It's worse than I thought."

"Afallon has not forsaken us." Figg's voice was gentle.

Alain snorted. "Doesn't look that way from here."

"You've lost your faith."

"I never had much to begin with."

The sound of Figg shifting on the settee whispered against Alain's ears. The majordomo was silent for a moment, then said, "Yet you support the Maiden of Lorrae?"

Alain lowered his arm. "Whether she's sent by Afallon, by the Weave, or by some other supernatural force—or even by her own delusions—will it do us any harm to follow her? If she can rally a proper army for Fraelin and give us one last chance to take back our lands and fend off the Crow, what does it matter what I believe? The people will decide whether faith is a sharp enough sword to fight tyranny."

"Faith has ever been that," Figg mused.

Alain grimaced. "It's also been used as a weapon *for* tyranny. I fully intend to support this young woman and stay close to her. I'll do everything I can to help her defeat the Thargundians. But if ever she uses her faith to overthrow my cousin, she'll find a knife in her back—whether or not Afallon guided her steps."

The head servant stood and moved to a small table where a water pitcher and several glasses had been placed earlier. "That's a dangerous oath, but one I would aid you in carrying out." He poured water into two glasses, then brought them over, offering one to Alain. "Let's pray we always find the right side to stand on."

Alain accepted the glass, watching water bead along the outside. He grimaced. "Let's *hope* at least."

INTERCESSION

The eventide bells ended the second grueling day of Jenai's examination. She'd expected all the same questions she'd already answered over and over the day before, but this time the priests focused more on her apparel. Though she wore one of the dresses the priestess had provided, the Council of Faith had taken her male attire as a personal attack against feminine purity.

In one way or another, they'd asked the same circle of questions again and again: Why do you wear male clothes? Do you not think Afallon is offended by such indecency? Do you prefer to think of yourself as a man?

She'd answered the same way she had the day before: It was a protection. It was easier to wear boy's clothing on horseback. It was purely practical. She didn't care whether she wore a dress or pants and tunic—she only cared that the clothing was clean and suited her purpose.

When the examination ended, she was excused and escorted to her room by the priestess. Neither woman spoke en route, and Jenai was left alone with a tray of food already set on her bed. She ate with fervor, ravenous after the long day of ceaseless inquiries. After cleaning her plate of every crumb, she moved to the window and unlatched it. A breeze teased her shoulder-length tresses, and she breathed in deeply, purging herself of the heaviness in her head.

"How long will this last?" she asked, uncertain whether the question was a prayer or a private musing. Setting her head against the stone window frame, she watched the clergy trailing toward their evening meal in a smaller building across the courtyard. As they walked in orderly rows, a chant rose toward the heavens. She closed her eyes and chanted with them. It was a prayer of thanksgiving, appropriate before a meal.

The last eventide bells fell still, and Jenai soaked in the quiet. The Voice had told her the Crane Prince would come today. She didn't doubt it, and her nerves stretched with every passing minute. The Voice hadn't revealed to her what she must say to him, and she had no idea how he would take the unknown words.

She found herself pacing, wringing her hands. How long until she could convince those with authority to let her fight? How long until—

The clatter of hooves outside sent her flying back to the window. She hoisted herself halfway out and leaned as far as she dared to see the courtyard. Three horsemen arrived, and several robed figures rushed to meet them. From here, Jenai couldn't see the heraldry on the horses, but only one man was in armor. Could it be...?

One of them must be him. Jenai sent up a prayer of gratitude, then returned to pacing, waiting with straining ears for any sound outside her door. Time dragged by, but she tried to keep her composure.

There. Was that a scuff against the corridor flagstones?

Yes, those were steps, coming closer. She found the center of the room, shook her dress skirt straight, folded her hands, and waited with scarcely a breath.

The steps came closer—at least four sets. Armor clattered. Voices rose and fell.

They stopped outside her door and her heart soared.

A knock sounded. "Jenai, you have a visitor." The priestess sounded bewildered.

"Be welcome," Jenai said in a clear, strong voice that belied her nerves.

The door swung aside, revealing the Crane Prince. Beside him was the priestess, and at his back stood the Duke of Clayre and a knight whose breastplate was embossed with a crane.

The crown prince of Fraelin took in the room with a sweeping glance, then stepped inside.

"I've been waiting for you, Your Royal Highness," Jenai said calmly, though her heart raced.

Prince Chartan arched his brows. "Have you? And did Afallon tell you I was coming?"

"He did, last night."

Wandering deeper into the room, the prince eyed the empty tray on the bed, then searched the room again. "Did He know that I would come even before I did? Are we bound to Fate, then?"

"He moves what must be moved, but He doesn't take away our choices," Jenai answered. "Afallon simply knows us better than we know ourselves."

The prince cast a glance over his shoulder, eyeing the duke. A strange smile crossed his lips, then fled. He turned back to Jenai. "I wish to examine you for myself."

She nodded. "May we speak privately?"

Eyebrows flew up all around. The knight stepped forward. "Your Highness—"

The Crane Prince batted him back. "Stand outside the door."

"What if she's a witch?" the knight asked.

The crown prince glanced at the priestess. "Is that possible?"

"Highly unlikely, Your Royal Highness," Kilay answered. "Jenai entered the chapel yesterday and prayed for a long time. Afallon above doesn't tolerate witches in His holy abodes."

Alain Clayre muttered something at the doorway, but no one asked him to speak louder. Jenai, her nerves stretched to their limits, looked between the priestess and prince. The memory of the earlier bells still rang in her ears.

The Crane Prince nodded to himself, then eyed the knight. "Remain outside. I will speak with this maiden alone. After five minutes, knock on the door. If I don't answer, come in immediately."

"Yes, Your Highness." The knight tossed Jenai a glare, then retreated into the corridor. The priestess swung the door shut, leaving the Crane Prince alone with Jenai. She tipped her head up to meet his eyes. He studied her as if she was a rare bird—one he'd never seen before.

"What do you wish to say, Jenai d'Arc?"

She bowed her head. "It's difficult to believe what we don't witness for ourselves. I can't reveal to you all that has been divulged to me, but I have been instructed by the Voice that guides me to tell you something."

Caution lit in his gaze, but he nodded. "Go on."

"It's a secret you've told no one. One you harbor close to your heart."

His brows flew up. "You think a prince is entitled to secrets? How naïve you are."

"I couldn't say, but the Voice of heaven knows."

"Speak, then," Prince Chartan said, "and let us view the power of heaven."

The words that poured forth weren't Jenai's. Power infused her voice, and the prince's eyes widened with each syllable. When Jenai went silent, he fell to his knees, staring up at her with wonder.

"You truly are sent by Afallon. Blessed be this day." He shook himself, then sprang to his feet and clasped her hands. "I will speak with the Arch Priest. You wish to have an army at your back? I'll get you one. You wish to besiege Lorion? I will give you every tool at my disposal." His eyes lingered for a long moment, awe mingling with fear. "I'm...not a righteous man, Jenai of Domrem. Why would the Voice of Afallon aid me?"

"Sweet Afallon above is accustomed to working with imperfect people, my prince. He provides opportunities for us to become better. We must simply seize them."

He tightened his hold on her hands, opening his mouth. A knock sounded on the door. "Just a moment," the prince called. He held Jenai's gaze. "Was there anything else you needed to discuss with me?"

"Not at this time, sweet prince."

He nodded, releasing her hands. "Then I must go immediately to speak with the Arch Priest. I'll see you taken from this place and given proper housing soon. My oath on that."

"Thank you, Your Royal Highness."

He strode to the door, wrenched it open, and came face to face with the knight. "We must speak with the Arch Priest posthaste. Follow me." He hurried off, and the startled knight followed right on his heels. The Duke of Clayre glanced into the room, a crooked smile on his lips. He inclined his head to Jenai, then hurried after his cousin. The priestess considered

Jenai, then shut the door, closing the young woman off from the world.

She sank to her knees, pouring out her thanks to Afallon. Soon, she would ride into battle and spark fear in the hearts of Fraelin's enemies. Soon.

A GRAIN OF HOPE

"What did she say to you?" Alain asked as he rode beside his cousin toward Chateau Darr. The knight rode at their back, keeping his distance to respect their private conversation. A crossbow rested on the knight's saddle horn.

"Something I'll share with no one," Prince Chartan replied after a long moment. "Suffice it to say that she couldn't have known what she told me. She couldn't have guessed. Afallon alone could divulge such a secret—and that convinces me she's sent by Him."

"You certainly surprised the Arch Priest." Alain smiled at the memory of the prince bursting in on the clergy's meal and announcing that the examinations must finish the following day, and Chartan expected a favorable answer for "his maiden." The Arch Priest and his closest advisors attempted to drag the prince into a private argument in the adjacent chamber, but Chartan wouldn't have it.

"I know for myself that she's chosen by Afallon and the Weave," he'd declared. "I've seen the signs, and I fully intend to send Jenai d'Arc into battle. Be quick about your work—no more dawdling. You should've reached a verdict by now. She has my sanction already. Have you all gone daft and blind?"

After that came the scraping reassurances that the rest was just a formality, and naturally, they recognized the same piety their prince did. She would be set free by noon the next day.

Alain grinned. He'd seen his cousin take life by the reins before, but since returning to Fraelin, Alain had begun to doubt that Chartan had kept his backbone. Apparently, these days it took more motivation for the heir apparent to sit upright and take notice. He'd learned the dance of politics and bureaucracy too well.

"Alain, will you see that the maiden gets apartments near the chateau? As a bachelor prince, I can't very well have her stay on the grounds. She'll also need a handmaiden and..."

"A page?" Alain suggested. "If she's to be your general, she should be properly equipped. She'll need armor and a sword. A banner, too, I should think."

"Yes, yes. See to it."

"As to money..."

"We'll commandeer the accoutrements we need if necessary." Chartan craned his head to catch Alain's eye. "I haven't felt so alive in years. We have a real chance, Alain. If Afallon has truly sent her..."

"You still doubt?"

"No. No, I don't. He must have. By the *Weave*, we can win, Alain! We can take back Fraelin. I'll be crowned at Reems. My mother's curse will finally be lifted from my shoulders." His shoulders straightened, and his eyes shone with fervor.

Alain's grin deepened, seeing his cousin restored to proper hope. "Yes, my prince. It seems things are finally turning in our favor. Even the people feel it."

"I should send out a decree." Chartan nodded to himself. "Let's see how many people answer the call to join *her* for the cause of heaven. If it's anything like the reports from Valcinay... Yes, this changes everything." He urged his horse faster, and Alain nudged his new gelding—a gift from his royal cousin—into a canter to keep up.

AT CHATEAU DARR, ALAIN LEFT CHARTAN TO PEN THE decree. He made his way out into the garden that he'd seen from the window of the parlor he'd taken over. Pebbles crunched under his boots, and a floral-scented breeze tugged at his short ponytail. Hollyhocks swayed to a private rhythm while bees darted by, humming. Alain made way for the busy insects, then carried on, letting the peace of the green world fill his senses until he had no room for his sequestered horrors.

He'd not slept the previous night. Nightmares of the dungeon, of what he'd seen in the Crow King's courtyards, and the stories other prisoners had shared with him had conjured up a nightscape to unsettle the strongest soul. Against someone as shattered as Alain, it had full rein. He'd been trapped among the dreadful images of death and madness, caught under the power of endless screams.

Another day of petitions had followed, each heartfelt story as egregious as the next, but Alain had heard as many as he could, making what promises he might to ease the load of each petitioner. Anything to keep his mind off his dreams.

Traveling to see Jenai had been a reprieve he dearly needed, especially after seeing the weight of defeat lifted from the Crane Prince. Though Chartan had spoken to the contrary, it was obvious now that he'd believed the war was already over—that he'd failed his ancestors and his people and lost the throne to usurpers from across the channel.

Will things be different now? Alain wondered.

His thoughts flitted to the tall, slender woman whose eyes shone with courage and faith. Could the Fraeli really put their lives into such delicate hands and expect to win?

He turned a bend in the garden path and found himself standing among enormous willow trees. They dipped their pendulous branches into a shallow stream burbling among the rocks. The sight was more natural than the cultivated gardens along the side of the chateau, and it moved something in his heart. Beyond the willows, the deep Redroot Forest climbed the hill, rolling over it to disappear down the other side. Evening birdsong filled the trees, and wind whispered through the boughs.

He drifted toward the stream, ducking under the weeping branches. A bench sat under the nearest willow, facing the flowing water. He took a seat there and inhaled the watery perfume. This was what he'd needed: a sanctuary away from people. Away from problems. Away from the hubbub of life and all the noise and strife.

The one perk during his time in the dungeon was moments for self-reflection. Perhaps too many of them—but he preferred that to not having enough time to think at all.

If it was only the petitioners—where he might do some good—he could handle it. But it was also the nightly banquets, the follow-up meetings where he ended up bickering with the Duke of Thame on every possible issue, and the questioning looks Alain got when people thought he wasn't paying attention.

It was all so much, and he'd only been back in Shinon a fortnight.

A branch snapped. Alain shifted on the bench to eye the forest beyond the stream. For a wild moment, he wondered if an Ilidreth would step from the wooded shadows, but so far south it was unlikely. The ancient Ilidreth had all but vanished since the fall of the Royal House of Wintervale in

Simaerin. It was said the line of Crow Kings hunted the fae remnant for sport, just as they did unicorns and dragons.

Must Simaerin destroy all the wonders of the world?

The first Crow King had also outlawed magic from his kingdom, and no doubt his descendant—the current tyrant—intended to swallow up Fraelin and snuff out magic here as well. When Alain had first set foot on Simaerin soil, he'd noticed the hollow where his wind magic ought to be. He'd not been able to tap it until he'd returned to Fraelin. The feeling of that magic swirling in his chest had finally convinced him he'd truly returned home—changed, but alive.

Leaf mold crunched. Rising, Alain squinted into the gloom. Something was coming closer, quiet and steady. Too loud for an Ilidreth scout. Wind tickled Alain's fingertips, answering his silent summons. He waited, taking shallow breaths, straining his ears for any sound that might clue him into the identity of the approaching form.

The footsteps halted. Silence fell. Even the birds were still.

Alain breathed through his nose, willing his heart to keep steady, even as adrenaline spiked.

Nothing happened.

Had he imagined the sound? Had it been a passing deer?

The fine hairs on his neck lifted. No, something was out there. He sensed eyes on him. Licking his lips, Alain lifted his hand, letting wind swirl into a ball above his palm. It created a breeze that fluttered his ponytail.

"Show yourself!" he called, dredging up the commanding voice he'd used during his military service. "I know you're there—I can hear you."

A feminine voice filled his mind like rain on a pond. *'Be at peace. I mean no ill will.'*

A woman?

He tensed, fingers throbbing for his sword while instinct

demanded he stand down. This voice was magical. With his rustiness at wind magic, he stood no chance against anything that could speak directly into his mind. He lowered his sword arm and willed his muscles to relax.

The sounds of steps resumed, and Alain blinked. They weren't *foot*steps at all. They were hoofbeats. A moment later, he saw her sapphire horn gleaming. A unicorn. She emerged from the shadows, lithe like a deer, but taller and more delicate. Her mane and tail flowed like water, and her sapphire-and-gold horn gleamed in the forest gloom. Her white coat shone like diamond dust.

'Hail, Alain, Duke of Clayre, son of two lands.'

He flinched. She *knew*. Somehow, she knew his secret. But that couldn't matter just now. She was a unicorn—a real-life unicorn—and she'd come to him of all people.

"What do you need of me, wise one?" he asked, fighting to keep his voice level. He bowed his head respectfully.

'I require your company in a matter most urgent.'

"I will do anything you ask." He knew little about magical creatures. They'd all fled into the deep woods and high mountains once the Crow Kings rose to power. Even in Fraelin, none had felt safe, especially once the Thargundians gained strength and began slaughtering anything magical for fear that the Fraeli loyal to Chartan might use the fae against them.

'Come with me.'

The unicorn turned and moved back into the trees. Alain followed at once, intrigue pushing out any doubts. If he couldn't trust a unicorn, he couldn't trust anyone at all.

STONE SCALES

The duke and the unicorn traveled in silence while the ground sloped toward the forested hills beyond Shinon. The sun was setting, casting red light on the boughs. Alain stayed a few paces behind the unicorn, studying her beauty with growing awe. She was like a precious gem whose facets flashed and sparkled at every angle—but more beautiful still, for she was a living creature: breathing, moving, shaped by a hand far superior to any jeweler.

"May I ask where we're going?" he ventured.

'*To a certain vale beyond Shinon. It is called* Annonenfa—*the Realm that Breathes.*'

He'd never heard of it, and he'd roamed Redroot Forest often as a boy. But he also knew that fae-kind had secret vales and pathways no human could find unguided. Childlike eagerness flooded his veins, and his step picked up. He'd so often daydreamed of visiting hidden Ilidreth villages and finding secret dragon lairs—but never had he expected any of those visions to come true.

Alain positioned himself beside the unicorn, careful not to

touch her. He knew most unicorns found men impure. That she stood so close to him at all was a miracle.

Maybe Afallon is out there somewhere after all. He almost laughed at himself. Now wasn't the moment to examine his faith.

"May I ask..." He hesitated. "Do you have a name, wise one?"

'*I am called Mirrasae.*'

"That's a beautiful name."

'*I have traveled here with Jenai d'Arc,*' Mirrasae said. '*I await her release from the human cathedral.*'

"That will happen tomorrow at midday." He found himself smiling. This was proof that Jenai wasn't delusional, wasn't it?

'*That is good news, Alain Clayre. I had hoped your intervention would assist. You heed the will of the Weave well.*'

He stumbled but caught himself. "The Weave guided me?" He knew about the source of magic in a vague way, enough to catch the threads and work wind magic, but even his mentor had known little about the true nature of the Weave itself. Most agreed it was no longer as strong as it had once been—that a great travesty had altered it. Many said it happened the moment Afallon was sacrificed. Others said it occurred long before that, or that magic had weakened when the first Crow King destroyed the House of Wintervale. Alain had never much cared either way, content to use magic as it was now, since he couldn't do anything to change the distant past.

'*The Weave is life. We belong to it, live in it, are part of it, just as it belongs to us. It is balance and breath.*'

"Do you believe in Afallon?" he asked.

'*Some believe that the Weave and Afallon are the same source using separate names. Others believe that the Weave was woven by Afallon to bring life to the universe. Others still believe in one, but not in the other.*'

"That isn't what I asked," he said. "What do *you* believe?"

She walked in silence for a time. *'I have believed different things at different times. For now, I will say nothing, for I do not yet know.'*

That answer rocked Alain. He'd expected a wise, ancient unicorn to have a straightforward answer—to perhaps guide his own wavering faith and point it toward a destination he could run to. But it seemed even magical creatures were subject to doubt.

"Thank you for your honesty," he said at last.

'I am not the unicorn you should ask such questions to, Alain Clayre. I am...not as I once was. Better to seek out the opinion of someone such as Aluem, prince of our kind. He would know better, for he has lived longer and seen more.'

"Would such a meeting be possible?" Alain asked.

'Not at present. Aluem is afar off, dwelling in the True Realm of Ilid. He seeks...something...'

"It's just as well," Alain said. "I'm hardly anyone, much like you imply about yourself. We're both broken, it seems."

'Cracked, perhaps,' Mirrasae said. *'But such things can be mended.'*

They said nothing more until they crested the hill, and Alain stared down into the trees. Most were in leaf, but a few ash trees still hadn't unfurled their leaves. He saw no sign of any valleys, but that wasn't surprising. He could see nothing beyond the denseness of the trees before him.

'This way,' Mirrasae said, changing her course to the southeast. He kept up, watching his step more carefully in the wild terrain. Fallen tree limbs and jutting roots were everywhere, some hidden under last autumn's decaying leaves.

Neither spoke while they traveled downhill. Alain found his thoughts returning to Jenai. If any corner of his mind had doubted her purity before, he certainly didn't now, knowing a unicorn had come with her from Valcinay. Mirrasae's movements were as fluid as water; she glided down the hillside, letting no tangled foliage or fallen tree slow her progress. He sprang over the obstacles with less grace, but he was relieved to find his body stronger after a decent diet.

At the bottom of the hill, a stream gurgled by, running north to south. Mirrasae followed it downstream while Alain did his best to keep up. He began flagging after an hour, his strength spent, his stomach hollow. But he didn't complain. He fell further behind, but Mirrasae never disappeared from sight among the trees, even as they grew denser. The netting of branches overhead tightened, shielding against the dipping sun's red-gold rays. Long shadows swallowed the earth. Though summer brought longer days, here night fell early.

Wordless whispers filled the ancient trees. Alain had the sense that he was being watched, but not by anything he'd call human. Did Ilidreth roam these woods unbeknownst to the Fraeli? Did their arrows track his steps, taut strings ready to release?

The unicorn halted, then turned her sapphire eyes on Alain. '*Art thou ready to enter a Vale?*'

"I...hope so," he whispered.

She started forward again. Her coat shone in the darkness, the only light visible in the forest. He followed it like she was all the hope left in the world. Shaking himself, Alain tried to dispel the despair cradling his heart. She slipped between two trees. Reaching the same trees, he squeezed between them, wondering how the unicorn had managed it—but then his mind froze.

A clearing spread before him, vibrant under a silver moon and diamond stars. The trees circling the space were adorned by silver-and-gold leaves while the pale trunks shone with a soft blue light. In the center of the clearing stood an enormous statue of a dragon, its appearance strangely lifelike for a stone construction.

Mirrasae trotted toward the statue, and Alain followed

belatedly, fixing his eyes on the dragon's face. The statue turned its head to stare back. Alain jerked backward, stumbled, and fell onto his posterior. His senses flared to life. Instinct demanded he unsheathe his sword. He reached for his hilt.

'*Do not draw steel in this Vale, human,*' Mirrasae said. '*It would be most unwise.*'

He froze again, fingers brushing the hilt. Every muscle trembled. The dragon was still watching him.

'*This is Yenntevar,*' Mirrasae said. '*He is a stone dragon, one of the last of his kind. He requested the opportunity to meet with you, Duke of Clayre.*'

"Me?" Alain winced at the high pitch of his voice. Swallowing, he tried again. "Why me?" He climbed to his feet, ignoring the urge to flee. Instead, he squared his shoulders and looked directly into the dragon's face.

Considering Yenntevar was a real dragon—not a depiction—he realized the beast was rather small. Most dragons were taller than trees and wider than houses. Some were rumored to be as large as mountains. Sea dragons could destroy an entire fleet of ships with one wing. But this one stood perhaps twenty feet high. His scales weren't the gleaming jewel-like surface rippling with light that Alain had observed when a rare dragon raced across the sky in his youth. Instead, these scales were a flat, deep gray, blending well with the shadows. Yenntevar's eyes were the only contrasting color on his body; they were a stunning yellow, blazing like flame, surrounding fierce slitted pupils.

A voice like tumbling rocks and soft quakes filled Alain's mind. '*You may call me Yenn, Duke of Fraelin.*'

Alain swallowed again, trying to force down his mounting fear. "And you may call me Alain." Good, his voice had held up that time, only trembling a little. "What do you need to—to speak with me about, majestic one?"

'The Weave has summoned me from the depths. Magic is stirring. It calls for aid. Are you the one who has elected to assist the Lily Maid?'

Alain frowned. "I know of no maid with that title. Do you mean the Maiden of Lorrae?" The official flower of Fraelin was the ember lily, but he didn't intend to make assumptions about Jenai's titles.

'If she is the one called by Weave and Wave to purge the taint of Simaerin from these shores, then yes.' The dragon's rumble grew louder in Alain's mind. *'I desire to aid you in this war.'*

Alain fell still, trying to decide if he was really awake. Had a *dragon* just offered to help him fight the Thargundians and Simaeri invaders? He shifted his stance, buying himself a few precious seconds, trying to make sense of this.

He inhaled. "You wish to help...how exactly?"

The dragon lowered his long neck, silver horns flashing in the moonlight, eyes pinned on Alain. *'The Lily Maid will be a symbol of peace and faith. She elects to ride a unicorn—and not a battle unicorn—to face her adversary. She has chosen to be a shield. But a shield needs a sword. Do you intend to become that sword?'*

Alain hadn't thought that far ahead, but it made sense to do so. He was a soldier, not a politician, and his pathetic attempts to live the latter kind of life were proving more frustrating than he'd predicted. The only thing Alain really understood was the battlefield. There, he could win arguments for a cause he understood. Who better for him to serve than the woman sent to cleanse Fraelin?

Nodding, he met Yenn's steady yellow gaze. "Yes," Alain said. "I do intend to become her sword."

'Then I will aid you, Alain Clayre. I will be your battle mount.'

Alain's jaw fell open. "But..." But what? He couldn't bloody well argue with a dragon—and why would he try? Wasn't this *ideal?* The Thargundians certainly didn't have a dragon.

They'd adopted the Crow King's law declaring that magical creatures should be hunted down and executed like vermin.

Just as soon as the Thargundians crushed us, they'd adopt the Crow's edict against magic as well. It's only a matter of time, unless we put a stop to this.

'*What say you?*' asked the stone dragon.

Alain set his shoulders, inhaled deeply, then nodded. "Anything that will bring victory to the Lily Maid, I will accept."

The dragon's mouth split to reveal a sharp grin. '*Then we have an accord.*'

BEGINNING THE WORK

At noon the next day, Alain swung down from his saddle, patted his horse's flank, then strode toward the front doors of the Holy Cathedral of Shinon. As he neared them, the doors drew back, revealing Jenai d'Arc dressed once more in boy's clothing, a satchel in one hand, and a grave smile on her soft lips. Her hair was pulled back into a tail. She looked up into Alain's eyes, and he faltered, feeling as if she could read his soul.

He slapped a fist to his sternum. "Maiden of Lorrae, I've come to bring you to your new quarters near Chateau Darr." He turned to gesture toward his horse—and toward Mirrasae, who'd ridden with him. Jenai followed his motion, and her grave smile brightened into something more alive.

"Hello, Mirrasae!" She raced to the unicorn's side. Resting a hand on Mirrasae's muzzle, she whispered something. The unicorn's ear flicked, but Alain couldn't tell if she replied.

Approaching, he said, "Your men—Bregger and Mercer, I believe? They've already been sent to your apartment. I've also taken the liberty of assigning a handmaiden and a page for your use. A second page may be necessary later, but one should be enough to begin with. This afternoon, once you've settled in, we can head for the armory to have you properly fitted up. You'll need a sword, too, which—"

Jenai held up her hand. "I will procure my own sword, Your Grace."

He arched a brow but nodded. "Very well. I'm at your disposal. His Royal Highness, Prince Chartan, has given me leave to remain at your side and handle whatever business is necessary while he assembles your army."

Jenai swung up onto Mirrasae's back with ease, though there were no stirrups or reins. She turned her dark eyes to Alain and inclined her head. "You have my thanks for your assistance, Duke of Clayre."

"Please, just Alain. My noble rank means nothing on the battlefield. If you're to become my general, you outrank me outside Chateau Darr."

"As you like. Alain."

He grinned. "Good. And what shall I call the Maiden of Lorrae?"

"Jenai will do, except at formal functions. There it would be best to answer to each other's titles. If I'm truly to be a general, please use that when needed."

He swung up onto his horse, grabbed his reins, and wheeled his gelding around. "Very well, Jenai. Shall we be underway?"

Her somber smile was back. "Indeed. Let us begin Afallon's work."

When Alain took Jenai to her new abode, she found the location acceptable, offering Alain a satisfied nod. He was glad of that.

The apartment was one of many within a building erected

for pilgrims who visited the cathedral. Alain had been forced to remove a family of refugees, but he'd found them another abode in a less reputable area. Jenai must be close to Chateau Darr. He hadn't explained the details of confiscating the apartment, and he'd ordered the neighbors to say nothing either. While he didn't pretend to know Jenai well, he could easily guess that she would have protested his actions.

He'd had to scramble this morning to accomplish what he'd intended to begin the previous evening. He'd returned far too late to the chateau and found a frantic majordomo ready to wake the house and assemble a search party. Reassuring Figg had taken time, but Alain had managed it before stumbling into bed and sleeping late. The mad dash to settle Jenai's affairs by noon had only been possible because Figg was more efficient than a legendary Royal Mage.

"If you lack anything at all," Alain said at the open doorway to Jenai's private bedchamber, "don't hesitate to ask."

She turned from the bed, her fingers running along the satin coverlet. "This is more than enough. Thank you, Your Gr—"

"It's Alain, remember?" He motioned to the page waiting at the end of the hall. "I made sure to get a lettered boy for your use. He can pen any missives."

"You knew I couldn't read and write?"

"Few commoners can." He shrugged. "A deficiency in Fraelin I'd dearly love to correct."

She blinked at that. "To what purpose?"

"To what— Well, for instance, wouldn't you like to write to your parents without having to dictate your private thoughts to a stranger?"

She shrugged. "I have nothing to hide."

He stared at her, then cleared his throat. "And your conversations with heaven. Would you not want to record those privately?"

"I don't dare record them. It would risk someone else reading what I consider sacred."

"But our scriptures were penned by men and women who spoke to the divine in secret."

She hesitated. "The clergy are learned, for they're required to pen holy writ. I'm only a farm maid, called to purge these lands of our enemies. I needn't write or read."

He had one last argument. "Wouldn't you like to read scriptures for yourself, Jenai?"

She paused for a long moment, her eyes bright with interest and perhaps a little fear. Finally, she shook her head. "The clergy read to us. That's their calling. I'll not step beyond my station."

"*That* you've already done," Alain said. "There's no going back from here, Lady General. You'll never be what you once were. You've strayed too far from that path." He brushed back his pale blond bangs, flashing an ugly scar that ran down from his temple. "We both have."

Her eyes pierced him with sharp interest. "What were you before, Alain?"

He ran his thumb along the door frame, trying to conjure words to describe his metamorphosis. At last, he shrugged. "An innocent boy. But the first time I ended another man's life, that boy vanished. It's the fate of all soldiers, I'm afraid. I've taken many lives since, and there are many faces I don't recall, but that first one..."

He grimaced, even now remembering the fear lining the young man's face just before Alain's blade stabbed between gorget and helm. Blood had spewed across the air, blinding Alain. His horse had cantered to the side while he'd wiped his visor clean. He looked down and found the enemy soldier fallen to the ground. The dead soldier's mare retreated into the haze of a misty battlefield. The corpse's helm rolled away, revealing a motionless face that stared into the sky, lips parted as though frozen in a prayer to stay alive.

Alain shuddered at the memory, recalling the hollow that opened in his stomach—one he'd wished he could fall into. Maybe in the abyss of his soul, he'd feel none of the horror, the regret, mingling with the haggard elation of still being alive.

A hand fell on his arm. Alain pried his gaze from the stone floor and found Jenai's eyes—lit with compassion—boring into his soul.

"Be at peace, Alain Clayre," she whispered. "His soul is with Afallon. He feels no pain, no fear, and no anger. Those things aren't found there."

He tensed at her words—a concept told a thousand times in his youth from pulpits by thunderous priests determined to ram truth into a wayward congregation, but never penetrating. Yet Jenai's soft voice smoothed his doubts like ruffled feathers under a gentle hand. Could Afallon be the loving God this girl followed? Did paradise await those who served heaven?

A flood of questions surged up Alain's throat, but he choked them down. Now wasn't the moment. He hadn't assisted Jenai to examine his shredded faith, but to save Fraelin from destruction. To put Prince Chartan on the throne. To shake off the shackles of Simaerin.

He smiled and stepped free of her kind grip. "I'm all right, Jenai. Thank you. Is there anything else you require?" He'd already asked that, hadn't he?

She shook her head, her hazel eyes still tinged with concern. "I'll make do quite well with what you've provided."

"Very good. Shall we head to the armory?"

She nodded. "Can you tell me where the Church of Saint Cethera is located?"

He hesitated, then moved down the corridor, letting her follow. "If it's the one I passed on the way here a fortnight ago, it's fallen into disuse. Thargundian swine destroyed the village around it. I doubt the clergy can justify relegating funds to maintain such a small structure in an abandoned province." He did a quick mental calculation. "It's less than a two-day ride from Shinon, out in the wastes."

"I must go there," Jenai said.

He turned to eye her, then stepped into the common room she would share with her retainers. Sir Mercer and Bregger waited there, their bags at their feet. Jenai smiled at them.

"I find the accommodations more than enough. Please feel free to settle in."

They saluted her, then Bregger took both bags and slipped by Jenai and Alain. Sir Mercer remained where he was.

"I heard you're going to the armory," the knight said. "May I accompany you, my lady?"

Alain caught sight of her faint wince at the unofficial title, but Jenai only nodded.

"Are you certain you don't want to find a sword for yourself today?" Alain asked.

"That won't be necessary," she said, moving toward the door. "I'll travel to the Church of Saint Cethera for that." She stepped out onto the wooden walkway which led to stairs going down to the street.

The three—Jenai, Alain, and Mercer—walked down the wooden stairs in single file. Mirrasae and the horses had been led to a nearby stable, but the armory was a brief walk. Alain took the lead across the road and down three blocks to the Royal Blacksmith's shop. It had been designated as such upon the prince's arrival in Shinon, after he'd abandoned Lorion to the Thargundians. That defeat had been devastating and pathetic by every report, though Alain had been imprisoned in Crowwell at the time.

The smells of iron, smoke, and fire billowed from behind the shop while the ring of hammers sang across the air. Alain ducked inside the front-end of the shop where armaments were on display in a smudged window. Jenai stayed close. Mercer positioned himself at the door. Alain noted that with approval. The knight seemed competent, especially for one of Lord Robarr's men. Most of what came out of Valcinay was said to be lax or inferior.

A clerk strode across the room, a leather volume in hand, a squinty look on his face. He was a lean man in his forties, with dark hair pulled back in a severe tail. "May I help you, my lord?" He squinted harder, then blinked. "Ah, Your Grace. A pleasure to see you again. This must be—" Alain had stopped by the shop on his way to retrieve Jenai, to give them forewarning, but the clerk still hitched when he saw her. The clerk tacked on a smile. "You must be Jenai d'Arc. Of course. Right this way."

She glanced at Alain who nodded his encouragement. The clerk led her into a back room where he would take her measurements for a custom suit of armor. When Alain had explained what he wanted earlier and for whom, the clerk and the blacksmith had stared at him like he'd gone mad, but he'd calmly repeated himself—twice. Brandishing Prince Chartan's declaration, which claimed Jenai as the leader of the Crane Army, helped them to make sense of Alain's demand for expensive armor made to be flashy, with special embossing. At last, they agreed.

While the clerk and Jenai were in the back room, Alain roamed the shop. Most of the armaments were kept under lock and key in a storehouse behind the smithy. Regular patrols discouraged ne'er-do-wells from breaking in and stealing from the stock of arms, but when Alain had inspected the supplies that morning, he'd been alarmed by how scant they were. How could Jenai lead an army if no one had proper weapons?

Feeling Mercer's eyes on him, Alain glanced at the knight. "I don't suppose Valcinay is better armed than Shinon?"

The knight shook his head. "Given the state of things on the border, I doubt it. But pitchforks work well in the absence of a sword."

Alain frowned. He knew what pitchforks could do. He'd seen enough combat to appreciate the morbid skill of a fierce farmer. But farm implements weren't enough against armored knights on horseback.

He began pacing again, trying not to dwell on the folly of Jenai's path. Even with her unicorn and—Alain's heart skipped a beat—*his* dragon, how could they hope to trounce the enemy? Especially with the Crow King backing the Thargundian side?

Put your faith where you can find it, he told himself. *Put it on her.*

A few minutes later, Jenai reappeared, with a rather flustered-looking clerk behind her. The man squinted at Alain.

"We'll have the armor completed as soon as possible. I assure you it's our top priority, Your Grace."

"Thank you." He looked at Jenai. "You're certain you don't want to select a sword—"

"The armor is enough. I will obtain my own sword." Her jaw was set. She wouldn't be moved.

"As you like, Lady General." He bowed his head.

"Is that all for today?" she asked.

"That's all. I imagine you're exhausted, and I could use a little rest myself. Allow me to escort you back to your abode."

She readily agreed, and they walked back up the hill, Mercer at their backs. Alain considered telling her about the dragon, but she looked lost in her thoughts. The news would keep. He was still absorbing it anyway.

Halfway up the hill, Jenai paused, listening to the mid-afternoon bells chiming from the cathedral. "Listen," she whispered, closing her eyes. "Afallon has set us on this task. The war begins now. We must be ready."

Part ii

THE CRANE MAIDEN

An army came to Shinon, answering the summons of their Crane Prince and the allure of the Maiden of Lorrae. At first, men arrived in a trickle, filling up the roads and byways like pebbles. But then a flood surged across the southern city, spilling out onto the fields where the prince's generals struggled to organize a proper war camp. Two thousand strong, then three thousand; more came every day.

Eager to begin her work, Jenai intended to head into the camp at once, but Alain persuaded her to wait.

"Let the generals get things tidy for you. You need to arrive in pomp, fully armed."

A swell of urgency filled her chest. She turned to meet his brown eyes. "Then I must go at once to the Church of Saint Cethera. Will you accompany me?"

"Surely," he said. "Anywhere you wish."

They left at dawn the next morning, with Mercer and Bregger in company. Mirrasae set the pace and the horses followed without complaint. Jenai and her handmaiden—a lively and sweet-tempered woman—had prepared food for the road. At Alain's urging, they'd all cloaked themselves in nondescript attire to avoid unwanted attention from brigands or deserters.

The going was quiet for the first few hours. Near noon the wide road narrowed as it approached a town that looked abandoned. Half its buildings had collapsed, some burned out. The odor of smoke lingered. Jenai's adrenaline spiked. This devastation was fresh. She glanced at Alain.

The duke was frowning, hand on his sheathed sword, eyes darting this way and that. His lips were pressed in a tight line. His tension was palpable.

Jenai found the dagger she'd hidden in her cloak. The cool feel of the hilt was strangely soothing. Behind her, Bregger loaded his crossbow.

"Careful," Mercer murmured. "We're being watched."

Jenai nodded. She could sense eyes on her. Examining the abandoned buildings, she tried to pick out where the onlookers were hiding. There were too many options. Some of the upper floors of the burnt-out buildings looked stable in places, and the shadows there were thick. Several houses still had their back walls. Five or six men could hide side by side behind each one. Beyond the town, the woods stood in silence, the foliage thick and absent of birdsong.

Her palm was slick against the dagger hilt.

"*It is not what it seems*," came the Voice in a gentle whisper.

Jenai tugged on the unicorn's mane. Mirrasae halted. The men on horseback followed her lead, tense, peering into every shadow to scrutinize it.

Swinging from Mirrasae's back, Jenai approached the nearest building.

"Wait, Jenai," Mercer protested.

She waved him off. "Remain here."

The pressure of the unseen stares grew stronger as she

inched around the husk of the house, but she couldn't tell if her imagination was playing tricks on her. Releasing her hold on her hidden dagger, she leaned on her faith in the Voice and moved around the building.

There she faltered, gasping. The person crouched before her wasn't human—that was obvious from the silver hair draping down the girl's shoulders in tangles, and the pointed ears protruding from the wild tresses. She looked young—perhaps twelve—but Jenai knew enough about Ilidreth to doubt her eyes. They were older than they looked, aging slowly across a lifespan of centuries.

The youthful Ilidreth stared at Jenai, fear bright in her pale gray eyes. She remained crouched, her motley clothes tattered and blood-flecked. One leg was twisted, clearly broken.

Jenai squatted before the fae girl and reached out a hand. "Don't be afraid. I will help you, not hurt you."

The Ilidreth canted her head, locks of messy hair slipping into her dirt-smudged face. She didn't speak, but the bright fear in her eyes dimmed. Alain cautiously stepped around the building, sword drawn. The Ilidreth tensed and started to crawl backward, dragging her leg with her.

"Stay back," Jenai said, glancing at the duke. "She won't hurt me." She turned back to the Ilidreth. "Alain is my protector. He means no harm to you."

The girl glanced between them, tension pouring off her taut shoulders. Her fingers dug into the dirt. Alain lifted his hands away from his sheathed sword, then backed up, giving the young women space.

Jenai pointed to the girl's leg. "The bone needs to be set. Will you—"

"*Beware!*" called the Voice.

The crack of a crossbow echoed over the air. The bolt missed Jenai's hand by a hair's breadth and smashed into the charred wall. Jenai whirled, expecting Bregger, but the projectile had come from the woods—her brain told her that belatedly.

Alain threw himself in front of her and the trembling Ilidreth. "Get down," he hissed, then raised his voice. "Reveal yourself, coward!"

Mercer and Bregger appeared around the corner, the former with bow and arrow, the latter with his crossbow. They inched closer while keeping their weapons trained on the trees. A second cracking sound sent the two soldiers diving for shelter in the rubble of the house. Another bolt smashed into wood, sending splinters flying. Jenai hunched over the Ilidreth girl, sending a prayer heavenward.

Alain swore under his breath, then lifted his head. "By Afallon's bones, reveal yourself or die! I'll offer no more chances!" His words were clear, despite being under fire. His eyes blazed, fearless, almost maniacal.

"Cowards indeed," Bregger spat.

Sheltered in the safety of the debris, Jenai glanced at the Ilidreth who peered fearfully into the woods. Jenai kept her voice low and calm. "Did these attackers injure you? Were you running from them?" She wasn't certain the Ilidreth knew the Fraeli tongue. Did the girl understand anything Jenai said?

Slowly, the girl nodded. "Hunters. Bad men."

"We'll protect you," Jenai said.

The fear was back in those gray eyes, and the girl shook her head. "Run away."

"Never." Jenai's voice was firm.

Mercer was belly-crawling toward an old stump, taking his bow with him. Alain drew close to Jenai, splitting his attention between Mercer's progress and the crouched females. "We're in a bad spot, but I've survived worse. How about you?"

Jenai caught the flash of humor in his eyes. "Nothing quite like this."

He turned toward Bregger who'd thrown himself around the corner of the house and was peeking out while loading his crossbow.

"Can I see that, soldier?" Alain asked.

Bregger grimaced, then shrugged. "Know how to use it?"

"Surely." Alain glanced at Jenai. "I'll return soon."

A third bolt slammed into a sturdy board against the wall and stayed there. A rain of splinters came down, and Jenai flinched. Alain took that moment to throw himself around the corner and disappear with Bregger.

Turning back to the Ilidreth, Jenai offered a calm smile. "I'm Jenai. What should I call you?"

"Aveyal," the girl answered, pain lacing her voice.

Wincing with sympathy, Jenai glanced at the twisted leg. A fourth bolt shattered a burned-out plank, sending shards of wood in all directions. They ducked down, covering their heads. Someone in the trees let out a curse, and the crunch of grit and snap of a twig followed.

Jenai lifted her head and glimpsed a handful of figures darting around among the shadowed trees.

"Who are they?" she whispered.

"Fraeli." The girl stared at Jenai, her distrust obvious in the narrowing of her eyes and the tightening of her lips.

"Bad Fraeli," Jenai replied. "Aren't there any bad Ilidreth?"

Aveyal frowned.

The house behind them groaned and creaked. Jenai glanced up, afraid it would crush them, but then she saw a flicker of movement. Alain. He was up on the roof. Was that why the men in the trees had scattered?

With a crack, Alain released a crossbow bolt. Mercer used that distraction to sit upright behind the stump and take aim with his bow. He let loose an arrow. A scream followed. Someone darted out from behind a tree, trying to flee. A bolt struck him in the back. He crumpled. Mercer took aim again and hit someone else. A string of curses followed.

A voice rose from the woods. "All right, we surrender! Don't shoot!"

Alain had promised no more chances, but he seemed not to remember that—or he'd been bluffing. "Get out here. Now!"

"I've got injured men here!" someone hollered. "They can't be moved!"

"Anyone who can walk, step out from the trees! Nice and slow!"

Three men stepped from the shadows, hands lifted, knife belts empty. Jenai searched for weapons, but they had none in view. They were dressed like hunters, with the sun-tanned skin and dark hair common to most Fraeli. Whether they were Thargundians or not, she couldn't tell.

"Closer!" Alain barked. They shuffled nearer. "That's enough. Keep in an orderly row, and stay right there. Mercer?"

"Got 'em." Mercer's arrow was trained on the brawniest man standing at the center.

Clay shingles slipped from the roof as Alain moved. One shattered near Aveyal, but the Ilidreth didn't even flinch. Jenai straightened up, gripping her dagger. Her palm was still sweaty, but her heart had settled into a quiet rhythm.

More shingles shattered on the side of the house, followed by the crunch of gravel. Alain stepped around the corner, sword in hand, with Bregger beside him. The older soldier held his crossbow and had it trained on the men from the woods.

Alain caught Jenai's eye, smiled reassuringly, then strode toward the strangers. His sword caught a strand of sunlight, flashing across the tall grass between the broken house and the trees. The birds took up a song, apparently sensing the violence was over.

Jenai smiled at the Ilidreth beside her. "I'll be right back to see about your leg." She stood, tugged her jerkin straight, and hurried after Alain. He glanced back, then slowed to let her catch up. Together, they drew close to the men.

"All right," Alain said. "Tell us why you attacked us."

"We weren't attacking *you*," the brawny man said. "We were after that creature." He jutted his chin in the Ilidreth's direction. "Filthy thing left the deep woods, and we didn't like that, did we, boys?"

They muttered their agreement.

Jenai bristled. "That *filthy thing* is a creature created by Afallon."

The brawny man's dark gaze settled on her. "Aye, lad, but so are cockroaches and venomous snakes." He shrugged. "I don't tolerate unnatural creatures in my woods, hunting my game, taking from my family."

The Ilidreth girl let out a dry laugh that carried to the group. "Your woods? Your game? All woods belong to the earth, not to men or Ilidreth. We are guests of the trees and should take only what we need! But you—"

"I won't be lectured by a monster!" the brawny man bellowed.

Jenai stepped between the man and Aveyal. "*Enough.*" Her voice rang with authority, and the birds in the trees fell silent. "What's your name, hunter?"

He scowled. "What—"

"Answer her," Alain said in a low, dangerous voice.

"I'm Tullo," the man growled.

Jenai's eyes narrowed. "The Crane Prince has summoned every able-bodied man to join his force-of-arms for the coming siege of Lorion. Why are you here and not in Shinon, Tullo?"

The hunter offered a shrug. "Maybe I forgot? Who follows the Crane Prince now, honestly? He's gone madder than a loon, that one. He's even got some woman leading his army. Probably a witch who's ensorcelled the foolish prince. What other kind of man would—"

"I am that woman, Tullo." Jenai stared into his widening eyes. "I am Jenai d'Arc, Lady General of the Crane Prince's Holy Army. And I'm no witch. These are my first orders to you and your fellows: You will return home, say goodbye to your families, pack your essentials, then travel to Shinon and register yourselves as soldiers fighting for Blessed Afallon. Do you understand me?"

His mouth worked, but he produced no noise.

"You heard her." Alain motioned with his sword in the direction of Shinon. "A new day dawns for Fraelin. Can you feel it?"

Tullo stared between them, then glanced at the man on his right.

"Many are following her," the man whispered.

"With many more still to come," Bregger said from the edge of the house, his crossbow still trained on the hunters. "Just you wait 'n' see. We're gonna win this time."

Tullo swung his gaze back to Jenai. "You're the Maiden of Lorrae?"

"I am," Jenai said, keeping her shoulders erect. "Will you join my cause, Tullo the Hunter? Will you leave your woods, leave your game, and hunt down Thargundian traitors in the name of Afallon? Will you help me take back our lands from the mad Crow in his faraway tower?"

"Tullo," whispered the man at his side. "A chance to repay them."

The large man wrestled against something, and his gaze settled on Jenai for a long time. She held that gaze, unwavering, waiting.

"You mean to fight them," he said at last.

"I do. They must be stopped. They've hurt and robbed us unchecked for too long." She glanced at the village. "What happened here? Was it Thargundians?"

"Aye, one week back," Tullo answered, his jaw tight. "Half the village burned up. We survivors fled into the woods." His eyes flitted to Aveyal. "We need game. Gotta feed our families, don't we?"

"The food will all run out if we don't fight back," Jenai said. "More villages will burn. The tragedies won't end. Tullo the Hunter, join me. Let us end this slow dance of death—let us stop these raids once and for all. Why waste your time hunting another victim—another creature who has been hurt by our proper enemy's vicious behavior—when you could be serving Afallon and hunting those that have robbed you of home and kin?"

"What of our families?" asked the man beside Tullo.

"Bring them to Shinon," Alain said. "Refugees are safer there."

"Tullo." Jenai stepped forward. "Afallon has called us. It's time to do your part."

"Aye," he whispered. Then he shook himself, the light of superstition sharp in his gaze. "Aye! We'll be hunters of men now, in service to the Crane Maiden!"

Jenai tensed at the title but smiled. "Thank you, Tullo. May Afallon bless you for your willingness."

He bowed his head, and so did the other men.

"Now see to your wounded," Jenai said, and turned toward the house. Her eyes fell on Aveyal, then she whirled back toward Tullo. "And see that you leave the Ilidreth alone. We and they aren't so different. Both have been beaten and starved by Crow sympathizers. If we're to be better than our enemies, let us start with kindness toward our fellow sufferers. Is this fair, Tullo?"

The hardness in his gaze dimmed. "Aye, lass. I'll be far too busy with the Thargundian swine anyway."

"Good." She inclined her head. "May Afallon attend your steps."

As she walked back to the house, she heard Tullo whisper "What is she?"

Alain answered: "A woman with a purpose."

A COMPANY OF FRIENDS

"Her leg must be set." Jenai looked up as Alain crouched beside the Ilidreth girl. "I've learned some healing craft, but not enough for something like this."

"I can do it, but I'll need splints and bandages." He considered the leg, then glanced at the trees. "I'm sure we can find what we need between the rubble and the woods."

Wordlessly, Bregger set off for the trees while Mercer began tearing off strips of his travel cloak.

Jenai smiled at the knight, then turned back to watch Alain examine Aveyal's limbs for any other breaks or open wounds. After a moment, he sat back. "Just the one leg."

"Are you a healer, Your Grace?" asked Jenai.

He snorted. "Not at all. I just know basic first aid. Any soldier worth his name should if he wants to keep his brothers alive, as well as himself."

"It's a commendable skill."

He shrugged. "Glad to have a use somewhere."

Hearing the tinge of pain and frustration in his voice, she set her hand on his arm. "I suspect you've more than one."

He opened his mouth, as though he might protest, then

shut it with the click of his teeth. He shrugged again, then felt around the twisted leg. Looking up into the Ilidreth's eyes, he said, "This will hurt a lot."

The girl nodded vigorously. "Do what you must."

Alain set his hands on her leg, and Jenai turned away. The sound of the bone moving, and Aveyal's accompanying scream, sent a shiver of sympathy up Jenai's limbs. She squeezed her eyes shut.

Boots crunched over grit. Jenai looked up to find Bregger coming toward them with a handful of long sticks. Soon the youthful Ilidreth had a tidy splint around her leg. Alain gingerly lifted the girl up and set her on Bregger's horse.

Jenai asked for Mercer's torn cloak and threw it over the girl's shoulders. "Wear the hood low over your face, Aveyal." She turned to Bregger. "Take her straight to my rooms in Shinon. Keep her safe until we return."

The older man nodded. "Certain you want me to leave you, Jenai?"

"We'll be fine. I intend to return by the morning after tomorrow."

Bregger bowed his head, then mounted the horse behind Aveyal. "Until then." He wheeled the horse around and headed for the road, crossbow cradled in one arm while he steadied the girl and clutched the reins with the other.

Jenai, Alain, and Mercer traveled on toward the church, each keeping their thoughts and weapons close. Though she tried to settle her nerves, Jenai jumped at little noises. Alain held the lead while Mercer rode in the rear.

Nudging Mirrasae, Jenai moved to Alain's side. "How much time did we lose?"

"Not too much. We'll camp in a glade I know of and rise before dawn to reach the church early. That should put us back on course. If that's acceptable to you?" He glanced at her with a raised brow.

She nodded. "I'd prefer to return to Shinon as swiftly as possible. There's a great deal to do ahead of our march to Lorion."

"You'll struggle to gain the trust of the Crane Prince's other generals. You know that, don't you?"

She nodded. "I realize that to many I'm an imposter. But I'll not let anyone keep me from Afallon's work."

Alain said nothing. Jenai studied his profile. He had a fine-boned face and a lean, erect frame, but was paler than most Fraeli, no doubt due to his long stint in an underground dungeon. Most Fraeli stayed out in the sun for long hours, making their skin bronzed and healthy. Alain's unusual pale blond hair and contrasting dark brown eyes also set him apart. Most Fraeli had both dark hair and eyes.

He glanced at her. "Did you have a question, Jenai?"

She ripped her gaze away from him and stared at the road ahead. Her mind raced for a polite answer. It settled on a question she could broach. "Is it strange to be free after so long?"

"Yes," he answered flatly.

Warmth blossomed on her cheeks. What a foolish question. "Does it...feel real?"

He sighed. "Sometimes?"

"You don't sound very certain."

"I'm not. Sometimes I'm scared to sleep because I fear I'll wake up in my tiny, filthy cell, awaiting a breakfast made from something I'd rather not guess the ingredients of. Sometimes I'll catch a whiff of something that puts me in mind of mold or stagnant water and I'm back there, waiting for the guards to come by and taunt me. Sometimes..." He shrugged. "I think that's enough of the picture."

Jenai frowned, unable to imagine five years under such conditions. She'd always had the fields and woods back home to run through. Always had the wind in her hair and clean water running somewhere close. And while she knew the taunts of immature boys and girls, she'd had a path of escape any time she chose to take it.

Searching for some response to his words, she settled on what would comfort her best. "With time, Afallon will heal your wounds."

"I'd rather he didn't."

Jenai stiffened. "Why not?"

"Because he's forsaken so many other soldiers. Why should he favor me—and belatedly? I'd rather not have the pity of an afterthought."

The bitterness laced into his voice stung Jenai as though he'd slapped her. She sought a response—something to reduce the sting and instill hope in a man whose faith had crumbled, if he'd ever had any to begin with—but her mind stumbled. What could she possibly say to cut through the pain? She was no priest. No orator.

For a long time, they rode in a silence that seemed to hush the very birds and insects. Jenai fell into a reverie, letting her thoughts drift where they would.

Nearly an hour later, Alain sighed and twisted toward her. "My apologies, Jenai. I'm not the best of company, and certainly I have no right to lay my troubles at your feet. Forgive me. I'll not speak of them again."

She shook her head. "You should be allowed to feel what you feel and speak of it, Your Grace."

He grimaced. "Maybe so, but timing is important."

"True. But I don't fault you, nor am I offended."

"I'm relieved to hear that." He offered a grin, tight at the edges. "You're a kind lass. And please, drop the title. It's just Alain out here on the road. Remember?"

She glanced at him. "Did you have a rank when you were an active soldier?"

"Several," he answered.

"Which was your highest?"

"Lieutenant-General under General Onrin Tarie."

"You intend to serve under me, do you not?"

"I do," he said.

"Then you'll be my lieutenant-general," she said firmly. "When we're with the army, that's the title I'll use for you."

He chuckled. "As you wish, Lady General."

"Not here," she said. "As we discussed, we're two people, equal on the road, equal in our purpose." She glanced at the knight riding behind her. "The same applies to you, Mercer. Out here, no knightly titles."

He inclined his head. "That suits me well enough."

"Call me Jenai," she insisted.

"Very well, Jenai."

Satisfied, she turned forward, feeling a weight lifted from her shoulders. She'd feared that, on Afallon's path, she might not stand in any company she could call friend; that she'd feel isolated from personal connections. But these two men stood beside her and treated her like one of their own, despite their shaky faith. Despite the fact she was a woman.

She found herself smiling. The road didn't feel so perilous.

A RUSTED BLADE

They camped in a glade bordered by a wide stream. The unicorn led the horses over to drink from it while Jenai and the two men rolled out their beds, started a fire, and set about warming a stew Jenai had packed for the evening meal. Without Bregger, there was more to go around, so Jenai made certain Alain got an extra share. He looked better than he had at the inn, but a gauntness still clung to him.

The meal was comfortable, though no one spoke much. Afterward, Mercer rummaged through his satchel, then extracted two small bells attached by a string and a tabor pipe. He smiled faintly. "Would you care for a little music?"

Delight pattered through Jenai's chest. She'd never heard the tabor pipe played outside of festival season. "Yes, please. I had no idea you knew an instrument."

He shrugged. "I couldn't risk any music on the road to Shinon."

Jenai tensed and glanced at Alain. "Is it safe to play it here?"

"I think so," said the duke. "We're far removed from the Thargundian sympathizers—few would live anywhere so remote—and anyone else would be daft to interrupt a concert."

Mercer flushed. "I'm not *that* good. But it's something I enjoy."

Jenai leaned forward. "Please, do play something."

Beaming, Mercer's gray eyes caught the firelight and glowed. He lifted the three-holed pipe, balancing it in one hand, with the string of bells dangling from the same little finger. He then held up a small mallet. Mercer set the pipe to his lips and began to play a jaunty tune. As he piped, he used the mallet to strike the bells in a steady rhythm, adding a tinkling sound to the folk song. Jenai admired the man's playing; his fingers flew up and down over the three holes, miraculously producing a melody she'd known all her life. When he finished the folk song, Jenai and Alain applauded.

"Do you know 'Away to the Sea'?" Alain asked.

Mercer nodded, set the tabor pipe to his lips, and played.

In a pleasant tenor voice, Alain sang:

> 'Away to the sea, away to the sea,
> We're off to distant lands,
> Where the sky meets the sea.
> To the sea. To the sea.
>
> 'Come water and wind, water and wind,
> We may never return,
> But onward we sail. The sea.
> The sea. Away on the sea.'

The lyrics went on. Jenai closed her eyes and listened, imagining the sea spray on her face, and the sound of the gulls, the way Papa had once described them to her. Alain's voice was pleasant, lulling her toward sleep. She settled down on her bedroll, letting the weariness of the day flow away with the imaginary tides. The world rocked gently, and she let herself succumb to slumber.

ALAIN SHOOK HER AWAKE BEFORE SUNRISE. THE WORLD WAS still, almost breathless. Only the bubbling stream gave any indication of life. Rising, Jenai found the horses already saddled and Mirrasae close by, waiting. Alain offered Jenai an apple, and she accepted it while he knelt and rolled up her bedding with practiced swiftness. Tying it off, he stowed it with his own upon his horse's saddle.

"We should reach the church by midmorning," he whispered.

Mercer moved around his own horse, double-checking the saddle straps. He smiled at Jenai. "Good morning." His tones were hushed as well, as though neither man wanted to break the spell of silence.

"And to you," she said.

She swung up onto Mirrasae's back and waited while the two men mounted their steeds. With a nod from Alain, Mirrasae started forward. They returned to the road and cantered on, racing the rising sun.

Several hours later, bright morning light stretched its beaming fingers across the woodlands on the east side of the road. And there, nestled among the trees, a white church stood with a steeple piercing the heavens. Around it was the remnants of thatched cottages, abandoned and put to flame at some point in the recent conflicts. The church itself remained standing, worn but unspoiled.

Jenai urged the unicorn faster. The horses did their best to keep up. Approaching the church, Jenai's skin tingled, as though she'd passed through an invisible spray of water. The air took on a hallowed feeling, much like the church grounds back home where she'd first heard the Voice. That brought her comfort. She was on the right path. Though the Voice had been the one to send her here, she'd heard nothing more until yesterday, and doubts had crept in.

Slowing, Mirrasae led the horses right to the front door of the holy edifice. The two men reined in, and Jenai felt their eyes settle on her. She bowed her head and prayed, seeking a sign of what to do next.

At once, the Voice drifted across her mind with instructions.

"Alain, Mercer, enter the church with me." She swung down from Mirrasae's back, offered the unicorn a weak smile, then turned to face the Church of Saint Cethera. Her nerves were in a knot despite the Voice's reassurances. She'd been promised a sword—something special to set her apart for her calling. But until now she hadn't known what that meant.

Striding into the church, she found the dusty chapel more spacious than it looked on the outside. It was also unscathed. The two men flanked her, and they moved together between the pews, aiming for the altar before the raised pulpit. The tingling sense of hallowed air returned, relaxing Jenai's nerves. This was her purpose. Her calling. She had a right to wield the sword waiting for her.

"Alain, go around the altar."

He hurried forward, one hand on his sword. As he halted on the far side of the ancient altar, awaiting her next instructions, he turned his eyes toward her: eyes full of trust, though they'd met so recently. Just like Mercer who stood faithfully at her side, tense and ready for an enemy strike.

Jenai held Alain's gaze, grateful for these men willing to obey a woman. "Kneel and seek a hollow place at the foot of the altar."

He stooped until she could only see the top of his blond head. The sound of thumping followed, at first solid, then the pitch changed. Alain peeked over the altar, his eyes dancing with delight, then he ducked again. "Should I force it open?"

"Yes."

He shifted, causing the floor to creak, then he waggled his boot knife in the air before bending again. Scuffing sounds followed, then the crack of wood. Alain grunted like he was prying something heavy loose. The cracking wood grew louder, then Alain fell backward into the space beyond the altar, clutching floorboards in his hands. His knife clattered at his side. He grimaced, rubbing his knuckles, then sat upright.

"It's a compartment," he said.

Jenai nodded. "Draw out the sword from its resting place."

Alain glanced at her, then bent over again. He inhaled a sharp breath, then stooped out of sight. Seconds later, he straightened, and rose to his feet clutching a sword in both hands. It was a broadsword, ancient and dusty from its golden hilt and crossguard to its dull steel blade. Rust riddled the blade, giving it a brittle appearance. Jenai strode forward, noting the familiar design even through the wear of time.

Alain stared at the sword as the other two approached. Mercer gasped and wheeled toward Jenai, halting where he was. She ignored him, her eyes locked on the hilt. This famous sword had belonged to the hero Varyon, first king of House Crane, Prince Chartan's ancestor.

Alain adjusted his grip on the sword, then pried his eyes from the sight to meet Jenai's gaze. "Lost its integrity, I'm afraid."

"Not so." She drew nearer, heeding the Voice's instruction. Taking the sword in both hands, she was glad of its balance. Not too heavy. She clutched it close, and the rust fell away like dirt. The blade gleamed. Both men froze.

Mercer fell to his knees, whispering a prayer to Afallon. He raised his head after a moment. "Lady Jenai, I vow to serve you for the rest of my days."

Trembling, Jenai managed to smile. "Don't make that vow to me, but to One far greater."

"I will serve Him through you."

Passing the sword to a startled Alain, Jenai rested her gloved hand on Mercer's shoulder. "Then vow to serve me only until this war is won or my life is forfeit." She released him, turning back to Alain.

"I, too, will serve you in the march to Lorion." The duke's voice was soft, almost gentle. "Whether you're called of Afallon or Thiavos, you've got the power to save us."

She inclined her head, then took the sword back. At the center of the crossguard was an intricate depiction of an ember lily. Fingering the royal flower, Jenai offered up a silent prayer of her own, then looked up. "Gentlemen, let's return to Shinon. We have much to do."

Mercer jumped to his feet. Both men threw their fists over their hearts. Silently, they followed Jenai from the Church of Saint Cethera.

THE LADY GENERAL

Prince Chartan and his cabinet had stayed busy in Jenai's absence. What had started out as chaos and confusion among the new recruits on the fields outside Shinon had become a well-ordered camp. Tents spread out in rows and corrals had been erected for horses. Armories were half-built, and the smoke of campfires and mobile smithies stained the cloudy sky as Jenai surveyed her army from atop a hill.

She and her two companions had ridden through the night, determined to return to their duties with all haste. Now the light of dawn cracked and spilled over the fields, painting everything in gold and pink.

"Do you think Bregger made it back safely?" she asked.

"That scallywag? Definitely," Mercer answered.

She nodded. "Let's return to my apartment. I need to change and see that Aveyal is well. Then we should head at once for the central camp. I wish to inspect my generals." She caught Alain and Mercer exchanging a glance. "What is it?"

"I'm certain they're eager to inspect you, too," said Alain, flashing a crooked grin, "and *I'm* looking forward to watching." He clicked his tongue to guide his horse around.

Jenai joined him, and Mercer took the rear, more protective now that they were back among civilization.

Studying Alain's back, Jenai reflected on his captivity again. He was a good man, and charming at times. She'd met no boys like him back home. They were all...simpler. But then, they'd known little beyond farming and faith. Even the few Thargundian raids had done little to turn the villagers' eyes from the soil.

That will change now. More men will set aside the plough and pick up the sword. They will answer the call of Fraelin.

Her thoughts flitted to her three brothers. Would they join the fight? Would Papa let them? Conflict rose inside her, lodging in her throat. Did she want to see her brothers among the soldiers gathered outside Shinon? Was it better if they remained home, helping to grow and harvest food for the war? She didn't know.

Riding through the empty streets of Shinon, Jenai let her personal life drift away in favor of what lay right before her. She imagined most civilians were preparing for the day—especially with the influx of men to feed, clothe, and shelter. Markets would be booming, but Jenai doubted many of the new recruits could pay for anything, and Chartan's coffers were notoriously empty.

"How will we care for the army's needs?" she asked, hoping Alain or Mercer knew the answer.

"Likely, Chartan will borrow more money from the Duke of Thame." Bitterness edged Alain's words.

She cast him a glance. "Is that problematic?"

"Very. He's among those who view you as a witch, for one thing."

"How man views me is not my concern," she said. "Only how Afallon views me matters."

"With all due respect, Jenai, that's bloody nonsense. You must lead Fraelin's army to victory. That means you need the admiration and trust of people in power. Which includes His Grace, the Duke of Thame."

"I can't possibly hope to win over every dissenter."

"No, of course not, but you must *try*. If you don't, dissension will grow. I'm sorry to say this, but your position doesn't require just a sword and an army. You need supporters. You need politicians backing you. You must play the game."

She shook her head, her stomach squirming. "I won't."

"Don't be naïve—" He cut off, sighing. "I don't mean to question you, but—"

"Please don't." She spoke gently. "What I do, I do by Afallon's sanction. He will guide and guard me. That I live is due to Him. If I die, it's by His will. I realize that you mean only to protect me, but it's best to put our faith where true power lies."

Alain was quiet. The clatter of hooves filled the space between them. At last, he shifted. His leather saddle creaked. "Jenai, do you think it's mere coincidence that I was released from the Crow King's dungeons and returned to Fraelin just as you set out for Shinon? Or do you think that Afallon had a hand in it?"

She considered his words. "I believe it was divine influence that led to it."

"To what purpose?"

She glanced at him, meeting his bright gaze. "To help me."

"Then *let* me *help* you. If Afallon willed our paths to cross, I doubt it was so I could bear your banner into battle. If Afallon uses mortals to meet His ends, then perhaps He sent me to guide you at court. Please let me. I won't press if you tell me not to, but I will suggest actions that I feel are important to take. I'll introduce you at court and help you make allies. Didn't Afallon Himself walk among men during His mortal sojourn, tending to the poor and stirring up the rich and mighty?"

"I'm not Afallon." Jenai smiled faintly. "But you're right, Alain. There's sense in your words. I hadn't considered what Afallon's design for you is, but it appears plain now. I'll let you guide me in such matters. Perhaps for a moment I let my pride stand between us, and for that I apologize."

"Thank you for listening, Jenai. Your trust won't go amiss."

AT HER APARTMENT, JENAI FOUND THE ILIDRETH GIRL comfortably tucked into her bed while Jenai's handmaiden fussed over her.

"Where's Bregger?" Jenai asked.

"Gone to escort the healer back to his abode and make certain he's said nothing of this wee darling, my lady." The handmaiden smoothed the sleeping girl's hair from her face. "She's frightened of everything, poor lass."

Jenai sighed. "Yes, and sure to be more so if anyone discovers her."

"What will you do, my lady?"

"Take her with me."

The handmaiden stared.

Jenai shrugged, then began to peel off her travel clothes to climb into her gambeson. She needed to be dressed appropriately to meet her generals. "We'll have to disguise her, but she'll make an excellent assistant for you upon the road."

The handmaiden's eyes brightened. "Ah, of course. I think charcoal will do the trick." She ran fingers through the Ilidreth's silver locks. "Yes, indeed. Worked for me when I hated my hair." She blew auburn curls from her face. She looked to be in her early thirties.

"You're not from Fraelin, are you?" Jenai realized she didn't even know the handmaiden's name.

"No, my lady. I came with my parents as a youth. We crossed from the Isles of Amri. Thought this land would be more friendly." Her laugh was ironic. "Ah, well. War strikes all lands, no matter."

Jenai couldn't tell if the woman was flippant or wise, but she liked her. "What's your name?"

"Tryla, my lady." She dipped into a practiced curtsey.

"I'm pleased to know you, Tryla." Jenai turned back to the Ilidreth. "This beauty's name is Aveyal."

"That's lovely in a foreign sort of way."

Jenai rested a knuckle against her lips, pondering how to handle the fae girl's transportation. "I think she'll need to stay with Bregger in the supply train until her leg is mended, then I'll have her stay near you."

"I'm with the supply train myself," Tryla said. "We can both see to her needs. Might be best that way. Bregger doesn't seem especially taken with her, if you get my meaning."

Jenai smiled. "Thank you, Tryla. Your good sense will be very welcome on our campaign, not to mention your feminine companionship. I hope we can be friends." Despite the gap in their ages, Jenai longed for a friend.

Tryla dipped another curtsey. "As it pleases you, my lady. I'm honored, as are my folks. Me, serving the Maid of Lorrae! Imagine it. My children's children will be speaking of this honor, no mistake."

Jenai's smile slipped. "First, Tryla, we must win."

"Oh, we'll do that, my lady. Take heart. By Afallon's will, He led you here, and you with all the sense most men never inherit. All will be well, just mark that."

Tryla helped her change into her gambeson and armor. The woman must've taken the time to learn how to put on each piece, for she didn't fumble once. The armor was light and sturdy. Tryla then attached a cloak of shimmering gold and blue. Jenai walked around her bedroom, getting used to moving under the weight of the metal plating.

Stopping before a looking glass, she took in the strangeness of seeing herself in full armor. She brushed her fingers over her breastplate—what Tryla told her was called a cuirass. An ember lily was embossed on the metal, just as she'd asked for. Alain had agreed that her armor should be bold and unique. If she was to be the banner for Fraelin, she must be distinct on the battlefield.

She flexed her gauntleted fingers, then eyed the sword laying on the bed. "I'll need a sheath," she said.

"Yes, my lady," the handmaiden replied. "I can send your page to request one made."

"Please do. But this sword can't leave my apartment."

"I understand. What a glorious thing it is."

Jenai paused at the door. "I will also need a banner made, Tryla. Can the page send for someone I might speak with on that matter as well?"

"Of course, my lady."

"Thank you." Jenai stepped from the bedchamber and met Alain and Mercer in the common room. "I'm ready."

Alain strode forward and circled her, nodding to himself. "Yes. It fits well. This should lend you some weight with the generals, whether they like it or not. Don't you think?" He glanced over his shoulder at Mercer.

The other man nodded. "It'll do."

Jenai smiled. "Every little bit helps."

They moved outside and down the stairs to where fresh horses waited. Mirrasae remained, looking rested despite the long ride through the night. The men helped Jenai climb onto the unicorn's back in her armor, then mounted their steeds. They rode back through Shinon, drawing the attention of the vendors setting up shop. A woman with a flower cart glanced up from arranging a bundle of white ember lilies. The woman's eyes widened, then she managed a clumsy curtsey. Others noticed Jenai's passage, and whispers of "Maid of Lorrae" and "Crane Maiden" chased the small procession up the streets and out into the fields.

"You're practically famous now," Alain said cheerily.

Jenai ignored him, trying not to cave to her nerves. She couldn't allow anything to distract her from what she must say to Prince Chartan's generals. She needed to earn their regard and loyalty. Without their support, she had no real army.

She glanced at the satchel tied to Alain's saddle. Within that case was every parchment Chartan had written up granting her superior authority where necessary. Would it be enough to sway the generals, or would they resent submitting to a woman with no battle experience?

Perhaps sensing her train of thought, Alain spoke. "The one to watch out for is General La Resh. He's the worst sort of scum, with innumerable war crimes to his credit. His reputation is one no Afallon-fearing soul can embrace. But he's a fierce warrior, and no one dares hinder him."

Chills climbed Jenai's fingers. "I've heard of General La Resh, and I have something to say to him when we meet."

Alain and Mercer exchanged a worried glance, which Jenai chose to overlook. They reached the outskirts of the war camp. Passing between shelters, she kept her eyes fixed on the circle of command tents far ahead. They arrived at midmorning, and a sentry moved forward to block their passage until Alain lifted the Crane crest. Saluting, the sentry stepped aside.

Between the circle of blue-and-white striped tents, a series of tables had been set up under a broad pavilion. Men in gleaming armor stood beneath the shade, gesturing to maps upon the tables while shouting at each other. One noticed the approaching riders and nudged his companion. Silence fell among the camp leaders. One man stepped from among the rest.

"Welcome, Maiden. I'm General Firro. We've been expecting you."

Jenai looked the man over. He was a broad-shouldered fellow in his prime, with a trimmed beard, cropped hair, and sharp eyes. "Thank you, General Firro. I know something of your reputation, and I welcome your skill in the coming siege." He'd been one of the heroes at the Battle of Rime, surviving near-fatal injuries and sounding the retreat before it turned into a massacre. Fraelin suffered a terrible blow that day.

He dipped his head, then offered his hand. She accepted, sliding from Mirrasae's back. Her armor clattered. She brushed back her glittering cloak and studied the other assembled men.

"Will you introduce me, General Firro?"

"Come this way." He motioned to the table, and she followed close, taking in the cluster of war leaders gravely. Firro gestured to the first man: a willowy fellow with an eyepatch. "This is General Teeg." Next, he motioned to a short, plump man with wild hair: "General Bastin." Next, an extremely tall and muscular man with no hair at all: "General La Resh." And last, an average-sized man with a full, tangled beard: "And Lieutenant-General Kirio." He grimaced. "These are all who answered Prince Chartan's call. Of course, Count Duron is housed near Lorion, holding off the Thargundian advance, so he and his forces couldn't answer."

Jenai knew of the count. Duron, the younger brother of the deceased Crane King, was illegitimate, but his battle prowess had distinguished him just the same. The Thargundians' fear of him had created a stalemate. Papa had credited Count Duron—Fraelin's marshal, called the Blackguard of Lorion—for the period of peace following the attack that caused Cetta's death. But eventually the raiding parties broke through, far away from Lorion, causing destruction and loss of life again. One count couldn't hold off a flood forever.

"We'll meet Count Duron on the battlefield when we take Lorion," Jenai said. "Meantime, we will work with those we have."

The men eyed one another, shifting their feet.

"The Crane Prince did mention that you intend to take Lorion," said General Firro, "but you should know that we haven't the military might to besiege that great city. We need more arms. Our catapults number only five. We have no siege towers."

"We will build more catapults," she answered.

"That takes time—"

"More so if we argue, General Firro."

His mouth snapped shut. He blinked, then nodded. "A fair point."

"Good. Then you'll see to the construction of five more? Best not to wait until we reach Lorion. That will alert the enemy to our presence."

His mouth worked, and he cast a glance toward La Resh. The bald and brawny man stepped forward. His stance was casual but his eyes were threatening.

"With all due respect to our lord prince," La Resh said, "we're willing to acknowledge your presence in our camp, but that's as far as our courtesy extends. You have no real power here, any more than the Crane Prince does. You're just a pretty face and a waving banner. We appreciate your efforts to reunite Fraeli—but that's where your work *ends*. War is man's province."

Nerves tingled across Jenai's body.

"*Be bold*," said the Voice.

Drawing back her shoulders within her armor, she seized

the man's gaze and stepped forward until she stood directly before him. The difference in their height was staggering. He had a foot on her, at least. But the Voice was with her, and she felt no fear, despite his reputation for butchery and debauchery.

"You're right to say that war is the province of man, General," she said. "Likewise, I'm right to declare that *peace* is the province of Sweet Afallon, and it's by His will that I stand here to seek it. I will not bow and scrape to our enemies. The Crow King would subjugate and destroy us. He sees us, not as equals under heaven, but as slaves to Simaerin. *That*, Afallon shall not abide—and to *that* end I've come to this camp.

"You and your fellows have a choice to make, La Resh. You can either stand before me as an obstacle and be hewn down by Afallon's will—or you may stand with me, and for the first time in your life, you will serve a glorious cause. Afallon has commanded me to tell you that today is your moment of reckoning. You, La Resh, have served darkness throughout all your grown days. You've done unspeakable things. Forsake them now and stand with Afallon—or He shall forsake *you*."

The hardness in La Resh's eyes deepened, and a vein pulsed in his forehead. He stepped closer, almost touching Jenai. "You little b—"

Alain and Mercer started forward, swords half-drawn, but Jenai held out her hand. "You cannot touch me, La Resh."

The bald man lifted his hand, fury flashing in his eyes, but halfway through his strike he faltered. She stared him down, unflinching. His fury flickered toward fear. He licked his lips, then lowered his hand. "What *are* you?"

"A mortal, just like you," Jenai said. "But we have until now served different masters. Will that change today? Will you serve in Afallon's army henceforth and rescue your soul from the grip of Thiavos? Verily, Afallon will cut you down in the siege at Lorion and send you into darkness if you do not turn from sin and fight for His cause."

He stood frozen for a long time, superstition growing in his eyes. Then he sank to his knees. "By Afallon's will, I serve the Maid of Lorrae."

She set her hand on his bald pate. "I accept your service, La Resh, and pray that one day it will be born from faith rather than fear." Glancing toward her protectors, she found Alain staring at her, dumbfounded. She smiled gently. "All things are possible with heaven's power."

The duke shook his head, still looking thunderstruck. Twisting away, he murmured something to Mercer who snorted in reply.

Turning back to the other generals, Jenai lifted an eyebrow. "Does anyone else have something to say to me?"

Firro glanced at his fellows, then grimly looked back to her. "It would seem not."

"Then let us commence with business. We have precious little time for in-fighting. I hope I can rely upon your expertise in warfare, gentlemen. Shall we begin?" She stepped to the table and examined the maps while the others gathered close. Quills and bottles of ink were strewn about haphazardly. Plucking up an eagle feather quill, she dipped it in the nearest inkwell, then proffered the quill to La Resh. He took it at once. "Please mark Lorion for me," she said. La Resh obeyed, circling a dot on the map. Jenai nodded. "And where is Shinon?" He circled another dot.

"Thank you, General." She tapped Shinon on the map. "We must leave these fields and aim for Lorion within the month, once the five new catapults are constructed. To delay longer than that will be to undermine our purpose. For now, the Thargundians and their Simaeri allies will think little of any rumors which may reach them regarding myself. They'll scoff and call it lunacy. But if we wait too long, their spies will begin to think differently. We must use our advantage while we have it."

"A month is a very short time to prepare for a siege, my lady," said General Bastin with some hesitation. "Not to mention the earthworks we'll need to dig once we reach Lorion's gates."

"I agree, yet it must be so." Jenai rested her hand beside the dot symbolizing Lorion. "And what *must* be done *can* be done."

INSPECTING THE CAMP

Jenai ordered her quarters to be set up among the command tents. Traveling back and forth between Shinon proper and the army wasted valuable time and made her feel too separate from her soldiers. Alain and Mercer argued with her, but she fended them off. This was important, and her privacy meant nothing compared to the stakes. Her handmaiden, Tryla, came with her, bringing Aveyal, as well as Jenai's page: an energetic but focused boy of twelve. Jenai moved into the tent two days after meeting her generals.

"You really should have a squire as well," Mercer said on her second morning in camp. "Alain is looking into it at Chateau Darr, though we're very short of trained lads, it seems."

Jenai looked up from examining her new sword sheath, delivered minutes before by courier. The sheath was beautiful. Tiny ember lilies were etched into the leather belt. She fingered them, glad the leatherworker had followed her instructions. The night before, she'd also spoken to a seamstress about her banner, but it would take a week to be made to her specifications.

"Will Alain return soon?" asked Jenai, sliding her sword into the sheath. It was a perfect fit.

"He intends to, but he said sometimes the prince requires that he stay longer than expected."

Tryla shifted Jenai's cloak to the side as Jenai buckled the sword to her waist. Fully dressed in armor, she was as ready for the coming day as she could be. Although La Resh had sworn his allegiance, she'd sensed reserve and resentment in the other assembled men throughout their first meeting. It would take time and the Voice's guidance for Jenai to earn their fidelity.

"What will you do today?" asked Mercer, moving with her to the tent flap.

"Inspect the camp."

"It seems in order."

"That's not my issue." She stepped out into the sunlight, squinting. The generals were waiting at the table. Striding toward them, she focused on balancing her steps. The armor was well made, but heavy enough to throw her footing off. Especially with the sword.

The generals looked up from quiet conversation. Subtle scowls flashed across several faces, but La Resh hurried forward, that same reverent fear in his eyes.

"Lady General, we're ready to discuss the march."

"First, I wish to inspect the camp," she said, working to keep her voice firm.

The generals tensed.

"We already have," said General Teeg tartly.

"I wish to see for myself." Jenai drew herself up, holding the gaze of Teeg's one good eye. She wouldn't let him bully her—she couldn't afford to relent even for a moment if it risked weakening her in their estimation. She must look strong and confident, for she was on Afallon's errand.

"Oh, let her look," boomed La Resh. "It's *her* army, isn't it?"

Teeg's eye narrowed, and someone else coughed as though in dissent. No one else stirred. Finally, Teeg nodded. "Very well. Inspect the camp, though I assure you it's a waste of valuable time. We need to discuss the logistics of the march."

"We will," Jenai said. "But first, we should see the men to know what they require for the march."

"They require everything," La Resh said with a bitter laugh. "The Crane Prince over yonder has provided almost nothing since these men assembled."

"The Duke of Clayre is discussing that matter with our sovereign prince at this very moment." Jenai turned toward the camp. "Shall we?"

Every man followed, with Mercer flanking her. La Resh took up her other side, walking casually, like war was as common as breathing. For him, she supposed it was.

"Where do these soldiers come from?" she asked, taking in the rows of blue and white tents. Though neatly arranged, many of the canvas structures were shabby and looked ready to topple in a strong breeze.

"From all over Southern Fraelin, milady," La Resh answered. "Many come from right near here, in the outlying villages and hamlets. Others, from closer to where the Thargundian brutes have made their camps. Most lads between fifteen and nineteen years of age itch for combat, so they were among the first to arrive. Them and the old men who remember Fraelin from *before* the Crow's invasion. You should hear their campfire talk: reminiscing on how wine used to taste like the honeyed mead of the heathen gods of Amri, before our best vineyards were burned down, and how our fish used to just *jump* into the nets, like trawling was no work at all in bygone days."

Jenai smiled. "'Memory stains all things gold.'"

"Aye, so they say," La Resh grunted. "'Cept the bad things. Those are stained red."

Thinking of Cetta, she silently agreed.

Most soldiers had already left their tents for the training grounds where they underwent exercises with swords, spears, and daggers. Jenai paused to watch them. Many of the lads were clumsy and barefoot. Further out, Jenai spotted the cavalry throwing lances. The knights on their horses looked well groomed, with gleaming tabards and shining boots. The hammering of wood suggested that more catapults were being crafted. The nearby bellows belched out smoke as the blacksmiths made basic armor.

Everything looked in order. Thirty-five-hundred men all organized into units.

She turned toward the edge of camp. There the uniform tents fell away to a haphazard array of colorful bivouacs. She grimaced, prickles running up her arms. "Are those camp followers, La Resh?"

"That they are," La Resh said fondly.

"They must be ordered out. I won't have my men living in sin."

La Resh and Teeg spluttered protests.

"That's *final*." Jenai's voice cracked over them. "Prostitutes are not allowed near this holy army, do I make myself plain?"

Firro piped up. "But the men need—"

"If the men *need* women, they can marry them and make themselves and those women respectable. This army will not cave to wanton lust. We will keep the statutes of our faith."

The generals glanced at each other in dismay. "The camp followers won't like it," Lieutenant-General Kirio muttered.

Resting her hand on her sword hilt, Jenai turned on her

heels. "If they have trouble leaving, I will see them out myself." She marched back toward the center of camp, letting the men decide whether or not to follow. Soon the rattle of their armor told her they were close. She never looked back, keeping her focus on the next discussion: that of marching to Lorion.

"AFTER A FIVE-DAY MARCH, WE CAN RESUPPLY AT BLOSS." Firro tapped the map. "Very likely, more recruits will join us there."

"How many more?" Jenai asked.

"I'd estimate five hundred spears or so."

Jenai studied the distance between the dot he was tapping and the bigger one La Resh had circled earlier. Lorion. "Does Bloss have enough supplies to provide for so many soldiers?"

"Oh, they do, even if we have to squeeze it out of them," said La Resh.

She leveled a look on him. "Remember that now you're in the service of Afallon, General."

His grin widened. "There are many ways of squeezing, and most I learned from the clergy."

She frowned but chose to address the comment later if necessary. They were still a five-day march from Bloss. "What of weaponry? Are we short?"

"Always," answered Kirio.

"But we'll make do," added Bastin.

She started to tell them that wasn't good enough, but the clop of hooves ripped her eyes from the map. She looked toward the path leading to the war pavilion. To her relief, Alain appeared on horseback, dressed in armor that glinted in the sunlight.

Someone at the table swore. Jenai looked sharply around

but couldn't tell by anyone's expression who'd taken Afallon's name in vain.

"There will be none of that language here, good sirs," she said. "Especially not directed toward one of my men."

"Nothing personal," La Resh assured her.

Teeg snorted.

Jenai turned her frown on him. "Do you take issue with the Duke of Clayre, General Teeg?"

He hesitated, watching the approaching duke. "Not in any way that will interfere with your province, Lady Jenai."

She studied him a moment longer, then nodded. "See that it doesn't. Duke Alain is a good man."

The generals exchanged looks, but no one argued. Twisting back around, Jenai smiled at Alain. He smiled back, though it was a fleeting expression. He reined in his horse and swung from his saddle.

"Prince Chartan sends his regards, Lady General," Alain offered. "He also sends the means to finish outfitting your army, compliments of the Duke of Thame."

Now she understood his grim mood. "I'm grateful for all you endeavored to do, Your Grace."

He lifted a purse from his saddle and tossed it onto the table. The chink of coins was a heavy thud. The generals eyed the purse with relief and interest.

"Well, Your Grace," said La Resh, grinning broadly, "seems you're good for something after all!"

"Don't thank me," Alain said. "I was against it."

Someone snorted. Jenai shot Teeg a sharp glance, but he shook his head in denial.

"Gold wins wars, Duke of Clayre." La Resh scooped up the purse and hefted it in one large hand. He grunted with approval. "No matter where it comes from."

"Not all wars require gold, General." Alain turned away in disgust. "Especially not at the cost of souls." He waved his hand. "It doesn't matter. The deal is struck. Time now to make the most of what we have."

Jenai took the purse from La Resh and offered it to Firro. "See that this gets to the paymaster."

"Gladly." He bowed and went off at once.

Jenai rested her gauntleted hand on Alain's shoulder. "Afallon's will matters most, Lieutenant-General. We will accept aid by whatever quarter he may send it."

Alain shrugged while fiddling with his horse's tack. "Just pray it *was* by Afallon's will, though I doubt it. All too often, men stand in the way of heaven."

THE PRINCE'S BLESSING

Jenai had no interest in attending the royal gathering at Chateau Darr ahead of the march to Lorion, but Alain insisted. He also brought her a blue silk gown to wear in lieu of her armor. She hoisted it with awe. Never had she felt such soft, watery material. Taking the gown from him, she tried to imagine donning the delicate thing.

"Please wear it tonight."

Jenai looked up into Alain's dark eyes. Unwilling to enter a woman's quarters, he stood at the doorway to her tent. Morning sunlight bled in behind him. Jenai was grateful for his inborn discretion. Few of the soldiers had anything approaching it, and Tryla had scared off more than one peeping youth.

"It's beautiful, but how can we justify spending coin on this frivolity?" Jenai asked.

Alain's mouth quirked up. "It's a gift from a high court lady, actually. Your handmaiden might need to take it in a little. You're more willowy than your benefactress."

Jenai nodded. "I will consider what's best for my presence at Chateau Darr."

He winced. "Just remember, while this gathering is to celebrate the coming march, it's also to give the nobility a chance to approve of the church's decision. Most still suspect you're a witch. We should dispel as many doubts as possible. This gown will work magic in their eyes."

She ran her thumb over the cool cloth. "I will consider."

"Thank you," he sighed. "I need to return to Chateau Darr to help with preparations, but I'll come back to escort you before dusk."

"That isn't necessary. Mercer will be my escort. It makes no sense to have you travel back and forth twice in one day."

He frowned. "Are you certain—"

She offered a gentle smile. "I'm perfectly safe. Afallon is with me."

He opened his mouth, then closed it and shrugged. "I don't know about Afallon's protections, my lady, but I've seen your unicorn's horn. That I can trust in."

Jenai's smile deepened. She was relieved to hear proof of Alain's pure heart. So few saw Mirrasae for what she truly was. "She's as fierce as she is gentle."

He bowed his head, then strode off, letting the flap fall and snuff out the sunlight. Jenai turned to where Tryla stood waiting. Letting the gown unfold, Jenai held it out for the handmaiden's inspection.

Cooing, Tryla hurried over and lightly brushed her fingertips against the gown. "It's stunning, milady. Just stunning."

"Yes. It is. Please pack it for me."

Tryla blinked. "You're not wearing it tonight?"

"For now, I'm a soldier, Tryla. No, I won't wear it. Please polish my armor. If I'm to instill faith in my fellow Fraeli ahead of this campaign, they must see me as Afallon intends me to look."

"His Grace isn't going to be happy." Tryla accepted the dress, handling it like it was a butterfly's wings.

"I can't choose Alain's feelings ahead of my instinct. I'll help you polish."

THE CHATEAU WAS LIT UP UNDER COUNTLESS TORCHES. A string of carriages rattled in through the gates, up the drive, and around the water fountain, off-loading important persons in their finery. Music floated out from the bright interior. Jenai rode beside Mercer through the gates in their turn, and the gateman saluted her. Helmless, she nodded back.

Riding up the short lane, gravel crunching under hoof, Jenai studied the grand edifice, dreading the coming hours. Alain had insisted she attend this formal soiree. It was important. To avoid it would offend the Crane Prince, and that wouldn't go well for her cause. Reluctant though she was, she agreed that respect for the prince's wishes mattered.

Reaching the chateau's front steps, Jenai waited for Mercer to help her down. Her armor faintly clattered. She'd been wearing it daily, and the weight was familiar now. Her balance was good. But climbing on and off Mirrasae's back still proved difficult.

"I'll be right outside waiting," Mercer murmured.

Smiling, Jenai nodded, grateful for his quiet and consistent loyalty. She started up the steps alone, her cape trailing behind her, gleaming in the torchlight. Nobles halted ahead of her, craning their necks to stare. A carriage rolled to a stop below and someone gasped. She felt the weight of their eyes on her. Reaching the wide-open front doors, Jenai paused and stared into the grand vestibule where gentry had gathered, waiting for their superiors to pass into the throne room ahead of them. Jenai wasn't certain whether she should wait, too, but before her nerves grew too tight, Alain came toward her.

Their eyes met. He shook his head slightly, reproaching her for the armor. She faintly smiled back in defiance. Reaching her, he offered his arm. In contrast to her glistening armor and gold and blue cape, he wore a slate blue brocade doublet, gray hose, and black boots. A saber was strapped at his side, reminding the crowds that he was more than a titled noble.

"Shall we enter, Lady General?" Alain asked.

"Whenever you think it appropriate, Lieutenant-General." She rested her gauntlet on his forearm.

Whispers followed them through the double doors and into the grand chamber where the throne stood empty above the gathered throng. Music played in one corner, the refrains elegant and sweet. Diamonds sparkled as men and women flitted about, gossiping.

"Where is the Crane Prince?" Jenai whispered.

"Fashionably late," Alain replied under his breath. "It makes a statement that he's not always at the beck and call of his subjects."

The myriad candles reflected off Jenai's armor, dancing and flashing. She allowed Alain to steer her around the room, catching every eye and setting every tongue wagging. Jenai felt like a stuffed pig on display, the way the butcher back home paraded his around at Harvest-tide. She endured it, though her insides writhed.

"I know you hate this," Alain said under his breath, "but you need to make a good impression on these people. They're funding this war."

"I thought the Duke of Thame—"

"He's the main patron, but others are starting to drop coins into the pot."

Jenai chewed on that, annoyance swelling at the idea that

so many nobles still had coin to hoard until they were interested enough to part with a few.

The Duke of Clayre led Jenai to a cluster of noblewomen wrapped in dazzling gowns and drenched in jewels. One of them—an elegant, plump woman—detached from the rest to approach, her white dress sparkling. Her dark hair, coiffed atop her head, glittered like stars with tiny pearls and diamonds.

"Uh oh," Alain whispered. "Brace yourself."

Jenai checked her posture. "Why?"

The woman arrived before the duke could answer. "So, this is the Maiden of Lorrae." She lifted a fan to her lips. "Introduce me, Your Grace."

"Of course, my lady." Alain inclined his head. "This is the Crane General Jenai d'Arc. General, this is Countess Ilua Nuvan. She was the generous benefactress who gifted you your gown."

Alain's warning made more sense. Jenai tensed, then tacked a smile to her lips. "Ah, thank you for that most elegant gift, Countess. I've never worn anything so beautiful in all my life."

The fan tapped against Ilua's lips. "And did you find it too stunning to wear here?"

"I prepare myself for battle, my lady," Jenai said. "The thought of sullying that beautiful gown with my troubled spirit was too much. I intend to save it for a more peaceful era."

The countess blinked, then a light caught in her keen gaze. "I was told you were a simpleton, Jenai of Lorrae, but I think someone underestimated you." Her eyes cut across the room to the portly Duke of Thame. "I'm very glad to know it."

"We see the world through our own experiences," Alain

replied. "The Duke of Thame finds only what he understands."

The countess snapped her fan open before her face, likely to hide a smile. "Vicious, Your Grace. Accurate, but vicious."

The flock of women inched closer, and Jenai had to repress a desire to back away. Countess Ilua turned and motioned them to approach. "You might imagine, Jenai, how enraptured the ladies at court are by news of a woman leading men to war. Your audacity is...quite something."

Jenai's smile slipped. Was the countess complimenting or insulting her?

A second woman spoke up. "If the war can be won, does it matter who leads the armies to victory?"

"Pragmatic rebuttal, Lady Nantay, as always," said a third, her voice dripping with sarcasm. "It's a wonder the men don't flock to your side."

Lady Nantay's smile could parry a blade. "I'd rather be pragmatic and alone than stupid and drooled upon, Lady Silian."

Alain gently tugged on Jenai. "A pleasure, ladies. Now, please excuse us. The Crane General must be introduced to a few more of her patrons." He inclined his head, and the women dipped into curtsies.

As they strode away, Jenai leaned close to him. "Are all courtiers so..." She searched for the proper term.

"Clueless? Only the majority. A few of us found our way out of the maze."

The smile that spread over Jenai's face was genuine this time, but it tumbled away as they approached the Duke of Thame. She recalled his mockery on the night she'd first met the Crane Prince.

"Must we?" Jenai asked.

Alain faintly nodded. "He's our most important patron. To avoid thanking him would send a poor message."

"Very well." The false smile was tacked back on. Jenai tried to conjure up gratitude to soften her expression, but the crowds, the lights, the elegant music, the perfumed air, and the tinkling laughter of courtiers who seemed oblivious to the starvation of their own people marched chills up her arms.

Have they even tried to win this war before now, or are they content to let Fraelin fall?

"Ah, the woman of the hour!" The Duke of Thame rubbed his meaty hands together. "Quite the spectacle you've created."

"This isn't my doing," Jenai said cooly.

Alain had gone rigid at her side, his dark eyes like coals in the candlelight. "Jenai wished to thank you for your generosity in outfitting the Crane Army."

"Yes," Jenai said, putting more warmth into her tones. Whether the Duke of Thame was the greedy man Alain painted him out to be was beside the point. Afallon used sinners as well as saints for His high purposes. "Thank you, Your Grace," she went on. "The coin you've supplied has been crucial in preparing Fraelin for battle."

"Think nothing of it," Thame said, flapping his ring-bedecked hand. "Glad to serve my country, and all that."

"Better late than never," Alain commented. "Your Grace."

The portly duke cast Alain a smirk. "My dear man, I've always wished to aid Fraelin in her need, but until now we've not had any hope for victory. Past calls to arms have gone unheeded. We needed a proper banner—and by Afallon's teeth, at last we have one!"

"More than His teeth are responsible," Jenai said coldly. "Please have more respect for your God, Your Grace."

The Duke of Thame hesitated, then let out a bellowing laugh. "She's the genuine article, isn't she? All piety and prophecy. By Afallon, she's magnificent. Just what we need."

Alain tensed, and Jenai glanced at him to find fire blazing

in his eyes. He opened his mouth, but the music abruptly cut off, then a new strain strummed across the throne room. The clusters of people shifted to face the dais. Alain steered Jenai to the fore of the crowd. A moment later, Prince Chartan strode from behind the curtained throne, one hand raised in acknowledgment of the room. The multitude folded into rippling bows. Alain and Jenai joined them.

The prince reached his throne and remained standing. The crowds rose to watch what might happen next.

"Jenai d'Arc," the Crane Prince said in a clear voice, "join me please."

Inhaling, Jenai released Alain's arm and strode up onto the dais. She carefully knelt before the prince, bowing her head low. "Sweet prince, may Afallon bless thee forever."

He set his hand on her head. "And you have my blessing, brave maiden. May your victory at Lorion be swiftly won. May angels strengthen your blade. May Fraelin soon be liberated from traitors and tyrants alike. Rise, my Lady General."

She stood with little difficulty and lifted her eyes to meet her prince's. "I'm yours to command, Your Royal Highness."

"I'm grateful," he answered. "Turn around and face your fellow Fraeli. Let them get a proper look at their champion bold."

Jenai turned.

"Behold, my beloved subjects," Prince Chartan said. "The Crane Maiden!"

Cheers erupted across the room, echoing off the vaulted ceiling. Feelings of bewilderment and fear churned in Jenai's stomach, but she held still and tried to ignore the din. Focusing on Alain, she found his steady gaze calming. Her nerves settled.

Soon the Crane Prince lifted a hand, silencing the crowd. "Tomorrow, our noble army will march toward Lorion.

Afallon has not forsaken us. Soon, we will take back the North. I will be crowned king at Reems. We will become a great kingdom once again!"

The roar was deafening. Jenai longed to step down. The prince's speech continued, speaking of the glorious past. Of thriving vineyards and lazy summer days. Of mild winters. Of the blessings once bounteously bestowed from on high.

Half-listening, Jenai thought back to her childhood and little Cetta, her beloved sister, killed out of cruelty, and for no better reason.

Soon, she thought. *Soon I will chase out the monsters who took you from my side. Not for hate, Cetta—for that's a poison to the soul. But for love: of you, of country, and of freedom.*

THE MARCH

The day of the march dawned overcast. Thunder drummed in the low-hanging clouds, but the rain held back. Seated upon Mirrasae, Jenai studied the soldiers standing at attention before her. Some stared at the unicorn, presumably because they saw her for what she was. Others were transfixed by Jenai.

As always, Mercer and Alain flanked her. The generals surrounded them, barking last minute orders to their captains and adjutants. Horses whinnied. Banners bobbed in the clutches of their human wielders. The air was charged with expectation. Jenai read determination and excitement in the eyes of the young and old alike. Too long, Fraelin had been forced to bend to the whims of the tyrant across the sea, allowing the traitors of Thargundy to steal ground. But no more.

"Looks like we're ready to march," Firro said above the din.

"Not yet." Jenai nudged Mirrasae forward. The faint commotion of the large body fell into silence. Jenai squared her shoulders, drew a long breath, and lifted her voice.

Mercer had explained to her that she could address the assemblage, and messengers stationed at intervals would carry it to the back of the army. Even so, she wanted as many to hear her as possible.

"My dear men," she began, "today, we change history!"

A booming cheer swelled through the ranks. The banners waved. Jenai waited for the cries to settle, then she lifted her hand and silence fell.

"For too long, we've allowed the traitors of Thargundy to bully us. They have rejected the rightful king of Fraelin, setting up their own imposter. Likewise, they have allied with the treacherous Crow King—" A storm of boos followed that. Jenai allowed the noise, then lifted her hand. Again, immediate silence fell. "By Afallon's divine decree, this shall no longer stand!"

More cheers. Stamping feet. Madly waving banners.

Jenai spoke over them. "We are His holy army, called and appointed to end this conflict, put the rightful king on the throne, and take back Fraelin!"

The thunderous response was enough to deafen the brewing storm.

Jenai lifted her hand one last time. "In Afallon's sweet name and that of our beloved Crane Prince, we shall be victorious!"

The resounding cheers lasted for a full minute. The generals eyed Jenai with reluctant awe. She glanced at Alain who was grinning broadly. He leaned toward her to speak above the shouts.

"By the Weave, you've got that special something that makes a true leader. Not blood, not wealth, not anything so superficial. I suspect it's your sincerity and faith."

She turned away to avoid his eyes. "I doubt it's me at all. I'm only doing the will of Afallon."

He shrugged, leaning back, though his eyes still danced with pride.

The cheering faded, and Jenai motioned for the generals to take command. They issued orders to march, and the men —though drilled for only a few weeks—fell into line fast and well. Many were seasoned soldiers from past conflicts, but even the raw youth appeared disciplined. Jenai was grateful for their dedication. She knew so little about war—only what the Voice told her during her meetings.

Marching at the head of the long columns, Jenai watched the sky, praying it wouldn't rain. Sure enough, the clouds held back, making the march a pleasant one. A breeze chased them, pushing them along and keeping them cool. The sun hovered beyond the clouds, preventing the coolness from turning into a chill.

"A perfect day," one of the generals remarked.

"You may thank Afallon for that," said Jenai.

No one contradicted her.

In the afternoon, Mercer offered food to Jenai. The rations were simple: an apple, a wedge of cheese, and a heel of bread. She ate slowly, studying the lay of the land, the swell of hills, and the swaying boughs of the trees they passed.

As the company marched alongside a stream, Alain moved his horse next to hers. "The prince was upset that you didn't join his dinner party after his speech last night."

Jenai grimaced. "On the night before our march, it was impossible to stay so long."

"So I told him. Still, I think he's offended. I tried to soften the blow, but..." Alain shrugged. "He's a sensitive soul."

"I will dictate a letter apologizing."

"Hopefully that's enough. More than anything, he hates to lose face, and you were to be his main attraction at that dinner. He wanted the Duke of Thame to speak with you more one on one. I believe they have a wager going about the source of your Voice."

Her grimace deepened. She'd not told anyone but the clergy about her Voice, yet word had spread. "More than ever, I'm glad I didn't stay."

"I don't blame you. While not the main attraction, I'm still something to gawk at." He absently ran a finger down his scarred temple. "Longtime prisoner, slightly emaciated. Makes for a thrilling draw."

"That's morbid."

"Most people are drawn to morbidity, you know. It fascinates us."

"Not me."

"Well, you haven't faced war yet, Jenai. It will change you —though I can't say in what way. Just be prepared."

Her grip on Mirrasae's mane tightened. "I'm trying to be."

Alain set his hand on her gardbrace, then retracted it. "May I see your banner?"

She glanced at her satchel. "I will unfurl it tomorrow."

"Why wait?"

"Today, we follow only the royal banner of Fraelin." Her eyes flitted to the pennant of the white crane on a blue field. "Tomorrow, I'll take full charge of my army, after they're more certain in their hearts that Prince Chartan is the rightful heir."

Alain fiddled with his reins. "It's true, many still doubt. His mother made certain of that."

Jenai had heard of the former Crane Queen's mad ravings. Her infidelity was well known—and the fact that she insisted her own son, the crown prince of Fraelin, was illegitimate, had rocked the whole country, causing cracks in the foundation of the Crane House's rule. She'd also been said to curse Prince Chartan on her deathbed, prophesying that he would never be crowned king at Reems.

"Jenai?" Alain asked, cutting through her reverie.

She fixed her eyes on the road. "That Afallon sent me to carve his path to the crown is sufficient for me."

"Most of us don't have your level of faith, Jenai. I envy your pure heart, unsullied by politics or time. I pray it lasts, I truly do. Virtue suits you."

She glanced at him, seeking any hint of mockery, but his smile appeared genuine. He turned his head toward the stream, and they rode in silence.

"The generals don't appear to trust you," Jenai said in a low voice.

He scoffed. "Apparently, living beneath the Crow's fell eyrie may have tainted me. Never mind I was his prisoner and have more cause to hate him than most Fraeli. That and... well, other things."

"For instance?"

"It's not important."

"You're my lieutenant, Alain. Should I know of these other things?"

He glanced at her, frowning. "I'm not sure they matter. They *shouldn't*, but somehow Fraelin has adopted the same prejudice that Simaerin has toward—well, *magic*."

Understanding dawned. "Yes, the church tends to view magic as witchcraft."

"Just so."

Jenai read the tension in his face. "Do *you* wield magic, Alain?"

He blew out a breath. "I do, yes. Wind." As though to demonstrate, a breeze rustled his hair. "It comes when I call —mostly. And often when I don't. Think I'm a witch now?" Humor danced in his eyes, but fear lurked there as well.

"No," she said. "I think you're strong and capable."

He snorted. "Thank you, I suppose. Either way, I don't like to use my talent in public settings. Last thing I need is a trial in the court of public opinion. Few survive that harrowing experience, and of those few, none are unscathed. Not even the saints."

"Not even Afallon," Jenai agreed. "We are, after all, fallible. Our judgments are murky."

"Even yours?"

"Surely." She ran her fingers through Mirrasae's silky mane, welcoming the coolness. "I'm only human. Why I've been called upon to lead this force against our enemies, I don't know. I can only make guesses."

"What are they?"

She shook her head. "This isn't the place to discuss them."

"But discussing magic is fine?"

She shrugged. "You could have refrained."

"I suppose I wanted you to know before I surprised you in an emergency." He glanced over his shoulder at the cluster of generals. The men were laughing and shouting at each other, all in high spirits. "They know about my *gift* and want nothing to do with me. It seems, in the last three years, a lot of Fraeli have been burned at the stake for using elemental magic. Prince Chartan warned me off using it where others can see, hoping they'd forget that I used to wield wind in battle. I used to be renowned for it. Now...it feels as though some folk find my imprisonment fitting because of that magic, as though I wasn't a prisoner of war at all, but some kind of heretical monster."

"That's a lot to deal with," Jenai said softly, sensing that there was more he wasn't saying. "I'm sorry, Alain. It isn't right."

His shrug was sharper this time. "Is anything right?"

"Yes—love, acceptance, forgiveness. The principles of heaven."

"Does marching on our enemies not contradict that?"

"Another principle of heaven is truth, unaltered by man,"

she answered. "And the truth is that the Thargundians are traitors selling their country out to a tyrant for their own gain. The Crow King has no love for the church or Afallon's teachings. He would imprison or kill any and all whom he finds unacceptable—as his forebears did to the Ilidreth in Simaerin, butchering and driving them nearly to extinction."

"By recent reports, the same's been happening here," Alain said.

"That's due to the Thargundians, not Prince Chartan. I hope he will hear my appeal on behalf of the Ilidreth once he's crowned."

Thunder rumbled. The sky looked ready to weep.

Mirrasae tossed her head. *"It will rain very soon."*

Jenai twisted around to eye the marching columns behind her. "Mirrasae says it will rain soon."

Alain sighed. "Great. Nothing I like better than being trapped in armor, drowning in a sopping gambeson."

She chuckled at that and pulled her hood over her head. Alain and Mercer followed suit. Thunder drummed again, then rain descended in sheets. Groans drifted from the generals, with echoing cries and curses flowing down the line.

"At least the camp will be ready for us," said Mercer, breaking his silence for the first time all morning.

"Will it?" Jenai asked, surprised.

"Surely," Alain said. "The supply train headed out long before we finished assembling for the march. Until we reach enemy territory, the army will travel thus: scouts, supply train, generals, cavalry, foot soldiers, camp followers, and lastly, a second scouting party to make certain we're not attacked from the rear unawares."

She frowned at the mention of camp followers, but that was something she would have to deal with later. Instead, she focused on the impressiveness of the organization. Though she'd been part of the marching plans, the order of the march hadn't come up. No one had seemed to feel the need to address it. She really shouldn't be surprised that the machine of war was well greased. "I'm glad we can get dry immediately. How far up the road will camp be arranged?"

"Ten miles is average for a complement of this size and range," Mercer said, "but with the threat of rain, the supply captains probably chose to find a campsite within eight miles."

She supposed it made sense that so many men on foot would bring the covered mileage to single digits. No wonder the generals had been eager to move things along, avoiding as many delays as possible. At this rate it would take several weeks to reach Lorion—and that was if fickle weather didn't slow them further.

She glanced at Alain. "I don't suppose you could use your wind magic to blow the storm away?"

He tipped his head to one side, wearing a wry smile. "I like to think I'm an able Wind Mage, General Jenai—but I'm not *that* good."

"Too bad," said Mercer. "If you managed that, you'd probably be more popular."

"I'm still nobleborn," Alain answered. "I was doomed from birth."

KEEPING A SECRET

The road was washed out in two places. That slowed the army's progress by several hours, and they limped into camp after dark, starved and soaking. Alain, knowing that Jenai didn't care for strong language, bit back the complaints that had settled on his tongue. She hadn't fared any better than her men, yet she remained pleasant, conversing and even making light of the bad conditions.

"Perhaps Afallon is cleansing us before we begin His holy errand," she'd said when she heard General La Resh utter a strong expletive. "Don't soil yourself so soon, good sir."

The supply train had been hampered by the same conditions and had made it to camp only an hour ahead of the main force. The hired hands were still setting up the foot soldiers' tents, but the generals' circle of tents had been erected, and a blazing bonfire welcomed them like a warm embrace. Flames hissed and spluttered, but the rain didn't win out.

Alain swung from his gelding's back, rubbed the horse's nose affectionately, then hurried to Jenai's side. He reached her at the same time as Mercer, and together they helped her slide from the unicorn's back.

"Thank you," she said. "It's nearly impossible to move well in this armor."

"You'll get used to it," said Mercer.

"But it will always be annoying," Alain added.

Jenai's pages raced up to her, bowed, then eagerly waited for her orders. She considered the boys, perhaps at a loss on what to tell them. Alain had found the second page two days ago, impressed with his keen wits. Every general ought to have two pages—it was practical.

"Why don't you bring her some food," Alain told the newcomer. The boy inclined his head, then shot off like a rabbit.

"Is Tryla in my tent?" she asked the second page.

"Yes, my lady."

"Has she laid out my dry things?"

"Yes, my lady."

She hesitated. "Can you write?"

"Yes, my lady."

"I'll need to dictate a letter to His Royal Highness."

"Yes, my lady." He raced off toward her tent.

"Good thinking," Alain said. "That apology shouldn't be put off."

Jenai shot him a grimace, then trudged toward her tent. Partway there, she turned back. "What will you do this evening?"

Alain shrugged one shoulder. "Dry off. Eat bland food. You know, *army* stuff."

Her lips quivered toward a smile, then she walked away, her short dark ponytail bobbing to her steps. Alain lingered a moment, watching her with a swell of awe in his chest, then he pivoted in the mud and went to find the officer's mess tent. There it was, smoke rising from the hole near the back of the canvas monstrosity, the scent of roasting meat heavy in the damp air. Food was more important than being dry; he'd learned that in the Crow King's dungeons. Even if it was army rations. Mercer slipped inside the tent ahead of him.

Hooves squelched mud behind Alain. He glanced over his shoulder and started. "Stalking me, O fair one?"

Mirrasae tossed her magnificent mane. *'Your mount is waiting for you.'*

Alain stared at her while the significance of her words dawned. With all that had happened since his visit to the otherworldly Vale, he'd half forgotten his accord with Yenn. *Though I don't know how I managed that.* Perhaps it was because of his preoccupation with Jenai herself—the Lily Maid, as Yenn had dubbed her. The stone dragon had called upon Alain to become her sword, and he'd taken that to heart.

Shaking himself, Alain smiled at the unicorn. "And where is our statuesque friend?"

'Yonder. Come with me.' She walked past him. Her inner glow was brighter than normal under the gloomy conditions. He trailed after her through the swirling puddles, glad he hadn't changed yet, but sorry he hadn't been able to eat something.

Soldiers scurried through the wet, setting up the smaller tents around the erected command circle. The din of shouts was muted under the steady rainfall, isolating Alain further from a company that didn't want him.

Stop feeling sorry for yourself.

He set his shoulders and hurried to Mirrasae's side. They descended a slope that led to the rising water of the stream. The supply captain had the good sense to set up camp on higher ground, though a few unlucky lads would likely be forced to sleep nearer to the water. Hopefully the rain would stop soon.

The unicorn came right to the water's edge, and Alain

slowed. Dread swelled in his stomach. "Do we have to cross—"

The water in the racing stream swelled, then burst apart in a cascade of droplets. Yenn emerged from the depths, though the stream was no more than three feet deep—except, wasn't Yenn a stone dragon, and hadn't he said he'd been called from underground by the Weave?

Alain inclined his head, then looked up to meet those fierce, intelligent eyes. "Hello, Yenn."

'Greetings, Duke of Clayre. Had you forgotten our pact?'

"Not entirely..."

The stone dragon grinned, bearing sharp fangs. Chills ran down Alain's spine. Small dragon or no, Yenn could still chomp Alain in two.

'Are you prepared to let me be your mount?'

Alain hesitated. "I'd say yes, but I do have a strategic question. The Thargundians aren't expecting us—yet. But once their spies discover we're marching on them, they're going to take a closer look. Isn't the element of surprise our best approach?"

The dragon fell still. Water rolled off his dull scales. *'A valuable point. You mean to keep me a secret—even from your forces—until we are near Lorion.'*

"I wonder if that's the cleverest way to ensure victory."

The dragon's wicked grin broadened. *'I like your mind, young duke. Very well, I shall follow at a distance. None shall spot me. But you must be watchful of the Lily Maid. Her dangers may lay closer than we suspect.'*

"Then, you, too, believe she has enemies within this camp." Alain nodded. "I'd be shocked if she didn't. She's bold and unwavering in her convictions. That doesn't win popularity contests, but it does breed lively foes."

'Keep her close.'

"I intend to." Alain bowed his head again. "Will I see you again before Lorion?"

'*Only if the need arises.*' Yenn slithered back into the water until the stream covered all but his head. '*Watch your own back, Duke of Clayre. Many eyes are fixed upon you.*'

"Yeah, I know that, too." He patted his broadsword. "Luckily, I'm a light sleeper and more than a little paranoid." He flashed his own grin at the dragon, then offered a bow before starting back up the hill. Halfway up, he paused and glanced over his shoulder. The dragon had vanished beneath the stream, leaving no trace behind. Mirrasae came up to Alain's side, and they returned to the center of camp. The smell of fresh rain was displaced by the fragrance of the roasting meat.

Turning his plan with Yenn over in his mind, Alain spotted a flaw. He glanced at Mirrasae. "Is riding a dragon difficult? Should I be practicing?"

The unicorn's laughter filled his mind. '*Fear not, Duke of Clayre. Like unicorns, a dragon does not lose his rider—no matter how maladroit they be—unless he desires it.*'

"That's some comfort, I suppose." Alain motioned to the officers' mess tent. "Here's where we part, fair one."

She nodded, then walked toward Jenai's canvas quarters.

Alain ducked into the mess tent, welcoming the warmth that tingled across his sodden limbs. Lanterns lit the interior while four braziers, placed in each corner, chased off the cold. The seasoning of smoked pork teased his nose. The roar of pleasant voices rolled over him; everyone was too busy with their meals to pay him any mind. He moved between the tables, aiming for the thin line of people that led to the tureens of food. He took his place behind a captain, locked his hands behind his back, and soaked in the ambience.

His stomach grumbled. The captain glanced at him, the

hint of a joke on his lips, but he met Alain's gaze, he paled and wheeled back around.

My reputation is worse than I thought.

Alain pushed that down, determined not to let anything spoil his meal. The line moved up, and shortly he was heaping smoked pork, steamed vegetables, and a fat chunk of buttered bread onto his plate. He also snagged a mug of ale. At least rations hadn't reached desperate levels yet, so soon after leaving Shinon, and the cooks appeared eager to use up the fresh goods before they spoiled.

He found a place at a table removed from the other officers, flopped down, and devoured his dinner in short order. The ale washed it all down well, and he shoved back his empty dishes with a satisfied smack of his lips.

"Dessert?"

He craned his head to find Mercer standing behind him, holding a white powder-dusted pastry in each hand. The man offered a smile, then sat across from Alain and proffered one of the delicacies. "Bregger's watching Jenai."

"Where by all the Ilidreth did you come by these?"

"Bakery in Shinon. This morning before the march. Raspberry filling."

Alain munched the pastry happily. "Mmm. I'm impressed they didn't drown in all the rain."

Mercer shrugged. "I know how to protect what matters."

"This is delicious."

The man nodded. "I sent Bregger for them."

"*That* is a clever man, and not one to cross," said Alain.

Mercer grunted his agreement. "He's basically a pirate."

"We'll need that sort before the end, I suspect. Every army does."

Mercer nodded, chewing a bit of pastry. He downed the last bite, dusted off his fingers, then rose. "I've got your back."

He dipped his head, then strode off. Alain watched him go, torn between shock and gratitude.

It seemed he had more allies than he'd thought.

ONE LAST WARNING

At dawn, Jenai was dressed, mounted, and ready for her personal bannerman to unfurl her pennon. The army looked on, awaiting orders. Already, the supply train had broken camp and trundled off along the puddled road.

The rain had stopped sometime during the night. Jenai was grateful for that. According to General Firro, there was still the risk of a washed-out bridge four miles on, but only the one. The scouts had been sent ahead to investigate.

Mercer and Alain, as well as Jenai's pages, stood waiting for her signal to proceed. She surveyed her army once more. The Crane banner was bobbing in a crisp breeze, the golden threads glistening. She nodded. Everything was ready.

The bannerman lifted the lance, and the gold-trimmed pennon unfurled, catching a current of wind. Jenai glanced toward Alain, but she couldn't tell if he was using his magic. She returned her gaze to the banner: three white ember lilies outlined with the first sign of autumn's red were emblazoned on the white field. She hadn't asked for gold trim along the banner's edges, but the seamstress had insisted.

Cheers rose under the sun. General La Resh grunted his

approval while some of the other generals glared at the pennon. Alain flashed Jenai an encouraging smile.

She patted Mirrasae's neck, and the unicorn strode forward a few paces. Clearing her throat, Jenai prepared to address her men. "My soldiers, do not forget that we march first for Afallon and second for our rightful king!"

The cheers crested higher, then rolled back.

"That you follow my banner into battle is not of great significance—it only exists to tell you that, as we enter the fray, I am still upright, protected by heaven!"

More cheers bubbled up, bright and clear. Fists pumped in the air. Jenai smiled, nodding at soldiers whose gazes she met. Soon the noise dulled, and she lifted her hand.

"We still have many days to march but let us use this time to strengthen our allegiance, to Afallon, to crown, to country —and to one another. We're brothers and sisters in this fight. We stand against tyranny and greed. We fight a holy crusade. With that in mind, look inward. What of yourselves do you approve of? What do you wish to shed? Let us use this march to become better, so that heaven may smile down upon us!"

The roar was resounding. Several soldiers traced the sign of Afallon across their chests. Others fell to their knees. Not every face was friendly or reverent. One man spat on the ground. Jenai didn't fault him. She wasn't certain how she would feel in his shoes, had she not heard the Voice for herself. Even her generals doubted her call.

That couldn't matter. She held her hand up one last time.

"We march!"

They fell into line quickly, and a cluster of them started to sing. It was an old battle hymn written by a devout knight, and one of Lucen's favorite songs. Jenai smiled at the memory of her brother, even as the hollow in her heart widened.

Turning to her generals, she said, "Shall we?"

As Mirrasae trotted to the front of the line, Jenai's

attention fell on a group of women beside a colorful wagon to the side of the road. Narrowing her eyes, she turned Mirrasae toward them. Mercer and Alain followed.

"Who are you?" Jenai demanded.

One woman squared her bare shoulders, her colorful apparel ornamented with a bright red shawl. Her brunette hair was loose and flowing. "We're women of the world, Your Holiness." Dipping into a brief curtsey, her lips lifted in a mocking sneer.

"Camp followers," Alain muttered.

"I'd suspected as much." Jenai held the woman's gaze. "If you persist in pursuing this army, I will run you off personally." She set her hand on her sword. "Don't test my honesty."

"We've got a right to the road," a second woman said, shoving her way forward through the bunch.

"So you do, but you don't have a right to stay with the Crane Army. And I will drag you by the hair from my camp *if I must*. I trust I make myself plain."

"We're earning our living," the first woman said.

"Then earn it elsewhere. You will not encourage my men to live in sin."

"Some of the generals won't like that," Alain said.

Jenai smiled coldly. "If the generals insist on these women joining us, then they will do the honorable thing." She nudged Mirrasae. "I mean what I say. Let's go."

She raced to the head of the army, past the singing soldiers, not waiting for Alain or Mercer. When she reached her generals, she eyed them fiercely. Several cowered.

"I requested that all camp followers be sent away," she said.

"We did ask them to leave—" Firro began.

"They obviously didn't listen, so let me be clear: Any

woman found in camp soliciting men will be thrown out. If *you* wish her to stay, *you* will marry her. Is this understood?"

Several jaws slackened. La Resh burst out laughing. Firro nodded solemnly.

"The men need—" Kirio began.

"This is a holy army. What the men *need* will wait for leave. Not before. Is that understood? If we're not disciplined enough to forgo our own lusts for the duration of a few weeks, then we are no better than a pig in his trough."

"Says the virgin," growled Teeg.

Jenai narrowed a look on him. "Aye, so she does. If you don't like the way I lead, feel free to write to His Royal Highness. Perhaps Prince Chartan will be interested in your love life. Or if you'd rather, you may write to the church. The priests will *certainly* take an interest."

La Resh hooted, slapping his cuisse. Metal on metal pealed over the air. "This one has a *spine*, she does! I like you, lass. Don't agree with you, mind. To be frank, men aren't much different than pigs, anyhow—but your spirit's bright and glorious to behold, and these men are fools if they don't see the hand of heaven in your design. What a woman!"

Jenai blushed, unsure whether to take his words as praise or condemnation. Breathing deeply, she managed a slight smile. "I appreciate your honesty, General La Resh—far more than a friendly smile that may hide a treacherous heart. Afallon keep you." She allowed Mirrasae to carry her ahead of her generals, glad that Mercer and Alain fell in between them.

"You truly know how to shake things up, Lily Maid," Alain said.

Mercer grunted agreement.

Though she was startled by the new title, she kept her peace.

THE ULTIMATUM

D inner was done, the evening prayers were finished, and a general quiet had fallen over the camp. Alain strode through the fog, whistling softly, lest a sentry take him for an enemy. He couldn't sleep. In the damp and darkness, his dreams were plagued by the Crow's dungeon. Better to walk all night to shake off the memories than succumb to them.

He'd already paced the entire camp one way and was heading the other way now. It was going to be a long night.

Passing tents, the soft murmurs of soldiers swirled through the fog, lending a haunted air to Alain's passage. He felt like a wraith, crossing paths with the living, drinking in their souls. Somehow, that made him crack a smile.

What a morbid thought. I really do need to get over myself. Since when have I relished melodrama?

Someone screamed. It came from the center of camp.

Jenai!

Unsheathing his blade, Alain raced toward the noise while others shouted in alarm. Men scurried from their tents at his back. Alain jumped over a shallow pit in the ground, careened around a corner—and came up short. Jenai stood in her armor in front of General Teeg's quarters, her sword drawn. Before her, the general stood in only his breeches just outside his tent, with his arms outstretched in defense. Behind him in the cold night air, a woman cowered, sobbing into his bare shoulder blade.

"I will not ask you again," Jenai said in commanding tones. "Either you will escort her from camp, or I will."

Alain stood frozen, trying to grasp the situation. It looked almost ludicrous. Jenai was a tall woman but compared to Teeg she was a reed. Yet the general looked terrified, and Alain couldn't blame him. There was something in the way Jenai stood—a kind of power in her posture. She held her sword as though she'd wielded one since birth. Even her hair, loose and billowing in the night winds, cast a kind of influence over the scene. She was otherworldly, but not like a wraith at all. She was a war angel, channeling the wrath of heaven.

She's magnificent.

Drawing himself up, Alain strode forward, sheathing his sword. "General Teeg, I'd do as she says—unless you truly want to marry the harlot."

Teeg glanced at him, scowling. "And if I do?"

"Then I'll find the chaplain to officiate." Alain stopped behind Jenai, giving her center stage. She'd earned it.

"What do you say, Charine?" asked Teeg. "Want to tie the knot?"

"You...want me to...marry you?" The woman peeped over his shoulder and stared at him like he'd gone mad.

"Why not? Bachelorhood has grown old. You're pretty enough. I think I might even have fallen in love with you over these past three years."

Clutching her shawl close, Charine stepped forward, splashing through a puddle, and circled to face him. "You love me?"

Teeg nodded curtly. She let out a squeak and threw herself into his arms, showering him with kisses. Alain grimaced, not as charmed by the man's supposed confession as the woman was, but he said nothing. To each their own taste.

Jenai turned to Alain. "Will you find that chaplain?"

"Surely."

Off he went, hoping that this wasn't a mistake. To swine like Teeg, nothing hurt a woman's value so swiftly as compulsory wedlock. But maybe Charine had the grit to make it work. Using the strictest threats, Alain's mother had warned him to avoid the company of prostitutes, so the duke had little experience with camp followers, but he respected their tenacity.

He returned to camp central with the sleepy chaplain and witnessed the slipshod ceremony between the two mismatched people. After that, Teeg swept Charine off her feet and into his tent—the woman giggling like a milkmaid— and the chaplain went back to his own sleeping quarters. The other generals slinked into their tents, apparently less eager than their comrade to partake of marital bliss. Jenai and Alain soon stood alone.

He stepped to her side, leaned toward her, and studied her expression. She was smiling.

"Happy?" he asked.

She turned, blinking at him. "Oh, Alain. Yes. Yes, I think I am."

"Why?" He couldn't hide his surprise. How she could find that match-up anything but off kilter, he'd never know.

Jenai nodded to Teeg's tent. "I chased off several other women tonight trying to beseech the men. One look at my sword and they scattered."

"Can't blame them," Alain said, eyeing the legendary weapon clutched in her hand.

She followed his gaze, and her smile widened. She twisted

the sword in her grip. The hilt caught a flash of torchlight and glinted. "It's not that I blame the women for trying to earn a living. The way Fraelin is right now, we must all make decisions we might not consider in a better world. Some of those women are heinous, others aren't. But Charine...she stayed. Even though she was afraid. I saw why at once. She's in love."

"She's a fool," Alain replied.

"Maybe. Or maybe people who *aren't* in love are the fools."

"But Teeg is..." Alain tried to find a strong word for the man that Jenai wouldn't consider offensive. "Well, he's a pig."

She laughed. "Possibly. But he protected her—and that says something. He could've sent her away. He didn't *need* to wed her."

Alain chewed on that. "I suppose this old world is full of all kinds, and somehow or other, the human race must go on."

Laughing softly, Jenai set her hand on his arm. "I see who you really are, Alain—an idealist."

"Am I?"

"Oh, yes." Her eyes danced with firelight. "Goodnight, Alain. Try to sleep now." She turned and walked gracefully back to her tent, leaving him in the swirling fog.

How had she known he couldn't sleep?

Do I look so bad as that?

He smiled, shook his head, and turned to find his tent. Now, full of Jenai's light and warmth, maybe he could sleep. She was so ethereal. Maybe Afallon really had called her to fight for Fraelin—and maybe, in some small way, she was fighting for Alain, too.

UNREST

Ten miles out from Bloss, at the end of the day's long march, Jenai remained in her armor and asked Mercer to join her in the evening for another camp inspection. She intended to keep a vigilant watch on everything, to make certain there was no bullying or unrest that could lead to injury.

As they started down the first row of tents, Alain appeared without a word and took his place at Jenai's right side. Mercer nodded to him. Jenai lifted her eyebrows, and Alain shrugged.

"Hope you don't mind," said the duke. "I'm looking for someone. I never had any luck in Shinon, but we've picked up a few recruits yesterday and today, so I thought I'd search again."

"You're welcome here," she replied.

There was a trace of some emotion in Alain's expression, though Jenai couldn't tell if it was pain or relief. He looked away too quickly to probe.

Most soldiers were already in their tents, resting for tomorrow's march, but few were sleeping. Nearing Bloss, where supplies and more recruits awaited, their excitement was palpable. Their murmurs were a steady hum as Jenai strode down the rows. Captains and other officers, not yet retired, saluted her in passing. Near the end of the third row, a sergeant spat on the ground near Alain's boot.

Jenai halted, turned, and stared the man down. "Was that an accident, soldier?"

"Er, yes, my lady." The man colored. "Just some turnip caught in my throat. H-had to get it out. Unfortunate accident."

Alain exhaled through his nose. "It's fine, General. I'm sure that's all it was."

Jenai stepped closer to the sergeant. Their eyes met. "I will choose to believe you, and I truly hope you've not lied to me. I can't tell the difference, but Afallon knows all. Whatever our disparities, we're serving the same cause."

"Y-yes, General—sir—ma'am." The sergeant bowed his head, snapped off a salute, then scrambled away with a hurried excuse.

Alain's hand fell on her gardbrace. "I'm used to it by now, Jenai. Forget it."

"No." She whirled and started for the next row, bristling. She'd prepared herself to handle the prejudice and disdain aimed at her, but it was something else to witness the disrespect Alain faced daily. "Who are you looking for, Alain? Mercer and I can help."

The two men hurried to catch up to her.

"He's a new recruit," Alain explained. "I heard an old woman's petition and promised her I'd try to find her grandson. He's all the kin she has. I can't send him home, of course, but I want to take him underwing as my aide, and perhaps keep him from any real fighting."

"He won't thank you for that," Mercer commented.

"Don't I know it." Alain grimaced.

"But you have no idea where he is?" the knight asked.

"I know his name and city of origin," Alain said. "I did ask Lieutenant-General Kirio for help, but he couldn't—"

"He refused to assist?" Jenai finished.

"Well...yes."

Jenai turned to face Alain, wrath coiling inside her. "All this over your magic use? Surely others in this force-of-arms are also elemental mages."

Mercer coughed into his hand, drawing Jenai's gaze.

"You have a comment, Sir Knight?"

Mercer shot Alain an apologetic look, then nodded. "Magic usery is bad enough. Few would reveal their element in the present public climate. But that's not His Grace's only alleged defect."

"I'd prefer not to speak about it if it's all the same to you." Alain kept his gaze averted.

Jenai's wrath quieted under a surge of compassion. "If it brings you too much pain, I will drop the matter this moment."

He only nodded, his brow knitted.

Drawing closer, she rested her hand on his forearm. "I only wish to help."

Bitterness edged his mouth. "Not even Afallon's Holy General can work such a miracle as that. Please let it be, Jenai. I'm quite used to public censure by now."

She almost argued. He was obviously *not* used to it, or the pain wouldn't be so vibrant. But she understood not wanting to discuss one's deepest pains. Removing her hand, she nodded. "Give me the information you seek about the woman's grandson. Mercer and I will investigate. If he's here, he'll be sent to you as your aide. If he's in Bloss, we'll discover his whereabouts tomorrow. All right?"

"Thank you." He held out a slip of paper. "His name is

here, along with his grandmother's name and their village of origin."

Jenai hesitated, but Mercer took the paper. She relaxed. She'd asked her pages to stay behind and handle answering the missives she'd received from Bloss, but thinking back, she should've kept one of the boys close for just this sort of thing. Thank the saints she still had Mercer.

"Go and rest," Jenai told Alain with firmness.

He started off, shoulders slumped. Jenai watched his retreat, then nodded to Mercer. They continued along the rows, stopping at each platoon leader's tent to ask after the young man in question. No one knew him.

Two rows from the end, near the edge of camp, Jenai stopped to speak with the captain of the seventh platoon. The moon had risen high, and the last tatters of sunset clung to the purple horizon. The captain reported that an altercation had broken out before dinner, and he insisted on disciplining every man under his command to teach them a lesson. As Jenai asked for details regarding the altercation, a booming voice called out.

"If it isn't the Crane Maiden herself!"

A smile caught Jenai's lips. She turned toward the hunter. "Hail, Tullo. You wouldn't happen to be responsible for the fight that broke out?"

The brawny man from the road to the Church of Saint Cethera grinned. "Not I."

"Tullo is my second," the captain said. "He's the one who stopped the altercation. Stepped right in and rammed those meaty fists against several thick skulls. One young soldier ran scared. We haven't caught him yet."

Tullo shrugged. "Just a bunch of over-eager lads getting too emotional about things they don't understand. Figured a knock on the head would rattle the sense back in place."

"What caused the altercation, exactly?" Mercer asked.

The captain and Tullo shared a look.

"It was about me," Jenai said, letting none of her discomfort show. Of course, not every soldier would rally to her without questioning her cause.

"That's true," Tullo admitted. "One lad dared to suggest you were merely the prince's pawn, paid to pretend you can hear Divine Afallon's voice in order to send us to our deaths. Another lad was quick to defend your honor."

"That's why I want to discipline my whole platoon," the captain said. "It will keep other lads from getting hotheaded or letting their tongues wag idly."

"I don't agree," Jenai said. "Only discipline those who engaged in the fight—"

"That would be nearly half the platoon," Tullo said.

Jenai fell still. "Do you mean..."

"I'm guessing they all came to your defense against the naysayer," Mercer answered.

"Right." The captain shrugged. "I must do something."

"Then punish the first two lads," Jenai said, "but not harshly. It's a first offense for each, right?"

"Under my command, yes."

"If they fight again, deliver a harsher punishment—and warn your platoon that anyone who participates will receive the same treatment. Is that fair?"

The captain nodded. "It is, yes, Lady General."

"Good." Weariness stole through her, weighing her down. "Before I leave you, do you have a lad in your company by the name of Tristel?"

The captain stiffened. "Aye, Lady General. That would be the troublemaker."

Jenai stared at him. "From the village of Leyn?"

"Aye."

She glanced at Mercer who wore the hint of a dry smile.

"I think we can take him off your hands," the knight said.

"The Duke of Clayre has been looking for him. He wants to make him his aide."

Tullo snorted. "That's exactly what the lad needs. I'd send him, Captain."

The captain nodded. "I'll deliver him to the duke at first light."

"Don't bother. I'll collect him for you," Mercer said. "I'd like to see how the duke handles the lad."

Tullo and the captain grunted their agreement.

"Thank you all," Jenai said. "If that's everything, I think I'll retire early tonight. It was good to see you, Tullo."

The hunter bowed. "And you, Crane Maiden."

She and Mercer moved on, and Jenai's thoughts turned inward. The long march was grueling enough without the added burden of command, the worry about what lay beyond Bloss, and the tension of troops divided on the subject of her.

I begin to understand Alain's isolation.

Being a woman without combat experience, striding through man's province in full armor, she'd anticipated standing out. But nothing, not even Afallon's Voice, could prepare her for how it felt.

Buoy me up. Keep me strong.

Jenai and Mercer reached the southern end of the encampment where a clear path cut diagonally through the tents to the command center. Three figures stepped in front of them, the lower half of their faces covered by kerchiefs. The strangers brandished swords in the moonlight.

Hand on his sword, Mercer stepped in front of Jenai. "If you have business with the General, I'd reconsider."

The evening was quiet but for the murmur of soldiers' voices inside their tents and the distant music of the relentless camp followers. Jenai would need to chase the women off again. The crunch of boots on grit brought her head around. Four more men closed in on her and the knight, cutting off their retreat.

"Mercer."

He glanced behind him and swore under his breath. "Forgive me, Jenai. This will get messy." He drew his sword.

"Nothing to forgive. Do what you must." She turned back to the three men in front of her. "Before I unleash my knight upon you, I urge you to stand down. I would prefer no lives were lost senselessly."

One of the men chortled. "Is that a prediction, O great prophetess?"

Jenai's eyes narrowed but she said nothing.

The men inched closer.

Mercer adjusted his sword grip. "One more step and I will strike."

A breeze played with Jenai's short ponytail. She'd left her sword in her quarters, relieving herself of its weight at the end of the long day's ride. Casting around the ground, she found no other form of weapon.

"NOW!" shouted one of the strangers.

The three men sprang at Mercer. The knight moved like lightning, cutting off the path of two men with his sword, then pivoting to catch the third. That man fell with a cry, blood spewing from his neck. The first two men tried to attack again, swords flashing. Mercer caught one blade with his own and kicked out, throwing the other man to his back.

Jenai wheeled. The four men jumped her. Weighed down in her armor, she fell with a clang. Dirt powdered the air before her.

Hands groped for the latches of her breastplate, and fear like cold fingers stole down her spine.

"Don't do this!" she cried.

A man straddled her legs. "Help me, Koyte. Let's expose this witch!" His breath was hot on her face.

Panic clawed at Jenai's mind. Someone screamed. Was that Mercer? Had he fallen? Was she alone?

Call for help! Let someone know! Fight!

She wrestled to break free, but more hands held her down. They unlatched the breastplate. Fingers brushed against her inner thigh where the cuisse didn't cover her leg.

"Afallon, protect me!" she cried.

The breeze brushed her cheek, then rose in a shrieking wind. The man pinning her down yelped and fell backward, knocked aside by an invisible hand. Other shouts rose, but the wind drowned out the noise—then fell silent.

More voices approached. Hands reached for her. Jenai flinched, turning onto her side to escape. She groped for purchase, her gauntlets digging into the earth.

"Relax, Jenai. It's me! Jenai!"

That voice—she knew that voice! Jenai rolled over. Alain knelt beside her. Mercer stood behind him. Several other soldiers looked on as well. She was encircled by allies.

"You're safe now," Alain whispered. "Five of your attackers are dead. The last two are in custody. You're safe."

He helped Jenai to sit up. She still had her breastplate on, though several latches were undone. They hadn't hurt her. She drew several breaths, severing the last threads of panic woven around her heart, then she met Alain's dark eyes. "Will you help me to my quarters?"

Wrapping his arm around her waist, he lifted her to her feet. Jenai steadied herself. A cold tangle of nausea pressed behind her ribs. Swallowing hard, she moved toward the center of camp. Alain and Mercer followed, though none of the others did.

"I'm sorry I didn't arrive sooner," Alain whispered.

"You came in time." Her voice was faint even in her own ears.

"Barely." He stared ahead, shadows deep beneath his eyes.

"It was enough," Mercer chimed in.

They reached Jenai's tent what seemed like an age later. At the flap, she turned to her protectors and offered a tight smile. "Tryla will help me from here. I'm deeply grateful for your aid this night."

"It's our honor," Mercer said.

"And our job." Alain's smile looked tight. "Going forward, I don't think you should walk anywhere without both of us in tow—unless it's with a full complement of soldiers. And guards handpicked by Mercer will be posted around your tent at night. Does that sound good?"

She nodded. "It seems sensible. Thank you again. Goodnight."

Jenai slipped inside before she let the tears fall down her cheeks, smearing the dirt on her face.

WITH A CRY, JENAI SAT UP IN BED, TREMBLING. SWEAT rolled down her back. She pressed her palms to her face, fighting back tears. Another bad dream, every time she closed her eyes. The attack from hours before felt surreal now, yet the hot breath on her face and the brush of fingers against her thigh left her reeling.

Breathe. You're safe. Alain and Mercer are nearby.

A gentle hand brushed Jenai's arm. With a yelp, she whirled to fend off her attacker—then halted, staring into Aveyal's silver eyes. The Ilidreth girl rested a finger to her lips, then motioned. "Come with me." Her voice was a faint whisper.

Jenai slipped from her cot, threw a robe on over her shift, then followed the girl, who moved slowly on a pair of crutches to the door flap. They stepped out into the midnight air. Stars winked overhead. Mist curled around their ankles.

Before them stood Mirrasae, a beacon even in the mist. Clarity filled Jenai up, banishing the claws from her dreams. She reached out, and the unicorn drew closer. Wrapping her arms around Mirrasae, Jenai drank in the sweet fragrance of her ethereal friend.

"Fear not, Jenai," the unicorn said in her fluting voice. *"You shall be safe this night against all comers."*

A sob escaped Jenai's lips. She tightened her embrace. "Thank you, Mirrasae." Cracking her eyes open, she sought Aveyal in the darkness. The Ilidreth girl looked wraithlike beside the unicorn's beacon glow. Jenai's gaze met Aveyal's. "Thank you, my friend."

The girl nodded, and the edges of her mouth curled upward. "You ride a unicorn, therefore I can trust you. You also saved my life, and I am in your debt."

"Afallon brought our paths together," Jenai whispered, stroking Mirrasae's cool coat. "We are all in *His* debt."

HARDTACK

Alain slipped from his tent and winced in the morning light. The summer day promised to be hot, and the idea of wearing armor under the grueling sun, cooking by slow degrees, was unpleasant to contemplate.

"Good morning, Your Grace."

Alain squinted to find Mercer through his blurry vision. The knight stood beside a lad of about seventeen years. The young soldier scowled at Alain, showing no regard for his title or rank.

"I think we found what you were seeking," Mercer said.

After the attack on Jenai, Alain had been too agitated to sleep well. Realization dawned like a winter sunrise, slow and dim. "What I—oh. You're Tristel? Evella's grandson?"

The lad's scowl deepened. "And if I am? Sending me home, are you?"

Mercer clapped his hand on Tristel's shoulder. "Add 'sir' or 'Your Grace' to the end of your next sentence. Yes?"

Fear flashed across Tristel's face. "Y-yes, sir."

Alain rubbed his scar, pushing himself to think clearly. "No, Tristel, I'm not sending you home. I don't have the authority—or, frankly, the desire. We need all the able-bodied soldiers we can dig up. Do you have any experience with a sword?"

"I..." Tristel wilted like a spring bloom at summer's first heat. "No. Sir."

"That's fine. I'll train you myself"—Alain smiled as Tristel perked up—"and in the meantime you'll be my aide. Is that acceptable?"

"Yes, sir. Your Grace. Gladly!"

"There's one more thing you should know, Your Grace," Mercer said. "Private Tristel hasn't been the most exemplary soldier since his arrival. According to his past *three* superior officers in his short tenure, he's started at least four altercations and finished two more. He also has no regard for General Jenai. His being sent to you is punishment for his actions last night."

Alain narrowed a hard look on the lad. "These are serious offenses in an army, Tristel, and unbecoming in a proper soldier. I could horsewhip you for any one of these accusations. The combination of them can eject you from the Crane Army at best, and court martial you at worst. You would return to your village in disgrace, and the only person who would deign to look at you would be your precious Grandmama. Do you understand the seriousness of what I'm saying?"

Tristel looked ready to argue. Alain held up his hand.

"Spare me the excuses. Those are for children. Do you understand what I'm saying, Private Tristel?"

The hard exterior cracked. Tristel's shoulders sank. "Yes, sir. Am I being ejected?"

"No. Not yet."

The lad tensed.

"I'm giving you one chance to prove to me that you're a man. In order to do this, you'll serve as my aide without complaint and without causing *any* issues. You will also show the Crane Maiden—as well as every other officer here—all possible respect. And if I hear one *hint* of your personal opinion of General Jenai—if I catch a whiff of any private disdain on your part—I'll whip you myself and leave you for the carrion birds. Is that understood?"

Tristel snapped off a smart salute. "Sir, yes, sir!"

"Very good." Alain grinned at Mercer. "I've got this from here, Sir Knight. Thank you for finding him."

A wicked gleam sparked in Mercer's eye. "It's my pleasure, Lieutenant-General. I look forward to witnessing Tristel's further education." He bowed his head, then strode off toward Jenai's tent a few spaces down.

Alain turned back to Tristel. "You'll start by bringing me breakfast and packing up my belongings. Then see to my horse. He's the dappled gelding nearest to the water trough. After that, you'll gather your own gear for my inspection. Look smart, private!"

Tristel raced to the mess tent, and Alain allowed himself a chuckle. In his past years of fighting, he'd rarely run into any truly heinous young soldiers, just undisciplined youths, and those could be reformed with proper doses of correction and the promise of respect. No one wanted to stay a boy forever.

Ducking back inside his tent, Alain washed and dressed himself. Then he slipped over to Jenai's tent where Mercer stood outside waiting.

"Any word on how our Lily Maid is today?" Alain asked.

The knight shook his head. "Despite how shaken she was, she handled last night with the grace of a saint."

"I'm beginning to suspect she's exactly that," Alain murmured.

"In the making, perhaps," Mercer replied.

Motion down the aisle between tents caught Alain's eye. He recognized Jenai's handmaiden—Tryla wasn't it?—coming toward them with a bucket of water in hand. Beside her, toting a pair of crutches, was a young girl with dark hair tied under a kerchief. Alain's eyes narrowed. He knew that girl.

"Greetings, my lords," Tryla said cheerily as she approached.

"I'm not a lord," Mercer said. "Just a 'sir'."

Tryla shrugged that off. "If you're wanting to meet with the Lady General, she's not here. She wanted time alone." Jutting her chin toward a copse of trees removed from camp, Tryla added, "I'd not disturb her if I were you, my lords. She's praying."

Mercer grimaced while Alain sighed.

"She's not to go off alone," the duke said.

"She says she's never alone," Tryla answered.

"But after last night—" Alain began.

"After a good night's rest, she looks much better. And her valiant steed is with her. Begging your pardon, but don't fret so, Your Grace. Afallon truly abides with her."

Sighing again, Alain snatched a handful of wind and sent it into the trees to keep a watch on the reckless young woman, despite the unicorn's presence. He'd done the same last night after he'd reached his tent, following a gut instinct, and that was how he'd been alerted to the assault. The stone dragon had been right: Enemies existed within the camp.

Alain turned to Mercer. "Any word on who the attackers were?"

"A few disgruntled soldiers who thought they'd expose the lady as a witch or a fraud, and maybe have a little sport meanwhile. They wanted an excuse to forgo the siege at Lorion, I think."

"Vile cowards." Alain glowered at the copse. "Do they *want* to become slaves to Simaerin?"

"Men like that don't think far ahead. They only consider today—tomorrow will care for itself."

"Vile cowards and fools." Shaking off his anger, Alain excused himself and returned to his tent where Tristel stood waiting with a tray of hardtack and boiled gruel. Eyeing the fare, Alain almost told Tristel to send it back—but five years in a dungeon made it hard to pass on any food. He took it, slipped inside his tent, and sat down to eat. Last night had proven to him that he needed to stay alert and maintain his strength. Jenai wasn't just stirring up hearts—she was stirring up devils.

APPROACHING THE BATTLE

They reached Bloss on schedule and resupplied. Despite La Resh's threat of squeezing the city for food and weaponry, Bloss opened its arms to Jenai, offering whatever she needed.

Twenty-four hours later, the army moved on with seven hundred additional recruits—more than expected.

Another week and a half's march brought them without incident to the banks of the wide, lazy Lué River. On the far side of the water, Jenai studied the fortress where Count Duron held off the Thargundian invaders. An army camp of loyal Fraeli sprawled across the green. On this side, signs of battle scarred the ground. Trees and brambles lay broken, and the smoldering remnants of cannon fire declared the battle a recent one.

"Looks like the honorable Count Duron Whoreson has been busy," remarked Kirio.

Jenai shot him a sharp look. "You will show the count proper respect."

Kirio flushed. "It's—it's what everyone calls him, General Jenai."

"That's true," Teeg jumped in. "If anything, it's disrespectful to his late unfaithful mother."

Jenai grimaced and turned back to the fortress. "How near are the Thargundians?"

"They'll be on the far side of the count's estate in one of their blasted forts, unless Count Duron drove them back to Lorion."

"Where is Lorion?" asked Jenai.

Firro nudged his stallion closer. "If we continued up this road, it would curve around to a bridge. On the other side of the Lué is the watch town of Lué-de-Trul, which the count holds. Three miles further stands Lorion's walls."

Jenai smiled. "Lué-de-Trul. Troll of the Sands, isn't it?"

"You speak High Frael?" Alain looked impressed.

"Very little," Jenai admitted. "The priest in Domrem was fond of teaching the children what he knew of the old tongue. Mostly, we learned fae terms, like trul for troll, epian for fairy, and dreyvio for the Ilidreth."

Kirio traced a hasty warding sign in the air. "Best not to speak of the Forest Folk using High Frael, my lady. It might summon them."

"Craven cur," growled La Resh. "I'd welcome a band of those foul creatures to ride out and meet us if only to alleviate my boredom!"

"Check yourself, General La Resh," Jenai said. "The Ilidreth are not our enemies." She scanned the road ahead. "We will camp here. We must contact Count Duron and see if he will meet us ahead of the siege of Lorion. I would also like to issue a formal demand of surrender to Duke Kon of Thargundy. I would prefer to avoid bloodshed if he will heed Afallon's will."

Doubtless, news of the Crane Army's approach had reached the captured city, and the element of surprise was no longer necessary to maintain. She ignored the generals' looks of skepticism. She knew her attempt to avoid combat would likely fail, but if she didn't try all the same, she was as guilty of murder as any Thargundian traitor.

Turning Mirrasae around, Jenai rode toward the supply train which awaited orders to the side of the wide highway. Alain and Mercer followed. Since the assault over a week ago, they were never far behind her. Bregger was likely somewhere close by too.

As she approached the wagons, the supply captain saluted, and Jenai commanded him to set up camp just outside the area of recent slaughter. She then moved to the wagon where Tryla and Aveyal sat waiting.

The Ilidreth girl had been transformed beyond recognition, just as Tryla had promised. Her silver tresses were coal-black, and she wore a light gray peasant dress and matching scarf to hide her pointed ears. Her leg was still mending, but the girl got around well on her crutches.

"How do you feel today?" Jenai asked the Ilidreth girl.

Smiling shyly, Aveyal dipped her head. "Well enough, Honored Lady."

Tryla beamed at her charge like a proud mother. "She'll be fully mended in no time, make no mistake, my lady."

"Glad I am to hear it."

Alain cleared his throat. Jenai glanced at him, and he tipped his head to one side, requesting an audience away from any prying ears. She nodded, then turned back to Tryla. "We'll set up camp over there in the plains. There's fresh water, so make certain you both bathe."

"Do we attack Lorion today, my lady?" Fear brightened Tryla's green eyes.

"No. First, I must sue for peace." She motioned for Mercer to remain with the wagon, then followed Alain to the burnt husk of an elm tree.

"What is it?" she asked.

"Two things. Firstly, why is the Ilidreth traveling with us?"

Jenai stiffened. He'd noticed her despite the disguise? Alain had sharper eyes than she'd thought. "I couldn't leave her in Shinon to be discovered and burned alive. She's a child."

Alain grimaced. "Never mind what she is. How is this a safer place for her?"

"I'm with her, and Tryla loves the girl."

"Tryla is a handmaiden—not a competent soldier."

"Don't be so quick to dismiss the skills of an accomplished handmaiden," Jenai said gently. "She must protect herself in ways you may not dream of."

He hesitated. "Fair enough, but it's still a great risk."

"We're at war. Everything is a risk."

Again, he hesitated. "Very well, I'll move on to my second order of business." He glanced back at the wagon. Mercer watched them, but everyone else was bustling to set up tents in the tall grass. "There's a secret I've been keeping—"

She raised her hand. "Don't tell me."

"But—"

"The Voice informed me that you had a plan, and commanded that you keep it to yourself, whatever it is."

"But, Jenai—"

She smiled. "I will fight this war in my way, and you will fight in yours. Do what you must. I trust you."

"But why—"

"Because Afallon trusts you, Alain, and that's enough for me. I don't ask why. I only do the will of heaven." She patted Mirrasae's neck, and the unicorn trotted off to see to the arrangement of Jenai's quarters. It took only a moment for Mercer and Alain to catch up.

Night fell. The communiqués to Count Duron Whoreson and Duke Kon Dragonclaw were sent. Jenai stood outside her tent, listening to the song of the crickets and the hoots of an owl. Within her private quarters, Tryla was singing a folk song from her homeland while she brushed young Aveyal's hair. They'd spent the evening washing up, and the Ilidreth would need to have her locks dyed again.

Campfires dotted the field, and voices rose and fell in excited anticipation of the coming siege. The generals were gathered together, discussing possible strategies to lay before Jenai in the morning. Mercer lurked nearby, watching over Jenai, but Alain was nowhere to be found.

She found she missed the duke's company. He was steady and alert, always ready to listen and to offer up a new perspective. Surrounded though she was by soldiers, she felt alone. Alain understood that. He was isolated as well.

Thank Afallon for Mercer, with his solid constancy. She glanced at him. "Are you ready for our fight to begin?"

Mercer took a step closer to her. "I've been ready for years, my lady."

"We've been through a lot together, in a very short time, you and I—and Bregger, wherever he is."

"Likely stealing chickens from some nearby farm," Mercer said.

She sighed. "Likely." She lifted her gaze to the heavens. "Do you trust more in Afallon now?"

"Yes. You've restored my faith."

"How could *I* achieve such a marvel? You alone dictate to your heart."

"Some of us may blindly lead, Jenai. Most of us must follow blindly instead. You're the fixed star of my faith, and I will follow you, always." He swept into a bow, then rose with a quiet smile.

She set her hand on his shoulder. "Your loyalty

strengthens me, Mercer. Thank you. I'll need it in the coming battle."

WITH THE DAWN, THE DUKE OF THARGUNDY'S REPLY TO the Maiden of Lorrae arrived.

> *To Jenai d'Arc, Imposter & Heretic:*
> *I do not acknowledge your claim as commander of Fraelin's army, first because no such army exists, and second because no woman will ever wield the banner that drives me from my stronghold. I would not surrender my place here to Afallon Himself—and to you, deceitful maid, I say blasphemy for using His name! Begone from this plain. Take your sticks and your wooden soldiers and depart—or rot in the waiting for these great walls to crumble.*
> *So sworn,*
> *Duke Kon Dragonclaw of Thargundy,*
> *Defender of the Faith, Heir to Fraelin, Friend to the Crow of Simaerin.*

Jenai asked one of her pages—the boy called Lio—to read the letter twice. Flames blazed in her stomach. She stood all at once. "Tryla, help me don my armor. We march for Lorion this day. Lio, gather my generals."

Lio was off like a flash to deliver the order, but he came back amid Tryla's preparations to dress Jenai. The page clutched a second missive, this one tied in a scroll.

"It's from the Blackguard of Lorion himself."

From Count Duron? Jenai nodded for him to read it before stepping behind a screen to let Tryla dress her.

Lio unrolled the missive and read:

> To the Lady General,
> I've heard of your daring-do in Shinon and commend you for your good showing. That you've mobilized the Crane Army does you credit. I will take over from here and lead His Royal Highness's force against Lorion, as is my sworn duty. Stand down. Return to your fields, gentle soul, and let men soil their souls in the bloody fight ahead.
> Afallon save this good and ancient land.
> Yours in the Faith,
> Count Duron Whoreson, Blackguard of Lorion.

Lio looked up with a sour expression. "Why don't they believe you were sent by Afallon?"

"The answer to that lies within their hearts alone." Jenai stepped around the screen, wearing her padded gambeson. Tryla picked up the pieces of armor, one by one, to attach them in the right places. The page hurried across the tent to bring Jenai's sheathed sword from its place on a wooden stand. He held it reverently.

From outside, Aveyal came hobbling in on one crutch, holding a plate of food, with the second page—named Mattis —walking at her side to help. Aveyal's scarf was askew but still hid her Ilidreth ears. Lio glanced at her and blushed. Jenai hid a smile. The Ilidreth girl was beautiful in a youthful way, with her angular features and almond eyes. She would turn many young heads among the pages and squires.

Turning to Lio, Jenai motioned to the door flap. "Go and tell the generals we leave within the hour. Tell them the Duke of Thargundy is a fool and must learn his lesson soon."

"What should I say about the Blackguard's reply?" asked Lio.

"I will handle that."

The page set the sword down on the cot, then rushed off, skipping around Aveyal with a shy smile. The fae girl offered Lio a grim stare. Mattis rolled his eyes, then carefully moved to set the plate of eggs and smoked pork on the cot.

"General," Mattis said, "I regret to report that your horse has slipped her rope again. I don't know how. I tied the knot myself after the last time, and no horse has ever slipped that before."

Jenai suppressed a faint smile. "No matter, Mattis. She'll return, as she always does."

Mattis sighed and nodded.

"Will the camp remain here during the siege?" asked Tryla.

"Yes. Lorion is only a few miles off. Best to keep our supplies away from the walls."

Tryla stepped back, examining her work. "All done, my lady."

"Thank you. Please hand me my sword."

Aveyal danced with surprising agility around Tryla, caught up the sword, and offered it to Jenai who smiled.

"Thank you, my young friend."

The girl nodded. "May the safety of the Vales accompany you, Lady of the Ember Lilies."

Surprised by the title, Jenai rested the sword against her breastplate. "I pray that they will, thank you." She strapped on her sword and left the tent, Mattis at her side. Mercer and Alain flanked her. She glanced at each of them. Their expressions were grave. They had likely heard every word of the messages sent from two powerful men.

"Are you afraid?" asked Alain halfway to the pavilion where the generals were assembled, waiting.

"No," Jenai said, surprised by her steady answer. Setting her shoulders, she continued: "Afallon rides with us. Are you afraid, Alain?"

"Not yet. That usually comes later."

Mercer grunted his agreement.

She nodded, glad she wasn't alone in the strange place she walked between fear and confidence. This battle wasn't up to her. Only Afallon knew the outcome.

They neared the pavilion under a bright blue sky. Already the day was warming.

"What did the Blackguard say?" asked Teeg before Jenai had even reached the table. He adjusted his eyepatch. "We saw his messenger crossing the Lué."

"He'll join us in combat," Jenai answered, then turned to the maps. "As for Duke Kon—"

"The page read his disgusting sentiments," Firro piped up. "That man always was an insufferable fool, just like his father."

"Let's pray that's the case," said Alain. "It's easier to win against a fool."

The generals grunted agreement.

"Are we really marching today?" asked Kirio.

"Of course." La Resh slapped the table. "If we don't besiege Lorion, there's no point in any of this."

"Doesn't sound like Kon intends to flee," Bastin said. "We might be able to sneak in and cut his throat. That would save time and resources."

"The attempt would fail." Jenai looked around at her men. "Afallon has told me how to take Lorion, and we will follow His Voice. There will be no deviations."

Doubt burned in most of their eyes—even La Resh's—but they nodded and murmured assent.

Jenai waved at the map. "We must besiege Lorion as discussed. Let us brook no more delays. I already tire of Kon's arrogance." More grunts of agreement. "Assemble the men. We move out at once."

'At once' was always slow when four-thousand soldiers were involved, but they gathered with more efficiency than usual that day. Mounted upon Mirrasae, Jenai measured the troops while the bannermen on horseback held the Crane banner and Ember Lily pennon with pride. The chaplain took his place and offered up a prayer of protection, then Jenai drew a deep breath to speak.

"Soldiers of Fraelin, take courage! We fight for our homes, our honor, and our liberty!" She held out her hand, accepted her pennon from the bannerman at her left, and held it as high as she could.

The army roared, pounding feet, lifting swords. Startled, ducks in the shallows of the Lué took flight.

"We march on Lorion!" She returned the pennon to the bannerman and wheeled to face the road leading toward their destination. Alain, Mercer, and Bregger flanked her.

To herself she whispered: "Afallon guide me."

ONE ARROW

The morning sun was bright and warm, promising a hot afternoon. Within a few short miles, the march was slowed by the bridge crossing at Lué-de-Trul, where the soldiers could only pass in fives, and each cannon had to be brought to the far side in single file. The catapults were towed through the shallows by oxen. Jenai waited on the road between the bridge and the watch town, observing the army's progress. Soon, horses from Count Duron's fortress approached bearing a ram pennant.

She rode to meet them and came face-to-face with the Blackguard of Lorion.

"Greetings, Maiden of Lorrae," the armored man said in a gruff tone. He was a barrel-chested, rugged man who bore little resemblance to his royal nephew the Crane Prince. But there was something likeable in his countenance, and Jenai suspected that they could work together if she could only gain his esteem.

"Greetings, noble-hearted Count Duron. I'm honored to meet the famed Blackguard of Lorion and Marshal of Fraelin."

A grim smile was his only reply, then he eyed the progress at the bridge. "I gave no orders to march today, General Jenai."

"No. I gave the orders."

He frowned, turning his dark eyes on her. "Did you receive my missive?"

"I did."

"You deliberately ignored my directive?"

"With respect," she said gently, "the Crane Prince has placed me in charge of this campaign, my lord."

"But—" He glanced at Mercer and Alain standing silently nearby. Bregger was polishing his crossbow. When they offered no clarification, Duron turned toward the generals looking on from the town. They avoided his gaze, speaking animatedly amongst themselves.

"I see you've won some approval," Duron said. "But surely, General, you see the sense in letting seasoned men lead the assault? I've won several sieges, and La Resh there—"

"I welcome your guidance, Marshall," she said, "and look forward to witnessing your expertise on the field. But as for leading—that isn't possible."

He stared. "Never have I seen the like among your sex. Though I suppose the hunger for power may affect even the loveliest of us."

A prickle of anger stirred in her chest, but she ignored it. "If this were about power, I would hang my head in shame at your censure, honorable Count. But I seek no throne, no title, and no empty accolades. I fight this battle at Sweet Afallon's command. By no other course, and for no other purpose, would I ride for war." She nudged Mirrasae closer to the count. "But mark this: hunger and thirst exist within each of our hearts, whether for light or dark deeds. If you've not seen any woman with such feelings, you've not looked well. Am I better than you because I'm weaker? Am I kinder because I look fairer? Am I gentle because I'm smaller? No, Count Duron—within me exists the same conflict between right and wrong that dwells in every breast, man or woman. Do not forget it."

He stared on, lips parting, then he bowed his head. "I'm well rebuked, Crane Maiden." Lifting his eyes, he offered that same sober smile. "Shall we ride into battle together, Jenai? There I will see whether your words are true or rehearsed. If the former, I'll apologize for my doubt. If the latter, I'll watch you fall upon the field, forsaken by your Afallon."

She held his gaze. "Don't put conditions on your faith, Count." She turned Mirrasae and rode to the watch town. Alain and Mercer rode after her in silence, with Bregger following and chuckling, leaving the Blackguard of Lorion to his own devices.

'*That was well handled,*' Mirrasae said.

Jenai set a hand against her breastplate, trying to slow her heart down. "Am I required to prove myself to every man?"

'*It is likely,*' the unicorn answered. '*Your life is an uncommon one, Jenai—and uncommon lives are rarely easy to believe. Doubters will dog you all your days. Be certain to heed your own counsel: Do not place conditions upon your faith or doubt will set in and canker the brightness within.*'

BY NOON, THE ARMY HAD CROSSED THE BRIDGE. BY midafternoon, in the high heat, they approached Lorion's outer walls across a wide plain. The ancient city was a sturdy stronghold, never before breached in battle. When Kon's forces had marched from Reems to besiege Lorion, Prince Chartan had fled the great city, never challenging his cousin. Once the Crane Prince, his entourage, and his protectors had left, the treacherous duke ambled in and took control. Since then, he'd slowly been expanding his territory, creeping ever closer to Shinon. Not even the Blackguard of Lorion—Kon's half-blooded uncle—could win back the city for the rightful heir, or long stop the advance of its reach.

In many ways, Lorion and most of Northern Fraelin were now colonies belonging to the Crow King of Simaerin, whether the present Duke of Thargundy acknowledged that or not. Whatever promises the Crow King had made to Kon and his late father, Jenai suspected that few would be kept in the end.

That is an ending we can't allow to happen.

Studying the distant city battlements, Jenai prayed for guidance. Behind her rose the bickering voices of her generals. La Resh spoke loudest of all, shooting down most other ideas.

Sighing, Jenai tapped Mirrasae's neck. The unicorn walked over to the command table situated on a swell overlooking the city. Alain and Mercer flanked her. Bregger had slipped off somewhere.

"Gentlemen," Jenai said, slicing through the debate. She waited until they all eyed her. "We will proceed as we discussed earlier."

"But, General," Teeg began.

Jenai shook her head. "As discussed, General. We begin digging the earthworks—"

"But—"

"No," Jenai said gently. "We follow Afallon's plan, or we fail."

"But Count Duron—"

She looked at Teeg sharply. "What about him?"

"He's already ridden out with his forces."

Jenai wheeled Mirrasae around. "I don't see him."

"He's taking the west side," Firro answered. "Trying to use

the element of surprise while we distract the city watch with our own forces."

Alain swore.

Jenai shot him a reproving look, then rode over to her bannerman. "My pennon, at once!"

"You can't go after him." Alain reached out to grab her arm, but Mirrasae danced out of the way with the grace of a deer.

"He will risk our operation if I don't. Let's go, Mirrasae!" Not waiting for her banner, Jenai and her unicorn raced down the hill, aiming for the western wall. Alain called after her, but she didn't catch his words over the whistling wind.

'*You endanger yourself*,' Mirrasae said in Jenai's mind.

"Better that than to endanger the outcome of this war."

'*You are the means of ending it.*'

"Please ride as fast as you can."

As they approached the stone walls guarding Lorion, the fallow westside fields came into full view. The city had been under enemy rule for years, blocking the passage to the northern half of Fraelin and starving the loyal citizens within Lorion proper. No fields had been tended these past few years. Any supplies the Thargundian forces needed came from elsewhere.

Someone on the wall shouted. Voices rose, watching her approach.

Ignoring them, she rode hard until she reached the western side. There, with lances and two trebuchets nearly ready, Count Duron directed his men for the coming assault.

"Stand down!" Jenai called.

The count wheeled toward her, his eyes widening. "You shouldn't be here!"

"You can't engage the enemy like this, Duron. Our plan must be a united front! How dare you move without my sanction?" She halted Mirrasae before him, anger writhing in her stomach. "You will withdraw your troops at once!"

"But we're already assembled! Let me strike—"

"This isn't Afallon's way."

"You mean this isn't *your* way!" Duron threw up his hands. "By Afallon, you've ruined the element of surprise with your ride. Who could miss a woman on a white horse?"

Jenai glared at him. "You think your small force, previously incapable of taking Lorion alone, could do so now with or without a distraction? You're the Marshal of Fraelin— a brilliant tactician! How could you let your pride blind you now and risk the lives of your men? Dissemble your force and return—"

The whistle of an arrow caught her attention too late. A stinging pain bloomed in her neck, and she clutched at her throat. Duron shouted something as a thick rain of arrows fell from the city walls. Jenai sank forward on Mirrasae.

"Away. Hurry!" she gasped out.

The unicorn sprang off, racing from the assault. Duron's voice rang out, calling for retreat under the bloody deluge. The sounds faded, then fell away. Jenai struggled to remain on Mirrasae's back. Her vision was dim, and blood pounded in her ears, but the pain was distant and growing softer...

'*Hold on, Jenai,*' said Mirrasae urgently. '*Keep breathing.*'

SHE'D CLOSED HER EYES. CRACKING THEM OPEN, SHE FOUND her surroundings changed. She was lying on her back, covered by a heavy quilt. The light of a lantern guttered, staining the canvas ceiling yellow, while shadows danced around the glow.

I'm in my tent.

She tried to sit up, but a hand gently held her still.

"Lie easy, my lady," Tryla said, leaning into view. "You're wounded if you don't recall."

The arrow. Jenai swallowed and pain throbbed against her neck, near her collarbone, but not as intense as she'd expected.

"It wasn't deep. You're lucky, my lady."

"Luck has nothing to do with it, Tryla. Can I move?" Jenai shifted to free her arms from under her blanket.

Tryla frowned. "The surgeon would prefer that you stay still."

"What of Count Duron? Did he—"

"He made it safely away, thank Afallon for that. Your warning came just in time. That little weasel of yours— Bregger isn't it?—he came back from somewhere and explained that the city had been watching Duron all along, letting him inch his way over. They intended to wipe him out once he'd gotten his trebuchets positioned just so, and after his force was destroyed, they'd burn all the equipment and leave us with much less than we had. As it is, the Duke of Clayre surmises that we got the advantage in the end, by making the Thargundian fools use up so many arrows. It's also likely that they think you're dead."

Jenai smiled faintly. "That *is* a silver lining, isn't it? Where's Alain now?"

"Outside, along with a bundle of other folk all worrying over you. The surgeon wouldn't let them in—and neither would your lovely Mirrasae." Tryla grinned. "Finest mount I've ever seen. Only you could ride a unicorn, my lady, no mistake."

Knowing that Tryla could see Mirrasae for what she was warmed Jenai through. That marked two such souls in Jenai's inner circle. "Please send Alain in, but no one else."

"Right you are." Tryla slipped from sight, and Jenai closed her eyes. Voices spoke from the gloom, many of them, all sounding upset. Tryla spoke over them, then silence fell. Footfalls whispered across the rug, then someone crouched before Jenai.

"I'm here, Lily Maid," Alain said in a soft voice.

She turned toward him, opening her eyes. "Tryla told me all."

"Good." He slipped her hand in his. "The surgeon says you can be up and about in a few days."

"No. Tomorrow."

He softly laughed. "I thought you'd say that."

"Alain."

"Yes?"

She held his gaze. "Do what you must do."

He was still, then nodded. "Thank you for your trust. Now rest."

Her eyes drifted shut. "I will. Thank you, Alain."

"For what?" A smile was in his voice.

"For your friendship."

There was a pause, then he squeezed her hand. "I cherish it."

BESIEGED

Morning brought a summer storm. Even so, Jenai sent orders to her generals, ate a hasty breakfast, then donned her armor. She winced as her movements stretched her wound. The surgeon looked on, having already lost the fight to keep her in bed. Tryla and Aveyal assisted Jenai in every way they could, then followed her from the tent out into the lashing rain.

Mercer joined her at the door flap, but Alain was absent. The pages, Lio and Mattis, huddled close, with Mirrasae and Aveyal beside them.

"Jenai," said Mercer, looking her over, "I'm glad you're well."

"My task isn't complete, Sir Knight. Heaven won't take me yet."

He nodded, the hint of a smile on his lips. "The soldiers are already on their way to Lorion, per your orders. Bregger and his team are also getting into position. But Count Duron remained behind. He wishes to speak with you before riding out."

Jenai squinted at the sky. "Send him into my quarters. There's no reason to become soaked through prematurely."

"These conditions will make battle more difficult."

She glanced at Mercer. "Afallon's will be done." Ducking back into the tent, she was glad of the reprieve from the deluge. A moment later, Duron entered, dressed in full armor. He fell to one knee and took her hand.

"Forgive my recklessness yesterday, Crane Maiden. My actions caused your wound, and I'm ashamed to the depths of my soul."

She stared, taken back by his change of attitude. "You're forgiven, Count, right heartily. Please stand. I'm no saint to grovel before."

He climbed to his feet, towering over her, shame bright in his eyes. "I saw the hand of heaven spare you. Your boldness and your censure have shaken my pride, and I recognize now that Afallon has indeed sent you. My hard words from yesterday are a pit in my stomach."

"Think no more about them," Jenai said gently. "War is a time of hardness, but by Afallon's will, we may soon enter days of peace where we'll learn soft words again." She rested her gauntlet against his vambrace. "Shall we ride together to forge this peace?"

"I would be honored." Duron inclined his helmed head, then held aside the door flap for her. Outside, the rain hammered the earth, carving out rivulets that ran toward the Lué. Jenai stepped into the gale while an unfamiliar page led the count's steed closer. With the aid of Lio and Mattis, Jenai mounted her unicorn, then aimed her steps for Lorion. Count Duron rode at her side. Mercer followed.

THE CRANE ARMY WAS AMASSED ON THE SAME SLOPE AS yesterday, but this time Duron's forces were among them. Oxen-drawn catapults were ready, including the count's trebuchets, and scaling ladders were in wagon beds, ready to be carried forth. Jenai inspected the troops, then glanced at the rising river alongside Lorion's east wall, flowing to the south. Bregger's boats were gathered downstream, though they looked precarious upon the lapping waves.

Still no sign of Alain. She let that go. The Voice had said to trust the duke, and she would always heed divine counsel. She'd wanted to ask what Alain's plan was, but the Voice seemed to desire that she exercise her faith on the matter. So be it.

Her generals approached on horseback while their captains hung back, awaiting final orders.

"Looks messy," Kirio observed, eyeing the foggy plains between them and the city walls. "There'll be a lot of mud. And the river is swollen. The boats could capsize."

Jenai nodded. "All true. But the city watch can't see us coming."

"True, that," said Bastin, studying the thickening fog under the pelting rain. "Those accursed traitors won't expect us to attack in this."

"Wonder why," muttered Teeg.

"Is everything ready?" asked Jenai.

"As can be," La Resh said.

"Then we begin." At a touch, Mirrasae brought Jenai around to face Lorion. Ignoring her throbbing wound, Jenai offered up a prayer, then started forward. The army tailed her, mounted lancers first, shields raised, followed by the archers on foot. The catapults and wagons rolled forth between platoons. Bregger's team broke off to enter the boats.

The troops moved slowly. The ground was spongy and puddled, though not as muddy as expected. Mirrasae handled the conditions as a matter of course, but even the infantry on Jenai's heels made steady progress, rarely slipping. Twenty minutes passed before General Bastin signaled that they'd come within shooting range. The archers at once fell into position behind the shielded lancers. Groups of men with shovels began to dig trenches for the earthworks.

Jenai avoided glancing toward the river. In the fog, it would be a pointless exercise. Drawing a dictated letter sealed with wax from her hip satchel, she held it out to Mercer. "Can this be sent over the wall?"

"At once, General." He twisted in his saddle and called to someone. One of the captains rode forward, saluting. Mercer handed him the letter. "Shoot this into Lorion proper."

The captain slung his bow from his back, plucked out an arrow from his hip quiver, and tied the letter to the shaft. Then he nocked the arrow, aimed, and sent it flying. It arced over the air, barely visible in the gray storm. The arrow vanished over the wall.

"Thank you, captain," Mercer said. He turned his horse around and returned to Jenai's side. "Delivery made, General."

She smiled her thanks.

"What does the letter say?" asked La Resh nearby.

"It's a call to the Duke of Thargundy to surrender to this holy force-of-arms," she said, "or we shall take apart this wall, stone by stone if necessary, then draw and quarter him."

The burly general whooped, slapping his cuisse. "Bold you are, lass. Bold indeed!"

The rain continued hard and fast, and the fog clung to man and horse, chilling the soldiers to the bone. But the workers dug on while the archers stood still, watching the wall. The ladders were off-loaded and carried as close to the wall as anyone dared without being spotted.

Jenai waited. The day crept on. Near noon, Jenai accepted a parcel of food: dried fruit, cured meat, and hardtack.

As she ate, the Voice came into her mind. *"The duke has received your letter and will not surrender. It is time to attack."*

Jenai tied her half-finished parcel up, tucked it into her satchel, and held up her hand. "The Thargundians will not surrender. By Afallon's will, begin the siege!"

Horns called out her orders. Archers took aim above the wall. Lancers calmed their mounts, then adjusted their polearms. The catapults and cannons were manned, awaiting further orders.

Shouts rose from Lorion. The army had been heard—too late.

"Fire!" Jenai shouted. Softly, she added "For Cetta."

The horns blasted across the field. The archers let loose their bowstrings. Arrows soared over the air like a flock of ravens, arcing perfectly before descending over the wall. Under the covering assault, infantry began lifting their ladders toward the towering ramparts.

Jenai nudged Mirrasae forward, eager to help.

From narrow slots in the walls, answering arrows peppered the Fraeli. The lancers held off most with their shields, but the screams of dying men cut Jenai to her core. At the nearest ladder, she flung herself from Mirrasae's back and helped the men hoist the heavy wooden structure to escalade the wall. It scraped against the louring sky, then fell toward the battlements. The ladder struck stone with a dense thunk.

Cheers rose around Jenai, then the infantry ascended the ladder. The first man in the line fell with a scream, an arrow lodged in his eye. He landed with a squelch at Jenai's feet. She stared at him, the horror of his gaping mouth and sightless gaze searing her mind. So much like her dead sister.

More cries filled the air. Arrows flew between forces.

Another man fell from the ladder.

War. Ugly, senseless...

'Jenai!' called Mirrasae, rearing up. *'Move!'*

An arrow whistled past her cheek, tearing Jenai from the gruesome sight. She swung up onto Mirrasae's back, adrenaline lending her added strength. Searching the chaos, she found her bannerman still holding her pennon up. Archers fired endless slues of arrows at the wall while a catapult cracked with the sound of assault.

Generals barked orders; captains echoed them. The count's men raised more ladders. Most failed to touch the wall before they clattered back to the earth. Other ladders fell in place, and soldiers poured onto the wall, cutting down enemies.

Jenai raced back to her bannerman. "Lift it higher! Let the men see we can win!"

The bannerman waved the pennon back and forth. Gold threads glittered in the rain.

"Fight on! For Afallon! For Fraelin!" Jenai's shouts brought a smattering of cheers and hoots.

Archers rallied, replacing fallen soldiers. The rivulets eddying around Mirrasae's hooves ran red.

"Let us gain the victory, Blessed Afallon," Jenai whispered.

With a crack, the second catapult sent a projectile careening over the air. It struck a battlement, shattering stone. Two enemy soldiers in Thargundian red fell to the earth with a crunch.

The bannerman beside Jenai gurgled, then fell, an arrow lodged in his chest. Blood foamed at his mouth. The pennon fell into the mud.

"She's fallen!" someone shouted in dismay. "Afallon forsakes us!"

"No, I'm still here!" Jenai shouted into the din. Scrambling to snatch up the pennon, she nearly fell from Mirrasae's back. At the same moment, Mercer appeared, jumped from his mare, and caught the pole.

Hefting the pennon, he shouted: "The Maiden lives! Take courage!" He waved the flag back and forth. "Rally! To arms!"

"To the lady!" boomed La Resh.

Others took up the call: "To the lady! The Crane Maiden lives!"

"Follow the Ember Lilies!"

Jenai wheeled Mirrasae around, then grasped the banner. "Take up your sword, Mercer! We shall claim Lorion by day's end!"

He swung back into his saddle, and they rode toward the city wall. More ladders struck the stone, and soldiers scaled Lorion's defenses.

With a loud crack, a ballista behind the walls flung a projectile into the field. It rammed into a catapult, crushing it. The soldiers manning the war engine jumped out of the way.

Jenai tore her eyes from the wreckage. Seconds later, Mirrasae reached the wall. Bodies lay in the mud, and Jenai averted her gaze from the gore. She'd thought she was prepared for battle after the skirmishes in Domrem, but this was so much worse than the losses of back then. Not because Cetta's death was somehow lesser, but because this was multiplied by so many.

Tears burned in her eyes. *Never forget the horror you see here. This is what war brings. This is the cost of liberty.*

Even so, she couldn't regret her choice, no matter how death weighed on her. Better to die in the mud than to live oppressed and enslaved to a tyrant who cared as little about the people of Fraelin as he did about the slaves in his own land—or perhaps less.

Thrusting her pennon skyward, she shouted "Fight! Fight on! Take Lorion: For Afallon, for the Crane Prince, for liberty!"

ON THE NORTH

The storm broke. Thank the powers for that, at least. Bregger and his boatmen had moored on the northeast side of Lorion, then carried their equipment with them to the north wall under cover of fog and deluge.

Long before the main force assaulted the south side, Bregger and his fellows pulled out their hook-end ropes. No one expected a small rear attack. The Thargundians had grown lazy sitting on their spoils, working the lesser Fraeli to the bone. They'd forgotten their own roots, and Bregger took great satisfaction in the idea of reminding them today. He might not be a young rooster anymore, but Bregger had never lost his skill from former, less-reputable days.

Throwing his rope to the battlements, he caught a solid hold, tugged, then began his ascent, walking the wall horizontally. The others in his team followed his lead. They had all been hand-picked for their strength and agility. They moved fast, silently, and soon escaladed without a single ladder or siege tower. It was slow-going, and Bregger's arms protested, but he never faltered.

Climbing onto the crenel, Bregger slithered down and

crouched in the shadows. His men mimicked him. Though winded, they controlled their breaths, staying quiet.

Two Thargundian guards stood looking south, perhaps sensing the tension of the coming conflict, rather than minding their watch. Shaking his head, Bregger drew a garrote from his hip satchel. He motioned to his second-in-command, a petite young man called Claw for reasons Bregger hadn't asked after. Claw nodded, taking out a garrote of his own. They sneaked up on the guards, slipped the wires between helm and cuirass, and strangled them without a sound.

After laying the guards across the flagstones, Bregger motioned to his men to tail him. They crept along the east side of the wall, taking out unsuspecting guards with the same wires. No one sounded an alarm. No one had the chance.

Bregger made his way toward the southern wall, aiming for the southeastern watchtower. The Duke of Thargundy would either be housed there or on the southwestern counterpart. Bregger had fifty-fifty odds. He could've separated his men, but that signified a death sentence. Better to stay together and take out the tower watch, whether or not Kon Dragonclaw was present.

If he'd gambled wrong, Bregger would have time to rectify his mistake only if he survived long enough. Fortunately, surviving was what he was good at.

42

A SLIGHT DELAY

Clad in brown leather armor, Alain had ridden out from camp early, after leaving his new aide with instructions to join Count Duron for the siege. There, Tristel wouldn't face combat—the count had given his word on that.

Alain hoped to find Yenn and mount up before the army ever reached Lorion. Surely the dragon was close, waiting for Alain's signal. The rain was a galling inconvenience, but he hadn't counted on further interference. Downstream, on the shores of the Lué, he dismounted and shouted for the stone dragon to emerge.

Instead, a dozen or more shadows rose on the far side of the wide swollen river. Alain lifted his hands at once, chills nibbling flesh. His horse whinnied. These weren't Thargundians. They weren't human at all. The Ilidreth company consisted of twenty men, all dressed in motley reds, purples, and blues. Their hair ranged from silver to gold to black. They trained arrows on Alain, and he knew better than to twitch.

Now would be a really good moment to come out of hiding, Yenn,

Alain thought, but he didn't dare speak. His father had claimed that an Ilidreth arrow never missed.

One of the fae stepped forward, plunging into the river up to his booted ankles. "You are Fraeli?" His voice had a faint accent.

Alain nodded once, blinking water from his eyes.

"You belong to the company of the *Lilerayai*?"

Hesitating, Alain finally shrugged. "Do you mean the Lily Maid?"

An arrow let loose and sank into the wet sand at Alain's left foot, missing by a fraction of a millimeter. His knees weakened, but he schooled his expression. If they wanted him to answer questions, he'd need to speak, dash it all!

The Ilidreth in the water turned toward his fellows and spoke in a musical language Alain had no hope of understanding. The one still holding his bow aloft answered back in clipped tones. They were arguing, that much anyone could see.

Alain held still, waiting. He had the distinct feeling he'd get himself killed if he interrupted, but he also felt time trickling away from him. Jenai must already be on the move, heading for Lorion. He needed to find Yenn.

The conversation went on. Other Ilidreth joined in, taking sides. They moved less than humans did; few hand motions cut across the air. When they did gesture, the Ilidreth were grace itself. Their otherworldliness was jarring to observe.

After too long, the conversation drifted off. Two Ilidreth moved toward the trees, but if they were upset Alain couldn't tell. A deeper stillness fell over the group.

The lone Ilidreth in the water turned back to Alain, searching his face. "You know the Maiden of Ember Lilies?"

Alain nodded, holding his tongue.

"You have been with her long?"

Alain shook his head.

Shadows gathered across the Ilidreth's face. "You will not speak?"

Alain pointed at the arrow by his boot, then shook his head.

Understanding lit the Ilidreth's light green eyes. "Ah. You needn't fear. We have agreed to spare you long enough to gain answers."

That was hardly comforting. Alain folded his arms, keeping his lips sealed. If they intended to kill him either way, he'd certainly not aid them first. Especially if they posed a threat to Jenai.

One of the Ilidreth on shore stepped closer to the water's edge. A female, Alain realized. Their alien litheness and angular features made distinguishing the two sexes almost impossible. She spoke with her companion in the water, her words a soft pattering rain. The male replied, nodding.

He turned back to Alain. "You fear we will harm the *Lilerayai?*"

Alain shrugged.

The female spoke again to her companion.

"Ah, you also fear for yourself," the male said.

Yeah, that too. Alain offered a nod.

"Very well. We will offer our oath not to harm you if you are truthful and steadfast. Will you answer our questions?"

Alain gave a curt nod.

The lead Ilidreth relaxed a margin. "Very good. I am called Ney'Nenamyn."

Alain tried to commit the long, strange name to memory. Before his dungeon days, he'd trusted his mind more on such matters. "Mind if I call you Ney or Nen?"

The Ilidreth's eyes narrowed.

"Never mind." Alain cleared his throat. "What do you want to know about Jenai?"

"Is that *Lilerayai*'s name?"

"If you're referring to the woman who leads the Crane Prince's forces, then yes."

"Jenai. It is a good name, if short."

Alain lifted a brow at that. "Please, time is pressing. She's...fighting at the moment." If they didn't know about the impending siege, he surely wasn't going to reveal her whereabouts to these beings.

"She has something that belongs to us." Ney'Nenamyn's eyes hardened.

"Ahhhh." Realization struck like a hammer blow. The girl, what was her name? Aveyal? "Yes, that's true. She—"

Ney'Nenamyn lifted his hand. "Where is the Ilidreth child?"

"Nearby. And well. She's perfectly well. Jenai treated her broken leg and keeps her close, protecting her from any harm. Other humans tried to make sport of Aveyal, but Jenai prevented that."

The female at the shore spoke in Fraeli. "Is she happy?"

"Yes, I think so. She and Jenai appear to be good friends, and another woman—Tryla I think—is also a good companion. They...they're all happy." He flushed at his own awkwardness. How had he come to this moment, answering for a decision he'd been opposed to?

"Take us," said Ney'Nenamyn, starting forward through the water.

Alain held out his hands. "Not so fast. Hold up. I can't just bring a group of Ilidreth into camp. We'll be killed by the sentries, no questions asked."

"Are you not the Duke of Clayre?"

He faltered. They knew? How long had they been watching him? Had their spies come into the camp itself? "I am, but even a nobleman would have to be a mad fool to bring your kind into a war camp. I'm sorry, it's not possible."

"Then bring the girl here. We will wait."

Alain blanched. "I can't just—"

Another arrow flew, striking the sand before his *other* foot. Alain choked down spittle, raising his hands higher. "All right! I'll bring her."

Why isn't Yenn interfering?

He glanced around, but none of the stones or hillocks resembled a twenty-foot dragon. Turning to his horse, he was almost surprised to find the gelding hadn't run off. He mounted quickly, lungs tight, nerves humming. He couldn't afford this delay. Jenai had a good plan to take the city, but using Yenn was a guarantee—and she'd told Alain she trusted him. He needed to answer that trust—to make a difference for Fraelin after five years in disgrace.

Besides, no plan was foolproof. Things could turn ugly in an instant.

She needs me.

He rode for camp, jumping brambles, working his horse as hard as he dared. The ride would still take time he didn't have. Wind whistled in his ears, tugging at his ponytail, loosening the ribbon holding it fast. As his horse jumped a burned tree stump, the ribbon flew away. His sopping pale hair whipped around his face. He hardly noticed.

Careening into camp, he waved off the sentries, then made directly for Jenai's tent. Apart from the few guards, only servants remained to mingle between the shelters. Tryla and Aveyal tended to remain apart, keeping close to headquarters. That much Alain could rely on.

"Tryla!" he shouted, reining in his horse outside Jenai's tent. "Tryla, for the love of Afallon, get out here!"

The redhead flew from the tent. "What's wrong? Is Jenai hurt? Did she fall?"

"Never mind that. I need the girl."

Aveyal peeked out from the tent, wearing her disguise. Alain turned his focus on her.

"Your people have come for you. They're waiting downriver. Will you come?"

Tryla shot a dismayed glance at the youthful Ilidreth but said nothing. Aveyal examined Alain for a moment, during which he wrung the reins, impatience and fear gripping his insides. Finally, she nodded.

"Thank you. Come on!" He held out his hand. Using her crutch, she limped from the tent and made her way to him as quickly as she could. She splashed through a puddle, unfazed. Nearing him, he caught her wrist and hoisted her into the saddle before him. "Wish me luck, Tryla!"

The handmaiden shouted after them, but the sounds of the horse's hooves thundered in his ears, drowning out her words. The gelding, though a newcomer in Alain's life, was strong and swift. He seemed to enjoy the race. Alain pushed him hard, but the horse didn't flag. Glancing northward, Alain saw smoke rising from Lorion. He swore under his breath. The siege had begun.

It was after noon before Alain reached the Lué downstream. Slowing the horse, he searched the far shore. This had been the spot where he'd come before, right? There was no sign of the Ilidreth. No indication they'd ever been there. Not even the two arrows lodged in the bank.

Shoving back his shoulder-length tangles, Alain dismounted and moved to the water's edge. The swollen river was gray under the dark sky. He stared into it, asking unspoken questions, though he didn't imagine he'd find any answers there.

"Help me down," Aveyal said.

He turned toward her. "I'm not sure this is where—"

"It is." She nodded toward the far bank.

He spun around. Standing there, as if they'd materialized

out of nowhere, was the same cluster of Ilidreth. Ney'Nenamyn moved forward, the female right behind him.

Aveyal called out *"Brei! Marya!"* She shifted, causing the saddle to creak. "Please, Alain, let me down."

He complied, hoisting her from the gelding's back. She adjusted her crutch, and he set her fully on the sandy shore. At once, she limped toward the river. *"Brei! Marya!"*

The male Ilidreth splashed across the river, ignoring the quickened current. At the highest point, the water only touched his thighs. He reached the near shore, caught Aveyal up into his arms, and swung her around while she laughed.

Understanding clicked. "You're her father."

Ney'Nenamyn glanced at Alain, his eyes bright with moisture. "I am." He looked over his shoulder, watching the female Ilidreth cross the Lué. She reached shore and flung her arms around Ney'Nenamyn and Aveyal.

"And you're her mother," Alain whispered.

Aveyal pulled back in her father's arms. "This is my *brei*." She touched Ney'Nenamyn's chin, then turned a smile on the female. "And this is my *marya*."

The woman hooked her palm under Aveyal's chin and whispered something in their liquid language. Then she turned to Alain. "You have proven honorable, young duke. We are in your debt."

He shook his head hard. "Not mine. Jenai's the one who rescued your daughter. If there's a debt, it's to her."

Aveyal spoke rapidly in the Ilidreth tongue while her parents listened. Once, the girl twisted in her father's grasp to point toward Lorion. Faint hope rose in Alain's chest, but he tried to push it down. No debt could compel these fae beings, hated and reviled by humans across the four continents, to fight for any human cause.

Ney'Nenamyn asked Aveyal a question. The girl answered firmly. Her father fell still, then turned and spoke loudly to his fellows across the river. They answered, then came marching through the water. Alain's hope fluttered in his ears.

A moment after the Ilidreth touched the shore, water sprayed up from the Lué in an explosion, and there stood all twenty feet of the dragon Yenn. He was grinning.

The stone dragon's voice rumbled through Alain's head. '*It seems you have a new ally in this fight, Duke of Clayre.*'

"Where have you been?" Alain demanded.

'*Observing. Fear not, there is still time to win. Shall we?*'

Letting his annoyance bleed away, Alain caught his sword hilt. "I thought you'd never ask."

43

FIGHTING ON

An arrow dug into General Firro's chest. He fell from his horse near Jenai, letting out a cry that slashed at her soul. She forced herself not to slide from Mirrasae's back to kneel at his side in the swirling mud. Instead, she held her pennon higher. "Fight on, men of Fraelin!"

The sixth Fraeli catapult smashed another projectile into the wall. Stone rained down on the Fraeli forces, along with Thargundian arrows. Hundreds were dead; maybe more.

Even so, more ladders had ascended. More men had escaladed into Lorion proper. They were breaking in.

"Afallon bless us," she whispered. "Guide us true in this dark hour."

The clash of arms above stirred Jenai's hope. Bregger must be approaching the southern towers by now. Hopefully, soon he would engage Kon Dragonclaw and convince the duke to surrender before more lives were lost.

A large stone careened from over the city wall. Another Fraeli catapult burst into pieces. Men screamed.

Jenai's hand fell to her sword, but she hesitated. She was a symbol, not a fighter. She knew nothing of swordplay, and she hated the idea of taking a life.

Even a Thargundian's? she asked herself.

"Yes," she whispered. "Especially a Thargundian. I must not kill in hatred."

"Watch out!" shouted Kirio from her left flank. An arrow glanced off her pauldron, denting the metal protecting her shoulder. She flinched back, then rode eastward along the wall, calling for her men to carry on. "Take courage! Afallon is with us! Drive out the Thargundian traitors!"

The men rallied, again and again. Ladders rose. Men fell. Catapults cracked. Arrows screamed. The rivulets ran red with blood. Sightless eyes stared heavenward.

Tears flowed down Jenai's cheeks, but she rode on, back and forth at the base of the wall. Calling the soldiers forward. Waving her blood-spattered banner.

The sun came out. The ember lilies on her pennon blazed in the light.

An arrow bounced off her right sabaton and lodged in the churned-up mud near Mirrasae's front hoof. Wheeling her unicorn around for another pass to the west side of the city wall, Jenai spared the arrow only a passing glance. She kept shouting, drawing the men to her. They answered, whooping and shouting, passing her to climb the ladders.

Reaching the east side, she turned again to ride west. "Take Lorion! Take the city!"

As she rode, her eyes strayed south toward the camp. Where was Alain? Had he been injured?

Sweet Afallon, please protect him.

A BAD GAMBLE

Stone debris from a catapult assault sprayed the air. At a run, Bregger reached the southeastern tower, slammed his shoulder against the side, and took a moment to catch his breath. Midway along the eastern wall, they'd encountered a half dozen Thargundians gathered together. In the skirmish, Bregger had lost one of his men, but he still had enough to finish the plan.

Using hand gestures, Bregger directed two of his men to scale the outermost side of the tower and cover the watch window on the east end. He took two more men with him to attack from the west side, where the tower door stood open. Bregger unstrapped his crossbow, ol' Baya, from his back and loaded a bolt. He wound up the tiller while making his way along the corner walkway bridging the southern wall.

Striding like he owned the world usually kept him from getting shot, and it worked now. The Thargundians were too busy fighting off scaling Fraeli soldiers to pay any mind to a man sauntering along the battlements like he belonged. His men followed his lead.

Arrows struck nearby guards. One tumbled from the wall

with a harrowing shriek. Bregger and his men didn't flinch. One Thargundian glanced his way. An arrow caught the man in the shoulder; he twirled in place, then slumped against the parapets. Bregger would have to thank his rear cover for his excellent aim later.

He reached the southeastern tower. A group of high-ranking soldiers stood within, issuing orders. A page cowered in one corner, jotting down notes. A haggard lieutenant snapped off a salute and spun to exit the tower. Bregger pulled his crossbow trigger. The bolt sank into the lieutenant's heart. The man spasmed, then fell to his knees.

That caught the attention of the officers within. One gave a shout, but another bolt caught him in the throat. Gurgling, he scratched at it. Then he fell, dead. Bregger had already loaded his third bolt, and he pointed it at the highest-ranking man in the tower.

"You the Duke of Thargundy?"

Wide-eyed, the man hastily shook his head.

"Where is he?"

The man started to open his mouth, rethought, and clamped it shut.

"Bad move." Bregger waggled the crossbow. "Tell me, or I'll sink one of ol' Baya's bolts into your eye socket. Won't lose a wink of sleep over it either."

"I'd listen," one of Bregger's men, called Frey, said. "He's a right bloodthirsty old git."

The other of Bregger's men—Gilim by name—snorted.

The officer stared at ol' Baya, then jerked his head toward the southwestern tower. "He was over there."

Bregger cursed. "We gambled wrong, lads."

"What'd you mean by *was*?" asked Gilim.

The officer swallowed. "Just that if he left, I never saw. I've been too busy on this end."

"That'll do." Bregger pulled the trigger. True to his word,

he didn't sink the bolt into the officer's eye socket. It was a nice clean shot right in the heart. Quick death, less pain. Probably.

Bregger whirled away. "C'mon, lads. We gotta get across this southern wall and take out that duke!"

TO THE MAIDEN

General La Resh was a monster in human skin. Jenai knew of his reputation from her brothers, but she'd never dreamed of witnessing it firsthand. He sent dozens of arrows over the battlements, never missing his target while making sure his company got all their ladders up. Then he scaled Lorion. Despite his bulk, he moved fast. At the top, he drew his claymore and cut down soldiers like a wheat thresher. Jenai found herself mesmerized by his movements.

'*Watch yourself, Jenai!*' called Mirrasae, dodging a spray of arrows.

She shook herself. "Sorry, keep going."

They raced to the corner of the west wall, with Mercer right behind them. How many passes they'd made from end to end, Jenai couldn't count anymore. As they swung back around, a bevy of arrows rained down. Baying, Mirrasae charged through them. An arrow tore through Jenai's pennon. Another plunged into Mirrasae's flank. The unicorn bucked and cried out. Jenai flew from her back, the world careering around her. Shouts and horns filled the sky. Wind exploded from her lungs.

She came to herself in the mud. The pole of her pennon lay snapped in two. Wincing, Jenai sat up. No arrows jutted from her chest. Mirrasae was nowhere to be seen. The taste of copper filled Jenai's mouth. She touched her lip but couldn't feel anything through her gauntlet.

A soldier splashed through puddles. "General Jenai, are you injured?"

She shook loose hair from her face. She'd lost her helm somewhere. "I think I'm well. Where did Mirrasae go?"

The soldier wrapped her arm around his neck and helped her to her feet. "Your unicorn?"

"Yes." Jenai still felt dazed. She'd probably struck her head.

"Ran toward the river, right through the arrows. I don't think any more arrows hit her though." The soldier was just a lad, no more than sixteen, young like her. A dusting of freckles attested to long days in the fields.

"What's your name, soldier?" Jenai asked.

"Runi, my lady." He moved away from the wall, guiding her past the archers toward better shelter.

"Runi, a good Fraeli name. I need my pennon."

"Got it with me."

"How many saw me fall?"

"A fair few. I ran over straight away to make sure you weren't dead—not that Afallon would let you get killed."

"No. Not yet." She was missing something... Oh. "Where's Mercer?"

"He got hit, but he's still alive."

Thank Afallon for that.

Foot soldiers raced over to assist while archers set up a perimeter of defense.

"I need a horse—or—or something." Jenai tried to shake off the many helping hands reaching toward her. "I must return to the battle."

A horn sounded.

Jenai stiffened. "What is that?"

"Retreat." Runi squinted. "Bastin is sounding it. Must've seen you fall."

"No!" Jenai pushed through the wall of soldiers. "If we retreat now, we'll never be victorious! Don't retreat. Keep fighting!" She whirled toward Runi. "My pennon!"

He thrust the broken pole into her hands.

Jenai held it as high as she could. "Keep besieging the wall! Take Lorion!" She raced toward the wall, running opposite of the retreating forces. Seeing her, men tripped, whirled, and rallied. A renewed cry swelled over the air like a roaring wave.

"Fight!" Jenai screamed. "Fight on!"

Tullo appeared at her side. "Come on, men! To the Maiden! To the Maiden!"

The roaring wave of men rolled toward Lorion. At the same moment, a second roar exploded over the sky. A blast of flame rammed into the southern wall. Chunks of stone burst apart, punching a hole into Lorion proper. Thargundians tumbled to their deaths.

Jenai spun, searching the heavens.

There he was, riding a dragon: Duke Alain Clayre, giving her the siege engine she needed. At last!

AERIAL ADVANTAGE

Jenai cheered with her men. The dragon raced past the wall, wheeled around, then blasted more fire from its maw. Enemy soldiers screamed. Several jumped from the wall to escape the fire, plummeting to their deaths.

At the same time, arrows with colorful fletching soared through the air, coming from the east side of the field, cutting down more wall sentries. Jenai spun, searching for the source of the attack.

There, near the east wall, came twenty strangers clad in motley colors. Awe filled Jenai's chest. Ilidreth. The company of high fae shot another horde of arrows at the top of the wall. Not one missed their mark.

The Fraeli soldiers hesitated.

"Our enemies are above!" Jenai screamed. "Fight the Thargundians!"

Pages carried the message to all the Fraeli platoons. Doubt filled most eyes, but they held to their course. Attack horns blared. The dragon gave another roar, capturing the attention of all. A third fireball smashed into the southeastern tower, toppling it. As the stones hammered the ground, none of the Ilidreth flinched and none were hit.

Reaching the wall, Jenai lifted her pennon in a second hurrah. Alain spotted her and pointed. The charcoal dragon soared low, wings beating the air. Wind thrashed at Jenai's hair.

Alain jabbed a finger at the western plain, mouthing "Follow!"

She nodded, her heart taking flight. Spinning toward her men, she speared her pennon at the sky. "Fight on! We're nearly there!"

With renewed strength, the Crane Army rolled over the walls. She hurried west while the flood of soldiers attacked. Breaking free of the army, she ran alone toward the duke and his dragon. The mighty beast gracefully touched down, folded his wings, and waited a few yards away. When she'd almost reached him, Jenai caught Alain's gaze. They smiled at each other, and he held out his arm.

She jumped and he caught her, hauling her onto the dragon's back. She sat behind Alain and wrapped one arm around his waist. She still clutched her pennon.

Alain's smile was liquid sunshine. "Sorry we're late. We had a bit of a detour." He patted the lusterless scales. "Jenai, this is Yenntevar—but call him Yenn for short. Yenn, this is the Lady of Lilies herself."

A voice like rolling stones rumbled in her mind. *'Greetings, Lady Jenai. I am honored to know you.'*

"And I you, mighty dragon. Thank you for your aid this day." She dipped her head, then shifted to eye Alain. "Where did the Ilidreth come from?"

"Compliments of Aveyal," Alain said. "And the source of my detour. Ready to go?"

"Yes." Jenai rested her cheek against his leather armor. "We have a surrender to accept."

The dragon lifted off, sending butterflies swirling in Jenai's stomach. Wind sang in her ears, and she clung tightly to Alain, careful not to look directly down. The dragon propelled forward, then banked to glide over Lorion. She risked a peek. Rubble littered the main thoroughfare, but damage was minimal past that point. Citizens ventured from their townhouses, pointing at the dragon.

"Quite a spectacle, huh?" said Alain, a smile in his voice. "Look what you've accomplished."

"Not I. This is all by Afallon's will."

Alain chuckled. "Well, I think we can agree He had some help. Give yourself a little credit."

Jenai turned to eye him over his shoulder. So close, the faint scruff of his pale stubble was visible. "And what of you, Duke of Clayre? What credit will you allow yourself?"

He grinned. "Me? I didn't do much. Just rode this warmongering dragon so he didn't get lost. He was already eager to fight. For you, I might add." He patted the dragon's neck.

A new cheer rang out from the southern wall. Yenn veered around, heading for the noise. And there it was: a white flag billowing atop the southwestern tower amid streams of dark smoke. The Thargundians had surrendered.

"Thank Afallon," Jenai breathed, tears welling up. "Heaven be praised."

"Finia," Alain whispered.

WITHIN THE CITY

K on Dragonclaw had fled ahead of the surrender. Bregger brought the news while nursing an arrow in his shoulder.

Jenai had taken residence in Lorion's cathedral. It was the best place she could think of to bring the injured, Mercer among them. The healers said the knight would make a full recovery. The Thargundians were still Afallon-fearing, generally, so no harm had befallen the sacred edifice. Several grateful priestesses had ushered Jenai into one of the stately upper rooms, where she and her generals, the duke, the count, and several captains had gathered to discuss damage control and logistics.

"That Kon's a sniveling coward of the lowest variety." Bregger spat on the flagstone floor.

Jenai looked at the spittle, then shot him a reproachful look. "Don't sully this holy abode, Bregger."

He had the decency to look ashamed. "Sorry, General."

Her expression softened. "Go on, Bregger. Care for your wounds."

"Right." He snapped off a smart salute, then pivoted and

left the room. Several haggard men followed him, presumably members of his wall-scaling team.

"A well-executed battle," Count Duron said, shaking his head. "By Afallon's blood and bones, what a day! We didn't even need the earthworks."

"Please don't swear, my lord," Jenai said, studying the city map spread across the mahogany desk.

Alain sat apart from the rest, a glass of wine untouched beside him. He'd been elated since arriving on dragonback, but once he'd returned to ground, his mood had darkened by degrees. Each time he was surrounded by these men, his sunshine countenance dimmed.

"The day was won through the merit of *all*, so yes, very well executed." Jenai tapped the map. "We'll need to secure this city so that the Thargundians don't try to take it again."

"Easily arranged," said Bastin. He'd been eager to jump at any chance to redeem himself since his shameful order to retreat.

"Good." Jenai eyed Kirio. "What is the death toll?"

"Still being tallied, but close to four hundred lost by my estimate."

So many. She leaned over the desk, her eyes misting over. "They must all be buried well."

"A mass grave would—"

"*No.*" Her voice rang across the chamber, cutting off Teeg. "Each will receive proper rites and their own plot. Let's not stoop to the level of that accursed Crow in Simaerin."

A murmur of assent followed that.

"What of Mirrasae?" Jenai was almost afraid to ask.

The generals exchanged looks.

Count Duron sighed. "No sign beyond the river. But we'll keep looking."

"Please do." Jenai was careful to keep her voice steady,

though her heart throbbed. "Is there anything else, gentlemen?"

"There is *one* thing," La Resh said.

"Yes?"

"The Ilidreth."

Following the official surrender by Thargundian General Hethroy, the Fraeli generals had surrounded the Ilidreth, placing them under arrest. The Ilidreth hadn't fought back. Only one had spoken, demanding an audience with the Ember Lily Maid.

"I will see them," Jenai said, looking up from the maps.

Protests broke out.

"They came to help," Alain snapped from his settee. "Don't forget that."

"Should've known you'd be a fae-loving—" Teeg's sneer was cut off by La Resh's elbow in his side.

"They *did* aid us," La Resh growled.

"Yes." Jenai straightened and glowered at her men in turns. "Let's not forget that the Crow King—a man we despise for his tyranny—has pushed the Ilidreth to the brink of extinction in Simaerin. Shall we do the same here? Are we no better than he? I will see them."

Kirio opened his mouth.

"I'll brook no argument."

He closed his mouth.

"Good." Jenai released the map, letting it spring back into a roll. "Leave me—all but His Grace, the Duke of Clayre. Please bring the leader of the Ilidreth here, Kirio." She lifted her hand against renewed protests. "Under guard, of course, but not in any way harmed. Is that clear?"

Murmurs of "yes, General" resounded in the room, then they all left like whipped dogs. The door closed. Jenai moved around the desk and sat beside Alain. Taking his hand, she waited until he lifted his chin. Their eyes met.

"Be proud, Duke of Clayre. This day you proved your mettle."

A slow smile brushed his lips. "To the one person who matters." He lifted his free hand and stroked her cheek. A spark ran up her spine, and Jenai released his hand, turning away.

"We're far from finished with the fight," she whispered. "There will be more battles. I won't rest until the Crane Prince is crowned in Reems, and every last Thargundian traitor is chased from Fraelin or bends the knee to the rightful king. Our kingdom will rise like a phoenix from the ashes."

"And I—"

A knock sounded at the door, cutting Alain off.

Jenai rose. "Come in."

It was Kirio. "Forgive me, General Jenai, but the Ilidreth have vanished." He swallowed. "Even though they were under guard."

Alain laughed. "They grew impatient."

Kirio held up a piece of parchment. "They left this. It's addressed to you."

"What does it say?" she asked.

Kirio unfolded it and read:

To the Lady of Ember Lilies —

We have begun to pay our debt for your service to our kin. When next you are in need, we will be there. Vien lo Fraelin.

— Lord Ney'Nenamyn
Marshal of Ilid-Jo-Nar, Keeper of the Eastern Vales.

Chills climbed Jenai's limbs. She stared at Alain who shrugged.

"You spared his daughter that day on the road. She vouched for you, I'm pretty sure."

"Thank you, Kirio."

The lieutenant-general slipped out, closing the door.

She held Alain's gaze. "The Ilidreth will aid us. Afallon grows his forces. And you, Alain—what were you going to say?"

He sank to his knees, caught her hand, and softly kissed her knuckles. "I was saying that my dragon and I are coming with you, Jenai. To the bitterest end. To the highest heights. I will be at your side."

Chest warming, Jenai set her hand on his pale head. "I welcome you with all my heart, Duke of Clayre. Thank you."

Continued in
THE CRANE MARTYR

FROM THE AUTHOR

Thank you so much for reading! The journey to bring this story into the world has been full of unusual pitfalls and miracles alike, and that feels fitting for the type of story it is. I hope you've loved journeying thus far with Jenai, Alain, Mercer, Mirrasae, and the rest of the characters! They feel so alive to me, and I pray I've captured that essence properly to share with you.

Please consider leaving your honest review online. It makes all the difference for a starving author.

ACKNOWLEDGMENTS

As I said in the foreword, this book has been among the easiest I've ever written. Which is funny to consider, thinking back. I had pneumonia as I wrote the climax, yet somehow it still came together in the first draft. Have there been plenty of changes since? You betcha. But even with research and sickness, this story came together with an ease that baffles me even now.

The fact remains: I couldn't have done it alone.

Firstly, heartfelt thanks to my Savior, Jesus Christ, for Your abounding love and gentle kindness. Greater love hath no man.

Deep thanks to R. K. Goff, Heidi Wadsworth, and Robert Zangari—my amazing alpha team—for coming through on yet another manuscript and helping me slay the most embarrassing mistakes. Equally big thanks to Andrew Platten who joined my alpha team for this project. Your notes all helped a TON!

Enormous thanks to my beta team: Beba Andric, J M Archer, Laura A. Barton, and Jaxon Charlton. Your enthusiasm and honesty helped in equal measures!

Epic thanks to Sarah B., who always comes through and gushes where I need her to gush. Sorry I can't let you have Alain, but I'm so glad you fell in love with him!

To my family—especially my parents and sisters—thank you for cheering me on, reading my books, and keeping me alive like your pet goldfish. I appreciate the food, movie nights, and rant sessions more than you'll ever know (maybe).

To my tiny niblings—Brylee, Finnley, and Tate—thank you for showing me a brand new vista of love and affection. I'll make good use of it in my stories!

And lastly, to Joan of Arc, that stalwart soul who inspired this author and this story. I'm in awe of you.

—M. H. W.

SPECIAL ACKNOWLEDGMENTS

Special thanks to the 121 Kickstarter backers who helped bring this book to life, including:

A. Vogel, Aaliyah Drake, Alexandra Corrsin, Amanda Thompson, Amena Jamali, Amy dowell, Annarose Willhite, April C, Arianna Johnson, Author David A Trotter, C. L. Allen, Carl Spitzer, Carol MacLennan-Gonzales, Catherine Holmes, Chase McGlinchey, Christa Niehot, Christine E. Schulze, Claire Banschbach, Corrie Pelc, Courtney Carter, Dayna C, Deborah O'Carroll, Deborah Torrance, Denise C. Allen, Derek Gorny, E.R. Paskey, Elaina J, Faith Drake, Gianna Christopher, Gordon Sturgeon, Greg Levick, Hannah Pennington, Heather Lueken, Heidi Wadsworth, Ian Brown, J. Lynn Else, J.A. Andrews, Jack, Jane McGarry, Janice Muehle, Jaxon Charlton, Jeanna, Jessica Johnson DVM, Jessica Tucker, John Idlor, Julian Vanidoso, K Hendrick, K. L. Warden, Kara Schmidt, Karyne Norton, Katelyn Fowler, Katherine Malloy, Katie Cherry, Kayla Cotrell, Kelly S., Castañeda Corona, Ken A. Baker, Kiñuruin, Kristen Schleif, Kyle Luke, Kyrie, Larisa I, Laura A. Barton, Liana, Lichelle Slater, Lisa Heiser, Liz Delton, Madelyn S., Madge Watson, Magnus S. M. Johannessen, Maira, Mandi Oyster, Marcel Hegler, Mari T., Mariah, Megi Perkins, Melinda Cater, Melissa B., Meredith Carstens, Michael Box, Michael Dubost, Michele Israel Harper, Morgan G., N. Gustafson, Natalie Wish, Nate & Meleena

Humpherys, Per M. Jensen, Rebecca M. Krogman, Rick Gagne', RLS, Robert Zangari, Samantha Newberry, Samuel Ray Lund, Sarah Rogers, Sean Gray, Shawn R Charlton, Sheldon Albertson, Spookies Books, Tawnee Wadsworth, Tracy Lee, ValerieAnne, Veronica Nguyen, Victoria, Victoria P, Vidi Castañeda, Z.R. McCormick

GLOSSARY

PEOPLE

Afallon – The God of Simaerin and Fraelin.

Alain Clayre – The Crane Prince's cousin. Imprisoned for five years in Simaerin.

Aluem – Prince of the unicorns.

Aveyal – A young Ilidreth girl.

Bastin – A General in the Crane Army.

Baya, ol' – The name of Bregger's crossbow.

Bregger – A city guard of Valcinay.

Cetta d'Arc – Jenai's younger sister.

Charton – The Crane Prince of Fraelin.

Claw – One of Bregger's men.

Dulen Thame – A duke of Fraelin.

Duron – Marshal of Fraelin, and also a count. Called Whoreson or the Blackguard of Lorion.

Edrin d'Arc – Jenai's youngest brother.

Evella – A widow from the village of Leyn.

Figg – The Crane Prince's majordomo.

Firro - A General in the Crane Army.

Frey – One of Bregger's men.

Gilim – One of Bregger's men.

Heshi d'Arc – Rowan d'Arc's wife.

Hethroy – A Thargundian general.

Huvarn – Gatekeeper for Chateau Darr.

Ilua Nuvan – A countess of Fraelin.

Issa d'Arc – Jenai's mother.

Jekan d'Arc – Jenai's father.

Jenai d'Arc – The main protagonist.

Kerch – Jenai's uncle and Jekan's brother.

Kilay – A priestess at the Cathedral of Shinon.

Kirio – A lietenant-general in the Crane Army.

Kon Dragonclaw – The treacherous Duke of Thargundy.

Koyte – A soldier of Fraelin.

La Resh – A General in the Crane Army. He has a bad reputation.

Ladia – Jenai's aunt and Kerch's wife.

Limmar – A young city guard of Valcinay.

Lio – One of Jenai's pages.

Lucen d'Arc – Jenai's second-eldest brother.

Mardry – Prince Chartan's cook.

Mattis – One of Jenai's pages.

Mercer – A Fraeli knight in service to Lord Robarr of Valcinay.

Mirrasae – A unicorn.

Nantay – A lady at the Crane Prince's court.

Ney'Nenamyn – An Ilidreth.

Onrin Tarie – A Fraeli general and Alain's commanding officer at the Battle of Rime.

Orry – Husband of the market baker in Valcinay.

Petray Havim - Lord Robarr's scribe.

Phren LeGre – A villager in Domrem. He has feelings for Jenai.

Priarre – The priest of Domrem.

Robarr – The governor of Lorrae Province.

Rowan d'Arc – Jenai's eldest brother.

Runi – A Fraeli soldier.

Runin – A barber in Candalar.

Sharisse – Jenai's childhood friend.

Silian – A lady at the Crane Prince's court.

Teeg – A General in the Crane Army.

Thiavos – The Devil.

Tristel – A young soldier. Grandson of Evella.

Tryla – A Fraeli handmaiden.

Tullo – A Fraeli hunter.

Varide – A priest on the Council of Faith in Shinon.

Varyon – First of the line of Crane Kings of Fraelin. A legendary hero.

Yenntevar – A dragon.

PLACES

Amri – A neighboring kingdom.

Annonenfa – An Ilidreth Vale. It means 'The Realm that Breaths.'

Boyan – A town in Fraelin.

Candalar – A village in Fraelin.

Chateau Darr – The seat of power in Shinon where the Crane Prince lives in exile.

Church of Saint Cethera – An abandoned church in Southern Fraelin.

Domrem – The village where Jenai was raised.

Fraelin – The kingdom where Jenai lives.

Hesh-Kassal – A neighboring kingdom.

Leyn – A village in Fraelin.

Londolin – The Silver City in Simaerin.

Lorion – A conquered city held by Thargundians in Central Fraelin.

Lorrae – A province in Fraelin.

Lué – A river near Lorion.

Lué-de-Trul – The watch town near Lorion.

Pira – A conquered city in Central Fraelin.

Redroot Forest – The southern forest near Shinon.

Reems – A city in Central Fraelin where traditionally the king or queen is always crowned.

Rishom – A neighboring kingdom.

Shinon – A city in Southern Fraelin.

Simaerin – The kingdom across the channel where the Crow King reigns.

Thargundy – A northern province in Fraelin.

Thray – A port city in Fraelin.

True Realm of Ilid – The northern forest above Simaerin where many of the Ilidreth dwell.

Valcinay – The capital city of Lorrae Province.

TERMS

Annonenfa – Ilidreth for 'The Realm that Breaths.'

Brei – The Ilidreth term for 'father.'

Church of Afallon – The title of the church that worships Afallon.

Council of Faith – An ecclesiastic cabinent heading the Church of Afallon in Fraelin.

Crane King – The title for the current ruler of Fraelin.

Crane Prince – The title of the heir to the Crane Throne in Fraelin.

Crow King – The title for the current ruler of Simaerin.

Crowsmen – Soldiers of The Crow King.

Dreyvio – *Ilidreth* in High Frael

Epian – *Fairy* in High Frael

Fraeli – The people of Fraelin.

High Frael – The old tongue of Fraelin. Few still speak it.

Lilerayai – The Maiden of Ember Lilies

Marya – The Ilidreth term for 'mother.'

Simaeri – The people of Simaerin.

Thargundians – Those loyal to the treacherous Duke of Thargundy.

Trul – *Troll* in High Frael

Vien lo Fraelin – High Frael for "Long live Fraelin!"

ABOUT THE AUTHOR

Writer of fantasy, magic weaver, dragon rider! Having spent the past two decades devotedly writing fantasy, it's safe to say M. H. Woodscourt is now more fae than human.

All of her fantasy worlds connect with each other in the Mithrinn Universe, forged with great love and no small measure of blood, sweat, and tears. When  she's not writing, she's napping or reading a book with a mug of hot cocoa close at hand, while her quirky cat Wynter nibbles her nose.

Learn more at www.mhwoodscourt.com

ABOUT THE AUTHOR

Writer of fantasy, magic weaver, dragon rider! Having spent the past two decades devotedly writing fantasy, it's safe to say M. H. Woodscourt is now more fae than human.

All of her fantasy worlds connect with each other in the Mithrinn Universe, forged with great love and no small measure of blood, sweat, and tears. When she's not writing, she's napping or reading a book with a mug of hot cocoa close at hand, while her quirky cat Wynter nibbles her nose.

Learn more at www.mhwoodscourt.com

ALSO BY M. H. WOODSCOURT

DRAGONS OF ROKAHN
Epic Fantasy/Adult

When Darkness Hunts the Dawn

A Silent Song in Winter

The Burden of a Broken Crown

MARK OF VALLIATH
High Fantasy/Young Adult

The Storyteller True

The Shattered Arch

The Marked Prince

The Blood Fountain

RECORD OF THE SENTINEL SEER
Science-Fantasy/Adult

Prince of the Fallen

Rule of the Night

Song of the Lost

Paths of the Broken

Heart of the Sentinel

9 781959 619192